WHAT HAPP

Pre-Final Edit copy.

Hope you enjoy

MW

Pre-Final Edit
Copy.

Hope you enjoy

MW

WHAT HAPPENED IN AUGUST

Michael Whiting

Copyright © 2024 by Michael Whiting
Copyright © 2024 Level 139 Publishing

All rights reserved. No part of this book may be reproduced or used in any manner without written permission of the copyright owner except for the use of quotations in a book review.

For more information,
please contact: level139publishing@gmail.com

First paperback edition: November 2024

Book design by Barış Şehri

ISBN 978-1-0369-0358-9

www.whathappenedinaugust.com

To my wife who always asked me "when is the book coming out?" Well…it's out. Thank you for always pushing me to finish this.

No. You can't have a free copy.

CONTENTS

Prologue	9
Act One	15
Chapter One	17
Chapter Two	28
Chapter Three	34
Chapter Four	41
Chapter Five	51
Chapter Six	57
Chapter Seven	63
Chapter Eight	69
Chapter Nine	78
Act Two	87
Chapter Ten	89
Chapter Eleven	103
Chapter Twelve	112
Chapter Thirteen	118
Chapter Fourteen	124
Chapter Fifteen	135
Chapter Sixteen	141
Chapter Seventeen	153
Chapter Eighteen	155
Chapter Nineteen	168
Chapter Twenty	176
Chapter Twenty-One	180

Chapter Twenty-Two	188
Chapter Twenty-Three	199
Chapter Twenty-Four	204
Chapter Twenty-Five	209
Act Three	213
Chapter Twenty-Six	215
Chapter Twenty-Seven	218
Chapter Twenty-Eight	226
Chapter Twenty-Nine	233
Chapter Thirty	245
Chapter Thirty-One	254
Chapter Thirty-Two	259
Chapter Thirty-Three	266
Chapter Thirty-Four	270
Chapter Thirty-Five	279
Chapter Thirty-Six	287
Chapter Thirty-Seven	299
Epilogue	305
Acknowledgements	311

PROLOGUE

In his final years, when he closed his eyes at night, Ulrich could still smell the blood on little Martin Drake's white shirt. All the good things had faded. Meeting Sarah. Sian's wedding. His father's face. But the events of that one summer's evening in 1968 would remain clear until his final day.

It was a languid bank holiday evening when Ulrich found himself in the sprawling garden of his mansion, nursing the last dredges of his whiskey bottle. In the lull between his bouts of sunbathing, he'd swivel and peer through the sliding glass doors into the wreckage of his kitchen. Cabinet doors hung off their hinges, a testament to his and Sarah's violent unveiling, while shattered glass and porcelain painted the floor, the fallout from another of their altercations. It wouldn't be their final spat, but the events of that day would forever shift the course of the retired banker's life. A mind once devoid of fear and packed with ego would soon be haunted by dread and uncertainty lurking in every shadow.

There he sat, shirt unbuttoned, liquor-soaked, gazing out at the garden that unfurled into the forest and the hills encircling the valley. At first, he dismissed the figure flitting between the trees on the forest's distant edge as a hallucination, an illusion brought on by the heat of summer and the alcohol seeping through his veins. Yet, the figure didn't vanish into the ether as he expected. It lingered, and with it, the chilling sensation of something being terribly wrong.

Unmistakably the form was edging closer, emerging from the forest's veil to reveal itself as a small boy. Ulrich remained frozen at the garden table, incredulity clouding his senses as the boy loomed nearer.

The morning's events and the dispute with Sarah had led Ulrich to believe his life was at a dead end. He had transformed into a bitter, pitiable creature, and all his friends and acquaintances had grown tired of his antics, scrambling over one another to find the nearest escape route. Perhaps the figure advancing towards him was the apparition of his inner child, finally breaking free from the dark forest of his tormented psyche. Such muddled, destructive thoughts plagued Ulrich, submerging himself in fantastical narratives to conquer the monsters confronting him. But no, the boy was real, soaked in blood and emitting a terrified scream as he scaled the fence into Ulrich's garden.

Startled, the inebriated banker leaped up from the table, upsetting the condiments and drinks, and rushed towards the boy who had fallen over the fence and lay crumpled. As Ulrich moved to help him up, he recoiled violently.

"GET THE HELL OFF ME!"

Ulrich retreated; hands raised in a defensive surrender.

"Kid, I'm not trying to hurt you! Is that blood yours? If it is, we need to—"

The boy shook his head, his breathing ragged and uneven from shock.

"Listen, my name's Ulrich. My wife, Sarah, she'll be back soon, and we can … Oh God!"

Another form was breaking free from the forest. Even at half a kilometre's distance, Ulrich could discern the crunch of undergrowth and the ominous rhythm of muddied footfalls. The figure seemed to lurch towards them, arms flailing wildly, emitting a guttural shriek that echoed with primal fury as if the boy had been torn from its clutches.

"Get inside," Ulrich murmured, first to himself, then louder, to the boy.

It wasn't an animal. It was a man, a ghastly figure garbed only in a rabbit mask, brandishing what appeared to be a machete.

"Get inside! NOW!"

Wasting no time, Ulrich seized the boy by his blood-soaked shirt and hoisted him up. The boy kicked and screamed as Ulrich sprinted through the garden door. The bone-chilling shrieks from behind swelled, growing louder and more insistent with each stride the figure took towards the house. Once inside, Ulrich set the boy down and quickly secured the doors. As he fastened the final lock, a heavy thud jolted it from the outside, nearly splitting the barrier that kept them safe from the assailant. The man outside continued to shriek, a wild, relentless sound, hammering against the door in a desperate attempt to reach the boy within. Ulrich turned to see Martin, who stood against the back wall, tears streaming down his face.

"Come on. Follow me."

With a sense of dread gnawing at his gut, Ulrich guided the terrified boy into the next room. All the while, their tormentor shadowed them, his silhouette moving from window to window, tapping his machete against the glass and letting loose unsettling, manic giggles. They made their way to the living room, then to a narrow landing with a steep, uneven staircase.

"Up there now! Quick!"

Without hesitation, the boy scrambled up the stairs, his heart pounding in his ears. Ulrich followed closely, adrenaline propelling every step. As they reached the landing, the boy, bereft of direction, darted into one of the secluded bedrooms. Ulrich lingered a few steps away, drawn unwillingly to the large glass window that dominated the landing. He watched specks of dust dance in the sunlight, a tiny spectacle that offered a fleeting distraction from the pulsating fear.

Taking a deep breath, Ulrich summoned the courage to peer down into the garden. His fleeting bravery was extinguished by regret as he locked eyes with the assailant below: a man in his late twenties yet strands of grey already threaded through his unkempt hair. His skin, an eerie pallor of white, stretched taut over prominent bones and his eyes gleamed with a manic fervour, a wild energy that spoke of chaos and unrestrained violence.

He held a blood-smeared rabbit mask in one hand, and in the other, a blade that told tales of savagery. Even from this distance, Ulrich could sense the unhinged malice emanating from the man below. A shiver of dread crept down his spine as he observed the assailant's eyes flick towards the bedroom window where Martin was concealed.

A dreadful, silent understanding wove its thread between Ulrich and the frenzied figure below, pulling tighter with every beat of his heart. Sprinting into the bedroom, voice scratched by fear, Ulrich commanded, "What the hell are you doing, kid? Get away from the window, now!"

Martin retreated from the window, his eyes an abyss of terror and some inexplicable emotion. A strange, silent interaction seemed to have passed between the boy and the man outside, a dark secret conveyed in a glance.

The relentless thud of machete against wood interrupted Ulrich's thoughts, and Martin's muffled sobs harmonized with the impending threat. And then, the door yielded. As the intruder's footsteps echoed like a death knell within the house, Ulrich, propelled by a desperate resolve, moved to the cupboard and retrieved a firearm, all while Martin trembled silently in the corner, a young mind in the throes of horror.

"They're going to kill me!" Martin's voice quivered, the raw terror palpable. "They're going to kill me like the rest!"

Ulrich's attention darted to the room's entrance, his parched lips clamping together, teeth grinding as the ominous figure crept ever closer to the door. He thrust out the gun, his grip quaking, and the weapon itself seeming to shudder in resonance with his dread. A desperate prayer rose unbidden in his mind—that the words exchanged with Sarah earlier wouldn't their final farewell. His finger trembled on the trigger. The monstrous apparition was at the precipice.

And then, it was no more.

A gasp escaped Ulrich's lips at the sound of footsteps; not encroaching, but hastily withdrawing. Time seemed to warp, twenty minutes elongating into an unbearable eternity before he could muster the fortitude to inch open the door. The menacing figure in the mask had vanished, leaving behind only the grim remnants of blood droplets from his weapon. Ulrich navigated towards the window, his grip on the gun now unwavering. He leaned forward, scrutinising the garden below. The lunatic was absent. His gaze traced a slow arc upwards, back to the dense shroud of the forest from where the horror had first emerged.

He spotted them lurking in the forest's depths. Where one had appeared, now there were two, each adorned with the same grotesque rabbit masks, each wielding identical blades. Ulrich's stare was unyielding, transfixed on the pair, and he sensed their cold, predatory stare in return. Gradually, with deliberate steps, they began to recede, melting back into the forest's embrace, disappearing, their return hanging in the air like a promise.

ACT ONE

CHAPTER ONE

Fifty Years Later

"So, Reuben. Let's start with what happened to your face, shall we?" DCI Elaine Walker posed the question, studying the nineteen-year-old male settled in the back of the car.

His right eye, radiant with a unique shade of green, was marred by a vivid, fresh bruise. It made for a stark contrast against his otherwise pallid complexion. His thin lower lip was unnaturally swollen from tonight's events. His tousled shoulder-length blond hair bore the pungent odour of stale beer, and his black Super Furry Animals shirt was torn at the neck.

She manoeuvred the car away from the now-shuttered pub, offering a courteous wave to a pair of fellow officers engaged in interviewing a congregation of young adults outside. Soon they found themselves ensnared in traffic, alongside a motley array of minibuses, taxis, and parents retrieving their drunk offspring, all journeying from Cardiff back to the valleys. Walker cast a glance at the rear-view mirror, only to find the young man's intense eyes reflected at her.

"Ready to talk about what happened?"

He looked towards the window.

"I could've walked home, you know?" he said back. "Fresh air would've done me good."

"Really?" she asked, swaying her right hand to the window like a tour guide. "If you fancy a stroll from here all the way to Caerphilly, go right ahead," she shot back. "Just don't think about dialling triple nine when you're wandering lost in the woods at four in the morning." The young man raked his fingers over his head, then mumbled a curse under his breath realising his hair was soaked in beer.

Feeling somewhat trapped, Reuben folded his arms across his chest in defeat. Though he generally enjoyed a good rapport with the Detective Chief Inspector, he sensed that there was no avoiding a deep dive into the night's unsettling events.

"Look, I had a minor scuffle with an old pal. It's no big deal."

"Friends fighting isn't a big deal, sure," Walker conceded, her focus on the road as traffic picked up and their car began to roll down the M32. "But friends generally don't leave each other looking like Picasso paintings. Was this friend of yours particularly close?"

"Morgan," Reuben replied, his voice growing softer. "I mentioned him before. He was the one I told you about from the funeral."

"Was that the one who made an inappropriate comment about your mother at the wake?"

"If by *inappropriate* you mean referring to my mother as 'a babe,' then yes," Reuben replied. "So, what did he say this time?"

He groaned.

"Christ. Okay fine …"

Reuben stretched in the car seat, as if physically bracing himself for the emotional labour of retelling the night's events.

"It was like a mini school reunion," he began, each word tinged with a palpable weariness recounting the story had already drained him. "We hadn't all been together in the same place for a while—Alice moved to Barcelona for her studies, while Tris and Morgan settled in Cardiff. I've stayed local. The get-together was sort of a catch-up, and also a way to maybe talk me into finishing college. I thought that maybe hearing about how good of a time they were having, it would give me the kick up the arse to apply. So we were talking and Alice floated the idea of us visiting her in Barcelona. Everyone was enthusiastic, except I had to admit I couldn't afford it. With my mom's night shifts barely making ends meet, there was no way."

He paused for a moment, gathering his thoughts before continuing. "That's when Morgan, sporting this absurd, drunken grin, says, 'Surely you had some inheritance from joining the Dead Dad Club.' The room went silent—Alice and Tris looked horrified. I tried to laugh it off, but then Morgan took another swig of his drink and added, 'I bet you got a grand for every stab.' That's when I lost it."

Walker shook her head in disbelief and disappointment, her face wincing at the words.

"The audacity some people have, making those kinds of comments after a tragedy—it's unbelievable," she said. "When my sister passed away, it was all 'I'm here for you' and 'if you need anything, just ask,' for like two weeks. After the funeral, it's like everyone expects you to just go back to normal, like they have. That's the big misconception about grief—it's not something you can just get over."

Reuben shot back, his voice tinged with bitterness, "Don't act like we're in the same situation. Your sister died in a car accident; my dad was murdered. You know what happened to your sister; I'm still trying to piece together the truth about my father."

Matching his tone, Walker shot back, "Are you finished?"

They descended into a reflective silence.

Six weeks before his lifeless body was discovered at London Paddington station, Martin Drake, a well-respected but otherwise unremarkable postal worker, mysteriously vanished from his home in Ystrad Mynach, Caerphilly. The abrupt disappearance left Reuben and his mum, Julia, in a torturous limbo of dread and uncertainty. Sleepless nights unfolded as they awaited news, any news, of what had become of Martin. Then, a devastating blow: Martin was found dead, hundreds of miles away from home, bearing multiple stab wounds.

The tragedy shattered the fragile peace of their lives, scattering fragments they'd never be able to fully gather again. The why and how of Martin's disappearance, the identity of his murderer, and the inconceivable distance his body had travelled—these haunting questions remained unanswered, persisting like open wounds. The weighty task of solving this perplexing and heartbreaking mystery had fallen on the shoulders of DCI Walker, who had yet to bring any closure to the grieving family.

As they crossed the threshold marked by the Welcome to Caerphilly sign, Reuben broke the silence. "I didn't mean what I said. It's just ……" He paused, fiddling with the frayed collar of his shirt. "Truth is, I feel old," Reuben confessed. "Every day, I'm tormented by the looming sense that I'm running out of time. I'm nineteen, and I'm just exhausted."

"Oh, for fuck—"

Reuben's body lurched forward as Detective Walker slammed the brakes, the abrupt halt almost launching him into the back of the front seat. His seat belt tightened like a vice, pulling him back just in time. Walker's hand came down hard on the steering wheel, her knuckles whitening from the force of her frustration. For a fleeting moment, the normally composed detective seemed almost overcome by a fierce, elemental anger. Reuben caught sight of her reflection in the rearview mirror: her eyes blazing, her expression transmuted into something bordering on the demonic. Then, as quickly as it had flared, her wrath ebbed away, leaving her countenance as impassive as ever.

"They'll hand out a licence to anyone these days," she spat.

Reuben couldn't really fault her for the outburst. Given her high-stakes, high-stress job—endless sleepless nights spent in pursuit of murderers and thieves—social niceties were a luxury she could scarcely afford.

"No, listen …" She collected herself. "I'm the one who should be apologising. By now, we should have had someone in custody, awaiting trial. I feel guilty that you're unable to move forward."

Reuben mustered a smile. "So, that's why you do all this? Drop by for tea with my mum every month? Act as my own private Uber? All because you feel guilty?"

Walker didn't respond to his questions, instead she went back to what he said earlier.

"You're too young. You have all the time in the world. More time than you think."

The police car gradually rolled to a halt at the peak of Central Street, a long incline lined with terraced houses in a spectrum of different hues. The street was deserted, the only sounds being distant echoes of inebriated laughter and the idling engine of the police car. "I should drop you off here. Your mum won't appreciate a set of flashing lights outside her house."

Reuben groaned as he gingerly stepped out of the car. The pain in his gut from Morgan's punch was now making itself known. He shut the door and ambled over to the front of the vehicle. As he did so, Walker rolled down her window.

Walker was a distinctive figure. Her slicked-back quiff reminded Reuben of Morrissey from The Smiths. She possessed a broad, youthful smile that contrasted sharply with the tiredness etched under her eyes and the lines creasing her forehead—evidence of too many sleepless nights.

As Reuben peered inside the car, his eyes drifted to her hand on the steering wheel, particularly the absence of a ring. At her age, somewhere in her forties, one might expect to see such a token, but there was none. His thoughts lingered on her guilt over not finding his father's killer. He visualised her spending countless nights besieged by a fortress of towering paperwork, each sheet a testament to the unsolved mystery that continued to elude her.

"Tell your mother I'll pop over sometime next week to say hello," Walker said, her smile providing a comforting warmth.

Reuben paused as if he were about to say something.

"Is there something else you want to tell me?" She asked.

A long five seconds passed. He shook his head.

"Just bring some biscuits or something when you come over next, alright?" he joked. "Bit rude showing up empty-handed."

With that he began to walk, the sound of the car pulling away echoing behind him.

He ambled down the centre of the pavement, following the same path he and his father would tread when he was picked up from school. As Reuben neared the end of the street, the blue pebble-dashed exterior of his house came into view. He took one last glance over his shoulder before quickening his pace towards the door.

There had been something he had wanted to share with Walker, a nagging worry that had been bothering him for the past few weeks.

He couldn't shake the feeling that someone was watching him.

*

Hey. Just wanted to check to see if you're okay. Look, I'm sorry about Morgan. You think a year out of the valleys and with other people would've sorted his personality out. I've had a word with Tris, and we've decided we won't invite him to our next reunion. We also agreed that we should have maintained better contact since the funeral. I'm not flying back to Barcelona until next month. Mum and Dad are still sorting the divorce, so they want to work some things out. You could stop by and see me on Apsley Road. Just let me know where and when x.

Reuben read Alice's message twice before switching his phone off. He laid in his bed, the rest of his room surrounded by the massive charity boxes that his mother had assembled of his father's belongings. He wanted to keep them even though he hadn't looked at anything since the funeral. But for Julia Drake, it was time to move on and this morning, they had the conversation he never wanted to start.

Julia, his mother, was hastily slicing a ham and cheese sandwich in half, throwing one half into her work lunchbox. "They're going whether you like it or not!" she told him.

"I haven't had the chance to look through anything yet!" Reuben retorted, his hands still wet from washing them at the kitchen sink.

"You've had more than enough time," Julia replied, her voice tinged with desperation. "I'd rather get rid of the stuff now and see if we can make money off any of your father's old things. Could help with the bills and everything."

"I've already checked!" Reuben snapped back, failing to mask his offense at the idea of selling his father's belongings. "There's nothing in there but old photographs and some history project nonsense."

Julia, steadying herself against the kitchen counter as if it were her lifeline, softened her voice. "So, why don't you want to get rid of them?"

Searching for the right words felt like trying to catch smoke with his bare hands. Reuben was at a loss for an answer.

"I wish we could bring him back," Julia finally said, taking a step towards her son. But Reuben backed away, keeping a distance.

"But we can't," he said. "I get that. I'm not the one trying to just move on and forget him."

The anger flashed in Julia's eyes, angrier than he'd ever seen her. "I don't want to forget him," she asserted. "But does everything … does everything have to be this sad? Is that it? Do we just spend the rest of our lives being defined by what happened?"

"His killer is still out there somewhere. Don't you get it? Am I the only one who cares about this?" Reuben's voice was a volatile mix of disbelief and frustration. "Some man murdered your husband, Julia. And as far as I'm concerned, you couldn't give two solid shits about it!"

The room charged with tension, Julia's hand struck his face with a resounding slap. For a moment, her eyes filled with regret, and she took a half-step towards him, perhaps to offer some comfort or apology. But Reuben was already moving.

Ignoring the sting on his cheek, he snatched up his brown leather jacket from the hook by the door and stormed out.

*

This wasn't the first time these conversations had happened. Tensions with his mother had risen shortly after the funeral. She wanted to talk about it. He didn't. The image of his mother collapsing at the front door, as the police delivered the grim news, was forever etched into his memory. It was a scene befitting a television drama, too surreal and heart-wrenching for his otherwise mundane life.

The subsequent details did little to ease the pain. His father had been discovered at London Paddington station by a group of drunken ~~football~~ [rugby] supporters. His body slumped on the floor of a cubicle in the men's station toilets. At first glance, he was mistaken for a slumbering homeless man, swallowed up in a large, dirt-stained mountain-climbing coat, accompanied by a bag filled with camping gear and food. The fact that his father, a man who in his later years barely ventured beyond the confines of their home, was found in such a state, only deepened the mystery and multiplied the unanswered questions.

Many times, Reuben would leave his room to use the adjacent bathroom, only to hear his mother's soft cries echoing from downstairs. He would perch atop the staircase, listening, aching to offer comfort but feeling paralyzed at the prospect. In his heart, he kept hoping Detective Walker would show up to declare a case of mistaken identity. He held on to the expectation that his father might walk through the door any day. But descending those stairs, bearing witness to his mother's grief, would shatter his denial and solidify the horrifying reality.

Now, sitting in the darkness ~~with a phone drained to one per cent charge and a lifeless Game Boy Advance~~, Reuben rose from the computer chair and flopped onto his bed. Closing his eyes, he casually swung his leg just over the edge of the bed, only to feel it brush against some cardboard.

That wasn't there before.

Rising from the bed, he flicked on the light, exposing the chaos of his bedroom. He looked towards the floor, where a half-open wooden box full of cassette tapes lay. A mixture of intrigue and confusion washed over him as he bent down to pick up the tapes. They bore the names of bands he had never heard of in his life. A small note, resting atop the wide array of cassettes, caught his attention:

Your father's cassette tapes. He wanted you to have these. He loved you very much. Mum xxx

Reuben tossed the note aside and took a seat on his bed, the box of cassette tapes beside him. His eyes looked to the collection of tapes sprawled before him: The Beatles, Rush, Genesis, Led Zeppelin, and an assortment of blanks. An idea popped into his head, and with his mother working the night shift, he saw an opportunity to bring his plan to fruition.

He ventured into the hallway and fetched one of the moving boxes. Back in his room, he opened the box, revealing a vintage vinyl/tape combo player. He swiftly set it up on his cluttered desk.

His eyes scanned the cassette tapes laid out before him. The classics were all there, but he found himself drawn to the unknown. With his eyes closed, he reached into the box and picked out a tape. Opening his eyes, he read the label:

"Marty's Master Mix 1992? Jesus Christ ..."

He took a deep breath, trying to push away the impending embarrassment. Positioning himself comfortably on his bed, he inserted the tape into the player. His eyes closed as the sounds of the cassette's wheels turning filled the room. Soon, the air was filled with the melancholic melody of a slow guitar-led ballad, its poignant notes enveloping every corner of the room.

"It's late in the evening, she's wondering what clothes to wear,
She puts on her makeup, and brushes her long blonde hair,
And then she asks me, 'Do I look all right?'
And I say, 'Yes, you look wonderful ton—'"

The tape began to falter. Rueben sat up in confusion, leaning towards the tape player, ready to stop the malfunctioning relic. But then a voice pierced through the crackling speakers:

"T-testing, one, two ... One, two ... Helloooo ... Well, the red light is on, so I guess it's working ..."

It was the voice he had been longing to hear for the past year, the voice of the man he wished would walk through their door any day now.

"Well, might as well get on with it then ..."

Reuben, still half-drunk and fatigued, wasn't in the right state to unpack all this now. He lethargically reached out to hit the Stop button, his eyelids drooping.

"My name is Martin Drake, and this is a warning to all of you."

His eyes snapped open, his finger hovering above the ~~Stop~~ button. An invisible force seemed to pull him upright.

"I have tried my best over the years to maintain a civil discourse with you, Eli. But your refusal to leave her alone and your insistence on involving Jonas and Maya has led us to a point of no return."

Reuben was confused at what he was hearing. Who were these people his father was talking to? The voice he heard didn't even sound like the father he knew. It was imbued with a kind of fierce determination that had never manifested before. He continued to listen:

"I pleaded … no … I begged for you to leave her alone. We had all accomplished so much in our time together. When is it more than enough?"

Reuben frowned, puzzled. Who was he talking about?

"You think she's showing signs. You think this is your chance to take her from me and her family. But by the time you hear this message, we will be gone. Consider this a declaration of w—"

The tape fizzled out again, but it sounded like someone had entered the room. Reuben heard the echo of stomps and childlike giggles.

"H-Hey, what are you doing? Where's your mother?"

Was this a recording from a time when Gary, his best friend from school, had been over? He didn't recall ever interrupting his father like this in the attic.

"Hey! Listen now!"

The laughter and the stomping ceased. The children's attention had been caught.

"I don't have to go to work tonight, so if you're good for Mum, I'll take you to McDonald's. Deal?"

A unified, enthusiastic "Yay!" followed.

"I want nuggets!" a young, high-pitched voice chimed. It sounded like a girl.

"Good. Daddy is busy at the moment, so Reuben, please can you and your sister wait downstairs?"

He froze, his hand over the Stop button. The same chilling sensation that had consumed him when he'd first heard about his father's death washed over him once more. The only part of him that seemed to move was his heart, hammering against his chest as if trying to escape. The rest of him was cemented in shock, his index finger tracing over the Rewind button. He rewound it a few seconds and hit Play:

"Daddy is busy at the moment, so Reuben, please can you and your sister wait downstairs?"

Again, he rewound and played.

". . . so Reuben, please can you and your sister wait downstairs?"

And again.

". . . please can you and your sister wait downstairs?"

He must have replayed that segment of the tape dozens of times. What sister? He had no sister. It was always just him, his mum, and his dad.

Wasn't it?

A horrifying conjecture sprouted in Reuben's mind for a flash of a second—What secret would make a man abandon his wife and child? What secret would a man die for?

"I don't have a sister," Reuben said to himself. "Do I?"

Another terrible thought came to him.

What if his father hadn't been the only Drake family member who disappeared that night?

He rewound the tape once more and pressed Play.

". . . please can you and your sister wait downstairs?"

CHAPTER TWO

Across the country in London, Dahlia Rose perched on a barstool, her elbows on the counter and her eyes on the door. The amber liquid in her mocktail glowed under the dim lights, untouched. A sense of anticipation filled the air—she's waiting for the journalist who's supposed to interview her before her band takes the stage at the venue just across the street. It was what Pitchfork had called their comeback.

Her phone buzzes for the umpteenth time today, nestled next to her on the bar. It's her landlord—again. The screen lights up with his name and instantly, her insides knot. She's behind on rent for the second month in a row. She glances at her phone but makes no move to answer it. The landlord's calls join a chorus of ignored reminders and overdue bills that play a constant, low-level hum of stress in the back of her mind.

"Hi! Dahlia, is that you?" The voice is effervescent, bubbling up like champagne. A woman strides towards her, her glasses perched on the bridge of her nose as if they might take flight. Her short, blonde hair seems almost damp, as though she's rushed here straight from a shower or a sprint through the rain. She cradles an iPad against her chest like a shield and thrusts her other hand forward for a shake.

Dahlia meets the woman's grip, smiling through clenched teeth. There's an almost immediate, visceral reaction that she can't quite put her finger on. Perhaps it's the woman's uncontainable cheerfulness, a stark contrast to Dahlia's own hard-fought composure. The effusiveness of this stranger serves as a jarring mirror, reflecting to Dahlia a version of herself she can barely remember—the enthusiastic young artist just breaking into the industry, filled with a naive sort of hope that now feels both foreign and painful.

"Nice to meet you," Dahlia manages to say, extricating her hand from the woman's firm grip. She takes a lingering sip of her mocktail as if the liquid could serve as a makeshift barrier between her and the palpable enthusiasm emanating from her interviewer. "You're the journalist?"

"That's me! Kim," the woman declares, her fingers dancing over her iPad to awaken it from Sleep mode. "Been counting down the days for this interview."

"Sorry to hear Tom's under the weather," Dahlia replies with casual indifference, mentioning her initial point of contact at the publication.

"Oh, he's getting better, thank goodness," Kim responds, matching Dahlia's tone of feigned disinterest. "Shall we take this outside? The noise level in here's a bit distracting, don't you think?"

Dahlia can't help but smirk at the suggestion. "I was kind of hoping the tunes would drown out the sound of your voice."

"What?" Kim looks genuinely confused, her fingers pausing over her iPad.

Dahlia waves her off with a playful grin. "Nothing, nothing." Setting her glass on the counter, she gracefully dismounts her barstool and gestures towards the door. "After you."

Taking her mocktail in hand, Dahlia follows Kim to the quieter oasis of an outdoor table, but her thoughts are anything but silent. The cacophony in her mind is a contrasting blend of annoyance and nostalgia, a reminder of who she once was and the jaded person she fears she's becoming.

As they settle into the outdoor table, shielded by a worn-out umbrella, Kim wastes no time. Her fingers hovered over her iPad as she glanced up.

"So, you're playing opposite the road at the Harp Tree tonight," Kim began. "This is your first real gig back in quite some time. Was there a decision behind announcing your comeback with an intimate venue?"

"It's the only one we could afford," Dahlia answers back nonchalantly, looking at her phone.

Kim, seemingly startled, looked back at her questions. "So, a few fans online are hoping to see you debut some new material. Will anything you play tonight be from your cancelled album from last year or would it be something completely original?"

"Oh shit! A few fans?" Dahlia asked, faking shock with a chuckle. "Can't wait for the money to come in from them."

Kim put the iPad on the table with a thud.

"Okay then. Should I cut the shit?" she asked.

"By all means," Dahlia replied with a smile.

"Okay, Dahlia Rose, singer of grunge band Soldier, why the sudden departure from Trainspot Records? You were scaling new heights—headlining the second stage at Glastonbury, cracking the Top Twenty in the US. Why leave when you're at the pinnacle of your career?"

Dahlia looked down at her mocktail, as if she could find the answers in its swirling colours. "Let's just say Trainspot got some new management last year. A certain Edward Velour. Oh, and I didn't choose to leave. I was let go."

Kim's eyebrows shot up, pausing her fingers midair. "Ah, Velour. Not the first time I've heard criticisms about the man or his empire, VelourTech. Controversial tax cuts masked as philanthropy, for one."

Dahlia smirked bitterly. "Well, add my name to the long list of people who think he's a total sleaze. But it's not just that. My new album touches on topics that Mr. Velour would rather stay buried."

"Intriguing. Like what?" Kim was visibly keen, her journalistic instincts kicking into high gear.

Dahlia hesitated. "Can we go off the record?"

Kim nodded and tapped her iPad, deactivating the recording function and showing it to her. "We're off."

Dahlia glanced around nervously, as if someone might be lurking in the shadows. When she spoke, her voice lacked its usual bravado. "Do you remember the story about the children who went missing in the Welsh valleys in 1968?"

WHAT HAPPENED IN AUGUST?

"I think I saw a BBC documentary as a kid."

"I had the idea to write a song from the perspective of the victims but wanted to do it in a respectful way. I thought maybe I could reach out to some members of the family. I heard there was even a survivor. So, I thought maybe I'll dig further, see what happens, maybe there's someone else I can talk to ... Then I found something peculiar."

Dahlia leaned in, dropping her voice to a near-whisper. "The land where those abductions happened? It's now owned by Edward Velour."

Kim blinked, needing a moment to absorb the revelation. "That's bizarre. What would a tech mogul want with an isolated piece of land in a forgotten village?"

Dahlia leaned back, a mix of pride and trepidation on her face. "Good question. I started digging. VelourTech has been acquiring land all over Europe. All similar places. Small towns that you would never visit filled with people who didn't have the money or knowledge to ever leave."

Kim looked bewildered. "But why?"

Dahlia's voice dropped again, tinged with a chilling certainty. "Murders. Disappearances. Every single one of those sites that are now owned by VelourTech are all sites of historical murders that were lost to history," she said, leaning back, almost proud of herself. "So, how do you think the label felt when I wanted to title the album *Edward Has a Secret*?"

Kim stared at Dahlia, the weight of the implications settling in. Her fingers returned to the iPad, but for a moment, they hovered, uncertain. Then, she tapped the screen, reactivating the recording function. "Shall we go back on the rec—"

Before Kim continued, she suddenly broke into a long wheezing, coughing fit. She tried to mouth *sorry*, but it kept coming. It gained the attention of a waiter who came over and handed her a tissue to cough in. After what felt like a minute, the cough soon subsided, and Kim took a long breath.

"Jesus. You okay?"

Kim nodded quickly and apologised.

"Sorry about that," she said as she composed herself and put the crumpled tissue next to her drink. Dahlia couldn't help but notice there were droplets of blood.

"As I was saying, she would go back on the record?" she asked

"Of course, just need to pop to the ladies' room first," Dahlia said, rising swiftly from her chair. ~~She navigated through the dimly lit crowd and pushed open the door to the restroom.~~ "You sure you don't want me to get you anything? A water, maybe?"

"No, I'll be fine. Thank you," Kim answered sternly ~~as if she wanted to get off the subject quick~~ly.

Dahlia nodded and then shuffled through the crowd to the right of the bar and then stepped into the ladies' room. The moment she stepped inside, she was bathed in a surreal, disconcerting red glow emanating from the overhead lights. It lent an eerie quality to the otherwise mundane space. Shaking off an uncanny feeling, she took care of business and moved to the sink to wash her hands.

As she glanced up to the mirror, her eyes locked onto a startling reflection—a man standing behind her, wearing a rabbit mask that concealed his features, stopping just below his nose. His formal suit contrasted sharply with the absurdity of the mask.

"Bit early for Halloween, don't you think?" Dahlia quipped nervously, attempting to laugh off the unsettling sight. "Also, you do realize you're in the women's restroom, right?"

As she spoke, her hand stealthily slipped into her pocket, pulling out a pocketknife she always carried for safety. But before she could fully extend the blade, the masked man lunged forward with alarming speed, pinning her against the cold tiled wall. The knife slipped from her grasp, clattering uselessly to the floor.

Her vision began to blur, her consciousness waning under the masked man's overpowering grip. Just as she felt herself teetering on the edge of unconsciousness, he leaned in, his whisper cutting through the red-lit haze.

"I'm here to show you where the bodies are."

And then darkness swallowed her.

*

Dahlia's eyes snapped open, her lungs gasping for air as if surfacing from deep water. She took in her surroundings: she was bound to an opulent dining chair in what appeared to be an expansive, lavishly furnished living room. A long, elegant dinner table stretched before her, set with gleaming silverware and fine china. Crystal chandeliers cast a soft, golden glow, and the mellifluous tones of a Bach concerto floated through the room.

In front of her, food was meticulously arranged on a plate, a gourmet spread that looked utterly incongruous given her circumstances. Her eyes darted upwards to find two men sitting across from her. Both wore masks, but unlike the disturbing rabbit disguise, these were elegant, almost Venetian in style—one of them golden, the other more understated but equally unnerving.

The man in the golden mask just sat there, watching her intently, not touching his own, equally lavish, plate of food. The other man, however, was eating with a sense of relish that made her stomach turn.

And then, almost as if on cue, another figure appeared in the dining room.

It was Kim, the journalist, sauntering into the room as casually as if she had just stepped out of a shower. Unfazed by the tense atmosphere, she moved to an empty chair at the far end of the table. With a practised motion, she reached beneath it and pulled out another Venetian mask. She sat down, donned the mask with a self-satisfied smirk, and propped her elbow on the table, her chin resting on her hand as she looked at Dahlia.

Dahlia Rose thought that the secrets she found could be used for the purpose of artistry. But all she had done was take a step forward into a dark world where she didn't belong.

"So, Dahlia, shall we continue the interview?"

CHAPTER THREE

Bleary-eyed and struggling to shake off the remnants of sleep, Alice staggered towards the relentless noise, cursing under her breath. Her bare feet slapped against the cold laminate flooring, a harsh reminder of the early hour.

"For God's sake," she muttered, clumsily pulling on her faded jeans and a threadbare T-shirt. The incessant banging only fuelled her annoyance, creating a headache that throbbed in time with the noise.

"Yes? Who is it?!"

She didn't expect any visitors at this ungodly hour. Her brows furrowed in confusion, she tugged a hairband around her unruly curls and shuffled to the door. A familiar sense of dread clawed at her as she reached for the doorknob.

"Who's there?" Alice demanded, her voice echoing unnaturally in the stillness of the morning. Silence followed her question, but it only lasted for a heartbeat before the knocking resumed, more frantic than before. Her heart pounded in sync with the knocking. She yanked the door a tenth of the way open, chain still on, revealing the last person she expected to see on her doorstep.

"Good god. Your eye!" Alice said, wincing. "You look like Quasimodo but worse. Did Morgan also damage your ear? Couldn't you hear me calling?"

"Sorry, I got a missed call just as I was knocking on the door," Reuben said, breathing anxiously, his eyes darting around the front door, behind him at the lone Cardiff street, and finally settling on Alice. Her jet-black hair fell in soft waves around her face, catching the light so it seemed almost like shiny obsidian. Her emerald-green eyes often had this playful glint in them, a direct reflection of her vivacious personality. Reuben looked down at the pepper spray can in her hand.

"Which ex-boyfriend were you expecting at the door? Steve? Rich?" His smile was unflinching.

"You think I would welcome Rich with this?" she asked. "I'd be carrying a bloody cricket bat!" She playfully brandished the can of pepper spray she had been hiding. "No," Alice sighed, her voice still husky with sleep and tinged with frustration, "This is my standard-issue greeting for unwanted interruptions. Now get in here before Mrs. Henderson across the street starts speculating."

With that, Reuben stepped across the threshold, following Alice down the hall. The hallway was shabbily dressed in a once-beige, now dirt-brown carpet, the off-white walls marred with years of smudges and scrapes, revealing a narrative of raucous student gatherings.

"Just a wee heads up, this is Andrea's fortress. She's a real stickler for cleanliness, so try not to cause any havoc, alright? Want a drink? Coffee? Tea?"

"Coffee would be lush, thanks."

She guided him into the kitchen, a slender space bristling with appliances that had seen better days. The walls were a shrine to athleticism, adorned with various sports medals courtesy of Alice's flatmate. Reuben settled at the far end of the kitchen, leaning casually against the chipped countertop while Alice occupied the other side.

As Alice handed Reuben a steaming mug of coffee, she gave him an ice pack as well. "You need to start taking care of yourself more. Remember when you cracked your head open on the way home from graduation?"

Reuben gingerly applied the ice pack to his eye, wincing at the initial cold shock. "Yeah, Mum keeps saying the same thing," he said with a lopsided smile, cradling the coffee mug for warmth.

"How is she?"

"Fine, I think," he said, taking a sip.

"You think?"

"She works nights most of the time so I might see her once or twice a week. I think it's a good distraction, all things considered."

"Christ. Walker may have moved in with us!"

Reuben had told Alice last night about the inspector's attention.

"I'm sorry. It's really shit that they still haven't found anything new for you to go on."

Reuben set his coffee down, his demeanour suddenly serious. "Well, that's partially why I'm here." He dug into his pocket, pulling out a battered old cassette tape—his father's tape. He presented it to Alice.

"Do you reckon Andrea's got a sound system we could use?"

Reuben replayed the tape for Alice, not once but three times in succession. They perched at the edge of her double bed, lost in the jumble of words flowing from the tape, a heavy silence hanging between them. Once the third replay came to an end, Alice remained motionless, her hand cradling her head.

agreement, to

"So, what do you think?" Reuben asked.

his shoulders, his eyes silently pleading for Alice to say something.

"you don't even have a sister." Alice finally voiced her confusion.

He responded with an eye roll. "I figured that part out. Cheers."

With a click, he ejected the cassette from the recorder, carefully placing it back into his pocket. He sank back onto the bed, his eyes drifting towards the paper-ball lampshade suspended from the ceiling.

"I heard this last night, and I haven't slept since," he confessed, his voice barely above a whisper. "It's been driving me mad."

"I mean, it's clearly your father's voice," Alice agreed, her voice wavering slightly. "But the things he's saying? It's hard to wrap your head around to be honest. Do those names mean anything to you?"

Reuben shook his head. Those three names. Maya, Jonas, and Eli. Three people who his father was going to declare war on were strangers in his eyes. Were they the ones who had murdered his father? And what about the girl?

"That's me on the tape, no doubt about it," Reuben confessed, raking his fingers across his face as if he could physically erase the unsettling thoughts bombarding his mind. "But this sister thing … I don't have a sister. It's ludicrous to even think that Mum and Dad would have considered another child."

"Let's put the sister conundrum aside for now," Alice suggested, her voice a calming beacon amidst the chaos. "Your dad admitted to leading a double life on that tape. Whatever he was hiding, he left you and your mum for it. And it seems like it wasn't a spur-of-the-moment decision."

"The problem is, the one person who could unravel this mystery isn't here anymore," Reuben noted bitterly.

He noticed Alice's shocked expression out of the corner of his eye. Her eyes were wide, mouth slightly agape as if a revelation had just dawned upon her.

"What?" he questioned, bemused by her reaction.

"That tape was recorded when you were about eight, right?" Alice asked.

"And it seems he followed through with his plan."

Reuben simply nodded in agreement.

"So, doesn't it make sense that there could be more tapes? If he was interrupted, he might have recorded another one," Alice reasoned, her voice teetering on the brink of excitement. "Have you checked the other tapes?"

Reuben shook his head. "I heard this one and rushed over here."

Rolling her eyes, Alice sighed heavily, "I'll get changed. We're going to your mum's."

Once she left the room, Reuben found himself alone. His attention was drawn to a half-broken photo frame on a nearby drawer. A throwback to a simpler time—him and Alice, grinning like fools while sharing a bottle of wine in a bathtub. He picked up the frame, running a finger over the cracked glass. He allowed the sharp edge to cut into his skin, a droplet of blood pooling at his fingertip.

Surrounded by mountains of worn cassette tapes and neglected boxes, the remnants of Martin Drake's life, Alice felt a whirlwind of emotions. They'd spent the last hour scouring through each tape, hoping for a shred of enlightenment to his baffling secret. However, all they seemed to uncover was an assortment of esoteric mixtapes.

"Anything noteworthy?" Alice asked, her voice barely audible over the din of yet another Eric Clapton track blaring from the speaker.

"Just more of Dad's classic rock collection," Reuben grumbled, his patience evidently waning. He'd been clinging to the vain hope that perhaps his father had concealed a message within these seemingly inconsequential melodies. But as time passed, hope gave way to frustration, and with a gruff sigh, he turned off the tape player.

"Hey! What about this?"

Alice held aloft an old, wide-framed school photo. It was instantly recognisable to Reuben; a similar one hung in his childhood home, displaying his enthusiastic portrayal of a starfish in a nativity play. But something about this one was peculiar.

"I'm not in this photo," Reuben noted, squinting at the faded image. "Where'd you dig this out from?"

"It was stashed at the bottom of that ninth box," Alice explained, pointing to a heap of discarded bags. "But why would your parents keep a school photo without you in it?"

Stumped, Reuben shrugged.

"Could it possibly be a photo of Mum or Dad from their schooldays?"

"Unlikely. For one, this is a Latymer Comprehensive School uniform, which didn't even exist when your parents were students. And secondly …"

Alice's finger hovered over an adolescent girl with a beaming, bucktoothed smile, her hair swept back in a neat ponytail.

"That's Emily Edwards. Remember Luke's sister? The bassist in John's band?"

Recognition dawned on Reuben. "Oh yeah, he was in Siadosa. They were the band who beat me and the boys in the Battle of the Bands. I hate that guy so much."

Alice rolled her eyes. "Reuben. You were twelve."

"Do you have his number?" he asked.

"I do," Alice answered, taking out her phone. "Don't worry, I'll speak to him. God forbid what might happen if he hears the voice of his Battle of the Bands rival."

As she spoke into the phone, Reuben found himself poring over the faces in the photo, each one a potential lead to his elusive sibling.

Alice's voice dropped to a hushed whisper; her complexion drained of colour.

"I'm so sorry … yes, I understand …" she murmured. "As long as you're sure that's okay. I don't want to put you under pressure … okay. I'll speak to Reuben and see what he wants to do. Okay, bye."

She put the phone down and looked at Reuben. Her face filled with worry.

"What happened?"

Alice seemed lost in thought as she gravitated towards the window.

"Emily … she suffered a mental breakdown last year," Alice informed him, her voice barely above a whisper. "She's in a psychiatric institution."

"Christ, poor girl," Reuben reacted. ~~He thought of his old friend from English class, Mark, whose brother had been sectioned when they were in school.~~ "When did it happen?"

"Last year," Alice confirmed, her voice filled with hesitation.

Reuben nodded, processing the uncanny coincidence that it was the same time his father had disappeared.

"He said we can come visit. He's going to be at the facility until the evening. Maybe her family knows something," Alice suggested.

"You sure he's going to be okay with that?" Reuben asked cautiously. "I don't know if I'd be happy letting strangers visit my ill sibling."

"To be honest, all I heard was a guy who was desperate to talk to someone," Alice said. "To not be alone."

Reuben agreed with a curt nod. He stood up and moved for the door. "I'll let Mum know we're going out. It's the afternoon, so she'll think we're going to the cinema or something. Be right back."

As he exited the room, Alice was left alone amidst the chaotic remnants of Martin Drake's life. She returned to the box that had yielded the school photograph. Alice paused for a moment and turned her head towards the door, ensuring that Reuben wasn't going to come back. She moved her hands through the box's contents and retrieved another photograph. The one she didn't want him to see.

Staring back at her, smiling gleefully through the faded sepia polaroid were four men, three women and what appeared to be a young boy. They were sat around a long wooden table, playing some sort of card game. Each adult was in formal dress. The men wore matching black tie dinner suits, and all three women wore identical dresses which appeared to be green in colour. The most disturbing aspect of the photo was what was disguising the top half of their faces. All of them seemed to be wearing a mask carved into the shape of a rabbit.

Alice looked to the child sat in the middle chair of the photo. Even though the photograph was aged, and its quality had faded, it was unnervingly clear that the boy was tied to the chair. It was also clear that he was screaming for help.

CHAPTER FOUR

The bus hummed along the road, leaving behind the energetic bustle of Cardiff. Gradually, the urban landscape and its inhabitants bathed in the warmth of pleasant sunshine began to fade. The sprawling cityscape gave way to the tranquil beauty of rural pastures, an unending sea of emerald serenity.

Alice was the first to break the silence, a hint of regret colouring her voice. "We should've explored this place more often," she mused. "Those summers during our university days could've been spent better than just downing Jager bombs."

"Can't change the past," Reuben retorted, his tone distant and dismissive. He kept his eyes closed, basking in the soft sunlight pouring through the window.

Pressing forward, Alice shifted the conversation to Reuben's mother. "It's surprising your mum chose to stay here after all that happened."

"Yeah," Reuben muttered, his eyes still closed. There was an edge of bitterness to his voice. "We still get photographers and podcasters dropping by. That's an improvement from the days when we had crowds camped outside our house all night."

Alice's eyes widened in surprise. "Really? I mean, I knew your dad's death was a big deal, but I didn't think it had turned into such a media circus."

Reuben merely shrugged in response, a silent indication of his familiarity with the world's unwelcome intrusion into his life.

"Dad's disappearance was unusual enough," he conceded,

the bitterness in his voice more evident. "One of his workmates said he'd show up at the office in tears weeks before he disappeared and was constantly on his phone." He paused; his words weighed down with resentment. "Then someone claimed they spotted him at a cafe with a woman.

Rumours of an affair spread like wildfire, and the media jumped on it. A perfect distraction. It's a vicious cycle: people get angry, then bored, then angry again. They're always looking for some sort of stimulation, even if it means making a mountain out of a molehill."

Alice moved closer, resting her head on his shoulder. "I really am sorry, Reuben," she murmured sympathetically. "This whole situation is so …"

"Fucked?" he suggested, finishing her sentence.

"I was going to say 'complicated,'" she corrected, pulling away to hold her phone in front of him. "I think it's these kinds of situations that drive us mad. We're so quick to react but seldom stop to think about why we're reacting in the first place."

Reuben managed a chuckle. "Did you get that from a George Orwell book or something?"

"I'm serious!" she insisted, pushing the phone closer to his face. "Look."

Expecting a social media post or a sensational news article, Reuben glanced at the phone screen. Instead, he found a short message typed into the Notes app.

His heart pounded in his chest as he read: *Man two seats behind us. Eyes have been on us since the bus station. Think he's following. Get off at the next stop.*

He returned the phone to Alice, trying to maintain his composure and keep his hand steady.

"Funny, right?" Alice joked, trying to lighten the mood.

"Hilarious," Reuben muttered, his voice barely a whisper.

He remained on edge until they reached the stop just before Larkhill Manor. Without skipping a beat, Alice pulled him to his feet, and they shuffled towards the exit, joining a family of four who were bidding farewell to the bus driver. As they stepped off the bus, Reuben couldn't resist a quick glance back. Their vacated seats were now occupied.

As the bus whizzed by, Reuben locked eyes with a mysterious stranger aboard, capturing an entire persona in the blink of an eye. Icy blue eyes meet his. The man was clad in a distinctive purple tweed suit, his lips curling into a devilish smile. And then, as quickly as the moment came, the bus vanished from sight.

The grand entrance to Larkhill Manor was defined by imposing iron gates, groaning softly as they parted to expose the estate's expanse. Ahead, the manor house towered, an edifice of historical opulence, the very embodiment of majestic grandeur.

The mansion, with its ornate architecture and imposing facade, was set in a sweeping landscape of manicured gardens, picturesque water features, and ancient trees. The stone steps leading to the entrance seemed to rise towards the heavens, a symbolic stairway into the annals of the manor's storied past. The magnitude of the estate was overwhelming, with the mansion's sheer size making them feel exceedingly insignificant in comparison. Alice and Reuben paused, taking in the spectacle, the breadth of the estate serving as a stark reminder of their daunting task.

As they slowly began their walk up the gravel path towards the mansion, Alice finally broke the silence. "Who do you think that man on the bus was?"

"I don't know," Reuben replied. "But … I couldn't help but feel like that was a warning."

"A warning? Do you think it could be someone who recognised you? Do you remember seeing him at the funeral?" Alice asked, her voice merely a whisper against the soft rustle of leaves.

"No," Reuben admitted, as he dredged up the mournful memories. "But I didn't recognize half the people there to be honest. Mum said it was loads of Dad's old school and work friends."

Alice sighed, running her fingers through her jet-black hair. "You think we're getting into something deeper, don't you? Don't you think you should tell that detective buddy of yours?"

Reuben shook his head.

"I half believe what's on that tape. They'll laugh us out of the station if we come in with just that mind. Not without any proof."

Reuben gave a resigned sigh, a hand moving to rake through his unkempt hair as if hoping to find an answer amongst its strands. His gaze was lost somewhere beyond the manor's imposing gates, his mind wrestling with questions too vast and enigmatic to put into words.

Alice, who had been quietly observing her friend, suddenly pointed towards the group gathered at the manor's grand entrance, a hint of familiarity lighting up her eyes. "Look, there's Luke!" she exclaimed.

Reuben saw a man garbed in a small leather jacket, his hair restrained into a tight man bun. His features were drawn, etched with the story of sleepless nights and exhausting days. His fidgeting fingers danced restlessly across his chin, portraying a mind deep in thought.

As they made their approach, Luke acknowledged Alice with a weary smile and a brief embrace. "Glad to see you, Alice," he said, his voice gravelly from fatigue. His eyes then moved to Reuben, a respectful nod serving as his greeting. "So, you guys are here because of a photo, right? That's what you said on the phone."

Before Reuben could stumble through an explanation, Alice intervened with a well-rehearsed lie. "Reuben's doing a university project on his old school and thought Emily might recognize some faces in a photo," she explained.

"Right, exactly," Reuben quickly agreed, attempting to keep his nerves at bay.

A shadow of sympathy passed over Luke's face. "Emily hasn't spoken for over a year," he disclosed, his voice heavy with resignation. "But I agreed to this because ... well, I thought it was worth a shot."

As they stepped into the building's mustard-yellow reception area, Reuben immediately asked the question.

"What happened to Emily? Why is she here?"

Luke stopped in his tracks and squared up to Reuben. For a moment, Alice thought she was going to have to break up a fight but instead, he relaxed himself and turned to face away from them.

"I wasn't there when it happened, but Dad was," he began. "The day was normal. We were going to have a quiet night in with the rest of the family, as she was off to uni the week after. It was in the afternoon, and she was outside the front door, talking to her one of her school friends. Dad didn't see who it was, but he passed the entrance while he was cooking. They were both laughing and seemed to be in good spirits. Next thing he knows, he hears her screaming. He runs to the entrance and Emily's on the floor. Whoever she was talking to was gone."

His upper body shook as he desperately tried to not break down.

"Dad blames himself, of course. Said he should have been there and known who she was talking to," he continued, his voice breaking. "The doctors think she's suffered some sort of mental breakdown. When she came to in the hospital, she didn't seem to know who we were. In fact, she didn't seem to know anything. Soon after that, she stopped saying a word."

Alice moved to the side of him and put her hand on his shoulder. "I'm so sorry, Luke."

Luke turned back to face Reuben, his eyes and face red from crying.

Reuben, deep in thought, steered the conversation back to the person Emily was talking to. "So, the person she was talking to? Did you ever learn this friend's name? Did your dad know who it was?"

Luke responded with a shrug, "Emily never really mentioned names. She had many friends. I don't think there's a day that goes by where we haven't received flowers or gifts from one of her school friends. And once I was back from university, it was hard to keep track."

Handing over the photo, Reuben asked, "Do any of them look familiar to this person next to her?"

Luke examined the photo briefly and then shook his head before handing the photo back to Reuben.

"No. Sorry."

"And when did this all happen?"

Luke didn't ponder to think of the date. He knew exactly when it happened.

"The twenty-eighth of July, last year."

Reuben and Alice shared a look of concern. That was two days before his father vanished.

"If you're okay with us doing this, Luke, we could see if this photo jogs her memory," she proposed. "If you want us to leave, mind, we get it."

"No. It's fine," he replied. "Even if there's a small chance I can get her back, I have to take it."

As they approached room 1309, Alice and Luke fell into comfortable chatter, while Reuben silently took in the surroundings. A tall nurse with cascading curls and a warm smile greeted Luke but stiffened at the sight of the two visitors. As she ran through the safety protocols, Reuben peered through the door's small window.

Inside, a petite figure with dyed red hair sat on the bed. The sight of the teenage girl, trapped within the sterile confines of this mustard-yellow room, was a heart-wrenching reality. She deserved to be far away from home, enjoying a new life at university, not languishing here in a silence too profound for her years.

Luke approached Emily, his familiar features radiating warmth and affection. "Hello, love. You alright?" he murmured, pressing a tender kiss to her forehead. Alice and Reuben lingered at the doorway, unease pinning them at a respectful distance from the familial scene unfolding before them.

In the corner of the room, a male nurse was carrying out his duties of changing Emily's bed.

"These are my friends, Alice and Reuben."

Reuben offered the photo to Luke with an outstretched arm which was then held in front of Emily's face. "Look, Em, this is a picture of you at school. Recognize anyone?"

Emily's eyes moved to the photo, slowly surveying the faces. Silence fell over the room like a shroud, the occupants holding their breath in anticipation. Time stretched to its limit as they waited for a reaction.

As the initial wave of hope began to ebb away, Emily's hand jerked slightly. Gradually, she pointed a trembling finger at one of the faces in the photo. Her eyes widened with fear and confusion, her lips parted as if she was grappling with unspoken words.

"Do you know her, sweetheart?" Luke asked softly, indicating the girl Emily had singled out.

The question seemed to trigger something in Emily. She let out a piercing scream, her terror-filled eyes locked onto Reuben. Amid the ensuing chaos, as Luke and the nurse struggled to calm Emily, her eyes remained fixated on Reuben. The nurse managed to administer a sedative, and Emily's screams faded into a barely audible murmur, repeating a chilling phrase: "She had to leave ... She had to leave, or you'd die ... She had to leave, or you would die."

Once Emily succumbed to the sedative, the nurse, stern and visibly shaken, ushered them out. Reuben started to apologise, but Luke, fuelled by protective rage, shoved him against the wall.

"You will never speak to her again! You understand?" Luke spat out, his eyes blazing.

"I'm sorry, I didn't know ..." Reuben started, but Alice cut him off.

"Luke! He made her speak for the first time in a year, and this is how you act?" she countered, her voice echoing her disbelief.

A security ward staff member swiftly intervened, his stern voice cutting through the tension. "Guys. Do we have a problem here?" He guided them away from the door, restoring a semblance of order to the hallway.

Once they were back in the reception area, Reuben broke the silence, his voice heavy with resolve. "I know why you're upset, but I wouldn't have come unless it was important. The girl we are looking for, she might be ... someone who's missing."

Reuben handed him the photo again

Luke looked up at Reuben and back down to the photo, a maelstrom of disbelief, confusion, and exhaustion reflected in his eyes. The words seemed to hang in the air, undulating in the silent reception area. The outburst, the unexpected revelation, had drained him.

Luke wordlessly extended the photo back to Reuben. Accepting it, Reuben's hand slackened around the image. The photo, once seen as a beacon of truth, now seemed to be a mocking testament to the twisted maze they found themselves in. He felt a pit in his stomach, a blend of exhaustion, frustration, and an all-consuming sense of defeat.

"Hey, wait." Luke broke the oppressive silence, his voice rough.

"After you guys left, she … she said a name—Lena."

Alice spun to face Reuben, her eyes wide. "Lena?" she echoed.

"Yeah, Lena," Luke confirmed, rubbing his temples. "Look I'm going to go back and check she's okay."

"I'm going to see Emily," Luke stated, his footfalls echoing ominously as he and a security guard disappeared into the mustard-yellow hallway.

Reuben went to follow him, but Alice stepped in front of him, her hand pressing against his chest in a restraining gesture. "Reuben, I think we should leave it for the rest of the day. Don't you?" she warned.

"Didn't you hear the guy? She mentioned a name. This could be the girl my dad is talking about on the cassette tape. She will be able to answer some of our questions!"

Reuben went to move, but Alice didn't back down, her arms folding defiantly across her chest. "I think she's been through enough."

"What, and I haven't?!" Reuben asked angrily. "I thought you were in this with me, Alice," he hissed. "I thought you wanted answers too."

"Not at the expense of someone else's sanity!" she fired back, her voice echoing in the sterile space. "This is your business, Reuben. I agreed to help, but this is going too far."

He leaned in close.

"Then maybe it would be for the best if you just leave."

The escalating argument was cut short by a terrifying scream and a thud from Emily's room. Panic instantly flooded the corridor.

Their hearts pounded in their chests as time seemed to both freeze and accelerate. They dashed towards the sound, fear fuelling their every step. Reuben was the first to reach the door, crashing into it in his haste. His foot collided with something solid, and he stumbled, looking down to see Luke sprawled out unconscious. He looked to the source of the commotion. Emily was on her feet, her body shaking uncontrollably. The male nurse who had simply been changing her bed only minutes before now had her in a deadly grip, the blade of a kitchen knife shimmering threateningly at her throat.

"Where is she?" the man growled, a frenzied look in his eyes that was impossible to ignore. "Where is the girl?!"

Reuben, forcing himself onto shaking knees, attempted to negotiate with the frantic intruder. "What girl? We don't know what you're talking about," he said, forcing calm into his voice.

The man responded with a guttural yell that filled the room. "LIAR!" His face was flushed and streaked with tears, twisted in rage. "I heard him mention her name! You've met her!"

Alice's sharp cry barely pierced his focus as Reuben stood slowly, bracing himself for whatever was to come.

"Let's talk this out," he said, maintaining a calm facade despite the rising panic. "If you let her go, I can help you find who you're looking for. Is that a deal?"

At the sight of the blade pressing into Emily's throat, her gasp echoing in the room, Reuben seized his chance. "I can take you to Lena," he proposed, seeing the man freeze in his tracks.

"Lena … that's the name, right?" he continued cautiously, "That's the girl you're looking for? Put the knife down, and I'll help you find Lena."

The room was caught in a churning sea of suspense, each ticking second seeming to play out in slow motion. The man's wild, fevered eyes oscillated between Reuben and Emily, his mind clearly wrestling with the choice before him. His grasp on Emily slackened infinitesimally, yet the blade of the knife maintained its threatening proximity to her pale throat.

"For God's sake, think!" Reuben erupted, his restraint buckling under the strain. "You're out of your bloody mind!"

His words were like fuel to the flame. A savage snarl contorted the man's face, and he released Emily, lunging at Reuben with unchecked ferocity. The pair crashed to the floor, a tangle of thrashing limbs, the glinting knife swinging precariously close to Reuben's face. The man's strength was formidable, his madness granting him a terrifying endurance.

Reuben struggled valiantly, warding off the deadly blade. But he was rapidly depleting his reserves, his strength waning. Time was slipping through his fingers.

Suddenly, the room was awash with harsh light as the door was kicked open violently. A wave of uniformed police officers flooded in; their stern faces set in grim determination. In a matter of seconds, they had the man subdued, his hands bound behind his back and the knife skittering uselessly across the tiled floor.

"Subject is secure," one officer announced, hoisting the still-raving man onto his feet while others rushed to assess Emily and Reuben's conditions. Though the immediate threat was neutralised, the room vibrated with the aftershocks of the confrontation. The tension, albeit ebbing away, clung to the atmosphere like a spectre.

CHAPTER FIVE

From the uneasy comfort of the reception window, Reuben found himself spectating the grim tableau as Jonathan, shrouded in silence yet visibly trembling, was led into the iron-clad clutches of a waiting police car. Nestled in a nondescript corner of the reception area, Reuben was marooned in a sea of tormenting thoughts and unanswered questions. A bitter cocktail of anxiety and anticipation curdled in his stomach as he awaited the impending scrutiny of the stone-faced detectives.

"Hey, mate," Luke's voice emerged softly from the whirlpool of Reuben's thoughts. He was standing there, a gentle, apologetic smile playing on his lips. Miraculously, he seemed unscathed by the earlier turmoil.

"Hey," Reuben replied. "You doing okay?"

Luke bobbed his head in affirmation. "On-site medics say I dodged a concussion. I suppose I should count myself lucky."

"And Emily?"

His smile waned ever so slightly.

"She's pretty rattled. Doctors said it's too early to assess the full psychological impact of this … It's grim, but at least she's still here with us."

A heavy silence descended, a wordless testament to the ordeal they had both survived. Eventually, Luke found his voice, a note of remorse colouring his words.

"Look, I was a bit harsh on you before, and for that, I'm sorry … I shudder to think what might've happened to Emily if you and Alice hadn't intervened. You have my eternal gratitude for that."

Reuben managed an awkward nod, taken aback by Luke's change of heart. "There's something else, though," Luke continued. "All of this … it's connected to your father's story, isn't it? Sorry if I'm bringing old shit up for you but I can't shake off the feeling that it's not merely coincidental." Reuben's eyes locked onto Luke's, questioning what the police might have shared. That familiar adrenal surge, the visceral fight-or-flight instinct, came rushing back. He was cornered once more, but this time, there was a clear choice.

"I've had more close shaves with a knife today than I'd care for," Reuben retorted, pushing himself up with visible effort. "If the cops have anything to discuss, it can wait till after I've caught some shut-eye."

Luke conceded with a nod.

"When you're ready to talk, you'll know where to find me." He extended a hand towards Reuben. After a brief moment, Reuben accepted it.

"Reuben, the police are ready for you," Alice informed him, her voice soft and understanding. He couldn't look at her. His eyes darting around the room, tracing the geometric patterns on the linoleum.

"I can't. Not right now, Alice," Reuben confessed, his voice barely above a whisper. The adrenaline rush from the confrontation was starting to wear off, replaced by an overwhelming anxiety. He felt foolish. He had naively thought he could play the detective, but instead, he'd nearly ended up as another casualty. "I nearly got us killed …"

Alice reached out, laying a gentle hand on his arm. "I know … I know it was terrifying. But you did what you thought was right. You can't blame yourself."

"What was I thinking? What was I hoping to achieve here?" Reuben muttered more to himself than Alice. The questions were rhetorical; he knew the answer. He was still a young boy chasing his father's footsteps.

He exhaled deeply, rubbing his hand over his face. "I need to go home."

Alice nodded, offering a small, supportive smile. "Maybe that's for the best. You should spend some time with your mum, Reuben."

✓

He frowned at her suggestion. "Why does everyone keep saying that?"

"Because she's your family. Because she's grieving too. Because she's not the only one who's been suffering through all of this," Alice pointed out, her tone gentle yet firm. "You've been so focused on finding answers, you've forgotten the people who need you the most. Your mother needs you, Reuben. Just as much as you need her."

Reuben mulled over Alice's words as he slowly made his way towards the exit of Larkhill. He was so engrossed in his own grief and quest for answers that he'd forgotten his mother was going through the same. He'd neglected her, blinded by his own desperation to solve the puzzle surrounding his father's death.

"You should ask your Mum about Lena," Alice called after him, her voice barely above a whisper yet piercing through the fog of his thoughts.

The cold evening air greeted him as he pushed open the doors. He looked at the photo one last time; the two girls, forever trapped in happier times, seemed unreachable now. A sobering reminder of the convoluted maze his life had become. With a deep sigh, he pocketed the picture, squaring his shoulders against the cold, harsh reality. He had a long night ahead.

Jonathan watched with a single eye cracked open as the sun disappeared beyond the distant valley. His hopes for this day to end differently had been dashed. He had hoped that handing over the information about Emily Drake would earn him a place within the family's fold, that he would finally be appreciated for who he was, quirks and all.

"This is what you've wanted all along, isn't it?" Eli's words echoed in his mind, his touch, that fleeting moment of connection that Jonathan had held onto since their first meeting. "For someone to love you back, to appreciate you for the person you are, faults and all. We can give you that. And more."

"We can set you free." His own words echoed back to him in a tear-choked sob.

Jonathan felt himself move forward as the car came to a sudden stop. The officers had exited the vehicle before he had time to question them. Left alone, he felt a tremor of unease curl through him. The darkness outside seemed all-encompassing, and he was miles away from anywhere recognizable. Naivete had dulled his senses to the fact that they had passed the closest police station an hour ago.

The door beside him was wrenched open abruptly.

The man who climbed into the vehicle wore a silk purple suit that screamed opulence. His fragrance, a blend of exotic aftershaves, was overwhelming. Blond hair cascaded to his shoulders, partially obscuring a neck adorned with intricate tattoos. The brief moment of eye contact felt like an unwanted obligation, as though merely looking at Jonathan was a laborious task.

"I know you!" Jonathan exclaimed. "You were with Eli … WAIT!"

But instead of revealing the knife that had haunted Jonathan's dreams, the stranger—Jonas to a select few—pulled out a small phone. He glanced at Jonathan once more, a cruel smile playing on his lips as he took in his captive's terror, before he began scrolling through the device.

Jonathan hesitantly accepted the phone, the screen black except for a red box demanding a passcode. Jonas took out a small paper packet from his jacket pocket, a satisfied chuckle escaping him as he did so.

"This is for you as well," he stated, handing over the mysterious packet. In Jonathan's right hand was the locked phone, in his left, the small packet containing a solitary pill.

As Jonas opened the door, the cooling summer breeze swept in. "The passcode is your date of birth. I'd recommend not opening the packet until you've finished watching the video," he instructed, standing up to leave.

Panicked, Jonathan grabbed him by the shoulder. "Where are you going?! You can't leave me to go to jail! Wait … what if I said something inside, huh? What if I told the police about you? About Eli? About all of you?"

Jonas stifled another chuckle, removing Jonathan's hand from his shoulder. "Oh, bless you," he smirked, raising a hand to Jonathan's face. "There's really not much going on behind those eyes, is there?" With an expression of distaste, he quickly withdrew his hand, wiping it on his trousers as if to remove a foul substance.

"Just watch the phone, Jonathan. Everything else will become clear."

He didn't look back as he shut the door, leaving Jonathan alone once again.

With nothing else to do, Jonathan keyed his date of birth into the phone, revealing a collection of photos. His stomach churned with dread as he immediately recognized the house displayed. Swiping left, the next photo revealed the side profile of a young woman entering her front door.

Jonathan flinched at the sight of the next photo—a masked man seated in a car; a gun pointed straight towards the camera. The backdrop to this scene was all too familiar—Daisy's house. The phone nearly slipped through his trembling fingers.

His thumb moved to the left again, revealing a final item—a voice recording. Jonathan pressed play.

"Jonathan." It was Jonas's voice, calm and collected as ever. "If you're listening to this, then it means you have failed your mission to retrieve details regarding The Collector and have thus placed the hidden existence of our family at risk. To make matters worse, you've now put yourself on a direct path to a jail cell."

Jonathan felt his breath hitch as he listened closely to the next steps Jonas outlined.

"You now have a choice. The woman in these photos is named Daisy Robinson. For the past two years, you have been stalking her and her young son. Despite police involvement and threats of a restraining order, you remain incapable of acknowledging your actions. You sought us out to help you overcome this obsession. This ... love."

As Jonas spoke, a wave of pins and needles spread through Jonathan, his skin crawling with both a momentary awareness and revulsion at his actions. But that feeling of disgust, the stirrings of a potentially healthier path forward, was quickly drowned by the fantasy that dominated his thoughts. He remembered confessing this to Daisy himself, on a rainy evening, soaked to the bone in his new three-piece suit, clutching wilting tulips. He had confessed his obsessive thoughts to her, begged her to help him, to extract them from his mind, right up until the police arrived to take him away. But she never understood their connection, something he was hoping to change.

"If you choose to go to prison and risk our family's identity, Daisy will die," Jonas continued. His words landed like a punch to Jonathan's gut. His mouth began to quiver, a mournful sound escaping his lips.

"Alternatively, you can make the other choice. Take the pill that you've been given, and Daisy will be allowed to live her life in peace," Jonas offered. "I can assure you, it won't be painful. Why not prove just how much you truly love her?"

Tears welled in Jonathan's eyes as he hastily tore open the small packet, revealing the tiny, mustard-yellow pill inside. His hand was shaking so much that he had to steady it with his other hand. His breathing became laboured, in and out, in and out, as he tried to control the panic that was threatening to overtake him.

Outside, rain began to pelt the windows of the police car, the first signs of an approaching storm. He was drawn back to the pill in his hand.

"Goodbye, Jonathan." Jonas's voice echoed from the phone. "We would like to thank you for your interest in the Blackwater Family."

An onslaught of rage and disbelief coursed through him, followed by vivid, horrific scenarios playing out in his mind. Then, suddenly, there was nothing but an eerie calm.

No, not nothing. A choice.

He closed his eyes, allowing the memory of the first time he heard her laughter in a bar to take over his senses. Then, with a heavy heart and the ghost of her laughter still echoing in his mind, Jonathan took the pill.

CHAPTER SIX

21ˢᵗ June 2018

Reuben rattled the entrance of ~~the Forest Oak~~ the pub, his anger reverberating through the locked doors. A light flickered inside, cutting through the darkness, and revealing the plump outline of a woman approaching. The opaque dance of purples and blues on the stained-glass panels of the door concealed her face until she yanked the door open.

"Alright, Reuben? Come in, love." Laura Butler, the proprietor of the pub, ushered him inside with a wave of her hand. Having known Reuben since he was a toddler, she often treated him more as a son than a customer.

The pub was shrouded in ~~semi~~darkness, save for the glow from the jukebox and a smattering of intoxicated regulars huddled around a figure at the bar. As Reuben approached, their raucous laughter and crude jokes dwindled into an awkward silence. They were used to this ritual—the son coming to collect his wayward father.

Laura offered water to Reuben, but his attention was elsewhere. The sight of his father, Martin, face down in his own spilt beer, half-asleep with strands of his brown hair spread out like a veil over the puddle, filled Reuben with a crushing sense of disappointment.

Martin stirred, his laughter echoing hollowly in the near-empty pub. "Oh, is it that time already?" he mumbled, barely coherent.

The sight of his father's unfazed reaction to his drunken stupor only amplified Reuben's anger. "Yes, Dad," he retorted, his voice hard.

57

"It's time to go home."

Martin's laughter ceased. He reached out for Reuben's offered hand and stumbled to his feet. As they walked out, Reuben felt the weight of his father's failures heavy on his shoulders, a burden he was far too young to bear.

The journey home was silent, save for the occasional mumbled apology from Martin. But the words rang hollow in Reuben's ears. He was done with the promises and the excuses. He knew something had to change, for both their sakes.

With the help of Reuben and John, a post-office worker known for his quirky humour, Martin was hoisted to his feet. As John shot Reuben a sympathetic grin, Reuben managed to keep his frustrations at bay. He knew his father would be tomorrow's gossip fodder.

"Thanks," he mumbled to John, who disappeared back into the warmth of the pub. Turning left, father and son began the familiar walk home, the sounds of merriment from the pub trailing behind them.

"Good night, was it?" Reuben asked, a touch of sarcasm in his voice. His father made a weak attempt to respond, but no words came out. With a roll of his eyes, Reuben continued on, preferring the silence over another empty apology.

As they walked past the local kebab shop, Reuben pulled his hood up, hoping to go unnoticed by his schoolmates inside. They trudged up the hill past the decrepit arcade, eventually reaching Central Street. Stopping in his tracks, Reuben took in the sight of the terrace houses neatly lined up before him, their yellow home at the far end. He gazed at the sprawling valleys beyond, a poignant reminder of his trapped existence amidst such vastness.

"Don't you think you should pick up some water from the corner shop or something?" Reuben suggested, his tone brimming with disdain. "You wouldn't want to get an earful from Mum, would you?"

"Ugh. Lighten up," Martin retorted, brushing his brown hair away from his face, a mannerism Reuben had seen him use countless times when cornered with an uncomfortable question from his mother.

Reuben was taken aback by his father's dismissive words. "What did you say?" he asked, disbelief creeping into his tone.

"Forget it," Martin mumbled, unwilling to confront his son's growing anger.

"No. Go on!" Reuben shouted, his voice echoing in the quiet street, challenging the distant hum of passing cars. "Say it again!"

Martin turned to face him, still swaying a bit from the alcohol, but his eyes, they were clear and serious. The usual passive indifference, his vocabulary confined to "Yes, dear" or "do what your mother tells you," seemed to have evaporated.

"I said, lighten up, Reuben," he said with surprising firmness. "You're constantly preoccupied with other people's lives. At your age, you should be focusing forwards, not sideways."

Caught off-guard, Reuben was momentarily at a loss for words.

"So what if your mum gets mad at me? So what if I want to go out and get blackout drunk on a Wednesday night?" Martin shrugged nonchalantly.

Reuben could feel his cheeks flushing with anger and frustration. "You just don't get it, do you?" he shot back. "I'm stuck here. It's going to be a while before I go to university and there's not much around here to do. If I don't want to work in a bloody shutter window shop, there's hardly any chance of me landing a job anywhere."

Pacing back and forth, hands behind his head, he continued, "What I'm trying to say is, I'm screwed. And the last thing I need is for you to be screwed too ... okay, stop laughing. That's not what I meant!"

Martin was shaking with laughter, the tension momentarily diffused by his son's poor choice of words. "Come on! That's funny!" he managed to gasp out between chuckles.

Reuben was ready to fire back, but Martin held up his hands in surrender. "Okay, okay ... I'll stop."

He moved closer to Reuben, his laughter subsiding. "I'll stop," he repeated, sobering up quickly. Lowering his head, he mumbled into his son's shoulder, "I'm a monster, Reuben. You don't deserve to have a monster like me for a father."

Reuben gave an embarrassed chuckle. "Hey, come on. You're a bit of a dickhead sometimes, but who isn't?"

Pulling back, Martin looked straight into Reuben's eyes. For a moment, Reuben thought his father was going to headbutt him. But instead, Martin pulled him into a firm embrace, so strong that from a distance, they could have been mistaken for wrestlers.

"Promise me something?" Martin asked, his voice a low murmur.

Reuben nodded, whispering, "Of course."

"When you leave this town," Martin said, his voice heavy with emotion, "I want you to do one thing. Stay as far away from me as possible. Do you understand?"

His words fell like a punch to the gut. Reuben watched as his father disengaged from the embrace, his arms dropping heavily to his sides. "Nothing good will come of being near me."

With that, Martin turned around slowly and began to trudge down the street towards their home. Reuben, feeling as though he was in a daze, simply followed. They spent the rest of the evening at home, eating reheated Chinese takeout in silence.

The next day, Martin acted as though the conversation had never happened. A week later, Reuben attempted to bring it up, but his father deflected every question. A month later, Reuben and his mum came home from an evening cinema trip to find him gone. He didn't show up for work the day after and he was declared missing at the end of the week.

Even though he died months later, Reuben always felt that it was in that raw and revealing moment, beneath the unforgiving streetlight, that he truly saw his father for the last time.

Present Day

In the Notes section of his phone, Reuben transcribed the haunting words his father had uttered that fateful night as one of his father's old pals from the pub casually strolled behind him. Having sought refuge in the pub from the chaos of the day, he had caught sight of his father's buddies huddled in a corner. Their eyes briefly met his before they turned away.

Even though his father had been a man of few words, maintaining a stoic exterior, the rare occasions he'd opened up to his loved ones left an indelible impression. His sudden disappearance carved a gaping void in the village as if he were a missing star in their shared constellation. Despite the passing of a year, Reuben had anticipated the villagers' attention to have shifted to world events like David Bowie's demise or Trump's ascendancy to power. But his father's name still lingered in hushed whispers, as if he were an elusive phantom haunting their streets.

Reuben's quiet musings were abruptly disrupted by the harsh vibration of his phone against the beer-slicked counter, nearly toppling his fourth pint. An exasperated groan escaped him, Alice, again. Ten unanswered calls in the last four hours. Looking skyward, he began to hum along with the melodic strains of Fleetwood Mac emanating from the speakers. Yet even amidst the clamour of the packed pub, the incessant buzzing of his phone was an unrelenting torment.

Reuben snatched up his vibrating phone, yielding to the unrelenting summons. "Alice," he responded, his voice raspy from both fatigue and an overabundance of alcohol.

Alice's voice trembled with urgency at the other end. "Reuben, I've just got off the phone with Luke ... it's ... it's the man from Larkhill, the one who tried to attack Emily." She hesitated, the following silence laden with a foreboding intensity.

He knitted his brows in confusion, trying to grasp the significance of her message amidst his inebriated state. "What about him, Alice?" he managed to ask, his words sluggish but focused.

Alice's breath hitched before she finally let the words tumble out. "He's ... he's dead, Reuben. They found him in a police car. He ... he took his own life."

Reuben's heart pounded in his chest. "No way." His voice wavered between shock and disbelief, the chilling news sinking its icy claws into him.

"Luke told me … The police are all over it, trying to piece together what happened. It doesn't make any sense."

The jovial buzz of the pub's background noise seemed to mute, leaving Reuben with nothing but his racing thoughts and Alice's distressed voice coming through his phone. The news was like a cold, biting wind, chilling him to the bone, sobering him up quicker than any coffee could. He was left speechless, the weight of the situation pressing down on him, suffocating him.

"This … This is insane, Alice," Reuben managed to croak out, struggling to comprehend the grim reality. His mind was sifting through the conversations, the encounters, each mention of this elusive Lena.

"What are you thinking?" She asked after a long pause.

"I'm thinking that we are a bit out of our depth, to be honest," he responded. "It's not even been twenty-four hours since I've found this tape and I've nearly got into a knife fight with a dead man. This is all too much."

"You're not thinking of giving up, are you?"

"I'm not sure," he admitted. "Part of me is still so angry that he lied to us that it's almost worth leaving these questions unanswered. But what if, and I know it's a big and silly '*if*,' but what if this Lena exists and she's in trouble? What if we're the only ones right now who knows she's alive? Surely pursuing that idea is better than sitting in a pub on your own wondering where everything went wrong?"

Alice took a while to respond.

"I agree that we are out of our depth," she said finally. "So that's why we need to ask for help?"

"Help?" Reuben asked alarmingly. "From who?"

Alice offered a firm suggestion. "Honestly, Reuben, the best person you can seek answers from is likely the woman who planned on spending the rest of her life with him."

Reuben bit his lip in worry. He was afraid that she was going to suggest this.

"Reuben. I think you need to tell your mum about this."

CHAPTER SEVEN

With a weary sigh, Jonas let the hotel room door close behind him, leaning his weight against it. The resounding click echoed the finality of Jonathan's fate. A wave of fatigue washed over him, pulling him downwards till he was nothing more than a defeated slump on the threadbare carpet. Jonathan's botched mission had only added to his burdens. Jonas was an outsider now, living in anticipation of Reuben Drake's next move.

After a moment of surrender to his exhaustion, Jonas peeled himself off the floor and began the painstaking process of undressing. He eased out of his suit as if it was an additional layer of skin. His reflection stared back at him from the bathroom mirror, naked and raw, a man beleaguered by a war of attrition with his own body. The shower knobs turned, hot water cascading over him, searing his eczema-wracked skin, blurring the line between ecstasy and agony. He thought of the condition not just as a physical affliction but as a curse, a haunting spectre from a past life, the payment for familial sins.

The fiery sting of the shower subsided, leaving him with temporary relief from his itching torment. He padded back into the room, digging into his suitcase for a fresh suit, this one a vibrant scarlet red. A matching robe slipped over his shoulders; the suit carefully hung for the morrow. Collapsing on the bed, Jonas reached for the remote, flicking through channels until a familiar face halted his hand—Jonathan Jenkins, the failed recruit, forever immortalised in his disgrace.

"Breaking news tonight, South Wales Police have opened an

investigation into the sudden death of a man arrested with attempted murder in their custody. Jonathan Jenkins, aged twenty-eight, was found dead in the back of a police car …" The newscaster's voice droned on, but Jonas had already switched channels. He felt no guilt over Jonathan's coerced suicide. He had given Jonathan clear instructions over a grimy cafe table—uncover what Reuben Drake knew.

People like Jonathan were often overlooked, their lives marked by dismal circumstances, languishing in forgotten villages, their dreams squashed under the weight of their realities. Ordinary people would greet them with half-hearted smiles at the corner shop or the public loo, barely acknowledging their existence. To them, these were people to be pitied but never to be regarded as equals. Yet, in their anonymity, people like Jonathan held the potential for stealth, the ability to make silent, deadly moves. Yes, he failed, but as far as Jonas was concerned, he should have been grateful for the opportunity.

With a drowsy blink, Jonas focused his semi lucid gaze towards his right foot. "What the …" His voice trailed off as he observed the abnormality. His bare right foot had inexplicably morphed into one suffering from trench foot, the flesh mottled and sickly under the spectral glow of the TV.

As soon as the realisation set in, the motel room began to transform. It dimmed progressively, shadows creeping in from the corners until darkness swallowed it whole. The muffled hum of late-night traffic morphed into a distant staccato rhythm of machine-gun fire. The motel's untouched-since-the-eighties beige walls dissolved, revealing an expansive battlefield unfolding all around him. The TV's inane chatter escalated, its laughter morphing into blood-curdling screams of war.

Staying true to the others' directives, Jonas refused to let the ensuing panic overwhelm him. He closed his eyes, grounding himself in the darkness, and began to hum softly under his breath.

The comfort of the bed beneath him gave way to the squelch of mud. The cacophony of gunfire and shouts of commands enveloped him as he strained to keep his eyes shut, singing aloud, his voice straddling the line between plea and prayer. He gasped as an urgent hand gripped his dressing gown, yanking him deeper into the hallucination.

"Charlie! Help me!" the man shrieked. "My legs! Oh god, my legs!"

Jonas's eyes snapped open. He was shaking violently, but remained mired in the battlefield fantasy, his legs shattered and riddled with phantom bullets. The teenager who'd clung to him, a boy barely seventeen with a jet-black bowl cut, was dressed in a military uniform. Tears streamed down his face, lips quivering in shock.

"Charlie ... help me ..."

Suddenly, another figure emerged from the smoke and chaos. It was his mother, her face pale and distraught, her long, grey hair flowing like a phantom's veil in the gusty wind. She was reaching out to him, her eyes mirroring the same terror as the young soldier's.

"Jonas ... help me, Jonas ..." she pleaded, her voice echoing painfully in his ears.

Jonas squeezed his eyes shut again, reciting the song lyrics like a mantra until they blurred into indistinct chanting. Abruptly, as though reality was a mere TV channel that someone flipped, he was back in the hotel room. He bolted upright, hastily flicking off the TV. He shimmied into his suit with manic urgency before dashing downstairs. Exiting the hotel, he let the crisp September air chill his fevered skin as he took a seat at the bus stop across the street. It was a family affliction. 'Think of it as watching someone else's PTSD nightmare, but your brain doesn't realise it's not yours,' Eli told him. The occasional trip was not a big deal but having them pile up was cause for concern.

Jonas regarded the desolate, lonely street, the air heavy with the metallic scent of decay that marked each alleyway and dilapidated block—a stark reminder of a community trapped in perpetual twilight. He remained cloaked in the shadow of the bus stop, an omnipresent spectre hiding in plain sight. His phone stirred in his pocket, buzzing with a new message from an unknown number.

He pulled out the device, unlocking it to reveal a disturbing image;

a terrified young man, no more than twenty, handcuffed to a chair. His location was somewhere underground, and next to him stood a large looming figure dressed in black, their identity concealed by a rabbit mask. A relic passed down through centuries. To the uninitiated, this image would inspire nightmares. But for Jonas, this was just another mundane part of the job.

A new message flashed on the screen.

Does this mean I got the job?

Jonas smirked.

Some, like Jonathan Jenkins, were fated to falter, unable to rise above their station. But there would always be others in the audition process, ones who would prove themselves exceptional, who'd heard the call of the Family and were prepared to fight tooth and claw to heed it.

His fingers moved swiftly across the screen, crafting a reply.

Most definitely.

Jonas retreated to the sanctuary of the hotel, a fortress against the reality of his blood-soaked visions. Ascending to his room, the sterile silence of the hallway replaced the cacophony of his nightmare. He unearthed a laptop from the belly of his suitcase, its cold metal a reminder of the world of technology and modernity, a stark contrast to the primitive terror he had just witnessed.

With practiced fingers, he powered up the device, his eyes reflecting the glow of the boot screen. He navigated his way through encrypted files and hidden applications until he arrived at an unmarked icon. A piece of software he had acquired from the darkest corners of the web.

Murmuring an expletive under his breath, he felt his heart rate increase. This call had the potential to either alleviate his concerns or send him spiralling further into uncertainty.

The figure on the other end picked up, his voice rolling through the speakers, measured and deliberate like a seasoned tutor, yet laced with a tone of sly insincerity reminiscent of a silver-tongued car dealer.

"You had another one, didn't you?"

The assertive certainty in his voice took Jonas aback.

"How did you—"

"You wouldn't be ringing me otherwise. When I'm trying to track you down, you're either off your face, got your head between someone's legs, or both." The man's words carried an edge, not just of accusation, but of knowing familiarity with Jonas's less than savoury pursuits. "What is this? Your third vessel trip this month? You should be reporting these to us."

"Seems I've got a good reason to sober up now," Jonas confessed, a hint of reluctance seeping into his tone. "It's about Jonathan."

"I'm up to speed," Eli interjected briskly. "Let's not waste time discussing failures. What's the status of the girl?"

Jonas responded rapidly, as if he were a schoolboy put on the spot to solve a complex equation. "She just sent through the photo—passed with flying colours. I've dispatched a team to retrieve her and your vessel. They should be back at the mansion by tomorrow."

"Good work," Eli conceded begrudgingly. "Anything else?"

"Jonathan indicated that Reuben is cognizant of Lena, at least by name. How he's come to possess this information and a photograph of her ... I'm baffled. I suggest we maintain our distance for now and monitor his actions to—"

"I think we should bring him in," Eli declared firmly.

Jonas was taken aback.

"Bring him in? And you're asking me if I'm the one who's drunk," Jonas retorted, his disbelief evident.

"Why are you opposed to it?"

"Reuben's father and Lena were our targets. Now, it's only her. We made a pact not to drag the boy or his mother into this. They didn't choose this."

"Jonas. We are racing against time. There's a high probability that she's already out of the country, and given her abilities, there's a chance we might never find her, despite all our resources. Like it or not, Reuben Drake holds the key to locating her. We need to uncover what he knows. You don't want history to repeat itself, do you?" Eli's words stung, striking a chord within Jonas.

He shook his head.

"In my latest vessel trip … she was there."

There was a moment of silence on Eli's end.

"The incident was a tragedy. But you can prevent another one from occurring. And another thing …"

Jonas looked up, expectant.

"His father betrayed us. There would be poetic justice in getting the son on our side."

A faint smile flickered across Jonas's lips. He looked up at the unresponsive computer screen, wondering if Eli was mirroring his smile.

"Bring him in."

CHAPTER EIGHT

As Reuben crept down the stairs, careful not to stir his mother who had returned from her night shift at the hospital mere hours before, his eyes were drawn to the photo array on the side table. One photo seized his attention. A small, pasty-faced boy no older than five at a sun-soaked beach, a guiding hand on each shoulder. One belonged to a woman with frizzy, nineties-style blonde curls and a soft green sweater, and the other to a man sporting a high-and-tight haircut. Both were in their early thirties and radiated happiness. All three beamed back at the camera, the beach forming a radiant backdrop. The sun shone so brightly behind them that Reuben was convinced it hadn't been as bright since.

His eyes slid towards the other pictures. The only remaining photo that featured his father was from graduation day. There was Reuben, draped in his graduation gown, one corner of his mouth turned up in a half-smile, his hands clasped. The man standing to his right, hands shoved in his pockets, hair now wild and untamed, his shirt half-tucked, regarded the camera as if the prospect of a father-son photo was a tiresome inconvenience.

At the time, Reuben had dismissed his father's attitude change as unimportant, attributing it to the natural process of aging, failing to realise that his father had been a perpetual sourpuss for most of his life. He overheard a late-night argument between his parents and assumed his father's demeanour was the result of marital strain. The truth was, something had happened that fundamentally changed his father, not only turning him into a stranger but also prompting him to abandon his family. The puzzle of who killed his father had haunted him, manifesting in his dreams as grotesque grinning monsters coming to finish what they started. After what had happened at Larkhill Manor, Reuben began to wonder if these monsters weren't entirely fictional.

Alice had been right. He had spent months dodging these uncomfortable confrontations. But it was time to face the inevitable. As he pushed open the living room door and stepped into the quiet expanse of the room, he failed to notice his mother, sitting at the long table in her pink dressing gown, observing him from the other end.

Across from her was Elaine Walker. His eyes instinctively gravitated to the centre of the coffee table, where, amidst wilting tulips, sat a brown porcelain mask identical to the one Alice had described. The presence of the mask dominated the room, and both women were inevitably drawn to it.

"What are you doing here?" Reuben asked, an edge in his voice that Inspector Walker clearly didn't appreciate.

"You left a questioning session after you were nearly assaulted, and you're questioning my presence here?" she retorted, her brow furrowed in disapproval.

"I'm sorry," he replied, his posture stiff, as if he were frozen midstride. He looked at his mother, their eyes locking in a silent exchange. "I should've informed you about what happened, where I was …"

"For the past year, you've been a disappearing act. Off to the pub. Off to mental homes. Sometimes, I've gone days without knowing where you are," his mother interrupted, her voice wavering. "You didn't answer any of my calls. My texts. Nothing."

"I know," he admitted, "and I realize it must've been extremely worrying, and you probably feel—"

She slammed her hand onto the table, cutting him off. Her outburst startled him, and he watched as she brushed away the tears streaking her cheeks.

"Let me make something clear," she interjected, her words laced with a bitterness he had rarely heard before. "I have lived in this house for a very long time, and for most of that time, I've allowed others, especially men, to dictate how I should be feeling. I think it's time I express my feelings in my own words. Is that too much to ask?"

Reuben nodded slowly, both terrified and somewhat impressed by the intense defiance she was displaying. He wordlessly took a seat next to her. When she glanced his way, the fire in her eyes tempered slightly, reassuring him that the loving mother he had always known was still there beneath the anger.

"I'm going to make some tea for us," Walker said sheepishly before quickly disappearing into the kitchen.

"Reuben," she began, reaching out to take his hand in hers. "I watched your father walk out of this house and never come back. I texted him, I called him, but he never responded. I'll never hear his voice again. I hope with all my heart that you never have to experience what I've been through, but the reality is, at some point, you will. Either you or someone you love will be left behind. But before all that, before your father left, I noticed he was drifting away from me. The little things—hugs, kisses, the 'I love you' he used to say before he left for work—they started to fade. The man I shared my life with was disappearing. Now, in retrospect, it feels like I was married to a ghost, a phantom just waiting to vanish."

Her grip on his hand tightened. "This year has been tough on you, but it's been tough on me too," she continued. "When you stopped answering your phone, stopped replying to texts … I don't want you to become a ghost too. Okay?"

Reuben could feel the tears trickling down his face. As he noticed his hand trembling under his mother's, he placed his other hand atop hers.

"I'm sorry," he managed to say, struggling to suppress the sob threatening to break loose. He wanted to say more, but for the moment, the words wouldn't come.

She gently pulled her hands away and wiped his tears. A small, shared smile passed between them, a brief respite from their pain. At that moment, DCI Walker returned to the table, holding three cups of tea on a dinner tray. As she sat down, Reuben looked at the brown mask in the middle of the table.

"What in God's name is that thing?" Reuben asked.

Walker turned towards Reuben's mother, her countenance firm and the warm, familiar tone she usually wore when visiting for her biweekly cup of tea was absent. "Do you want to tell him, or shall I?" she asked, her voice icy. The friendly confidante who had felt more like a sister than a family friend to his mother had now fully morphed into the stern, no-nonsense police officer she was at her core.

"This all happened before you were born," his mum began, her voice holding an edge of uncertainty as she reached back into her past. "I reckon it was somewhere between '68 and '70. I was just a young girl then. There was this girl from our street, Jenny Lewis. She left for school one day, a ten-minute walk away, and she never made it back home."

Reuben remained silent, waiting on every word.

"Jenny wasn't the only one. By the end of that week, seven more kids from our valley had vanished. It felt like we were living in some kind of TV drama. Curfews were set for anyone under eighteen. Police were a constant sight around schools and in the village. And the teachers ... they'd threaten us with getting 'caught' after school if we didn't behave. Looking back, it sounds downright horrible."

A distant memory resurfaced in Reuben's mind. "I think they mentioned this in one of our history classes. A kid in the class brought it up, arguing we should learn more about local history, not just the Tudors. So, it's true then? Eight kids went missing?"

His mum nodded, a hint of surprise flickering in her eyes at his sudden interest in the story.

"Yes, eight kids just ... disappeared," she confirmed.

"But why isn't it talked about more?" he asked, puzzled.

She sighed and looked down. "Forgetting is sometimes easier, don't you think? We both know that."

Reuben picked up the peculiar mask and turned it back and forth. An eerie aura seemed to emanate from it, stirring an unsettling feeling within him.

"What's this got to do with everything?" he questioned, looking back and forth between the mask and his mother.

"There was no hope. No sign of anyone being alive. Until an old man at the top of the valley saw a young boy running for his house, being chased."

"Was he one of the missing?" asked Reuben.

"That's correct," Walker answered, passing him a fragile, folded paper.

His pulse quickened as he gently unfolded the aged newspaper, its yellowed edges crumbling slightly under his touch. The bold headline appeared stark against the faded black-and-white print, sending a chill down his spine: *One of Valley Eight Found!*

Reuben glanced at the subheading below. *Martin Drake, Aged Ten, Found Alive and Well.*

A lump formed in his throat as his eyes darted across the print, grappling with the jarring revelation. The room felt as though it was closing in around him, the air turning thick and stifling. As the reality of the situation set in, Reuben was engulfed by a wave of anger, a fiery flush spreading across his features. "You're telling me that Dad disappeared as a kid, and you didn't think it was worthwhile to mention it when he vanished again? How could you not tell me this?" His voice rose, echoing around the room, the hurt evident in his tone. "You want us to build a better relationship, but you withhold something like this from me?!"

"I was trying to protect you," his mum responded softly, her own pain surfacing.

His anger simmered, bitterness coating his words. "Yeah. Seems like there's a whole lot of *Don't tell Reuben* mentality going around now. Really making things better."

"Keeping you in the dark seemed like the best way to keep you safe at the time," Walker added, her tone measured.

Reuben whipped around to face her, his face a picture of disbelief. "You knew about this too? Jesus Christ."

Walker met his glare with an unwavering stare.

"It's my job to know, Reuben. And look what happened when you decided to strike out on your own. You nearly got yourself killed."

"You didn't answer my question. What does this mask have to do with everything?" Reuben persisted.

"After finding your father, the police conducted a search in the nearby area. It was mostly farmland, so a small team did a door-to-door search of the few residences. Nothing was found until they came upon an apparent holiday home belonging to a Mr. Richard Vaughan. They managed to get a warrant and broke in."

"And what did they find?" Reuben's voice was tense.

Walker leaned back in her chair and ran a hand through her hair. "A horrific sight—six men and women in their fifties and sixties, all deceased, and all wearing masks just like this one. And one child strapped to a cross. Your father was questioned on numerous occasions about this throughout his life, but he had no recollection of what happened. The man who found him confirmed that whoever was chasing him were wearing the same masks. The rest of the children were never found. They had disappeared in plain sight. Whatever happened to them, it was a tragedy."

Julia took a final sip of her tea. "Your father insisted over and over that he didn't remember anything about what transpired," she relayed to her son. "Your grandparents tried therapy, but it didn't seem to help—only served to stir up painful memories."

Reuben rose from his chair, pacing to the corner of the room as he processed the information. "So, let me get this straight," he began, trying to wrap his head around the ordeal. "In the sixties, eight local children were kidnapped. My father was the only one found alive. The people who allegedly committed this heinous crime …" He glanced at Walker, "… or those whom you believe were responsible, could they potentially be involved in my father's recent disappearance?"

"What makes you think that?" the detective inspector inquired. Reuben slid his left hand into his pocket, clutching the cassette tape. "There's something you both need to hear."

". . . Daddy is busy at the moment, so Reuben, please can you and your sister wait downstairs?"

The voice of his father echoed from the worn-out tape, resonating through the room.

The tape fell silent, the soft hum of the cassette player serving as the sole soundtrack to their collective shock.

Reuben instinctively looked towards his mother, his heart aching at the sight of her, engrossed in the audio recording. Each syllable uttered by his father seemed to ensnare her, tethering her to a past she longed to revisit. Her eyes glistened, reflecting a tempest of emotions—longing, pain, perhaps even a glimmer of hope—conjured by the echo of her beloved.

The room sank into an oppressive silence, its weight only heightened by the intense emotions floating through the air. Reuben reached over and pressed the Stop button on the cassette player with a tremble in his hand. He looked at his mother again. She sat frozen in place, staring at the tape player as if she could summon her late husband back through sheer willpower. He could almost see the whirlwind of confusion and unanswered questions swirling in her mind. A pang of remorse cut through him, sharp and unexpected. He had shown her the tape to mend their strained relationship, hoping that some shared understanding could bring closure. Instead, he feared he'd shattered the fragile peace they were beginning to forge, catapulting her back into a world of uncertainty and pain.

Reuben shifted his attention to Detective Walker, seeking some form of reassurance. But she was as captivated by the haunting echoes from the cassette as they were. Her usually stoic eyes looked unsettled, her stern countenance marred by an expression that bordered on despair. Her hands, once casually resting on the coffee table, now gripped its edges like a lifeline.

"I think I need another tea," she managed to murmur, her voice barely audible, before abruptly standing and making a beeline for the kitchen. Reuben watched in surprise as the typically unflappable inspector made a hurried exit.

"Maybe I should suggest the vodka instead," Julia mumbled under her breath, still visibly shaken by the resurfacing ghosts of the past. Reuben instinctively placed a comforting hand on her shoulder, trying to provide the support she needed.

"Are you okay?" he asked.

Julia let out a hollow laugh. "Okay? Can you remind me what that feels like? I seem to have forgotten …"

Amid this emotional turmoil, Detective Walker returned to the table with fresh drinks, her face a mask of shocked confusion. Handing out the beverages with a faint smile, she settled back into her seat.

Julia finally broke the tense silence. "Could you do me a favour?"

Reuben turned his attention back to her.

"When you grow up and find someone you want to spend your life with, make sure they're honest with you. Completely, utterly honest. You deserve nothing less. The last thing you want is to bury them and be left with nothing but the skeletons they hid in the closet."

Reuben hesitated before speaking.

"When you hear the words that Dad is saying, what does it make you think?" he asked.

Julia vehemently shook her head with no answer. "Reuben, you're our only child. Just you. I've got no idea who your father might've been referring to … God, he kept so much from me. So many secrets …"

"Mum, you alright?"

Something was wrong.

Her eyes starting to roll back slightly.

"There was … so much … he didn't…" she mumbled, her voice fading into a pained groan.

Without warning, Julia slumped sideways, her body tumbling from the sofa and hitting the carpet. "MUM!" Reuben sprang towards her, knocking over their teacups in his haste. He tried to wake her up, but she remained limp and unresponsive. "Elaine! Call an ambulance, now!" he shouted, his eyes fixated on his unconscious mother. "Mum … you're going to be okay … Elaine, call them, she needs help now!"

"I can't do that, Reuben."

The calm reply was disconcertingly out of place in the current chaos. Reuben's eyes shot upwards, landing not on an intruder, but on Detective Walker. She stood over him, her expression unreadable amidst the commotion unfolding at her feet. It felt as though a sinister shadow had invaded the room, taking possession of the woman he thought was on their side.

Reuben's eyes darted to the shattered teacups. His mother had been drugged. But before he could even digest the horrifying revelation, he looked back up at Walker, just in time to witness her draw a gun from her jacket pocket.

"No," she commanded. "You're coming with me, Reuben. And you're going to tell me everything you know about your sister."

CHAPTER NINE

He cautiously rose from the floor, his hands lifting in surrender. "What the hell is happening? What did you do?" he demanded.

"It's just a mild sedative. In about half an hour, your mum will be waking up, wondering where we've vanished to," the DCI replied, her tone flat as if she were merely relaying someone else's message.

"If you've hurt her, I swear—"

"I have no intention of hurting your mother and I have no intention of hurting you if you do as I say," she answered, looking down at the unconscious woman dismissively as if she was just a piece of discarded rubbish.

Reuben's eyes searched for a way out. He considered the garden door; it was always open. All he would have to do is knock her to the ground and run for it. It would only take—

"Oh, Reuben dear …"

He caught her eye and the manic stare back at him. He felt naked. It was as if she could read his every possible move.

"You could hardly handle a madman with a knife. What chance do you stand against me?"

A chill coursed through Reuben's veins as reality settled in.

"It was you? You were the one who sent that man after Emily?"

Walker rolled her eyes and shifted her head back and forth as if keeping still was near impossible.

"I *really* wish we had time to discuss the ins and outs of who did what, but time isn't on my side," she said. "Now be a good boy and get in the corridor."

With her pistol digging uncomfortably into his temple, she dragged him into the hallway. Under her stern watch and demanding tone, Reuben fumbled with his keys, attempting to unlock the exit as swiftly as possible.

They stepped out into the torrential rain that immediately soaked through Reuben's grey joggers and Smashing Pumpkins T-shirt. He yelled out as he was forcefully dragged towards Walker's police car, his arm twisted behind his back at an excruciating angle. "Stop being difficult!" Walker hissed at him, her voice barely audible over the downpour as she yanked open the car door.

"Oi! What in blazes is going on over there?"

Reuben's heart plummeted. He recognized the voice behind him instantly: Terry, his neighbour. A former boxer now in his mid-fifties, Terry had come to his front door upon hearing the disturbance. Without missing a beat, Walker swivelled to point her gun at him.

"Get back inside, Now," she ordered sternly.

Reuben locked eyes with Terry, his hands raised and trembling in the pouring rain, and wordlessly begged him to comply. With a final glance of disbelief, Terry nodded and slowly shut his door.

He was roughly pushed into the backseat of the vehicle, his heart hammering in his chest as Walker hurriedly made her way to the driver's seat. As she started the car and abruptly sped off, Reuben was left reeling, fearfully watching as his familiar neighbourhood faded into the distance, replaced by the unsettling uncertainty of the dark, rain-drenched roads.

After a long hour of fruitless attempts at escape, Reuben had no choice but to admit defeat. He was well and truly trapped. They had long since left the familiar surroundings of Caerphilly, the landscape outside the car window now completely unrecognisable to him.

His attention turned once again to the woman seated in front of him. For the past year, ever since the day she had first turned up to the Drake house to offer her condolences, he had seen Detective Walker as a figure of empathy and support, a woman whose sense of duty was rooted in her inability to protect his family. He had lived in constant fear of being pursued by some unknown threat, yet the reality of his situation was far more horrifying—the real danger had been in front of him all along.

"Did you … did you do it?" Reuben's voice was a shaky whisper, barely loud enough to break the oppressive silence in the car. His words hung heavily in the air, yet she offered no response, her attention seemingly consumed by whatever or whoever she was looking for in her rearview mirror.

Feeling his frustration rise, he found himself demanding, "Answer me, Elaine! Did you … did you kill my father?" His voice filled the confines of the vehicle, the tension in his question only heightening the charged atmosphere.

"Maya."

"What?"

"My name is Maya," she answered, her voice a blank slate of emotion. "We've got this far, you might as well call me by my real name. It's quite nice to say it out in the open. I've had to be called Elaine for so long. I had to be Kim a while back. It's exhausting."

Reuben reeled in disbelief. "You're the one my father mentioned on the tape … the one who was trying to find him."

"It wasn't him we were after. If he'd simply handed her over, he'd still be breathing. I'd advise you to be smarter than he was and not make the same mistake." Frustration surging to its peak, Reuben slammed his palm against the car door, desperate for answers.

"I don't know anything about a sister! I'm as clueless as you are!" he exclaimed, his voice ricocheting within the confines of the car. "What on earth do you think I know?"

"Do you really expect me to believe you've gotten this far without clues from what your father left you? All we need is the girl, Reuben. Your father tried to hide her; you know how that story ended."

"What do you want with her?"

Maya glanced at him, visibly wrestling with what she should divulge now versus later. "That's a conversation for another time."

Reuben groaned.

"What if I refuse to help? I don't even know if my mother is safe."

Maya sighed, clearly irritated. "I hate repeating myself. Your mother is perfectly fine. We have no intention of harming her. She's merely a disposable character in our story. But you? You're different. That's why I'm telling you all this. Unlike your parents, we don't want to keep you in the dark anymore."

"You were acquainted with my father, weren't you? For how long?" Reuben pressed on, the knots in his stomach tightening with each evasion.

Maya let out a startling, somewhat unsettling laugh. "You won't believe me if I tell you," she said, grinning at him from the rearview mirror.

His frustration was mounting, growing into a rage that threatened to consume him. He was tired of riddles and evasions, tired of the looming questions that refused to be answered. He felt a feral instinct rising within him—a primitive fight-or-flight response awakened by desperation.

"So, was it you?" he asked again, his voice hard and unyielding. "Was it you who killed him?"

"When you come back with us and understand everything that has happened," she responded coldly, "you'll wish you'd had the chance to gut the bastard yourself."

What happened next was a blur, as if his mind and body were no longer one. He could see himself lunging forward, feeling the shock of skin on skin as he struck her across the face. She shrieked, her hands clawing at him as the car began to swerve wildly. The world outside was reduced to a blur of indistinguishable colours as the vehicle careened off the road. The screeching tires and Maya's shrieks merged into a haunting symphony of terror. Then everything went black.

Reuben opened his eyes and his world spun back into focus, an unwelcome collision of chaotic sights, sounds, and sensations. His body throbbed with pain that pulsed in time with the beat of his heart. The air tasted of iron and gasoline, stinging his lungs and throat with each shaky breath. He was alive—he was sure of that—but in that moment, he wished he wasn't.

Maya's limp body slumped over the steering wheel was the first thing he saw, her usually imposing figure now deflated. Her top half dangled precariously out of the driver's seat, suspended in a haunting display of vulnerability. In the dim light, he could see her chest rise and fall in shallow, laboured breaths. For the time being, she was out.

He squinted out the window, the world outside reduced to a hazy blur of swirling grey and mist. Rain pelted against the shattered windshield, streaking down in watery rivulets that refracted the weak, early-morning light. His mind was a whirlwind of shock and disbelief, but one thought cut through the maelstrom like a beacon: escape.

With great caution, Reuben stretched out his arm towards Maya. She hung motionless behind the wheel, a chilling portrait of peace amidst chaos. Blood traced a crimson trail from a gash above her eyebrow, meandering down her face and ending at the corner of her mouth in an eerie hook-like form. He was unable to see the other side.

His heartbeat thrummed in his ears, matching the rhythm of the downpour outside as he leaned over her. The car keys glinted faintly in the gloom, seeming to mock him with their proximity. His breath hitched with each inch he closed in on the keys, his muscles coiled tight as if he was ready to bolt at the first sign of Maya's stirring.

His hand trembled as he finally closed his fingers around the metal, pulling them slowly from the ignition. The quiet jingle they made seemed loud in the tense silence of the car, causing Reuben's heart to leap. But Maya remained still.

Now for the gun. With the same painstaking caution, he eased his hand into her jacket, his breath holding as his fingers closed around the cold grip of the weapon. The weight of it was both terrifying and empowering. He had it. He had a chance.

With a hefty push, he managed to force the car door open against the rain-slicked asphalt. The cold rain instantly drenched him, turning his clothes into icy shackles, but he welcomed the shock. It brought clarity, sharpened his senses.

Stepping out onto the deserted dual carriageway, he couldn't shake the feeling of being the last man on earth. The fog was a living thing, wrapping around him, hiding the world away. He looked back at the wreck. The car had veered off the road and smashed against a crash barrier, teetering dangerously on the edge of the steep embankment that dropped off into the frothy river below. A few more inches and they would have plunged into the water.

His attention went back to Maya, still unconscious in the driver's seat. His heart pounded a rhythm of conflict within him. She had taken everything from him, robbed him of his father. Yet, as he watched her bloodied, vulnerable form, he couldn't help but feel a strange pull to help her. How could he feel compassion for this woman?

The sound of an approaching engine broke the desolate silence, compelling Reuben to swivel around. A sudden flicker of hope was extinguished as he saw the car slowing down ominously behind Maya's car. He tensed, raising the gun in reflexive defence as a man disembarked from the vehicle, hands held up in apparent surrender. The figure was familiar: dressed in an eye-catching scarlet tweed suit, it was the man from the bus.

"Hold up there, lad!" The stranger's voice, jovial and nonthreatening, clashed horribly with the dire circumstances. "Are you certain you can operate that thing?" he asked, nodding towards the gun.

"Sure as hell, I can!" Reuben snapped back, trying to suppress the shivers of fear coursing through him. "I pull this trigger and your head comes off. Am I wrong?" His voice was full of bravado he didn't feel.

The man merely chuckled, his eyes shifted to the mangled car resting precariously on the edge of the carriageway. "Is she alive?" he inquired, unfazed by Reuben's threat.

"Don't know. Don't care," Reuben spat out, his eyes darting warily. "Who the hell are you?"

"Jonas," he responded with an amiable smile that felt grossly out of place. "And trust me, I can explain all of this much better than she ever could!"

Reuben eyed him sceptically, the gun still aimed squarely at Jonas.

"You and her killed my dad, didn't you?" Reuben spat out, his voice shaking with rage. "You lot and them bloody rabbit-masked nutters come to finish what you started?"

Jonas chortled, his laughter piercing the tense air. "Those rabbit masks! The old gang loved a bit of drama. Used to tell your old man we needed a fresh look!"

Reuben's confusion was evident on his face, a stark contrast to Jonas's casual demeanour. Jonas responded with a nonchalant eye roll. "Your dad, he was part of our crew, kid. That is, until he decided to bugger off and go solo and—"

"LIAR!" The accusation erupted from Reuben, raw and powerful. His hand trembled as he clung to the gun.

"You've had a gutful of lies, haven't you?" Jonas continued, unruffled by Reuben's outburst. "Well, believe me, your dad was a master of spin. Come with us, we'll lay it all out for you."

Reuben felt a swell of raw emotion threatening to overwhelm him. "Why'd my dad have to die? Why'd you lot go after him?" he yelled, the last word barely more than a broken whisper. "Don't I bloody well deserve to know?"

Jonas let his hands fall to his sides, confident that Reuben wasn't about to pull the trigger. He took a bold step forward. "Bet there's been loads of times this year, since your dad passed, where you just wanted to vanish. And I don't mean running away, I mean really disappearing. No one looking for you, no one even remembering you. Imagine that, the power to start over."

Reuben fired a shot into the air, frustration boiling over. The force and reality of discharging the weapon made his hands shake, and the gun slipped from his grasp.

"What's that got to do with my dad?!" he demanded.

"Your old man believed that gift was his and his alone," Jonas explained, his voice heavy with disdain. "He got up and left you and your mum to keep it all for himself. What kind of beast does that to his own family?"

His dad's words echoed in Reuben's mind, uttered on that fateful night a few weeks before he vanished: "You don't deserve a monster like me as a father." Suddenly, it all came crashing down on Reuben—the power to vanish into thin air.

My sister, he thought frantically. *Is that what happened? Is that why no one can remember her?*

His mind raced back to Emily, isolated and forgotten in the asylum. *When she saw her, Lena ... it sparked something. Could that be why she can't recall her own friend? Did she ...?*

The chilling realisation caused Reuben's heart to plummet.

Did she have her memory erased?

The implications were simultaneously horrifying and ludicrous.

Feeling cornered, Reuben staggered backwards until he collided with the metal barrier. Out of the corner of his eye, he noticed the flashing red and blue lights approaching from his left. As the police car pulled up behind Maya's wrecked vehicle, a flicker of hope sparked within him.

"Need a hand there, sir?" One of the officers smirked at Jonas, a twisted pleasure evident in his voice. But as soon as the two men stepped out of the car, Reuben's hope evaporated.

"Looks like a badge means nothing these days."

Jonas merely laughed. "Sure as hell doesn't hold a candle to money," he retorted. With a theatrical wave of his arm, the two officers reached into their pockets and withdrew their tasers. With nowhere else to turn, Reuben climbed onto the railing and perched himself on the edge, a single move away from plunging into the tumultuous river below. The scale of his predicament and the encroaching danger poised to tip him over the edge, quite literally.

"Last chance, Reuben." Jonas's tone shifted, a steely edge cutting through his prior mirth. "You can either plummet into that river, cutting your narrative short, or you can join us and track down Lena. By tomorrow, we'll be a memory in this town. You decide whether you want to disappear with us."

Reuben swung his other leg over the railing, peering down at the inky blackness of the swirling waters beneath him. Fear gnawed at his gut, but beneath that fear was a quiet calm, a certainty of what he needed to do.

"When Maya wakes up, I want you to tell her something," he called back over his shoulder. "Something I wish I said before this happened."

His eyes fluttered closed as he pictured his mother, splayed out on the floor of their home. Alice came to mind next, her voice a soothing balm he yearned for in this moment.

So, this is it, he thought, resignation creeping into his heart.

Reuben's eyes narrowed, ablaze with a fierce resolve. "I want you to tell her that I'm going to kill her."

Jonas relaxed his arms, letting them fall to his sides, his eyebrows arching in feigned curiosity. "Oh yeah? Why don't you tell her yourself?"

Just then, Reuben's attention was snapped back to reality; he was yanked forward off the railing and thrown back onto the asphalt. As he lay there, disoriented, rain drummed down on him, each droplet like a cold caress from the gunmetal-grey sky overhead. Two figures loomed into view against the backdrop of the heavens. To his left, Jonas, his face carved into a maniacal grin; and to his right …

Oh my God.

A vivid flashback assailed him: a childhood memory of his school friend Taylor, who had gruesomely torn open his leg while they naively played on a construction site. He remembered the sickening sight of flesh hanging from bone, the raw screams of agony. That gut-churning memory resurfaced now as he beheld Maya's face—or what was left of it. Her skin had been sheared away, revealing the monstrous visage underneath.

A thick fog seemed to descend, not just in the air but in his mind, obliterating all thoughts of escape. Reuben closed his eyes, bracing for what was to come. Jonas let out a deranged laugh.

"Welcome to the Family."

ACT TWO

CHAPTER TEN

1973

"Come on, Martin! He's had enough, mun!" Scott Williams yelled as he dragged his friend away from the fight.

"Get off me!" Martin spat, struggling against his friend's hold. But Scott was a boulder, immovable and unyielding, his wide rugby player's shoulders a barrier between Martin and his target.

The boy Martin had been fighting was on the ground, crouched in a protective ball as he coughed and sputtered, blood trickling from his split lip and swelling eye. A circle of onlookers had formed around them, drawn to the spectacle like moths to a flame.

Scott's grip on Martin's arm was iron, his voice clear over the murmurs of the onlookers. "And you taught him a lesson, didn't you? Let's split before the old bill show up."

"But he—" Martin began to argue, the words choked in his throat.

"He deserved what he got." Scott cut him off, taking one last look at the injured boy. "But we don't need to make it any worse."

Scott's usually jovial manner had given way to a serious demeanour that seemed to cool the heated atmosphere. As they weaved their way out of the crowd, the bystanders parted, and a quiet murmur replaced the earlier commotion.

Martin scoffed, brushing the grime off his bag. "Gobby little git," he muttered, noticing the mud stains on his jeans and jacket. "Bloody hell, Mum's going to have a fit."

Scott chuckled, patting Martin's back. "Oh, pipe down. Your mum thinks you walk on water, mate. Just say I pushed you down a hill or something. We can't have you getting grounded and missing the cinema this weekend."

Martin shot Scott a dry look. "Yeah, right. Wait till next week, someone else will be asking me about what happened!" He huffed, annoyed. "How long am I going to have to answer for this rubbish?" his sister

Scott's expression softened. "Yeah, she did disappear around the same time you did, didn't she?" He sighed, looking up at his friend. "Can't blame the lad for connecting the dots. Plus, his parents are a right mess. My old man works with his dad and says he's down at the pub every night. And his mum's up and left, hasn't she?"

Martin let out an exasperated sigh. "And for the millionth time, I don't remember what happened! I was a kid, Scott! I can hardly remember who was chasing me in the first place. If anyone wants answers, they should be pestering Old Man Mr. Ulrich, not me!"

Scott chuckled, shaking his head. "Old Man Ulrich, eh? Don't you think the man who saved your life deserves a better nickname?" His smile dimmed, eyes shifting from Martin's face to the muddy ground. "His wife told my parents at the pub around Christmas. Said some blokes came to their house that night … said they were wearing some mad Halloween masks. Is that true?"

Martin exhaled, a wearied expression drawing lines on his youthful face. "Let's head this way," he suggested, pointing towards the forest area skirting the park's edge.

"The Log path?" Scott raised an eyebrow, unease flickering in his eyes. "That's where Andrew Poole's gang hangs out. What if they spot us?"

Martin shrugged nonchalantly, a spark of rebellion dancing inside his mind. "So what if they do? You planning to spend the rest of your life avoiding places because you're scared of a few bullies? Bugger them."

Traversing the verdant stretch, they moved past afternoon strollers walking their dogs and straggling schoolkids rushing home. The soft grassy carpet beneath their feet soon morphed into a muddy terrain as they veered onto a secluded forest trail. At the trail's terminus, a large gate stood sentry, partitioning the path from the grounds of the local college. Sprawled before the gate, like a fallen warrior, lay a massive, half-shattered tree. Over time, it had morphed into a natural bridge between the two distinct tracts of land, colloquially christened *The Log*.

The Log had a notorious reputation. It was the clandestine rendezvous for various groups of adolescents on Friday nights. It played host to their illicit shenanigans, brimming with underaged drinking, blaring music, and reckless attempts at setting parts of the forest aflame under the cover of night. As nonchalantly as if he were lounging on a home sofa, Martin swaggered over to The Log and plopped himself down. Meanwhile, Scott remained standing, his nerves frazzled.

"Toss me some baccy, please, bruv?"

Scott, after a wary glance over his shoulder, fished the tobacco out of his bag and handed it over. Martin rolled his eyes at his friend's paranoia.

"Why are we here?" Scott's voice was an uneasy whisper.

Without answering, Martin abruptly hoisted himself up onto The Log, leaning casually against the college fence. He whistled to get Scott's attention and then pointed at a distant object perched atop a hill. Scott followed his friend's gaze and made out the silhouette of a gothic mansion looming ominously on the horizon.

"That's where it happened, right? Where you were taken?" Scott ventured, his voice shaky. "I thought they would've knocked it down by now with no one being there."

Before he responded, Martin meticulously rolled his cigarette. His tone was serious when he finally spoke. "What I'm about to tell you, you can't go blabbing to anyone else. You got that? If you do, you'll end up like Adam Lewis. In the mud."

"I won't, I promise!" Scott hastily assured him, his voice rising in intensity. "I won't tell a soul, honest!"

Martin sparked the cigarette to life and slouched on The Log, his usually assertive demeanour dissolving into something more pensive. "I remember everything about that night ... well, at least everything up until I bolted from the house."

"But you said—" Scott started to interject, confusion creeping into his tone.

"Yeah, I know what I said. Mum and Dad didn't buy a word of it. They thought I was just talking out of my arse. Thought I might have hit my head, they told Nan and Grandad. Thing is, if I started telling people about what really happened, I'd be locked up somewhere."

"So ... what happened?"

Martin flicked the end of the cigarette.

"You remember Robyn from Maths class, right? I've fancied her for years. She said no one had dared to approach that house in years. So, to impress her, I bluffed and said I had. Of course, she didn't believe a word, so she dared me to hike all the way up to the house and etch my name on the nearby tree. So, I told Mum and Dad that I was bunking at yours ... sorry once again for that by the way."

"Apology accepted, mate. Go on," Scott encouraged him, his eyes wide with curiosity.

Martin took another long drag of his cigarette, the embers glowing in the dusk.

"So, there I was, trekking all the way up through the forest, expecting to get back home around one in the morning. I get there, I scratch my name into the tree bark, and just as I finish ..." He snapped his fingers for dramatic effect. "Everything turns pitch-black. Someone hit me in the back of the head, I think."

"Jesus Christ."

"Oh, don't start fretting yet. This is where things get seriously messed up," Martin smirked, another puff of smoke billowing from his lips.

"First thing that hit me when I came around was the sound of applause. It was deafening, man. Everyone in the room was clapping and hollering like mad. Felt like I'd just woken up in some mad dream where I'd hit the bloody lottery or something." Martin chuckled in disbelief, the memory still as vivid as ever.

"I come to, and the first bloody thing I notice is that I'm sitting at this grand dinner table. There are wine glasses filled to the brim and a feast fit for a king spread out before me. And around the table, guess what, seven other terrified kids my age. Every one of us was in tears ... crying for our parents," he admitted, his voice shaky. Abruptly, he swore and got to his feet, pacing restlessly back and forth on The Log to keep his overwhelming emotions at bay.

"Everyone adults were clapping ... they were all dressed up in suits, wearing those masks. These damn rabbit masks that stopped just below their noses, and you could still see them smirking, laughing at us," Martin continued, the haunting memory of the moment reflected in his eyes. "I tried to move, but we were all tied down to our seats. There was nowhere to go."

Scott merely nodded, unable to find the words to respond.

"And then ... I black out again. When I wake up, I'm naked, lying on the cold floor of a dark basement." Martin paused, and there was a weighted silence between them. The wind rustled the leaves around them as they waited for him to continue. He took a long drag of his cigarette before going on.

"I get up and see the other kids around me, they've been awake longer. And that's when I noticed something ... bloody strange." He let the words hang in the air, the tension between them rising.

He looked at Scott, his eyes dark and serious. "They weren't screaming or crying anymore. No, they were smiling. Grinning from ear to ear. Just like the kidnappers." The words hung heavy in the silent forest around them.

"Did you recognize any of them? Jenny, perhaps?" Scott ventured to ask.

Martin nodded sombrely.

"Ed McCarthy."

Scott's head snapped towards him, his mouth agape.

"Did you say Ed McCarthy? The first one who disappeared?"

"Yep. First one of the esteemed Valley Eight," he replied through gritted teeth. The name that the journalists had given him and the other seven kidnapped children always made him sick.

"There was something off about him," Martin continued, his voice low, as though afraid the trees might be listening. "The way he embraced me was as if we hadn't seen each other in years. As if we shared a past. And then, I remember as clear as day, he called me Arthur. 'Welcome back, Arthur,' he said." Martin swallowed hard, the memory lodging in his throat like a bitter pill.

He paused, looking into Scott's eyes, trying to gauge if the man before him believed a single word. "I didn't reply. Just stared, my mind spinning with confusion and terror. He told me to 'walk it off.' Whatever that meant."

Martin's voice wobbled a bit, but he pushed through it. "I just nodded, too bloody scared to say anything, and I backed into this hallway. Place was eerie as hell, echoes and all, with old fancy stuff covered in dust. Then I saw the front door. There was this guy, all suited up, mask on, just chilling with a blade in his hand."

He absentmindedly rubbed his arm, trying to shake the shiver from his spine. "I had to think quick, so I go up to him, trying to sound all calm and that, telling him there's trouble downstairs, that their creepy ritual thing or whatever it was, went sideways." The word *ritual* seemed to stick in his throat, like he could still see those weird symbols they'd drawn out. "He bit it, thank God, and he's off down the stairs in a rush, dropping the blade, thinking there's some emergency."

Scott leaned in closer, the firelight flickering shadows across his intent expression.

"And that's when I went for the door. It was bloody stuck, but I was freaking out and somehow, it budged a little." Martin's words sped up. "But then—there was this creak on the staircase behind me. My heart just stopped, man. I turned around, and there's this person, wearing a mask, standing at the top of the stairs. Half-naked and all, just standing there in this creepy dim light."

✓

Martin's hands worked together, scrubbing absently, as if he could erase the touch of memories too cruel to bear.

"The last thing I heard when I cracked open that door," he whispered, a shadow of fear flickering across his eyes, "was the sound of him lifting that machete. Everything after that … you already know."

"And your folks didn't believe you?"

"Would you have believed me if I'd returned home that day?" he retorted. "Only Old Man Ulrich didn't treat me like I was mad. He saved my life."

"Anything else you remember?"

"Mad cult stuff, man. Weird inscriptions on the floor, a black bible in one corner. Bizarre … I've been mulling it over. Maybe I should approach them again, sit my folks down and tell them everything. What do you reckon?"

As he massaged his face with rough hands, he called out, "Scott? What do you think, mate?"

He glanced upwards towards Scott and noted the boy frozen in place; his back turned. His eyes were locked onto three figures emerging from the same path they'd just travelled. Martin's cigarette slipped from his lips and landed on The Log as his mouth fell open, recognizing the trio of teenagers dressed in head-to-toe black. On the left was a blond lad with a ponytail, on the far right a girl with shoulder-length brown hair, and in the centre, a towering lad with a shaved head, his stern features belying his age.

The figure in the centre was undeniably Ed McCarthy.

"Hello, Arthur," he said, in a voice almost unrecognisable as his own. His eyes shimmered with unshed tears, and his smile resembled one that would welcome a long-lost friend. "It's good to see you again."

Martin rose to his feet.

"What did you call me?" he demanded, feeling a strange mix of surprise and suspicion.

The three remained disturbingly silent.

"Where the hell have you been? You guys have been missing for years! Don't you know that? Shouldn't you be with your families?" Martin pressed, his heart pounding with urgency and confusion.

"We could ask you the same thing," retorted the boy to the left, his smirk seeming out of place in the situation.

"Jonas, quiet!" snapped the girl on the right, her voice trembling slightly.

"I don't know what the hell has happened to you three up in that mansion, but you shouldn't be here." Martin pointed an accusing finger at the boy in the centre. "Why on earth do you keep calling me Arthur?"

"Why would I forget my own brother's name?" the boy in the middle responded, his tone firm and challenging.

Martin could only laugh, though the humour didn't reach his eyes.

"Sorry, mate. You've got the wrong bloke."

"Listen to me," the boy growled through gritted teeth, commanding the attention of both Martin and Scott. The tension hung heavy in the air, making Scott shake. "My name is Eli. You … you think you're Martin Drake, but you're not. Your name is Arthur Blackwater. You're my brother. Something went wrong in the ritual, and your vessel … it's malfunctioning, making you believe you're someone else. We're leaving tomorrow and we need you to come with us. To be with your real family."

"Your head's full of fucking screws, lad," Martin responded, struggling to keep his growing rage at bay.

Eli paused, studying Martin's face carefully. "Having trouble sleeping? Dreaming about a different life? Memories that don't quite fit. When you look in the mirror, do you see a stranger staring back?"

"Enough …" Martin muttered, his voice barely above a whisper. "Come on, Scott."

Grabbing his bag and Scott's arm, Martin began to walk away, aiming to pass the group. "When you wake up, do you believe you have a different name?" Eli called out, his voice echoing in the silence.

"I SAID ENOUGH!" Martin's rage exploded, turning him around to punch Eli squarely in the face. As Eli fell to the ground, his eyes never left Martin's. Jonas and the girl rushed to Eli's side as Martin and Scott hurriedly walked away.

"You okay?" Scott asked, his voice shaky. Martin didn't respond, simply walking with one hand on his bag and the other wiping away the tears streaking his face. His expression was a volatile mix of raw anger and deep sadness, suggesting that the words weren't a lie after all. Behind them, Eli's voice carried in the wind, resounding with an emotional intensity that seemed to fill the entire forest.

"Don't you walk away from me, Arthur!" Eli shouted. "You're my brother, Arthur! You hear me! You're my brother!"

1995

He lingered beside the grave, enveloped in a solemn quietude. His hands were buried deep in his suit pockets, a vain attempt to ward off the biting chill of the January air. So engrossed was he in his thoughts that he hadn't noticed the crowd of mourners gradually dispersing.

It was the daughter of the deceased who finally approached him, a small blonde woman in her mid-fifties, gently breaking his reverie. "Excuse me," she said softly, her voice tinged with respectful sorrow. "We're moving on to the pub for the wake, if you'd like to join us."

He looked up, meeting her eyes for the first time, and nodded. "Thank you, Sian, I'll be there shortly."

Recognition dawned on her face. "Oh, Martin, I didn't realize it was you," she said as she moved closer.

"Unfortunately, Julia's back home with the kids," he replied, looking back towards the grave. "Reuben's caught himself a cold. The joys of having a two-year-old."

"Gosh! Lena must be walking by now," Sian observed, her blonde hair dancing in the wind.

[line break]

"Yeah, she's walking alright—mostly into trouble," Martin quipped, though his smile quickly faded. "I was deeply saddened to hear about your father. He saved my life; that's more than most can say."

Standing beside Martin, Sian looked down at the headstone where her father Ulrich's name was etched beside her mother's. "You know, Dad could be a real piece of work sometimes, but he told me that the afternoon you ran to our house was the first time he felt true fear," she said softly. "He described it like a scene from a horror film—boogeymen in the forest, chasing a child."

"It's a tragedy they never found the others," Martin sighed.

"At least they found you," Sian responded, her hand settling gently on his shoulder. [full stop]

"Martin said, "As I watch my children grow, I think about those who didn't make it. They'd be about the same age now. I'll never forget their faces, and I'll always wish I could've done more."

As they walked down the cemetery path, two elderly figures caught Martin's eye. Both men were dressed in sombre black suits; one leaning on a walker, his posture bowed by time, the other, although upright, bore a weariness in his eyes that spoke of endless years burdened by sorrow.

"Are we really doing this again, Alex? On a day like today?" Martin's voice rose in frustration.

Alex Stevens and his son Kristian had been fixtures in the same house for what seemed like an eternity. Martin imagined them, frozen in time since Cassie disappeared, their hands clenched on armrests, eyes glued to the TV, bitterness accumulating year after year.

"Have you got something to say?" Martin challenged, his voice loud enough to carry.

"Martin, let it—"

"You tried to intimidate me in the restaurant last week, making my wife and daughter uncomfortable. Now you're trying to do the same to me here?" Martin interjected, moving Sian aside and confronting the two men, whose faces looked etched in perpetual misery. "I'm sorry about what happened to Cassie. I'm sorry you don't have answers. But you don't get to blame me for surviving. You don't get to blame me for your lack of closure!"

Martin Drake still vividly remembered that day, the day after his inexplicable escape from captivity. He was at the police station with Ulrich and his own parents, staring at a collection of photographs laid out before him. Each picture captured the smiling innocence of the other children, a cruel irony considering how he last saw them—bound to chairs, eyes wide with terror, as if aware that their young lives could end in that very room. Those faces haunted him, vanishing as they had into the abyss, leaving a town and countless families with gaping voids.

He told the police he didn't know what had happened to them, and that was the truth. But the truth didn't seem to matter to some in the town. As he grew up and continued to live there, Martin couldn't escape the accusatory glances, especially from older townsfolk or families who still didn't have answers about their own missing children. Even mundane activities like a trip to the supermarket could suddenly erupt into confrontations—screaming matches, accusations hurled, tears shed. For Martin, survival wasn't a miracle. In the eyes of many, it was as if he had committed a crime simply by living when others had not.

Alex, the older of the two men, slowly made his way towards Martin, leaning heavily on his walker. Muttering something in a low voice, the words were indecipherable at first. Martin leaned in closer, straining to hear. Suddenly, Alex's voice escalated into a scream, and the words rang out clearly in Welsh: "Mae'r felltith yn cerdded ymysg ni!"

The sheer intensity of Alex's proclamation made Martin recoil, instinctively covering his ears and taking a step back. The curse that had haunted the town, and Martin himself, seemed for a moment to be embodied in the old man's venomous cry.

"Let's go, Dad," Kristian interjected, gently guiding his father by the arm as they retreated from the graveyard. Alex continued to chant the eerie Welsh words even as they moved farther away.

Martin turned to Sian; his face etched with apprehension. "What did he say?"

She lifted her eyes to meet his, then looked to the gravestone before which the two men had stood—a stone that bore the name *Cassie Stevens.*

"*The curse walks among us,*" she translated, her words hanging in the air like a chill.

After attending the wake ~~at the Forest Oak pub,~~ Martin made the long trek home, feeling the delayed effects of the alcohol he'd consumed. He finally reached his house, a journey that should've taken him just ten minutes but had extended to half an hour in his inebriated state. Pushing open the front door quietly, he stepped into the dim corridor. A soft glow emanated from the kitchen, slicing through the darkness. When he entered, he found Julia sitting by the television, cradling a sleepy Reuben in her arms. A suppressed smile tugged at her lips as she took in her husband's slightly dishevelled appearance.

"Have fun?" she whispered, mindful of their son's light slumber.

"You'd be surprised. It was actually a good time, given the circumstances," Martin replied, his voice unintentionally loud. Realizing his mistake, he quickly mouthed the words "fuck" and "sorry." He slumped onto the sofa and shared a rueful smile with his wife.

Julia got up to make herself a cup of tea and poured a glass of water for Martin. As she moved, she handed Reuben to him.

Settling into the soft cushions of the sofa, Martin took his young son into his arms. Reuben's wispy blonde hair caught the gentle light of the room, and Martin felt a profound sense of peace and warmth flood over him, overpowering the lingering buzz of alcohol. At just over two years old, Reuben had a serenity about him, as if he were an old soul in a small body. He looked up at Martin with eyes that seemed to understand more than they should, and for a moment, the weight of the day, the wake, and the past seemed to lift.

Julia returned to the living room, carefully balancing the drinks. As she sat down, gently nestling Reuben back into her arms, Martin's eyes grew heavy, and he succumbed to sleep within minutes.

The television flickered with soft light, casting moving shadows across the room. Just as Julia was settling into this peaceful moment, she heard the unmistakable patter of small footsteps descending the staircase. She turned to the figure who crawled into the room and smiled.

"Oh, hello, sweetie! What are you doing?"

There, standing at the bottom of the stairs, was their fair-haired five-year-old daughter, Lena. She was dressed in Power Rangers pyjamas, her thumb nestled in her mouth. Lena paused, her eyes meeting Julia's before flicking to her slumbering father on the sofa. The weight of the moment hung in the air, answering a question that had loomed large in their lives, confirming Lena's existence as real, as tangible as the very air they breathed.

Julia turned back to the television.

"Is Daddy sleeping?" Lena's innocent question broke the silence, her small voice tinged with curiosity.

"Yes, darling, he's had quite a long day," Julia answered with a weary smile, attributing Martin's stupor to the wake and the drinks that followed.

"Daddy's head is broken," Lena announced abruptly, her childlike face serious.

Confused, Julia turned to Lena. "No, honey, he's just tired, that's all."

Lena wasn't deterred. "No, Mummy, Daddy's head is broken. He can't see all of it."

The air seemed to thicken; the ambient noise from the television now felt like a low, droning buzz. Lena began to climb onto the sofa, her every movement laden with a gravity that made Julia's heart start to race. Slowly, with the deliberate care that children reserve for their most solemn undertakings, Lena reached for her father's head.

The tension was palpable, each second stretching on as Julia found herself caught between disbelief and a rising sense of dread. What could Lena possibly mean? And as her small hands approached Martin's head, Julia's breath caught, waiting.

Julia watched as Lena's small fingers gently touched her father's forehead. In an instant, Martin jolted awake, eyes ashen, as if void of all colour. For a split second, Lena clung to his face before tumbling to the floor as he convulsed forward.

"Oh my God," Julia gasped. Swiftly setting Reuben in the nearby crib, she rushed to lift Lena up.

When she turned back, Martin's eyes had regained their familiar hue. But when their eyes met, something felt profoundly wrong. "Babe … are you okay?" she ventured, her voice quivering with concern.

For a moment, Martin seemed to stare right through her, as if she were a mere wisp of air. It was as though a switch had been flipped inside him, illuminating long-lost memories in a flash of mental imagery. He felt it all—every pivotal choice, every triumphant success, and heart-wrenching loss. Memories he had forgotten or suppressed were suddenly laid bare before him, rushing through his consciousness like a torrent.

All that Martin saw was the face of Cassie Stevens, but this time he experienced the image from a harrowing dual perspective. A floodgate of long-buried memories burst open within him, each one sharper and more vivid than the last. And with that, he began to scream.

CHAPTER ELEVEN

Present Day

Amidst the kinetic wave of bodies, a figure in an oversized sky-blue hoodie elegantly navigated the pulsating dancefloor, her frigid demeanour a stark contrast to the vibrant chaos that enveloped her. She prowled with an intentional grace, her piercing eyes meticulously dissecting the room in search of her prey. [Full Stop]

"Three o'clock, by the DJ booth," she muttered under her breath. To quell the loneliness and stave off the creeping anxiety of getting caught, she often imagined she had a Cockney sidekick speaking into an earpiece, guiding her movements. He would have been a character straight out of one of those BBC detective dramas her mother used to binge-watch on Sundays. "That's him—wearing the brown linen shirt, captivating the singer from the last set."

She caught sight of his smug grin, a sensation of rage immediately stiffening her resolve. Their target, Edward Velour, bore the mixed heritage of Albanian and Croatian ancestry, standing at an unremarkable height with a somewhat slender build. His pallor was ghostly against his dyed bleach-blonde hair, usually kept short and swept to one side, rendering him the air of a rogue scientist from a nineties video game. There he was, bearing the self-satisfied grin of a reckless heir squandering his father's fortune, jesting with a woman who would have paid him no mind had he not been the beneficiary of such wealth. He wore sunglasses indoors as if he were the star attraction at his own album release party, rather than just another opulent philanthropist at one of his many charity fundraisers. She scanned the room, taking in the frenzied revellers, their dance a hedonistic display of their willingness to spend beyond their means.

The world is falling apart. Everyone is in on the game, and all they're doing is scrambling to claim their share before they're faced with the Game Over screen. She knew Velour as the unrivalled maestro of money laundering on a national scale. Her mission was concealed within the details of his client list—a handful of names connected to a certain family of notoriety. The same family that had shattered her life into irreparable pieces.

She continued to make her way towards the front of the DJ desk, blending in with a section of fans who had started moshing as Slipknot's "Duality" christened the speakers. Edward was still high-fiving the organisers, unaware of what was about to happen next.

The pulsating rhythm of the music did little to drown the mounting tension as Lena watched Velour detach himself from the DJ booth. A cloud of uncertainty cloaked him as he meandered towards the backstage, each step gradually amplifying the stakes. Her eyes remained locked on his receding figure, never faltering.

She let a few fleeting moments pass, allowing the environment to craft a perfect diversion. When the time was ripe, she glided past the gaudy security detail. Unseen. Unheard. Like a shadow drifting in the twilight.

As she ventured farther into the restricted zone, a burly security guard appeared in her path. His eyes narrowed, the unwelcoming glint in his eyes a clear signal that she was trespassing on forbidden territory. But Lena was prepared for this.

She moved towards him, her body language subtly switching from an onlooker to a silent assailant. In a swift, almost invisible movement, she reached out and brushed her fingers across his face. Something changed in that moment. There was a strange, almost imperceptible ripple in the air, a flicker of light reflected in the guard's widened eyes, and then it was over.

The sensation was ephemeral, an anomaly in the sea of normalcy, leaving a trace of intrigue that would leave any observer questioning what they just witnessed. Then she was past him, her form disappearing into the labyrinth of backstage.

She cast a glance over her shoulder, the adrenaline pumping through her veins making the world seem like it was moving in slow motion. The security guard, to her satisfaction, was continuing his vigil unperturbed, as if she had never crossed his path. It was as though he had never seen her.

Trading the throbbing neon chaos of the club for the drab, grey corridor of backstage, she stayed on Edward's tail. Here, the sheen of glitz and glamour was brutally peeled back to reveal stark, industrial simplicity. The corridor was lined with nondescript boxes, supplies for the decadent celebration. Harried young servers dashed past, trays of untouched canapes and freshly poured drinks threatening to tip from their hands, prepared to feed the insatiable guests hidden behind the soundproof doors.

Following him up a narrow staircase, she slipped into the stealth mode of a seasoned hunter. Her eyes focused on the target, she trailed behind Edward, careful not to alert him to her presence. She navigated the dimly lit, claustrophobic passages with an eerie calm, her breath steady and her movements fluid.

The staircase ended in a small, utilitarian office space, devoid of the faux luxury seen downstairs. She held back as Edward veered left, disappearing through a nondescript door. Pressing herself against the cold wall, she peered around the edge, her eyes glued to the door that had just swallowed her prey. Her heart pounded in her chest, yet her expression was as unreadable as ever. The thrill of the chase heightened, transforming the mundane setting into a high-stakes game of hide and seek. The hunt was on, and she was ready to close in on her quarry.

She approached the door, her footsteps soundless against the unassuming carpet. She eased her way up to the small window set within the door and risked a glance inside. The room beyond was a stark contrast to the mundane office space she'd just navigated. An opulent VIP suite unfolded before her eyes, its most arresting feature being an expansive glass wall offering an aerial view of the pulsating nightclub below.

Edward stood with his back to her, arms folded in an air of authority. His figure was silhouetted against the neon glitz of the club visible through the window, lending him an almost spectral aura. He appeared to be in deep conversation, his head nodding and shifting occasionally, clearly engaged with an unseen interlocutor.

Her heart pounded in her chest. This was it.

Go for it

Without a second thought, she reached for the door handle and stepped inside. The moment her foot crossed the threshold, a force slammed into her stomach, knocking her breathless and sending her sprawling onto the floor. She looked up, her vision blurring as she tried to make sense of the sudden assault.

Hovering above her was a man who seemed more mountain than human, his bald head gleaming under the harsh overhead lights. He was clad in an intimidating ensemble of military-grade camo gear, a visual testament to his formidable capabilities. A cruel sneer played across his face; his searing eyes devoid of any hint of empathy.

Undoubtedly, this was one of Velour's bodyguards. Lena's pulse quickened as she met his icy glare, the pain in her stomach momentarily forgotten. This was not an obstacle she had anticipated, yet she knew she had no choice but to confront it head-on. She would not be deterred so easily.

"You know, typically I wouldn't mind a pretty lass tailing me. But that Sinead O'Connor haircut? It's giving me weird vibes," Edward mused, pacing back and forth, his arms crossed tightly over his chest. His back was turned to her, his demeanour deceptively relaxed.

Lena lay on the ground, her hand pressing against her aching stomach, trying to reclaim her stolen breath. She kept her eyes locked onto Edward, her mind racing to form a plan.

"I would rather not have Javier lay another hand on you,"

Edward continued, stopping his pacing to stand menacingly over her. His tone turned harsh, his patience evidently wearing thin. "So, why don't you tell me who you are and who sent you?"

Silence was her only response. A non-verbal challenge that spurred Edward into action. With a subtle nod from Edward, Javier prepared to exert more force. But just as he reached for Lena, she swiftly caught his arm. A moment of sheer silence ensued, and then everything seemed to freeze.

Javier abruptly released his hold on Lena and backed away, clutching his head, a guttural scream escaping his lips. Edward watched in shock as his usually unfaltering bodyguard crumbled.

"Hey! Hey! What did you do to him?!" Edward demanded, his tone filled with surprise and not a small amount of fear. Lena slowly rose from the ground, her expression unreadable.

"Those who endure traumatic experiences often push what they remember so far back, they eventually forget it was there in the first place. But all it takes is a little pull, and suddenly ..." she paused, her chuckle tinged with dark irony, "... it's the only thing they can see."

Still nursing her aching chest yet clearly asserting her dominance over the room, Lena stepped forward. The tormented cries of Javier had subdued, the large man now silently shaking in the corner. "We could have made this simple, Edward. Your client list," she confessed candidly, dismissing his accusations. "Just a few specific names ..."

Edward, fear mounting, retreated until he was pressed against the window.

"You think I'll just hand over confidential information?"

"If you'd rather not share Javier's fate, you'll tell me where I can find these individuals," she retorted, advancing on him with grim determination.

"Jonas Blackwater," she demanded "Where is he?"

A bolt of surprise flashed across Edward's face, that particular name visibly unsettling him. His lower lip trembled as he grappled to construct some form of convincing denial.

"Don't even think of bullshitting me, mate," Lena interjected, cutting through his mounting panic. "I'm well aware that he's been employing your services to funnel his family's wealth. The kind of wealth that builds dynasties. A tempting commission, I'm sure. You have a choice. Spill where he is and his method of communication with you. Or I'll pry the information out myself."

A defiant grin spread across Edward's face. "Give it your best shot."

Lena sauntered towards him. Edward eyed her warily, hands slowly raising in a defensive stance. But it was already too late. As Lena laid her hand on his arm …

She was in. A rush of memories, thousands of them, streamed past her, appearing like simultaneous movies playing on adjacent screens. Each significant moment in Edward's life, the highs of pure joy or the lows of hidden trauma, were absorbed within minutes.

"God," she whispered to herself, repulsed by certain actions of Edward that were now vivid in her mind. "Hold on …"

She detected something, a flutter in the current of memories. With a flick of her wrist, she slowed the flow of the screen to her left. The image stopped. A man sporting a blond ponytail, a grin plastered on his face, was caught mid handshake. She reached into the image …

Leaning against the cool metal of the large black van, Edward frequently glanced at his watch. Someone was keeping him waiting …

Edward's eyes shifted as Jonas materialised from the shadowy depths of the parking lot, carelessly flicking a spent cigarette away. He was clad in a velvet suit, an air of unrest subtly evident in his demeanour.

"Kept me waiting, huh?" Edward queried.

"Oh please! You would've waited the entire night," Jonas countered with a smirk.

They stepped inside the backseats. Edward took a laptop from below the chair.

Their fingers danced swiftly across the touchscreens; the series of digits that represented enormous sums of wealth quickly transferred with just a few taps.

"Triple-check the accounts," Jonas ordered, his eyes never leaving the screen of his device. "I don't want any mistakes."

"Relax, Jonas," Edward replied, attempting a nonchalant smile. "You know I don't make errors with these things."

The van was filled with a tense silence, only broken by the intermittent beeping of their devices as the transfer processed. After a while, Jonas broke the silence, casting a sidelong glance towards Edward.

"Heard about your court case," Jonas casually mentioned, the corner of his mouth tugging into a sardonic smile. "Keeping out of trouble these days?"

Edward's smile tightened, his hand pausing momentarily over his device. "Trouble seems to find me, no matter where I hide." He chuckled lightly, a forced sound in the otherwise silent van. "But that's behind me now."

His fingers resumed their dance across the touchscreen, finalising the last of the transfers. In their world, even a conversation laced with tension couldn't distract from the task at hand—the business of handling vast amounts of illicit money.

With the transfers complete, Edward leaned back in his seat, the digital glow from the screen painting his face a sickly blue. "And how's the situation with ... the girl?"

Jonas's fingers froze on his device, his eyes slowly turning to Edward. "I told you not to bring that up again," he said, his voice low and cold.

Edward pushed on, undeterred. "I saw the news ... in Wales. A man got stabbed at a train station. Was it ... ?"

His words were cut off as Jonas's icy glare locked onto him. "You think because you inherited your father's fortune, you can stick your nose into anyone's business?" The question, delivered in a lethal whisper, hung in the air, a quiet threat.

Edward held Jonas's gaze, but the defiance in his eyes wavered. After a beat, he nodded, retreating into silence. Jonas's attention returned to his device, but the air in the car remained heavy, an unspoken reminder of the boundaries Edward had overstepped.

"Money is no match for time, Edward. And time is something we have in abundance," Jonas voiced out, his tone easing slightly as Edward recoiled *from the reprimand.* "We'll continue meeting every fourteenth of the second month. Let's try to keep these exchanges as concise as they've always been."

"We have our Tech Gala on the fourteenth. Be good for you to join and see how your investment is being handled."

Jonas nodded reluctantly, rarely wanting to carry out business in public. "Very well."

The pair exited the vehicle, Jonas retreating into the obscurity of the parking lot, his footsteps resonating ominously in the vacant space.

"I suppose now I understand your unusually sombre demeanour!" Edward called out after him. Jonas froze and turned his head. The grin on Edward's face was brimming with arrogance as he proposed the question that felt like a mocking punch to Jonas's gut. "You've lost her, haven't you?"

Edward's laughter echoed in the deserted car park, a haunting soundtrack to Jonas's silent fury. A crack in his usually unshakeable veneer was clearly visible now. Without a word, he turned and disappeared into the engulfing darkness …

The connection was severed as suddenly as it had been established. Lena and Edward slumped to the ground, both drained by the intensity of the mind meld. She was panting heavily on her knees; the expenditure of energy was significant, but she was invigorated.

For the past half a year, she had been wandering aimlessly like a spectre across different cities, searching for her next move. But now she had a lead. Today was the eleventh of July. In three days, Jonas Blackwater, one of the culprits behind her father's death, would be meeting Edward Velour for a clandestine transaction.

Leaning forward, Lena set about the delicate task of erasing their encounter from Edward's memory, her fingers gingerly tracing the contours of his unconscious form. Once her task was complete, she straightened up and moved towards Javier, preparing to repeat the process.

However, as she lowered her hands towards Javier, she froze. A flicker of movement from the adjacent room snagged her attention, her heightened senses detecting an intrusion in the otherwise empty space. A figure concealed behind the door of the SoundStation, silently observing.

Her heart pounded as she cautiously rose, her gaze darting between Javier and the door, the task momentarily forgotten. Every instinct screamed danger. The atmosphere was electric, the air thick with anticipation. She neared the door, her hand trembling slightly as she reached for the handle. Gathering her courage, she steeled herself for the inevitable confrontation. She thrust the door open, her body tensed and ready.

But ... nothing. The room was vacant, devoid of any human presence. Was her mind playing tricks on her?

With a heavy sigh of relief, she turned back to Javier, her task still incomplete. But as she looked down at him, she found his eyes fluttering open, consciousness returning. There was no time. She made the decision to abandon the process and leave.

She descended the stairs and reintegrated herself into the pulsating crowd on the dancefloor. Her time of reckoning was drawing near, and she could practically taste it. Immersing herself in the energy of the music, she closed her eyes, dropped her head, and let herself sway with the rhythm, lost in a world of her own.

CHAPTER TWELVE

2017

"Lena! Can you come down for a moment?"

Seated at her desk, deep in the mind-numbing labyrinth of A-level Maths, Lena relished the excuse for a break. She was idly tracing the frost patterns on her windowpane, her eyes straining for the first hint of a promised snowfall.

"Lena!" The second call had an undertone of urgency.

Springing to her feet, Lena took the stairs two at a time, made a beeline across the lush crimson carpet of the living room, and into the kitchen. There sat her father, dwarfing the old wooden chair he was perched upon, arms crossed over his barrel chest. Lena observed the tendrils of steam curling up from his *Dad's Army* mug, coiling around his silver-streaked ginger beard.

"Uh … Hey, Dad. All good?" she asked her father, noticing the telltale signs of exhaustion in his hunched posture. He was a far cry from the cheery man captured in the family photo that graced the living room table. His recent bouts of irritability and marathon drinking sessions hadn't escaped Lena's notice. The job was likely taking its toll, she mused. Even her brother, who usually had a stronger connection with their father, was in the dark about this transformation.

"Where's the rest of the gang?" she probed.

His eyes avoided her. Martin replied, "Sent them off to Tesco's for dinner supplies. I'm thinking of attempting a Thai curry tonight."

Lena's eyebrows shot up. "That's a bold move for a man who can't handle a Nando's medium sauce."

Her comment elicited a brief smile, assuring her that things were not as bad as she feared. She walked behind him to the sink, washing her hands before grabbing a glass from the lower shelf. Just a tough day at work, she decided.

"Work's been a bit crazy, huh?" she ventured.

Martin took a long sip of his tea.

"Yeah, I'm doing overtime for the next few weeks. Steve, our manager, is away looking after his daughter. I think you are in school with her, actually? You heard of Casey Alford?"

Lena put the glass underneath the tap.

"Yeah, she's in the year above me," Lena said with a slight strain in her voice.

Her father looked down into his mug of tea, rubbing his index and thumb across the edge quickly, trying to remove an invisible mark.

She turned on the tap.

"I called Steve to hear what happened. The man is so work obsessed he would probably miss his mother's funeral if the team needed him. Don't worry, I know how horrible that sounds! Anyway, I called him to see what happened. He told me that Casey was in hospital. She had fainted in her house They don't know what's wrong with her now. Apparently, she woke up not being able to talk or remember anything. They think she might have had a stroke."

"Sounds horrible," Lena remarked, concerned about lacing her words. "Hope she gets well soon."

"Well … I guess that would depend on if she gets her memories back, wouldn't it?" he suddenly said, a strange undertone to his voice.

Lena stiffened, the water from the tap pooling in the glass.

The tap sputtered to a stop, the silence in the room hanging heavy.

"I'm sorry, I didn't catch that," she stammered.

"You took her memories, didn't you?" he asked, a serious note replacing his earlier warmth.

"I … I think I should get back to my studies," she mumbled.

"Your hands are trembling," he noted, getting up swiftly and blocking her exit.

Lena tried to form a response, but the words stuck in her throat. She felt her body betray her, shaking uncontrollably as it struggled against her deceit. Her father had never been a threatening figure—no raised fists or fiery outbursts. But now, his stern expression seemed to convey that things were far graver than she had imagined.

"Listen to me," he began softly. "I understand that you may not have intended to do what you did, but Casey's in the hospital now. She needs help."

"Wait? What?" Shocked, Lena took a step back, gripping the edge of the table for support. "How … how do you know?" she stammered, her voice rising. "How in the hell do you know what I can do?"

In response, Martin raised his hands in a placating gesture. His eyes darted back and forth anxiously, as though caught in a fierce inner struggle to share an unspeakable truth.

"A member of our family once had it before," he finally confessed. "I can't do it myself, but I've seen it happen. And because I've seen it, I can help you. You need me to guide you before things get worse."

"ENOUGH!" Lena shouted, her emotions boiling over. She tried to push past her father. "I need some space; I'm going to Emily's!"

But Martin was quick. He positioned himself between her and the entrance corridor, his voice echoing through the quiet house as he spoke. "Lena. You're sixteen years old. You can't simply run away from this!"

She froze, turning sharply to face him, her face a mix of bewilderment and fear. "What are you—"

"That girl you put in the hospital. You took something precious from her. Whether that memory was something good or bad, it was a piece of her. You understand?"

The car keys clattered onto the tiled floor as Lena backed away, a strangled cry escaping her lips. She staggered, placing her hands on her head, her breathing ragged. It was as if the walls were closing in, threatening to engulf her. Her father stepped forward, pulling her into a comforting embrace. She wept into his shirt, the harsh reality of her situation finally sinking in.

"How long has this been happening, Lena?" he asked gently.

She slowly pulled away from him, wiping away her tears with the back of her hand. "Six months," she whispered; her voice barely audible.

"Come, sit with me. Tell me everything that happened."

Reluctantly, she moved to the table, taking a seat as her father went to make her a cup of coffee. She looked towards the rain-splattered window. Her own reflection stared back at her, a grim reminder of the situation. The thought of her father finding out about her powers had been unthinkable, and yet here she was, forced to face the reality.

Lena clutched the mug in her hands, the warmth seeping into her cold fingers. "Me and Casey met at Costa after school. She ... it's so stupid."

She paused for a moment, leaning her full head back and putting her hands through her hair. She took a deep breath and continued.

"She thought I liked this guy called Josh from our English class who she had been seeing for a few weeks and we just wanted to clear the air. Anyway, after we cleared the air, we hugged it out. And ... in that moment, as we pulled apart; I knew ... I knew about her necklace. I knew it was a gift from her grandmother when she was seven. She got it the day she fell from her bike, and her grandmother gave it to her out of sympathy."

Martin frowned, leaning forward.

"And you felt as if you had lived that moment yourself?"

Lena nodded. "Exactly. But Casey didn't remember any of it. I thought she was playing a prank at first, but she genuinely didn't remember. We went to her mum's place later, and her mum confirmed what I knew. You should have seen Casey's face when she realised she couldn't remember where her necklace came from. I still remember her looking down when her mum said, "You always tell that story."

Lena fiddled with her hands, scratching on her skin as she tried to find the words. She then told her father what happened.

"Her mum called me a few days ago to tell me she was in hospital. I asked what happened and I think that they had an argument about the necklace and—"

"You should've come to me as soon as this happened," he said, the edge in his voice clear. His fingers drummed against the wooden table, a clear sign of his inner turmoil.

"Oh, yeah, because that would've gone down so well. "Hey, Dad, guess what? I turned into one of the mutants from the *X-Men* today. How was your day?""

"Hey, I'm still your father." He reached across the table to take her hand. The tears had dried on her cheeks, replaced by a stubborn set to her jaw. "That means you can come to me about anything, you understand? I get why you felt you had to hide this, but I am both your parent and your best friend. You do get that, right?"

She was silent for a moment, then gave a small nod, her eyes fixed on their entwined hands.

"You said you had seen this before? What did you mean by that?" she asked.

Lena watched a shadow fall over her father's face, his features tightening as if grappling with an unseen adversary. He looked to a point beyond the room, locking onto a distant horizon only he could see.

"What I'm about to tell you may frighten you, Lena," he answered slowly. "But you must know that I'm going to protect you from whatever happens. Do you understand?"

"Dad. You're scaring me. What are you talking about?"

He stopped looking into the distance and instead locked eyes with her.

"This power you have is a gift," he began. "And there is a group who will do everything in their power to obtain it. You could hide in the very depths of Hell, and they would walk through fire just to get to you. That's how much they want to control this power. They are called the Blackwaters."

There was a rage behind his eyes that she hadn't seen before. She didn't dare ask her father if he was joking.

"Do you know who they are? The Blackwaters?"

Her father scoffed and finally, a small hint of a grin grew on his face.

"That's what makes this so ridiculous, Lena," he answered. "We are related to them."

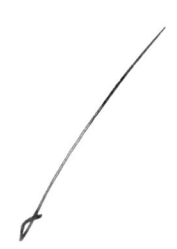

CHAPTER THIRTEEN

Present Day

Hidden within the cocoon-like comfort of her hoodie, Lena strolled through the bustling city streets, eyes glued to her phone, fingers mindlessly swiping through endless notifications and messages. Lost in her thoughts, she barely noticed the sensory bombardment of the city's morning routine: the cacophony of car horns, indistinct chatter, and the shrill cry of distant sirens.

A tangible rhythm pulsed through the urban landscape. Men and women, still shaking off the morning haze, hurried past clutching cups of takeaway coffee, their tired faces buried in their phones or darting through the sea of bodies rushing by. Workers hunched in outdoor cafes, laptops open, their eyes darting between screens and wristwatches. A group of students, too youthful for the morning grind, huddled on a park bench, sharing headphones, and whispering excitedly over a shared screen.

Yet, amidst the routine chaos, Lena felt a profound sense of isolation. Her secret, the bizarre and dangerous ability that marked her as different, created an invisible barrier between her and the bustling world. Surrounded by teeming masses, she had never felt more alone.

London's anonymity was both a solace and a torment. Among these multitudes, Lena could lose herself, blend into the anonymous human tide. But she was more, different, and unique. This indelible mark of otherness was something she couldn't evade, nor escape.

Her thoughts meandered back to the hospital visit, the sole instance she had successfully managed to restore a memory. If only he had spent more time teaching her, unravelling the mysteries of her power. But in the years before his sudden disappearance, he had avoided those conversations. He hadn't held back on warnings, though. He had often spoken of certain individuals who could potentially target her, as they had him in his youth. Jonas, Maya, and Eli. Names etched into her memory like cautionary talismans.

From a distance, she could see the towering silhouette of the city's train station—a sight she deliberately avoided. The sight, sound, even the mere smell of trains, painfully evoked memories of her father's lifeless form on a similarly cold platform

Attempting to suppress the unwelcome resurgence of memories, Lena focused her attention back on her phone. She opened a Welsh news app to check the latest happenings back home. She scrolled through the headlines, taking in the daily chronicles of her former home from a distance.

Lifting her eyes from the screen, Lena found herself standing on a familiar street lined with terraced houses, each painted in a different, vibrant colour. The rainbow-hued row of homes seemed to echo the energy and diversity of the city itself, a symbol of its resilience and spirit. Each house boasted a distinct colour, from fiery red and sunflower yellow to deep indigo and gentle mint green, lending the street a bright, cheerful aura that contrasted sharply with the monotonous concrete of the surrounding cityscape.

Lena approached the mustard-yellow house, a bright splash of colour that seemed to radiate warmth and comfort. Without a second thought, she walked up the narrow path and opened the front door, stepping into her haven.

The moment Lena crossed the threshold, she narrowly avoided stumbling over her flatmate, Sophie's mud-encrusted Doc Martens. A soft sigh of exasperation escaped her lips. Carefully, Lena tiptoed up the worn staircase towards her first-floor flat door, making sure not to alert Mrs. Parish. The old woman, with hearing as acute as a bat's, was easily disturbed by even the slightest creak from above. The red door, somewhat chipped and faded, was warm under her touch as she pushed it open and stepped into the flat.

Inside, it was a charming amalgamation of eclectic and vintage aesthetics, the kind of space that seemed to perfectly capture the spirit of young adulthood. The hardwood floors were often strewn with colourful throw rugs, each one with a different pattern, telling a story of a different time or place. The walls, painted a warm and inviting off-white, were adorned with a variety of art and posters—some from indie rock bands they'd seen live, others were prints of famous artwork Sophie liked to collect.

A mishmash of furniture—a thrift store couch, a mid-century modern coffee table, a shabby-chic bookcase—were strategically placed around the room. On the bookcase, novels and philosophy books sat side by side, evidence of their different tastes. The couch was usually draped with a cozy throw blanket, perfect for those nights of movies and popcorn.

A small kitchenette occupied one corner, its aged cabinets filled to the brim with crockery and an assortment of spices. The refrigerator was almost a piece of art itself, smothered in colourful magnets from around the world, concert ticket stubs, and small reminders scribbled on Post-it notes.

Upon closer inspection, it was abundantly clear that Lena had few to no personal possessions in the apartment. The eccentric trinkets, the abundance of books, the vast collection of posters and artwork, and even the myriad of refrigerator magnets, they all were a testament to Sophie's vibrant personality. The apartment was a canvas, and Sophie had painted every inch of it with her essence.

As for Lena, her presence was felt, but not seen. There were no remnants of her past, no personal keepsakes or favourite items, and certainly, no photographs. Her lack of belongings was a stark contrast against Sophie's personal trove of memorabilia. It was as if Lena was a shadow residing in the apartment, always present but never leaving a tangible trace.

In some strange way, their living arrangement was a perfect reflection of their lives. Sophie, fully immersed in her existence, embraced every facet of her life, leaving a vivid impression everywhere she went. On the other hand, Lena's life was one that was constantly on the move, leaving no room for the accumulation of material things. Her life was a series of disconnected moments, an existence defined not by what she had, but by what she didn't.

Emerging from her bedroom, Sophie appeared in the hallway, dressed in a soft, faded dressing gown that had seen better days. Her hair was a striking ginger hue, a wild, untamed cloud around her face, setting off her fair skin and adding to her vibrant personality.

Sophie was tall, but not in a looming way. It was a natural height, accentuated by her slender frame that seemed almost delicate. Yet, her lanky limbs moved with a confidence that suggested a sense of comfort in her own skin, of being aware of her own physicality and being unafraid to take up space.

"Ah, there she is, the night owl herself," Sophie called out as Lena entered the room. Her ginger hair shone in the morning sunlight that spilled from the window. "Ever heard of this phenomenon called the sun, Lena? You should see it sometime."

She leaned back against the counter, sipping her coffee with a teasing grin. "You do realise you spend more time unconscious than conscious, don't you? I'm surprised you're not permanently comatose."

Lena gave her a dry look, leaning against the doorframe. "Well, I'm sorry my job doesn't adhere to normal business hours," she fired back. "Not all of us can clock out at five. Some people need help at ungodly hours, you know."

Sophie chuckled, her coffee cup paused midway to her mouth. "You're right, those desperate souls who ring Samaritans in the middle of the night must be in dire need of your wisdom. But tell me this, are you going to continue this nocturnal existence and miss my birthday bash tonight?"

"*Ma chérie*, I wouldn't miss it for the world," Lena replied, dramatically affecting a French accent, a hint of amusement in her voice.

"Just grant me a few hours of shuteye, and I'll be ready to dance the night away," she added, padding towards the bathroom.

"Oh, Jamie!" Sophie called out after her.

Lena paused, her hand on the bathroom doorknob. She was still adjusting to her pseudonym, the artificial name that replaced her identity, always a split second behind in recognizing it as her own.

"I noticed you're paying rent in cash again. Is something happening?" Sophie's voice echoed behind Lena.

"Having issues with the bank ... Thought this wouldn't be a problem as discussed when I moved in," Lena replied, not bothering to turn around.

"Oh no, it's not a problem, it's just—"

"Good." Lena cut her off before she could finish, effectively ending the conversation. She disappeared into her room, shutting the door quietly behind her.

An hour later, Sophie quietly tiptoed towards Lena's door, pressing her ear against the cold wood. The loud, rhythmic sound of snoring reassured her that her elusive flatmate was indeed asleep. With a sigh of relief, she retreated from the door and headed to her own sanctuary.

Sophie's bedroom was a stark contrast to Lena's, which bore the bare, austere resemblance of a prison cell. Here, the room was a kaleidoscope of memories and connections. The walls were adorned with pictures, some in elegant frames, others simply taped on. Each image told a tale of laughter, friendships, family reunions, and memorable moments from Sophie's past.

Family photos with her parents and siblings, taken at parks, holiday dinners, or during random candid moments, filled the walls with warm familial bonds. Each image was a testament to her outgoing, vibrant nature, a nature that Lena seemed to lack or, at the least, kept well hidden.

Sophie, seated on her terracotta-hued bedspread, found herself wrestling with an unavoidable decision. Extracting her phone from her drawer, she drew a deep breath before unlocking it and navigating to her photo album. She found the photo she had taken in the early hours of this morning. As it turns out, Lena wasn't the only one who had been out until the early hours.

The photo depicted a scene from a concealed vantage point between an assortment of boxes in a nightclub's VIP area. It showed Lena—almost unrecognisable—wielding power over Sophie's boss, Edward Velour. Lena's hand was positioned ominously above Edward's bent head, an undeniable testament to her dominance. Sophie's finger hovered indecisively over Jonas's contact in her phone. The stories, the rumours, the half-whispered tales she'd dismissed as fantasy—it was all real. She had found The Collector.

CHAPTER FOURTEEN

"Hello?"

"Good day. This is Inspector Alex Osbourne from the London Metropolitan Police. I was hoping to speak to DCI Elaine Walker. Is she available?"

"I'm afraid not. Regrettably, she's on sick leave. This is DCI Owen Moody filling in until she recovers."

"That's unfortunate. Tell her I wish her the best," Osbourne expressed sympathetically. The line fell quiet, absent a response.

"Anyway, I'm getting in touch because we've got someone at our precinct who claims to have insight on a past case of hers."

"Do you have a case number?" Smith inquired.

"Sure do, it's case RD1309."

Moody's tone sharpened with surprise. "The Martin Drake murder? Are you certain?"

"Indeed, we have an individual by the name of Finian Evans in custody. He's adamant that he saw the perpetrator on the day Drake was stabbed," Osbourne relayed.

"Hmm. You sure?" Moody asked with a tone that suggested he would rather be talking to anyone else. "I'm checking through the file right now and can't see anything regarding witness interviews. Sounds like you've got someone trying their last 'Get Out of Jail Free' card," Moody countered.

"I would usually be on the same page as you, but Evans seems quite certain he remembers what he heard."

"And what exactly did he hear then, Detective Osbourne?" Moody replied, not attempting even slightly to hide his impatience.

"Well ... Mr. Evans was hired as transport security during the football match in August last year. As you can imagine after the incident of Mr. Drake's murder, there were a lot of people that were left feeling unsafe. Didn't exactly help the teams or the game's already damaging reputation either. They had to blame someone."

"I guess Mr. Evans got let go, then?"

"Yes, he did. He showed back on our radar this month, arrested on a drug charge. Looks like this job was an intermission between two downward spirals. Anyway, he's facing some hefty prison time. Soon as I start speaking about the amount of years, he starts talking about the murder from last year. Says that someone had bribed him to look away from the area where Mr. Drake was eventually found."

"Well, this all sounds very eventful, Detective. Look, as far as I'm concerned, this is Walker's case and I'm sure she'll be happy to listen to you when she's back. That's unless you got anything else to think about that's worthwhile?"

There was a pause.

"Does the name Jonas Blackwater mean anything to you?"

The line went silent.

"According to Mr. Evans's account, this is the man who approached him the night before. Paid him enough to ensure the men's toilets on Platform Six were closed off. The same place they believed Martin Drake was first attacked," Osbourne said.

"Hmm. Interesting. I haven't heard the name before," Moody lied. "So, this man has suggested to you that he was paid by a man called Jonas Blackwater to ... ensure that the platform toilets were shut off where Martin Drake was later stabbed? If this is the case, why didn't he mention this to the police before?"

"Well, that's why I wanted to speak to Walker in the first place," Osbourne answered quickly, showing the slightest hint of impatience at DCI Moody's passiveness. "According to not only Mr. Evans's account but our records of the case at the time, Elaine Walker actually interviewed him the week after the incident."

Another pause came much longer than expected.

"I see," DCI Moody answered.

"So, there's two things I need from you, DCI Moody. I need you to go through all the information Elaine had and check any references to Jonas Blackwater. Don't worry about checking any of the details of her interview with Mr. Evans because I've already done this myself. We have a tape recording of Mr. Evans giving the name to her. Therefore, we need to determine if she ever investigated this further and if not, why. There's a good chance this Jonas Blackwater may be the man we've been looking for all this time."

"Well, look. If me and my team have time this week to go through this, I can assure you we'll do our—"

"Let me know what you've come up with by the end of the week. The superintendent and I are going to pay a visit to you and the rest of our South Wales counterparts on Monday. That should be enough time for you to get things ready."

The phone line went dead.

Jonas took the phone in his hand and smashed it into the coffee table. Attired in a sleek green shirt, Jonas sprang from the table, his energy irrepressible. His polished shoes clicked rhythmically against the pristine marble floors as he strutted, his loud gasps of anger piercing the pervasive silence. The normally bustling mansion was nearly deserted at this hour, amplifying the echoes of his jaunty tune.

He strolled up the emerald-green carpeted staircase and headed down the first floor, into a corridor of luxurious paintings. Each frame held a captivating piece, some with vivid colours that seemed to pop off the canvas, others with intricately detailed portraits whose eyes seemed to follow him as he moved. The ornate designs on the borders were just as awe-inspiring, their golden sheen reflecting the soft glow from the chandeliers above. The elegance of the hallway was overwhelming, and he revelled in it, knowing every art piece told a story, every colour held an emotion.

As Jonas advanced farther down the corridor, the evolution of the artwork became more striking. The early works were grandiose and dramatic, brimming with the dark opulence of the Gothic era. Large family gatherings were depicted, austere patriarchs and poised matriarchs framed by an array of children, all draped in inky blacks, their stoic features accentuated by the backdrop of deep purples and rich crimsons.

Next came the Victorian era with its smaller family groupings, their attire now touched with shades of deep blues and vibrant emeralds, hinting at a change in times and aesthetics.

As the timeline of paintings unfolded, the family groups shrunk further, reaching the twentieth-century portraits, where the Family was now distilled to just five figures. The once dominant black had given way to more cheerful colours—the warm hues of oranges, the optimistic yellows, the fiery bursts of red.

But it was the last painting in the sequence that drew Jonas's gaze the longest, a piece starkly different from its predecessors. It was a modern monochrome portrait, stripped of all colour, that depicted a single figure dressed in a stark black tuxedo.

Jonas's hand gripped the brass doorknob, its cool surface grounding him momentarily. The faint rustle of movement from the other side heightened his sense of anticipation. He drew in a deep, steadying breath, preparing himself for the sight that awaited him, and gently pushed the door open.

The grandeur of the master bedroom had been replaced by an almost clinical austerity. The lush fabrics and ornate furnishings were supplanted by a hospital bed, a heart rate monitor beeping rhythmically in the corner, and an IV stand that hovered like a ghost at the bedside. The air bore the faint scent of antiseptic, a stark contrast to the usually comforting smell of Maya's perfume. All the trappings of a fully equipped hospital room, strangely out of place in the sprawling mansion.

His eyes shifted towards the centre of the room where two nurses busied themselves around the bed's occupant. These women, chosen for their professional competence and discretion, were the best in their field, their services secured at a premium by Jonas using the Family's sizable fortune. Their uniforms, impeccably clean and starched, contrasted sharply with the situation's inherent disarray. Each moved with a purpose, their efficiency and attentiveness born from years of experience and a commitment to their patient.

Maya was situated in the heart of this domestic medical hub, seated on the bed. The fierce, lively spirit he knew seemed to have dimmed in the wake of the accident. Her face, once brimming with vivacity, now bore the brutal signature of the car crash—a jagged scar that etched its way down the left side. Her eyes, unfocused and distant, was drawn to the window, affording a view of the sprawling garden below. Its lavish beauty was a stark contrast to the confinement she currently endured. It was as though the lush greenery, vibrant blossoms, and soaring trees served as a silent, cruel reminder of the world she was temporarily barred from—a world still teeming with life beyond the room's sterile confines.

"I'm not ready to talk right now," she murmured, her voice barely audible, devoid of its usual confidence.

Jonas leaned back against the wall with his arms crossed tightly.

"Oh, trust me. You don't get that choice anymore. Not after what I have to say."

"Don't you think we should wait for him?"

Her eyes remained fixed on the window, trailing towards the garden. Jonas did the same, and they both found their attention drawn towards the solitary figure practising archery in the distance.

Attired in impeccable white, Eli stood out against the garden's green backdrop like a stark silhouette. The tension in his arms was palpable even from this distance as he released a single, perfect shot. The arrow sailed through the air, lodging itself squarely in the centre of the stationary target fifty feet away. In the stillness that followed, it was as if he sensed them looking down at him. He paused, his hand frozen midway to his quiver for the next arrow, and slowly, he turned to face the mansion window. His eyes were steel grey, matching the sky overhead, with a certain coldness that made one shiver even on the warm summer afternoon. His hair was dark and slicked back, adding an air of calculated precision to his features. His jawline was strong, and his lips were a thin, straight line.

One particular aspect of his appearance, however, was strikingly off-kilter with his immaculate attire. The sleeve on his right arm was hitched up, exposing an expanse of skin that bore the patchy, raw evidence of severe burns. The discoloured tissue, a mottled array of pink and white, stretched from his wrist up to his elbow, a vivid testament to a past trauma that contrasted harshly against his otherwise flawless white ensemble.

They watched him disappear from their view and waited for his arrival. As they waited, they remained silent as if they would only be allowed to speak once Eli allowed them to do so.

The unbearable silence was soon shattered by the soft sound of the door creaking open. Each click of the latch echoed in the room like a gunshot, amplifying the tension that already lingered. Into this charged atmosphere, Eli stepped, his arrival making the air in the room seem to grow thicker.

Accompanying him was a butler, balancing a tray loaded with fresh orange juices and an assortment of teas. The tray seemed mundane, almost out of place in contrast to the palpable tension that Eli carried in his wake.

Every movement was followed by the watchful eyes of his siblings. The butler, a beacon of professionalism, efficiently manoeuvred around the awkward stillness, placing the tray on a table before making a hasty retreat.

Once the door clicked shut behind him and they were alone again, it was as if the room dared to breathe. But the silence that filled the room was far from comfortable—it was heavy with words unspoken, and secrets that threatened to spill.

"How are you feeling?" Eli answered with a chilling calm.

"Better," Maya said simply turning back to the window as if she was having the conversation with her brother outside.

Jonas smiled. "Well now that you're feeling better, maybe you'd like to explain why you never thought to mention my name being dropped into the Martin Drake murder case? I've just had an inspector on the call wanting me to investigate myself! Because of you, some simpleton in the valleys knows my real name!"

"Ugh. Once I'm back on my feet, I'll handle it. Don't worry your little head, nephew."

"Like you handled Reuben Drake? If maybe you had taken your time getting him to us and not panicked, you would still have half your face."

Maya winced as she pulled herself half up in bed.

"Well maybe if you thought for one moment about anyone but yourself, you would realise that rational thinking isn't on the top of my list regarding my circumstances. Did you forget that I'm running out of time?"

"Oh please! You think you're the only one running out of time?!" sneered Jonas. "We're all running out of time!"

"Enough!" Eli spat. "The both of you."

They did as he asked.

He turned first to Jonas.

"This inspector who contacted you. What was his name?"

"Alex. Alex Osbourne."

He spun to Maya.

"Know him?"

She nodded.

"Tell me."

He approached her bed slowly. Each step measured as if navigating the critical moves of a chess game.

"What type of man is he? One to know when to shut up and turn his head when he's told?"

He sat on the bed.

"Or another hero we're going to make disappear?"

"Sorry!" Jonas interrupted. "Two secs."

Both watched Jonas suddenly slip out of the room. The door slamming behind him.

"That means seconds by the way."

Eli rolled his eyes. "Fully aware, sister. I'm not a hermit."

"Your answer?"

"The man wouldn't take his lunch break, let alone a bribe. Isn't this a problem we could get our soldiers back in the valleys to sort out?"

Eli shook his head. His expression was blank.

"They're too busy looking after Mrs. Drake. Making sure she behaves until she gets her son back."

"And when exactly will that be?"

Eli chuckled slightly. His head tilted in confusion.

"Don't tell me you still care for him? You did your job well, but let's not keep the performance up."

"I wasn't referring to that. It's just … this needs to be over soon, Eli. Not only for my sake. But for all of us. The walls are closing in and she is our way out. We need to find her."

The door flew open, and Jonas stormed in with his phone held in front of him in one hand and his other raised in victory.

"She's in London!" he yelled.

"She's implanted one of her memories into someone in the past few days. Someone I know from London."

Maya turned towards him. "Was it Edward Velour?" she asked, her voice barely a whisper.

Jonas shook his head.

"An associate of his. The man thinks he was there when … when Arthur died."

"Seems funny for her to target someone so closely associated with you, brother," Maya said, looking pointedly at Eli.

Jonas's face remained impassive, betraying no emotion. "What are you trying to say?"

Maya, having turned fully from the window now, her scarred visage bringing a certain intensity to the conversation, replied, "What I'm saying is, have we found Lena Drake, or has Lena Drake found us?"

"If she knows about us, about me, it could be turned into our advantage. Think about it, what if she's aware of me and Velour's relationship? What if she's aware of when I'm visiting him next? We could take her right there and then," Jonas retorted, his voice steady despite the tension in the room.

Maya groaned in frustration. "Do you need a reminder of what this girl is capable of? If you want to plunge into this without proper planning, be my guest!"

Jonas laughed, a sound lacking any genuine mirth. "That's rich, coming from you, isn't it? If not for your overreaction, you wouldn't be confined to that bed."

"Watch your words," Maya warned, her voice a low growl.

"I'm not going to sit here and listen to you two squabble like children again. Jonas? Get to the point." Eli finally intervened, his voice a chilling calm amidst their fiery exchange.

Jonas gave a curt nod, unable to look at Eli. Eli eased into a chair and served himself some orange juice. He sat there, sipping slowly, staring off seemingly at nothing. Yet, behind those vacant eyes, his mind whirred with strategies, contemplating their next course of action.

"If Edward is oblivious to what happened to his bodyguard, then it's likely she accessed his memories too. That implies she knows about your interactions and your scheduled rendezvous," he spoke, eyes fixed on Jonas. "I agree, that's our window to apprehend her."

He finished his orange juice in one swift gulp, the glass landing back on the table with a soft thud. Leaning back into his chair, he continued.

"Travel to London. I recommend you keep Edward in the dark about the situation until your meeting on the fourteenth. We don't want to disrupt a scenario she's already aware of—it might spook her into fleeing."

Jonas gave a nod of affirmation and made his move towards the door.

But he was stopped in his tracks by Eli's voice.

"This issue with the detective isn't one we can ignore. Even if we find Lena Drake on the fourteenth, we need to make sure the detectives go away before we begin the rest of the plan. We might have to use Mrs. Drake to our advantage."

"What happened to leaving those in Arthur's family out of this? We left her alone for years and now want to use her as bait."

Eli's glare latched onto Maya with venomous gravity.

"Am I the only one who knows what is at stake here?" He asked, his head snapping to Jonas and then back to her. "This mansion, its maintenance, the staff working within, the wealth we've accumulated, this entire operation … our entire existence. Every bit of this family and what little remains of it, everything we've established over time hangs in the balance. After the way both of you have dealt with the police and Reuben Drake, you're walking on very thin ice," Eli warned, his voice laden with sombre seriousness.

He looked to Maya. "Both of you," he clarified, leaving no room for misinterpretation. His stern eyes then returned to Jonas.

"The next time I see you, it better be in the same room as Lena Drake. Do you understand?" His words were delivered with such finality that they echoed in the room long after they were spoken.

Nodding again like a chastised schoolboy, a mix of anger and hurt written plainly across his face, Jonas stormed out of the room. A few seconds passed and Eli got up as well. He moved to the door.

"And you," he called back. "Since you've been back, every word you've said has sounded like him. I've already had to deal with the betrayal of one sibling. Don't make carry out a similar punishment for you."

Eli exited the room, his steps firm yet unhurried. He descended the grand staircase, its once-vibrant colours now dulled from years of use. He navigated through the expansive mansion, its opulence bearing silent witness to the centuries of power and influence that had once resonated through its halls. His destination lay below, within the mansion's hidden underbelly.

As he descended into the basement, a stark contrast to the rest of the house greeted him. Gone was the grandeur, replaced by the chillingly utilitarian aesthetic of a clandestine prison. The basement was divided into four separate chambers, their interior mirroring the austere comfort of repurposed hotel rooms. Behind each door, the air vibrated with the echoes of muffled screams and frantic thuds.

The captives within these chambers pounded on their confines relentlessly, their pleas for mercy swallowed by the cold, impassive walls. But their cries, instead of triggering empathy, seemed to stir a perverse satisfaction within Eli. The cacophony, the display of fear and desperation—it was all part of a twisted performance that he revelled in.

With an eerily serene demeanour, Eli navigated to the centre of the basement. He settled onto the floor, crossing his legs in an almost meditative posture. The screaming continued, building to a fever pitch. Yet, amid the chorus of despair, Eli sat unaffected, almost tranquil. Each desperate plea, each anguished wail, was nothing more than a note in his sinister orchestra.

His lips curled up in a smile, a macabre reflection of the pleasure he derived from this cruel display. He closed his eyes, his breathing steady, seemingly feeding off the discordant screams that filled the room.

In this symphony of fear, Eli found peace.

CHAPTER FIFTEEN

Sophie's voice was barely above a whisper, laden with a weariness that seemed too heavy for her years. "I don't know how much longer I can keep doing this," she confessed, her chopsticks trembling slightly as she tried to focus on her yakisoba. "It feels like everyone is watching me."

She cast a nervous glance around the garden of the restaurant, nestled in the heart of Chinatown. The din of the city felt miles away in this secluded spot, yet to Sophie, danger lurked in every shadow. The family of four at the next table, struggling to feed their restless child; the elderly couple in matching outfits, quietly celebrating decades of togetherness; the young, laughing couple locked in an arm wrestle—any one of them could be an agent of the Family she dreaded.

During her time working for Edward Velour, the enigmatic business, once painted a vivid picture of the Blackwaters' reach, a network so vast and deeply entwined in society's fabric that it seemed inescapable. *"They've permeated every aspect of our lives,"* he had told her, a hint of admiration in his tone that she had never forgotten. *"Even the police aren't beyond their influence, manipulated to serve their ends without even knowing it."*

Why did he know all this? It's because Edward Velour wants to be a member.

He had inherited his father's tech company and had used that money to start a number of businesses including a range of nightclubs around the country. But he had grown bored with the inheritance and now wanted something more valuable. When Edward was approached by Jonas Blackwater and asked to help launder the Family's money through his business, he laughed them out of the room. Then Jonas showed him the amount of money he had and was willing to pay him to do this. It would've put his father to shame.

Edward always treated Sophie to an after-work lunch on Friday night. Since being drug-free and being introduced as a Blackwater Candidate (at least that's what Edward had called it), he had wanted to hear everything about her task.

"What have you got to be so afraid of?" he said as he doom-scrolled through his phone with one hand and downed a mojito with another. Edward's bleach-blond hair was slicked back, and he was wearing a £200 oversized plain grey jumper. "I gave you a job. Jonas's money gave you a place to live. We got you in a rehabilitation program and away from that shitty ex-boyfriend of course. I mean Christ, think what will happen if you deliver what Jonas asked for as well … come on, toast me!"

Sophie reluctantly raised her drink and clinked her glass with her boss who smiled briefly before returning to his phone.

Six months ago, Sophie wouldn't be seen anywhere near a place like this. It would be her and her ex-boyfriend trying to get by on pot noodles and cigarettes with the rest of the money being spent on any drug she could get her hands on. She would spend her days sleeping, dreaming she would wake somewhere else entirely. Be somewhere else entirely. And her nights would be spent travelling on the bus route back and forth across Croydon because the night bus was warmer than her own bed. The things she did. It made her want to take her own heart out.

That was, until Jonas Blackwater approached her.

He took her to a restaurant just like the one she was sitting in now and she wolfed the food down just like she did now.

"Your boss says you're a good worker. Says you take photos for his events and jump by the bar when needed. Is it true that you once even chucked two men out of the club yourself?"

"Sure did," she told him. "I had to learn to take care of myself."

She remembered how the waiting staff and the other visitors looked at her as she ate. They saw nothing but a junkie. Nothing more than something to be disposed of. But Jonas was the only one who would look at her in the eyes and talk to her like a friend. That conversation with Jonas was the most genuine one she had in months.

"I'm looking for someone to work for me," he told her. "In return, we'll get you somewhere to stay and will get you in a programme. If that's what you want?"

She would happily have stabbed the waitress to death right in front of him if it meant no longer having to live on a sofa.

"That's good," Jonas had said with a smile. "The first job considers your boss, Edward. I could do with someone on the inside, making sure that he isn't doing something he doesn't want to. I'm sure you know when to get involved when someone's double-crossing, right?"

She thought back to one night. Two A.M. Outskirts of London. Breaking a thirteen-year-old's face open with her fist over a bag in the rain. His blood mixed with the rain. She'd take what she knew from that life. But she didn't want to take matters into her own hands again.

"Is that really *all* you want?" she asked him. "My life is a mess, I'll admit, but it's given me quite a good bullshit indicator. You want to hire me to do this job? I'm nothing. There must be more to this surely."

Jonas looked at her and she couldn't tell if he was impressed or annoyed by what she said. He began to shuffle his hands as if they'd suddenly become beyond itchy.

"There is a woman around your age who is currently on the run. She is low on money, starving, no family or friends, but she also may be one of the most dangerous people on this entire planet. Her last sighting was right here in London at Paddington train station. Last August. The rest of our organisation believes that she's miles away, she could be on a beach in Morocco for all we know, but I believe she is still with us right here in the city. We've stationed people around this entire globe looking for her, we've profiled other candidates of …"

He looked her up and down.

"… Similar circumstances, in hope that she will reveal ourselves to us."

Sophie had leaned back in her seat.

"*Similar* circumstances?"

"We're going to set you up and get you better so that you can be the only person she would reach out to. The only person in the entire world who would understand what she's been through. The only one who will open up."

"And what if she doesn't?" Sophie had asked. "Why can't you guys find her anyway with your type of backing? Surely a Google search, one passport photo later, and—"

"This woman's identity no longer exists on any major database anywhere in the world. She's a ghost and she plays that role really well due to her unique gift."

Sophie folded her arms.

"What gift?"

Jonas leaned over.

"Did you believe him when he told you?" she asked Edward.

"Told me what?" His response came with a sly grin, as though testing her knowledge.

Mirroring the gesture once shown to her by Jonas, she leaned in closer. "That she could erase memories. With merely a touch."

At her words, the playful smile vanished from his face.

"Frankly, no. But as long as the money keeps coming in, who am I to judge if it's real or not? I'll continue living in Jonas Blackwater's fantasy as long as I get to thrive as well."

"If that's how you feel then why do you want to become a member so badly?" Sophie asked.

Edward looked at her as if she had grown two heads.

"Because, my dear, the one thing better than a shit ton of money is influence. I've watched Jonas shake hands with politicians, investment bankers …" Edward stopped himself. He had gone red with rage. "… people who wouldn't even bat an eyelid at me. If I asked someone on the street if they knew who the Blackwater Family were, they would shake their head. But everyone who is worth knowing, they call him 'Pal' or 'Buddy.'"

Edward turned to the waitress who was passing back with full hands and asked for another mojito.

"Apparently you have a new flatmate," he finally asked. "What's she like?"

Sophie had prepared to be asked this question but still, the expected anxiety rushed up her body. She looked down at her plate. She seized her knife and fork, stuffing her mouth with food to silence the confession threatening to escape. She wanted to reveal to Edward the discovery of The Collector. That Jamie, her flatmate, was indeed Lena Drake, the very person the Blackwater Family had sought tirelessly. A simple phone call to Jonas was all that stood between them being initiated into the world's most exclusive circle. Yet, making that call meant betraying the genuine connection she shared with Lena; the kindness and love exchanged, the countless nights filled with laughter and camaraderie. All of which would be sacrificed for a chance at a fortune. Holding the metaphorical lottery ticket, she faced the dilemma of losing the only true friend she had ever known.

"It's too early to tell yet," she finally answered. "She doesn't fit the criteria."

"How so?" Edward asked quickly.

"I don't know. She just … I just don't like her," Sophie replied strongly, her arms flailing in frustration. "Jonas told me this person who would approach me would be like me. Come from 'similar circumstances,' as he put it. She's literally a yuppie from Exeter who came here to study art. Give it three months. She'll get tired of working in a coffee shop and she'll move back home into the house her landlord parents bought for her! She's a twat, basically."

Edward laughed and held his hands up in defeat. "Fine … if she's not her, then you're going to have to tell her to move out. Just be careful in the future, you know this person can mess with your memories, right?"

Sophie rolled her eyes and grinned. Edward hadn't brought up at all how he had woken up in the nightclub on the floor with his bouncer, Javier, or how he had no recollection of why they couldn't remember anything. She wondered if he had told Jonas. Maybe by telling him, she could divert attention away from Lena.

Is that what you want to do? she asked herself. *Don't forget what he asked you.*

As Edward turned the conversation towards his favourite topics of finance spreadsheets and upcoming MMA fights, Sophie's mind was consumed by Jonas's final proposition. The ultimate offer he made if she could deliver Lena Drake.

"Tell me, Sophie," he asked her. "How would you like to live forever?"

CHAPTER SIXTEEN

Edward's limo dropped her outside of the house at one a.m. She left the warmth of the all-purple-LED-lighted limo and stepped into the cold morning outside. She was just putting her keys through the door when Edward called her back.

"Wait!"

She turned around and saw him swaying back and forth carrying a large cardboard box.

"It's an early birthday present," he slurred with half a smile.

She took it from him and was surprised at how light it was for its size. Before she could ask any further questions about its contents, the limo zoomed off down the road, turning left. She exhaled in delight as she finally shut the flat door and took her heels off. She glanced once towards her flatmate's closed door and then went into hers. She sat on her bed and opened the box. She didn't want the anxiety of waiting to see what he had given her. She was wondering if it was something expensive. Some ridiculous thousand-pound watch just because she complimented him on his Omega watch two weeks ago?

"Holy shit," she whispered to herself as she reached into the box and pulled out a semiautomatic gun.

How could Edward give her something like this? Was he crazy? Was this a joke? As soon as she checked the rest of the box, she was going to ring him and ask him what he was up to. She looked down into the box and retrieved two more objects. One was a small video camera. One of those that could be loaded up to your doorbell or behind the TV.

The final "present" was a new iPhone with a new SIM card. Why had he gone to all this trouble? She reached through the rest of the wrapping paper inside the box and found a small, folded envelope inside.

She opened it up and her heart dropped. The present wasn't from Edward.

"*Happy Birthday, candidate.*" the note read. "*For your role to continue, I would like to assess your current situation and that of your flatmate. Please set up your new phone and contact me with the number on the back of this note, letting me know you received this. Once that's done, we can discuss the webcam setup. And the gun? That's for your protection, of course. Just in case she finds you first. Speak soon, Jonas.*"

Sophie could feel her breathing become short. She left the room and went straight into the bathroom. She washed her shaking hands and rubbed water on her face. She stared in the mirror. The face that was once spotted and riddled by a drug addiction had been helped tremendously but at what cost? She was now working with criminals, looking to find the identity of a girl that she herself knew lay sleeping next door. She returned to her room and began to think, energy returning to her even after being up for so long. How would she explain the webcam setup to Lena? Wouldn't she become immediately suspicious? This was something she needed to discuss with Jonas.

No, she thought. *I need to give him something to take his mind off things. Just for a few days before I decide what to do next.*

She reached for the phone and waited for it to turn on. In her first meeting with Jonas, it was clear that he cared more about the Blackwaters than anything else. He wouldn't be too happy to know that someone they worked with didn't believe in their mission.

The phone turned on. She rushed to the messaging section and began to type.

Three Days Later

A whirlwind of black balloons bobbed and danced in the strobe-lit air. The room pulsed with the throbbing bass, making the floor vibrate beneath her heels, creating an intoxicating rhythm that threatened to sweep her away. Around her, ecstatic shrieks punctuated the heavy beats while splashes of champagne baptised the revellers in the throes of hedonistic merriment. Shouts of "Happy birthday!" echoed through the space, bouncing off the walls and colliding with the high-energy music.

Yet, in the heart of this frenzied celebration, her heart remained untouched by the joyous contagion. Her eyes, wide and alert, were locked onto a singular figure—Lena. A solitary entity amidst the boisterous crowd, an anomaly that demanded attention. Lena, known to her bosses as "The Collector."

As the party raged around her, she kept her eyes rooted on Lena. The Collector. The woman with a deadly touch and a penchant for memories. A woman who could strip a person of their past with a mere brush of her fingers. The woman whose very existence she had been tasked to help solve.

While Sophie was ensnared in a forced performance of normality, plastering on a warm smile, and nodding engagingly as if in agreement with the world, assuring others that "everything's fine," even though her reality was far from it, "Jamie," or Lena as she was truly known, stood in stark contrast.

Lena was at the opposite end of the crowd, conveniently located in the middle of the dancefloor. With an air of laid-back nonchalance, she was busily rolling a cigarette, an activity that felt strangely anachronistic amidst the throbbing music and swirling bodies. Laughter danced on her lips as she shared a light-hearted moment with Rita, one of Sophie's old university friends who had journeyed all the way from Edinburgh to partake in the festivities.

There was a paradoxical simplicity in Lena's demeanour, an air of unaffected charm that belied the danger lurking beneath her skin. The stark contrast between Sophie's strained pretence and Lena's breezy ease added an unnerving undercurrent to the party, charging the air with anticipation and unease.

Sophie watched anxiously, her mind spinning with scenarios, as Lena leaned in closer to whisper something in Rita's ear. The eruption of hearty laughter that followed was a jab to Sophie's heart. Was Lena fabricating yet another deceptive narrative about her life to beguile Rita as she had done with Sophie three months ago? The layers of deception seemed to grow thicker and murkier with each passing moment.

Or was the plot even more sinister? Had Lena already gained access to Rita's memories, penetrating the intimate folds of her past and using that stolen knowledge to insinuate herself further into their lives? The possibilities were unsettling.

Lena finally approached her. "Having fun?"

"Not really," she said. "I think we should've picked somewhere quieter. Something about coming to places I used to party in my late teens just makes me feel ridiculous."

"I can see that. I never got to experience anywhere like this."

Sophie's eyes seemed distant as if she were lost in thought. "You never did? That's hard to believe. You seem like someone who would fit right into a place like this."

Lena smiled, but it was a careful, guarded smile. "I grew up … differently. My brother and I never had the luxury of spending nights out like this."

"Your brother?" Sophie pounced on the opportunity, trying to sound casual. "I don't think you've ever mentioned him before. What's he like?"

Lena's eyes flickered, and her smile tightened just a fraction. "He's … unique. We were very close, but we were separated when we were younger. It's a long story. Maybe I'll tell you about it one day."

Sophie's curiosity was piqued, but she sensed that pushing too hard might shut Lena down completely. "I understand. It must be tough not knowing where he is."

Before Lena could respond, her eyes suddenly widened, fixating on something above Sophie's head. She seemed to go into a trance, her attention drawn to the balcony above.

"What is it?" Sophie asked, confused by the sudden change in Lena's demeanour.

Above her, clear as day even in the pulsing lights of the nightclub, was Reuben. Her brother. Without another word, Lena pushed through the crowd, her eyes locked on the balcony. She seemed to be following a phantom, a ghost from her past that had momentarily materialised in the chaos of the party.

Lena's heart pounded in her chest as she made her way to the packed top floor, weaving through the crowd with determination. Her eyes were fixed on Reuben, her long-lost brother, who was heading into a room down the hall. Her breath caught in her throat as she realised the gravity of the situation. What was Reuben doing here? Had he found her after everything that happened? Was this a coincidence, or something more sinister? Lena's mind raced with questions and possibilities, but she knew she had to act quickly.

Ignoring the pulsing music and the laughter of the partygoers, Lena made her way to the room Reuben had entered. The door was slightly ajar, and she could hear voices inside. She hesitated for a moment, uncertainty washing over her. Taking a deep breath to steady herself, Lena pushed the door open and stepped into the room, her eyes wide as she took in the scene before her.

"Hey, you can't be in here!" a stern-faced bouncer snapped, moving towards her.

She was met with the disapproving glares of well-dressed patrons occupying what appeared to be a VIP lounge. The room was decorated in plush velvet and filled with the low murmur of conversation and clinking glasses. Her brother was nowhere to be found.

"I'm sorry," Lena stammered, her eyes darting around the room in search of any sign of Reuben. "I thought I saw someone I knew. Sorry."

"You must be mistaken," a woman in a glittering gown said, eyeing Lena with suspicion. "This is a private area."

"Alright, calm yourself! I'm leaving!" Lena said, backing towards the door, her mind racing. Had she imagined seeing Reuben? Was her mind playing tricks on her because of the emotional turmoil she was experiencing?

She retreated from the room, the door closing behind her with a soft click. The pounding music of the club engulfed her once again, but Lena hardly noticed. Her mind was a whirl of confusion and doubt. Had she really seen her brother, or was it a figment of her imagination? The pieces of the puzzle were not fitting together, and Lena knew that she had to find answers. But where to begin?

She made her way back to the dance floor, her eyes still searching. Before she could comprehend anything further, Rita was rushing up the steps towards her in a state of panic.

"What is it?"

"Ian's here!" she yelled over the thumping music. "He's followed her into the toilets!"

Ian was a figure Lena had come to dread. Once Sophie's partner, he now existed like a persistent ghost, haunting their lives long after the relationship had ended. Every week, like clockwork, he would show up at their flat, usually inebriated, his eyes glazed over and voice slurred, demanding to speak with Sophie. His presence always carried an aura of unsettling volatility, a mixture of desperation and pent-up aggression.

Lena had been the one to handle these unwelcome visits, standing between Ian and the apartment door, trying to defuse the situation without knowing all its intricate explosives. Despite her persistent queries, Sophie never divulged the reason for their mysterious split. She would only look away, her eyes clouding over as if touching the memory could make it come alive again, too dangerous to be let out. And so, Lena dealt with Ian, never knowing what fuse might set him off but always fearing she would find out.

Now, that haunting figure was here, in the same club, and had followed Sophie into the toilets. Panic gripped Lena, and she could see the same fear mirrored in Rita's eyes.

"Go find security. Now. Tell them what's happening. I'm going to check on Sophie."

Rita's eyes widened, but she nodded, recognizing the seriousness in Lena's tone. "Okay, be careful," she stammered before darting off in the direction of the club's security personnel.

Lena's heart pounded in her chest as she made her way towards the toilets. The festive atmosphere of the club had turned into a nightmarish scenario, and she knew that every second counted. Her thoughts were consumed with concern for her friend, and she pushed her way through the crowd, determined to reach Sophie before Ian could cause any harm.

Lena stepped into the bathroom, and the immediate sight and smell hit her with revulsion. The floor was sticky with spilled drinks and littered with wads of tissue paper. Grimy handprints stained the mirrors, and a couple of the flickering fluorescent lights were out, casting the place in an eerie half-darkness. Several stall doors hung open, revealing cracked and unflushed toilets.

From the far end of the line of stalls, Lena could hear the unmistakable sounds of distress: a girl's muffled crying intermingled with a man's enraged shouting. Her heart clenched with fear and anger, recognizing Sophie's sobs and the venomous tone of Ian's voice.

Pushing past the disgust and the fear, Lena moved swiftly towards the source of the commotion.

As Lena edged closer, the voices became clearer. Ian's voice was a furious, pleading whine.

"Look! I haven't touched anything in months! I don't even drink anymore! You owe me this conversation, Soph. You can't just throw me away like a used toy!"

Sophie's response was filled with both terror and defiance. "Leave me alone, Ian. I don't owe you anything. I don't have to explain myself to you."

But Ian was not listening.

"YES, YOU DO!" he said, slamming his hand into the side of the stall.

Lena's patience snapped; her protective instincts fully engaged. She rounded the corner to confront Ian directly, her voice steady and commanding.

"Leave her alone."

Ian turned, and Lena took in his appearance: a green shirt sticking to his sweat-soaked body, a haircut that suggested he watched too much *Peaky Blinders*. His eyes were wild, and distress was etched across his face.

"It's you, isn't it?!" he spat, lunging at Lena and grabbing her by the arm. "You're the one who's with her!"

The instant Lena's fingers grazed Ian's skin; an electrical charge surged through her. She felt as if she were plummeting through an endless tunnel, her senses suddenly and intensely alive. Then, like a movie switching scenes, she was no longer in the club but seated in an intimate restaurant.

She was seeing through Ian's eyes. The atmosphere was suffused with the warm glow of amber lighting, reflecting off elegantly set tables adorned with crystal glassware and fresh flowers. A quiet jazz melody played softly in the background, filling the air with a sense of romantic expectation. Ian's nervous eyes darted to Sophie, who sat across him on another pub table, radiant in a dress that shimmered in the soft lighting. She was the most beautiful person he'd ever seen.

The jazz melody twisted into a long loud drone and the scene shifted. A half-painted living room. Sophie and Ian leaned back on a red sofa. Eyes closed. Two used syringes on the table in front of them. Sophie watched as the living room around her changed as time moved forward. The purple-painted walls began to rot, the desk became scattered with alcohol, cigarette butts, and more used syringes. The carpet beneath her started crawling with ants. She looked up. Sophie and Ian began to change as well. Their skin had grown pale, spotty, and bruised while the clothes they were wearing (which they seemed to never change) became covered in substances. Lena could have cried when she saw Sophie. The person staring back at her looked three decades older than she did now. Her eyes were hidden by the large sandbags beneath, her teeth looked as if they were rotting away, and her forehead was covered in various red marks and spots.

The image spared up and suddenly … Sophie was gone.

Ian was still on the sofa, rocking back and forth, his eyes lingering on the mobile phone in front of him.

"I-I know you've told me to stop contacting you! But I need to talk to you!" he cried pathetically with tears streaming down his face. "Why have you left me, Soph? Why can't you come back and be with me?"

"I'm sorry, Ian. I can't," Sophie replied over the phone, the confidence in her voice matched the woman that Lena knew today. "This relationship. It's not good for either of us. I've started a new life now. You should do the same."

The call ended, and, in a rage, Ian picked up the phone, kicked the living room table, and chucked the phone. Lena watched it pass her and then …

She was on a train station platform, surrounded by oblivious commuters. Against the wall, she saw a man being violently stabbed. Panic welled up inside her as she recognized the man as Ian. But something was horribly wrong; the man doing the stabbing was Sophie, and both were grinning at her.

Lena's heart pounded in her chest, and she felt her breath catch in her throat. This wasn't right. This wasn't what happened. The scene was surreal, nightmarish, and entirely out of place.

She tried to pull away, to escape the horrifying vision, but it clung to her, persistent and unyielding. The grins on Ian and Sophie's faces widened, their eyes gleaming with malevolent delight.

Reality seemed to slip away as the panic rose higher, threatening to consume her. Lena's mind screamed for release, for an escape from the impossible scene that had intruded upon Ian's memories.

She was momentarily overwhelmed by the warmth of the scene, the golden glow of the Christmas lights reflecting on her younger face. She watched as her younger self tried, and failed, to pull the controller away from Reuben, both of them giggling madly.

The nostalgic scent of pine mingled with the comforting aroma of her mother's special roast wafting through the air, making her stomach churn with both hunger and longing. The familiar clatter of dishes and utensils set the backdrop as her father fumbled around, placing cutlery and napkins. The gentle hum of the PlayStation 2 was in the background, a familiar and comforting noise from her childhood. She remembered the countless hours she and Reuben spent on it, arguing over whose turn it was next or which game to play. Her younger self, with a mock expression of determination, was trying once again to snatch the controller from Reuben's hands. Their laughter was infectious, reminding Lena of the simple joys they used to share.

"Reuben, you've been hogging it for hours!" she heard her younger self complain, pouting dramatically. "Mum, tell him!"

"Reuben! Let your sister have a turn!" her mother's voice echoed from the kitchen, its tone half-exasperated, half-amused.

Lena could see the mischief in her father's eyes as they met hers, the unspoken camaraderie of shared moments, his eyes playfully rolling upwards. It was a snapshot of happier times, of innocence and family, a memory she had clung to during her darkest moments.

The vividness of the memory felt almost tangible, as if Lena could reach out and touch the past. The juxtaposition between the safety of this memory and the danger of her current situation couldn't be more pronounced. But as with all things, the vision began to fade, pulling Lena back to the present with a painful jolt.

She was at the precipice of a vast mountain. The winds howled around her, amplifying the sensation of being on the edge of the world. Two enigmatic figures in red cloaks stood on the cliff edge, looking down at the endless expanse of water that stretched out beneath them, merging with the horizon. The taller of the two glanced over their shoulder, revealing the face of a terrified woman.

And then, in an instant, the ethereal landscape collapsed, and Lena was back in the grimy confines of the bathroom. She and Ian were sprawled on the ground, both gasping for air, their eyes wide with the shared terror of their unexpected connection.

Sophie's voice pierced through the fog that clouded Lena's mind. "Hey! We've got to go!" She hurriedly helped Lena to her feet, guiding her out with urgency. As they moved, Lena's vision darted from side to side, catching glimpses of alarmed faces. She wondered how long she'd been in that trance. Did Sophie witness the whole ordeal?

Sophie's gentle but frantic touch anchored Lena amidst the chaos of the nightclub. A sensory overload engulfed her as she was jostled by revellers, the pulsating lights warping her perceptions. The din of laughter, conversations, and music played a jarring symphony in her ringing ears.

Then, as if a curtain had been drawn, they were in the relative quiet of a taxi, the muffled noises of the city outside replacing the deafening roar. Lena blinked, trying to focus, but everything felt distant, almost dreamlike.

"It's okay. It's going to be okay." Sophie's voice washed over her like a calming balm.

Suddenly, a soft touch on Lena's face made her turn, only to see a blood-stained tissue being held to her nose by Sophie's trembling hand. The metallic tang reached her senses, and reality began to creep back in.

The familiar hum of the car's engine and the soft glow of the streetlights, interspersed with shadows, pulled Lena into a trance of memories. Each fleeting light was reminiscent of the stolen nights she had spent on the run with her father, away from prying eyes and seeking shelter. Those nights, filled with a mix of fear and security, where their old car became a cocoon, keeping the world at bay.

It wasn't just the sights but the sounds and smells too. The hum of the engine, the scent of the worn leather seats, and the soft murmur of the radio playing in the background. It was their little world, both a prison and a sanctuary. She remembered how they would sometimes talk, other times just drive in silence, always moving, always looking over their shoulder.

"You bloody idiot," Sophie muttered to her. "You shouldn't have got involved."

Lena smiled slightly and answered with something her father always used to say.

"We take care of each other. That's the deal."

As the memories washed over her, the weight of the evening and the exhaustion from the past few months caught up with Lena. Nestling her head against the cool windowpane, she let the rhythmic motion of the cab lull her into a deep, much-needed sleep.

Sophie groaned in relief as she finally dropped Lena onto her bed. This was the second time she had been a witness to her unusual abilities. Was it a mere lack of control on Lena's part, or was there a deliberate intention to assist her against her menacing ex-boyfriend?

The woman that Sophie had come to know as the formidable Collector had momentarily unravelled before her eyes. In the past, Lena had always been the picture of stability and control. The very essence of unpredictability and danger. Yet tonight had displayed a vulnerability Sophie had never expected to see.

She sat on the edge of the bed, looking down at Lena's sleeping face. Her fingers involuntarily brushed away a stray hair.

Sophie glanced down at the glowing screen of her phone, her fingers hovering over the opened conversation with Jonas. Messages filled with assurances and promises from the past year scrolled beneath her touch. It would take just one message to reveal Lena's whereabouts, and in return, she'd receive the protection she had been promised.

Yet, as she turned back to Lena, sprawled vulnerably on the bed, she couldn't deny the pang of guilt that gnawed at her insides. Tonight, Lena had shown a different side of herself, stepping in, potentially risking her own well being to protect Sophie from a haunting figure of her past.

Sophie grappled with the internal conflict. Loyalty and survival entangled in a dance. For tonight, the scales tilted in favour of the bond they had, however fragile. With a heavy sigh, Sophie set the phone aside, leaving the messages unread, the promises unfulfilled. Tonight, at least, she chose trust.

CHAPTER SEVENTEEN

In the dead of night, Lena jolted awake, her heart pounding like a drumbeat in her ears. The room was awash in an eerie, indigo glow from a neon sign outside her window. Her throat felt parched, as if she'd swallowed a handful of sand. With shaky hands, she reached for the glass of water on her bedside table, her fingers closing around it as if it were a lifeline. She took a gulp, hoping to drown not just her thirst but the gnawing anxiety that had wrested her from sleep.

Sophie saw me use my power.

The thought looped in her mind, each repetition amplifying her disquiet. For years, her secret had been a solitary burden, something she carried alone, apart from her father. But she had thrown that all away for someone she barely knew.

Her father's voice echoed in her head; his words edged with caution. *Sometimes, to stay alive, we have to do things we'd rather not do. The fewer people who know, the safer you are.*

He'd been teaching her all her life about the grave responsibility that came with her unique abilities. She'd always assumed his warnings were exaggerated, the cautious overtures of a parent. Now, they resonated with her, a grim counterpoint to her thoughts.

Unable to bear her racing thoughts any longer, Lena pushed back the covers and padded softly across the hall to Sophie's room. The door creaked open with a soft whine, revealing her friend's sleeping form, a peaceful island in a sea of rumpled sheets. Lena stood over her, her hand hovering in the space above Sophie's forehead. All she had to do was reach down, make contact, and she could erase Sophie's newfound knowledge. She could make things as they were, ensure her own safety, and protect her secret.

But look what happened last time, she told herself, causing her hand to falter. *What happened the last time you did this to a friend?*

Lena removed her hand and slowly crept away back into the corridor. Rejuvenated by her near-comatose sleep and knowing it would be morning soon, Lena shuffled her way into the living room and turned on the TV. Keeping it at a low volume, she flicked through the channels. Reality TV shows, shopping channels, B movie horrors. She kept flicking back and forth until she saw a face staring right at her through the screen. She dropped the remote and then immediately grabbed it to turn the volume up.

"We've had some breaking news in the last hour," said the presenter. "The son of Martin Drake, the victim of last year's most talked about murder, has gone missing. South Wales police have confirmed an incident involving gunfire took place at the Drake household this evening where four bodies have been found."

CHAPTER EIGHTEEN

28th July 2018
The day of the disappearance

The Sundown Cinema had been a cornerstone of the town for decades. Its marquee, a relic of neon lights and flashing bulbs, announced the latest blockbuster titles to the passersby. Flanked by newer establishments, the cinema stood proud and nostalgic, its brick facade whispering tales from the golden age of film. The ticket booth sat like a sentinel at the entrance, a glass cubicle that had witnessed countless movies and countless more filmgoers.

The night was mild, with a faint breeze carrying the scent of popcorn from the cinema's entrance. The streets were aglow with the soft luminescence of streetlamps, but it was the cinema's warm, buttery light that drew the crowd in.

The Drake family found themselves amidst a line that snaked its way out of the door. Martin checked his watch, subtly masking his worry. Outings like these were a rarity, and though he loved these moments of normalcy, the events of the past still weighed on him. He placed an arm around Julia, who leaned into him, enjoying her husband's unusual comforting presence.

Ahead in the line, Reuben was engrossed in his phone. Lena, meanwhile, was the most restless of them all. Her eyes darted around, taking in the ornate details of the cinema's entrance, the colourful movie posters, and the various faces in the crowd. She was doing her best to be present, to enjoy the outing, but the shadows of the past were never too far away.

As they inched closer to the ticket booth, Martin leaned down to his wife.

"Do we know what we are watching?"

"Surely the kids want to see *Spider-Man*. Right, guys?"

"As long as you guys are happy to sit through a two-and-a-half-hour film. You can barely get through an episode of *The Simpsons* without falling asleep," Lena chimed in from behind.

"Twitter's saying it's rubbish," Reuben said with his head still down in his phone.

"You listen to Twitter far too much, my friend. You going to jump off a cliff if they do it as well? *Hashtag pretty please!*"

Reuben diverted enough of his attention to remove one of his hands from his phone and raise his middle finger.

The queue for the concession stand wasn't particularly long, but it gave Julia and Lena a quiet moment away from the crowd. Martin and Reuben were engrossed in their own discussion, leaving the two women to their own devices.

Julia began by examining the array of snacks, but her attention quickly turned to her daughter. "You know," she started, the scent of freshly popped popcorn in the air. "Once you're off to Edinburgh next month, we won't have these little trips anymore."

Lena picked up a tub, weighing it in her hand. "I've been thinking about that. It's going to be strange … being away from all this." She filled the tub with popcorn, the kernels tumbling in. "I'll probably be living off instant noodles and missing your home-cooked meals."

Julia chuckled, selecting a couple of drinks. "I'll send you some recipes. But, you know, university is going to be such an adventure for you. New experiences, new friends."

Lena sighed, picking up straws. "I'm looking forward to it, really. It's just … all this time still means a lot to me."

Julia smiled, touching her daughter's arm gently. "And to me.

But remember, Edinburgh isn't a world away. We'll come and visit soon!"

Lena's face lit up with a playful smirk. "Are you saying you're going to crash my student life, Mum?"

Julia laughed, nudging Lena playfully. "Occasionally! And when you're back, we'll have our cinema dates."

Lena hugged her mother briefly.

"Deal. Let's be honest, you're probably going to enjoy the peace and quiet without me!"

Julia raised an eyebrow playfully. "Peace and quiet? Have you met your brother?" she replied with a laugh.

Before Lena could respond, Reuben interrupted, slightly out of breath from rushing over. "Mum, Lena," he said urgently. "Dad got a call. He doesn't look good."

The two of them turned in sync to find Martin. Even from a distance, his stance betrayed his distress: hunched shoulders, a hand gripping the phone tightly against his ear, and the clear look of disbelief painted across his face. It was a sight that made Lena's stomach churn.

Julia's jovial mood evaporated instantly. She exchanged a concerned glance with Lena, both sensing that whatever the call was about, it wasn't any ordinary conversation.

"Who's he talking to?" Lena whispered, trying to gauge more from her father's body language.

"I don't know," Reuben replied, a hint of worry in his voice. "But by the looks of it, it's not good."

Martin made his way back to the group, his steps heavy and face drained of colour. As he approached, Julia instinctively reached out, her fingers brushing against his arm in a gesture of comfort. "Babe? What's wrong?"

He took a deep breath, struggling to find his words. "It's someone from work," he began, hesitatingly. "Someone in my department … They've passed away."

Julia's eyes filled with concern. "Oh, honey, I'm so sorry," she murmured, pulling him into a comforting embrace. Reuben, usually reserved, clapped a hand on his father's shoulder, nodding sympathetically.

But as the family exchanged condolences and words of comfort, Lena watched her father intently, sensing that something was amiss. The hesitation in his voice, the way he wouldn't meet her stare—something wasn't adding up.

Martin must have felt her scrutiny, for he eventually lifted his eyes to meet hers. In that fleeting moment of connection, Lena saw a flicker of something in his eyes: fear, perhaps, or guilt. It was clear he wasn't revealing the whole truth.

"Who was it?" Lena asked, her voice neutral, though the suspicion was clear. "I've been to the office a few times. Anyone I know?"

Martin hesitated, avoiding her look once more. "No. They're a newer member of the team."

Martin's eyes darted between Julia and Reuben, both of whom looked on in concern, and then back to Lena. He opened his mouth to respond, but no words came out. The weight of the unspoken truth hung heavily between them.

The dim light from the cinema screen barely illuminated the Drake family as they hurried into the theatre, the booming sound of a trailer playing greeting their entrance. The scent of buttered popcorn mixed with the faint aroma of worn leather seats. The room was already populated with eager viewers, their faces illuminated in the soft glow of the trailers.

Finding a free row, they quickly shuffled in. Julia and Reuben took the middle seats, Lena sat next to Julia, and Martin chose the endmost seat, distancing himself slightly. Lena could hear the subtle sounds of Reuben munching on popcorn and Julia sipping her soda, but her attention was primarily on her father.

The trailers highlighted the next big blockbusters: vibrant explosions, heart-tugging romance scenes, and comedic one-liners that made Julia chuckle softly. Yet, throughout the kaleidoscope of stories flashing before them, Lena noticed her father's stoic demeanour. He sat rigidly, staring straight ahead, seemingly lost in thought, his fingers tapping a quiet rhythm against his armrest.

The memory of their recent conversations replayed in Lena's mind, distracting her from the spectacle on the screen. The nature of her powers. The Blackwater Family that tried to take him when he was younger. This hidden history of unanswered questions kept her up at night.

The opening credits had just begun to roll, casting their trademark glow on the cinema screen. Just as the audience started to settle in, Martin suddenly leaned over, catching Lena's eye. He mouthed the word "bathroom" and, without waiting for a response, rose abruptly from his seat.

The cinema corridor was dimly lit, the faint hum of the movie's soundtrack audible in the background. Martin, however, moved swiftly past the other screening rooms, his footsteps echoing with a sense of urgency.

Reaching the restrooms, he pushed through the door, the overhead fluorescent lights a harsh contrast to the cinema's ambiance. He moved to the sink, turning on the cold water and letting it flow over his trembling hands. The coldness of the water jolted his senses, but he welcomed the sensation, desperate for anything to anchor him to reality.

He splashed water onto his face, taking a moment to look up into the mirror. The reflection that stared back was one of a man on the verge of breaking, eyes red-rimmed and face pallid. He leaned heavily on the counter, taking deep, shuddering breaths to calm himself.

As he splashed his face again, trying to rid himself of the rising panic, the phone call he had received earlier replayed in his mind.

"It's me," came the hushed voice of Jonas, his nephew. There was a tangible urgency in his tone. "Eli and the others have taken a vote. They're coming for Lena. Stay calm! Don't give anything away. They could be watching you right this second."

Martin remembered gripping the phone tighter, his heart rate spiking.

Jonas continued, "I can help you both, but you need to move fast. There's a safe house in Paris that we can use. Grab her, get out of the theatre, and call me once you're safe."

After several moments, he took one final glance in the mirror, attempting to compose himself. Martin froze, his eyes locked onto the reflection of the man standing behind him. A chilling recognition washed over him.

"Hello, Arthur," the man's deep voice echoed throughout the restroom.

Martin slowly turned around, his heart pounding in his chest, his throat constricting. The height difference was evident; he had to crane his neck slightly to meet the man's piercing eyes.

His presence was domineering, an air of authority and power evident in his posture. The open black-and-white suit hung perfectly on his broad frame, contrasting starkly against his tanned skin. The neatly trimmed grey beard and hair added an air of distinction and wisdom, but there was something in his eyes—a sharpness, a hint of menace—that belied his age.

"Hello, Viktor," Martin replied, washing his face. "To be honest, I was expecting Maya to pay me a visit. Or at least someone a bit higher up. This your audition to be a part of the next cycle then."

Viktor laughed, shuffling out of the cubicle with his hands in his pocket. "Both me and your sister know you aren't going to come back quietly. Not that it isn't too late, of course."

"Bless my sister. I always thought it should have been her running everything, you know? Instead of me and Eli. It's been so long since I've seen them."

Viktor didn't reply but Martin could feel his resentment.

"You know, last year, Lena ended up having an incident in school. Because of what happened, Maya came to see me. When I saw her, I felt this immense dread of what this person was about to do or what they wanted to do to my child. But when I saw her, I just felt … I felt warmth. To feel that way about someone who wants to hurt your child. I'm still struggling to make sense of it."

"You could've told her everything then," Viktor said. "Told her about your daughter's powers. We wouldn't have to take her now."

"You never had kids, Viktor. You wouldn't understand."

"You were happy enough to remove children from their parents for so many years with us. What makes you better than them? May I remind you of the face you see when you look in the mirror?"

Martin looked down before drying his hands and took a hard look at his cousin, thinking back to their childhood all those years ago.

"You sure I can't persuade you once again to see my side of the story?" Martin asked.

"What side would that be?"

"Leave this stupid family tradition behind and let my daughter live," he said sternly. "Think of everything we've seen, everything we've accomplished ... isn't that enough? Enough to not hurt us?"

Viktor was unphased. "You really did come back haunted, didn't you? I remember the little psycho I used to run around with who loved this family. Loved the power we had and would refuse to let anyone even think for a second of taking it away from us. Now look at you with all that conscience and remorse. It's pathetic."

"Is that why you didn't take me from Ulrich's house?" Martin asked. He thought back to that fateful day in 1968, peering from the top window down at the masked machete-wielding maniac below, who now stood across from him.

"I didn't have to talk to you to know the truth. It was in your eyes, the same eyes of all the other children taken over the years. I only had to look at you once to know that you weren't one of us anymore."

Martin chuckled. "*Us.* You know what, Viktor? Even after all I've done, I could walk into that mansion tomorrow and be embraced as a brother while you will be where you've always been. On the outside looking in."

Viktor's piercing eyes met Martin's, and for a moment, the weight of years of history, rivalry, and resentment filled the air. "So, I suppose there's only one way for this to end?"

Martin nodded, a look of quiet determination on his face. "It seems that way."

Their standoff was interrupted by the abrupt entrance of a young man, earphones dangling from his neck. He whistled an upbeat tune, seemingly oblivious to the tension that thickly veiled the room. He went about his business, though the silence from the two older men was palpable.

While the faucets ran and the young man washed his hands, he glanced into the mirror, catching the fierce stares of both Viktor and Martin.

"Um …"

He quickly dried his hands, avoiding eye contact, and hustled out of the restroom, letting the door swing behind him.

"Last chance then. You can both come with us. You can come home."

"Not a chance," Martin replied. Taking a deep breath and clenching his fists. "I can never go home again."

The movie droned on, its vivid colours splashing across the screen and merging with the dim ambient lighting of the cinema. But for Lena, the vibrant visuals and dynamic sound were just background noise. Fifteen minutes had passed since her father had left, and the weight of his absence bore down on her with every passing second. The film's plot, characters, and settings became a blur as anxiety knotted her stomach.

Giving a sidelong glance to her brother and mother engrossed in the film, Lena slowly got up from her seat, whispering, "I need the toilet." But once out of their line of sight, she made a beeline for the men's restroom. Every ounce of her screamed that something was terribly wrong.

The entrance to the men's restroom was dimly lit, its silence broken only by intermittent sounds of distress—grunting, smacking, and something disturbingly akin to thuds of meat being tenderised. As she drew nearer, the gravity of what those sounds might signify sunk in, fuelling her dread. She had a sneaking suspicion that "they" had come. And they had come for her.

Lena's heart raced, her fingers trembling. Still, determination overpowered her fear. She prepared herself, flexing her hands, her fingers glowing slightly in readiness for a confrontation. Her powers surged within her, responding to her heightened emotional state.

Suddenly, the noise ceased. An eerie, tension-filled silence blanketed the space, broken only by Lena's own shallow breathing. The seconds felt like hours.

The door to the farthest cubicle opened slowly. It was Martin, his face pale and tired, eyes weary. There was a tiny, almost imperceptible speck of blood on his collar. As he stepped aside, Lena caught a brief, horrifying glimpse of Viktor—his grey hair and beard contrasting starkly with the grim surroundings—seated lifelessly on the toilet. But before the grim reality could fully sink in, the cubicle door swung shut, hiding the gruesome sight.

The dim lighting cast eerie shadows across the restroom, but Martin's eyes shone clear and bright, filled with pain, guilt, and an overwhelming sense of love and protectiveness. The sight of his daughter, her face a picture of desolation, struck a deep chord within him. All the warnings he had given her, all the stories he had shared, had culminated in this singular, defining moment.

Lena's eyes, wide with fear and disbelief, were fixed on her father.

"He's one of them, isn't he?" Lena's voice trembled slightly, her anxiety evident. As she uttered the words, she unconsciously rocked back and forth on the balls of her feet, her eyes darting between her father's face and the cubicle door.

Martin's eyes were sorrowful as he gave a grave nod. "I'm sorry, kid. We wished this day would never come."

Lena's body went rigid, the weight of his words settling in. The reality seemed surreal.

"Lena. Do you understand what I'm saying? Do you understand what you must do?" Martin prodded, a desperate edge to his voice.

She took a shaky breath, fighting the tears. "All my plans, I'm going to university … I *was* going to university … what about Emily? What about Mum? They won't know who I am …"

Gently, Martin reached slowly for her shoulder. "I know it's rough …"

But Lena, raw emotions bubbling up, wrenched away from him. "That's one word for it! You're asking me to erase myself from their lives! My own mother! You're asking me to never see her again!"

Martin's expression tightened, his voice a whisper of urgency. "Had Viktor finished what he started with me, he would have gone after Reuben and Mum. You need to understand, they're still in danger. It's your power they're after, Lena. It always has been."

Lena took a shaky breath, her voice barely above a whisper. "How long? How long until we can come back?"

Martin looked away, struggling to find the right words. "I don't know."

She stared at him, desperately seeking assurance. "So, what? We just keep running? Start a new life? What about school? My friends? What about Mum and Reuben?"

He looked at her, pain evident in his eyes. "We'll cross that bridge when we get there. For now, we need to stay safe. For all of us."

Lena's eyes filled with tears. "Can I make them remember? After all this, can I bring their memories back?"

Martin sighed deeply; his voice tinged with sadness. "I wish I had an answer for you, sweetheart."

A lump formed in Lena's throat. The weight of what lay ahead sank in. She'd have to leave everything behind, including her mother and brother.

"What now?"

Martin looked down, hesitating for a moment. "I've listed out all the people you know. Tomorrow, go to school, but only for the first hour. Act like everything's normal. Jonas … he's got people who'll handle the rest. The … surveillance thing."

She just gave a small nod, clearly lost in thought.

Martin sighed. "We should probably … try and say goodbye, right?"

"No," Lena shot back, her voice carrying a cold firmness.

He raised his eyebrows in confusion. "But isn't this our last chance?"

Without turning to face him, Lena responded, "Just go to the car.

When it hits you that you didn't get your chance to say goodbye, maybe you'll get what I'm feeling right now."

She headed for the door but paused just before exiting, casting a final glance at Martin. "Don't worry about you though. They'll remember you. And I hope you can live with that."

Lena made her way back to the dimly lit cinema, the emotional weight in her steps contrasting the mindless buzz of the ongoing movie. While Reuben was thoroughly engrossed in the plot, her mother's intuitive gaze immediately picked up on her turmoil. She watched with furrowed brows as Lena practically sank into the seat next to her.

Her mom leaned in, her voice a concerned whisper amidst the background noise. "Is everything alright?"

Holding back the flood of emotions threatening to spill, Lena gave a hesitant nod. She purposely avoided her mother's eyes, fearing that one deep look might unravel all her bottled-up secrets.

"Can I … can I sit between you and Reuben?" Lena's voice was almost inaudible.

Her mom, puzzled but always accommodating, responded, "Of course, sweetie."

As Lena shifted between them, she caught Reuben looking at her. For a moment, there was an unspoken exchange, a connection that only siblings share. It spoke of years of shared secrets, laughter, arguments, and unconditional love. But as quickly as the moment appeared, it vanished. With a playful roll of his eyes—their shared inside joke—Reuben refocused on the screen.

"Lena, is everything alright?" her mum asked again, sensing the unease in her daughter.

Lena managed a weak smile, trying to reassure her mother despite the turmoil inside. "Yeah, Mum, everything's fine. Dad's just grabbing some drinks. We'll all be okay," she murmured, trying to convince herself as much as she was her mother.

Seeing the worry still evident in her mother's eyes, she added, "I love you, Mum. Just … enjoy the movie, okay?"

She moved her hands delicately, placing one atop her mother's and letting the other gently rest on Reuben's arm. She took a deep breath, the weight of the world pressing on her young shoulders. Then she slowly began to remove everything.

It was as if she held the threads of their shared memories, delicate silken strands intertwined with one another. And with each breath, she began to pluck herself out of them.

First, she removed herself from the birthday parties. Reuben's tenth birthday, when Dad had joked about eating all the cake before the candles were even lit. Now it was just Reuben and Mum, with Dad smiling, the chair where Lena had been now empty, and the cake only shared between three.

Then that Christmas morning when they'd all woken up to fresh snow, Dad suggesting they build the tallest snowman on the block. Lena had fashioned the perfect snowball for the head. Now, it was just Mum, Dad, and Reuben in the yard, the snowman standing there, finished, but no one remembered who had placed the last piece.

Family dinners came next. The evening when Lena had laughed with Reuben over Dad's attempt at making Mum's new recipe, and they'd both struggled to swallow it down without bursting into laughter. Now, Reuben sat quietly with Mum and Dad at the table, the awkward silences filled with polite conversation, no shared glances, no suppressed giggles.

The beach trips, where Dad had chased them both into the waves, and Lena had dared Reuben to swim out farther, always competitive. Now, it was just Reuben, walking quietly beside Mum and Dad, the air still and calm. No one to challenge him. No one to laugh with him.

And with every memory, Lena extracted herself from, she felt an excruciating emotional tug, like a piece of her soul being wrenched out.

But she continued, determined, until there were no more shared memories left. It was as if she had never been a part of their lives, a ghost that had never existed.

"Everything's going to be okay," she whispered to these now-future strangers, her voice almost lost in the backdrop of the film's score. "Just watch the screen."

CHAPTER NINETEEN

The woman who met Detective Osbourne at the door bore little resemblance to the vibrant figure on that cinema outing a year ago. Julia Drake, clad in a pink dressing gown that hung loosely on her frail frame, was a stark contrast to her previous depictions. Her hair, once a lustrous shade, had turned to dark grey, unkempt, and giving the impression it hadn't seen water in days. Her appearance was one of neglect, emphasised by the pallor of her skin and the slight tremble that coursed through her body, as if she was perpetually caught in a cold breeze. She stood there, the door half open, a figure marred by recent hardships, her eyes reflecting a turmoil that shook her to the core.

"Can I help you?" she asked vacantly, her eyes barely meeting there for no more than a brief second.

The curly ginger-moustached man who side eyed his partner, Officer Doran, a man not much older than his twenties, stocky with facial features scrunched up by worry.

"Good evening, Mrs. Drake. I'm Detective Chief Inspector Osbourne, and this is Officer Doran. We're here on behalf of the London Metropolitan Police. You were informed this morning regarding our visit. Correct?" Osbourne introduced himself with a blend of professionalism and underlying concern.

"Oh yes, they did tell me. How wonderful," she responded, her smile unsettlingly out of place given the gravity of the situation. The detectives exchanged another glance, the air thickening with tension.

"… We were hoping to discuss this matter further inside. There are several questions we have concerning your son and your husband," Osbourne suggested, stepping forward, only for the door to narrow slightly at his advance.

"Right here is fine, thanks," Julia retorted hastily, a hint of panic lacing her voice. "What would you like to know?"

Officer Doran, visibly frustrated, moved forward, but Osbourne's firm grip on his shoulder signalled him to hold back.

"That's perfectly alright, Mrs. Drake," Osbourne continued, his tone steady yet insistent. "Firstly, we were hoping to speak to your son Reuben. Is he about?"

"Well … I think he's gone camping with his friends."

"Camping? With friends? And when was the last time you spoke to him?"

"Must have been … well, three weeks ago now."

"Camping? With friends? For three weeks?"

"Well, yes. Since his father's passing, he's taken to disappearing for days without a word," she offered weakly, her explanation ringing hollow.

"Mrs. Drake, I'm finding this difficult to comprehend. Your husband goes missing, and within twenty-four hours, you're at the police station. Your son has been gone for three weeks, and you chalk it up to him being with friends?" Osbourne pressed, his tone sharpening with scepticism.

Julia's voice suddenly rose in defiance. "Are you accusing me of neglecting my son, Detective Inspector?"

Osbourne remained calm. "I've made no such accusation."

"It's not your words, Detective Inspector. It's your tone. It's the same tone I've endured from everyone in this village, the same tone my son used! Accusations of apathy towards my family's plight! Have you any idea what it's like to live with unanswered questions about a loved one's fate?" Her voice broke with emotion. "If you have nothing further, I suggest you leave my property."

Yet, Osbourne stood his ground, as did Officer Doran. The atmosphere was charged with an unspoken ultimatum as Osbourne prepared to delve deeper.

"I have two more questions, Mrs. Drake. After these, we won't bother you again," he assured, his voice devoid of its earlier warmth. "The first concerns Elaine Walker, the police officer you and your son had dealings with regarding your husband's case."

At the mention of Walker's name, Julia's reaction was one of stark alarm.

"You see," Osbourne continued, his narrative weaving a tale of mystery and suspicion around DCI Walker's inexplicable absence, aligning with the timeline of her son's disappearance. "When was the last time you saw DCI Elaine Walker?"

Julia's attempt to respond was futile, her voice trapped by fear.

"My conversation with your neighbour raised further alarms," Osbourne pursued. "He hasn't seen you leave your house in weeks but reported hearing disturbing conversations from within."

Julia remained silent, her expression one of terror, as Osbourne delivered his final, chilling inquiry.

"My last question, Mrs. Drake, and it's one I hoped not to ask. But given the circumstances, I must." He positioned himself so they were eye to eye, his voice dropping to a whisper that cut through the tension like a knife.

"Is there someone else in the house with you?"

Julia's head shook vehemently, a silent battle to articulate her fear as words failed her.

"There's not? Okay," Osbourne responded, his voice intentionally raised. "Let me give you my number, in case something comes to mind later."

He reached into his pocket, extracting a notepad. With swift, deliberate strokes, he jotted down a message. But as he extended the note towards Julia, it was clear it bore no number. Instead, scrawled across the paper were covert instructions.

"If there's someone inside with you, signal with three fingers on your left hand."

The gravity of the situation weighed heavily in the air as Julia looked to the note. A moment of hesitation passed before her left hand tremulously rose, three fingers extended. Her hands shook violently, a silent testament to her terror. Mouthing the words, "They'll kill me." Tears began streaming down her face, etching paths of despair.

Acknowledging the signal, Osbourne and Doran prepared to breach the sanctity of her home. Julia, mustering every ounce of courage, stepped aside to grant them entry. The detectives moved forward with cautious strides, their senses heightened for any sign of danger.

Inside, the house told a story of recent occupation and chaos. No immediate threats were visible, yet the evidence of intrusion was undeniable. A rifle lay abandoned on the dining table, amidst a scatter of documents and the remnants of fast food—the detritus of a makeshift encampment. The living space, once a sanctuary, had been commandeered by unseen forces, transformed into a command post for those with nefarious intent.

The air was thick with the residue of hurried activities, the documents scattered across the table hinting at plans and secrets untold. Takeaway bags, discarded carelessly, spoke of days spent in the shadowy confines of the house, a temporary refuge for those plotting in the dark.

With the house eerily quiet and no immediate threats in sight, Osbourne and Doran instinctively drew their firearms from their holsters, a silent affirmation of their readiness to confront whatever dangers might lurk within. Osbourne, with a measured nod, signalled towards the staircase, suggesting they explore the upper level, where the true nature of the intrusion might reveal itself.

The ascent was tense, each step deliberate, their shoes pressing against the carpeted stairs with a softness that belied their grave purpose. The air seemed to thicken with anticipation as they divided at the top; Osbourne, drawn by an ominous creak, veered towards the bathroom, while Doran steered himself into the main bedroom.

Doran entered the room with a palpable sense of caution, his gun leading the way. The bedroom, under the circumstances, appeared deceptively normal. A double bed anchored the space, its covers slightly askew as if left in a morning hurry. A bookshelf stood guard against one wall, its shelves a testament to varied interests and moments of leisure. Dominating the room, however, was a long glass cabinet that consumed an entire wall, its contents shadowed from view, suggesting both the mundane and the mysterious.

Doran's initial sweep of the room revealed little out of the ordinary, leading him to probe further beneath the double bed. The sight of mere storage boxes offered a momentary reassurance, a glimpse of normalcy amidst the chaos. However, his attention was soon drawn to the long glass cabinet, its reflective surface casting back his own apprehensive gaze. With cautious hands, he opened one of the cabinet doors, only to find it empty. The false sense of security shattered in an instant as a sharp pain erupted at his ankle—a scream tore through the silence as he fell to the ground, grasping at the sudden wound.

From the shadows beneath the bed, obscured cleverly by the mundane storage boxes, emerged a figure—a bald man adorned with tattoos, his grin malicious in the dim light of the room. The surprise attack, cunningly executed from a hiding place overlooked, sent a rush of adrenaline through Doran's veins.

Reacting with trained reflexes, Doran managed to discharge his firearm, landing two shots into the attacker's shoulder. The impact staggered the assailant, yet, propelled by desperation or madness, he continued his advance. With grim determination, he crawled over Doran, the gleam of the knife poised for another strike. In this close-quarter struggle, the sharp blade found its mark, sinking into Doran's stomach with a cruel precision.

Pain and survival instinct collided within Doran, culminating in a decisive, almost reflexive action. With the assailant looming over him, Doran fired once more, the bullet finding its target in the attacker's head, silencing the threat permanently.

As Detective Osbourne emerged from the bathroom, alerted by Doran's agonised screams, his senses were immediately assaulted by a new threat. From the shadows to his right, a figure burst forth with startling speed, the force of the attack smashing Osbourne against the wall. The sheer unexpectedness and brutality of the assault left him disoriented, barely registering as he was hoisted and then hurled back into the confines of the bathroom.

Gathering his wits, Osbourne looked up to see a towering figure advancing towards him—a man cloaked in a grey hoodie, his features grotesquely deformed, instilling an immediate sense of dread. The size difference was stark; the assailant stood at an imposing seven feet, his presence dominating the cramped space of the bathroom.

The ensuing struggle was fierce but desperate. Osbourne, trained and experienced, fought with the ferocity of someone cornered, yet the assailant's sheer physical superiority quickly became apparent. With alarming strength, the attacker seized Osbourne and threw him into the bathroom mirror, the impact shattering glass and scattering shards across the floor. As Osbourne hit the ground, the figure loomed over him, hands closing around his throat in a grip that threatened to extinguish life itself.

In a frantic bid for survival, Osbourne's hand found a piece of broken glass, its jagged edge a slim hope against the overwhelming force he faced. With a surge of adrenaline, he thrust it towards his attacker, only for the man to catch his arm with ease. The sight of the giant hand effortlessly crushing the glass, while simultaneously tightening its chokehold, was a chilling testament to the futility of Osbourne's resistance.

The fight, though fierce, was unequal from the start. The assailant's frustration at Osbourne's persistent defiance culminated in a final, ruthless act. With a brutal efficiency, he twisted, breaking Osbourne's neck with a sickening snap. The life extinguished from Osbourne's body in an instant, his struggles ceasing as his killer stood over him, a silent sentinel in the aftermath of violence.

The hulking figure stood, leaving Detective Osbourne's lifeless form behind, his mind set on completing the mission. He made his way to the bedroom, where a scene of carnage awaited him—his accomplice,

Till, lay motionless, a testament to Doran's last stand. Doran himself, pale as death, reached feebly for his weapon, a final act of defiance despite his fading strength. Recognizing the futility of finishing off a man already on death's doorstep, the assailant turned away, his focus now on Julia Drake.

Thundering down the stairs with menace in each step.

"MRS DRAKE! WE'VE GOT A FEW THINGS TO TALK ABOUT!" he bellowed.

His voice, thick with a northern accent, echoed through the empty house. A frantic search ensued—living room, kitchen, back garden—each room yielded nothing but silence. Frustration mounting, he limped to the front door, his anger spilling out.

"WHERE ARE YOU HIDING, BITCH?" Yet the outside offered no sign of Julia.

In a storm of fury, he burst back into the living room, his anger blinding him to the figure lurking in the shadows. There, in the dim corner, stood Julia Drake, her arms awkwardly cradling the rifle he'd left behind in his haste. The intruder began to smirk, a cruel taunt forming on his lips, but the words would never escape him. Julia, with a resolve forged from weeks of fear and desperation, levelled the rifle at him and pulled the trigger without hesitation. The report of the gun was deafening, a scream ripping from her throat as she witnessed the bullet tear through the man's neck.

"This … is my … home!" she declared through gritted teeth, her voice a low growl of defiance. Her hands trembled, the weight of the rifle mirroring the heavy burden of her actions.

The man staggered backwards, clawing at his neck as his lifeblood gushed forth. Julia watched, the rifle still poised for another shot, as he stumbled over a clutter of shoes in the hallway and collapsed, disappearing from her view. She remained frozen, a statue of vigilance, as curses whispered past her lips, her entire body quivering with adrenaline and shock.

Minutes stretched into an eternity as she observed the eerie stillness of the man's feet, waiting for any sign of movement. Finally convinced of his demise, she inched closer, the horror movie clichés she'd laughed at with her son now echoing ominously in her mind. Yet, as she rounded the corner, the stark reality greeted her—the intruder lay lifeless, his eyes void of any spark.

With a deep breath, she stepped towards the door, never turning her back on the man who had invaded her sanctuary. The cool night air brushed against her skin as she emerged onto the street, the tranquillity of the night stark against the chaos she'd left behind. Across the way, a neighbour's door cracked open, a sliver of light piercing the darkness. It was then, under the watch of the silent night, that Julia's pent-up anguish and fear cascaded out in a soul-wrenching scream.

CHAPTER TWENTY

"Excuse me. Are you Ian's father?"

The question pierced the quiet of the waiting area, targeting a plump man in his late fifties. Engrossed in his phone, clearly preferring to be elsewhere, he looked up to see two younger men imposing their presence.

"What's it to you?" he responded slowly, his voice saturated with a posh drone, revealing a mixture of irritation and detachment.

The taller figure, clad in a distinctive red tweed suit, extended his hand, a gesture of peace in the unfolding drama. "I came to pay my respects." He introduced himself warmly. "My name is Johnny, and this is my partner, Sam. We are the event managers of Ocean One. A part of the Velour family. We were deeply saddened by the news about what happened to Ian at our venue and wanted to see how he's doing."

"How is he …"

Mr. Andrews, identified through his terse demeanour as Ian's father, stood up in a huff.

"How do you think he's bloody doing?" His anger was palpable, his finger jabbing the air towards Johnny as he voiced his accusations.

"You wait! Just you wait until my solicitors hear about this! My son is a recovering drug addict! I went on your Facebook group, and you can tell instantly it's a place for cokeheads! Look at the way they're dressed! I won't be surprised if your bouncers were offering him a line on the bloody door!"

Jonas, trying to infuse the tense atmosphere with a semblance of calm, raised his hands in a placating gesture, his laughter doing little to ease Mr. Andrews's fury. "Now, now, Mr. Andrews, there's no need to start throwing accusations!" He answered. "We're just as upset as you are about this," he said, attempting to soothe what was happening. "That's why we called you. We want to get your son's side of the story so we can ensure this doesn't happen again!"

"You can go and talk to him, but he'll tell you exactly what he told me! He had one drink! One drink! Next thing he knows he goes to the men's toilets, and he falls unconscious. Someone spiked him! Maybe one of your bartenders! I've seen them on your website, you know. Is being covered in tattoos a part of the bloody job spec?!"

"Okay, let's leave it there," Jonas said slowly, a final attempt for calm. "We'll go and have a chat with Ian. You're more than welcome to be with us when we do so."

Mr. Andrews's frustration seemed only to deepen, prompting him to grab his jacket and attempt to depart.

"I'm afraid I have some other business to attend to. God, you sound exactly like his Mum! He's in his bloody twenties, you know! I always used to tell that girlfriend to stop mothering him! Maybe she's the crux of all of this. Trust me, if you ever go to a jazz bar in the future and get approached by a Sophie Thomas, make for the exit! Trust me!" he spat out before he stormed off towards the elevator.

Jonas's partner turned to him and rolled his eyes.

"Bloody boomers … You okay?"

Jonas stared off into the distance with a knowing grin on his face like a child on Christmas Day.

"Let's have a chat with Ian, shall we?" Jonas said decisively, a glance around the corridor ensuring privacy before they moved to enter Ian's hospital room, stepping into the uncertain aftermath of the confrontation.

Jonas and Sam entered Ian's hospital room, their steps measured, their anticipation palpable. The room was stark, illuminated by the harsh fluorescent lighting typical of such places, making Ian's pallid complexion stand out even more. Amidst the sterile environment, Ian lay in bed, his green shirt plastered to his body by sweat.

Jonas cleared his throat softly, initiating the conversation with care. "Ian, I'm Jonas, and this is Sam. We heard about what happened at the nightclub and we're really sorry. We just wanted to see how you're doing and ask you a few questions about that night. Do you feel up to talking?"

Ian's eyes, darting around the room, finally settled on Jonas, a flicker of recognition—or perhaps confusion—passing through them.

Jonas continued gently, "Do you remember anything from that night, Ian? Anything at all that stood out to you?"

Ian's response was disjointed, his eyes unfocused. "It was all a blur … so crowded … I saw Sophie … I didn't mean to talk to her," he murmured, his voice barely above a whisper.

Encouraged by any response, Jonas ventured further. "Ian, we heard from your father about this Sophie. Are you able to tell me more about her?"

For a moment, Ian's agitation seemed to peak, his words tumbling out in a rush. "Reuben, you've been hogging it for hours!" he exclaimed suddenly, his voice sharp with irritation.

Jonas's reaction was immediate and visceral. For a fleeting moment, shock painted his features, a testament to the unexpected revelation from Ian's lips. "Reuben, let your sister have a turn!!" Ian had cried out, seemingly oblivious to the significance of his own words.

Jonas's shock quickly morphed into a palpable excitement, a glimmer of opportunity during Ian's manic state. He turned to Sam; his earlier surprise now replaced with a fervent gleam in his eye.

"You know what this means, don't you?"

The young man, whom Jonas had addressed as Sam, fixed him with a look of resolute determination. He crossed the room to stand by the hospital window, gazing out at the sprawling landscape of London. The city's skyscrapers pierced the early morning sky, a forest of steel and glass bathed in the dawn's first light.

Turning back towards Jonas, the clarity in his voice left no room for doubt.

"Yes, I do" he answered. "We found her."

CHAPTER TWENTY-ONE

15th August 2018

In a tucked-away corner of the service toilets, Lena and Martin found temporary refuge inside a locked, disabled-access cubicle. It was a clandestine meeting place, scarcely more than a hiding spot, lit only by the flickering fluorescent light overhead. Their faces were shrouded in hoods, their eyes darting back and forth for the appearance of security cameras and patrolling guards.

As they unfolded crumpled pieces of paper to reveal their makeshift meal, the aroma of stale bread, half-eaten sandwiches, and overripe fruit filled the air. Lena hesitated before taking a bite from a bruised apple, its sweet and sour taste mingling with the lingering bitterness of their situation. Martin dug into a forlorn turkey and cheese sandwich, its edges hardened but its core still soft—much like them.

The atmosphere was suffused with a tension that was palpable yet unspoken. Each was lost in their thoughts, mentally retracing the convoluted pathways and grim decisions that had led them to this precarious moment. Just as Martin was about to break the silence, a sudden noise from outside the cubicle froze them both.

Footsteps. Heavy, deliberate, stopping just outside their door. Lena's eyes met Martin's, a silent exchange that screamed caution. They held their breath, listening as the door of the adjacent cubicle creaked open, followed by the sound of a toilet flushing. A janitor, perhaps, oblivious to their presence but so dangerously close to discovering them.

The seconds stretched interminably until finally, the footsteps receded, growing fainter until they were swallowed by the ambient noise of the building. Lena exhaled quietly; her breath shaky. Martin nodded, his eyes clouded with a mix of relief and lingering dread. And so they sat, taking another moment to regain composure.

"You are sure we couldn't use even a one-star hotel?" Lena broke the silence, her voice tinged with defeat.

"Jonas said that they would be able to track us," Martin responded, cautiously peeling back the wrapper of a half-melted Mars bar. "He believed they were getting help from an outside source in monitoring surveillance."

"Oh, great. Let's listen to Jonas, the man who communicates to us by text and someone you haven't met in god knows how long," Lena retorted, her tone dripping with sarcasm.

"You don't know him," Martin said defensively.

"You're goddamn right I don't!" Lena's response was a touch louder than intended, eliciting a stern glare from her father.

"Ugh. Just promise me that as soon as we get to Paris, I can shower, because this isn't what a woman should have to put up with!"

Eventually, the tension proved too much, and they both dozed off into fitful slumbers. Lena woke first a mere half hour later, slick with perspiration. She glanced at her father, who lay beside her in a deep sleep. Her patience for his cryptic manoeuvres had waned, and her desire for transparency had reached its limit. With a contemplative expression, Lena regarded her slumbering father. She knew she couldn't delve into the labyrinth of his thoughts, but there might be another way to glean some insight into his mysterious motivations.

"If only," she murmured softly to herself, wary of waking him.

"But I can do the next best thing."

Her eyes shifted from the backpack to her father's peaceful face, and she decided. Gently, almost reverently, Lena leaned over and placed her hands lightly on his temples. It was a risky move, delving into another person's memories, especially her own father. As she closed her eyes, she felt the initial resistance give way, and suddenly …

The grandiose gates of the mansion swung closed with a resonant thud, shutting out the world they once knew. Four children—two boys and two girls, brothers and sisters, all with grimy faces and malnourished frames—stood awestruck, their eyes widening as they took in the towering doors that had just closed behind them.

"This is your home now," announced a voice, rich and booming. They turned to see the man who had led them there: an imposing figure dressed in black, his bald head a canvas for intricate tribal tattoos that danced across his skin. From the deep wells of her father's memories, Lena knew him as Father Hishaya. He had ushered them around the mansion, greeting more than thirty men and women in robes.

Suddenly, the environment around them underwent a surreal transformation. Light flooded the scene, escalating in intensity until all Lena could see was an overwhelming whiteness. Yet, even in this blinding expanse, she heard voices with crystalline clarity.

"You said we could live forever," spoke one of the boys, his voice tinged with a blend of incredulity and yearning.

"Let me show you," the priest had replied.

As Lena observed, entranced, the four siblings convened around an ornate chessboard, intricately carved and laid upon a grand wooden table. Their hands, in various stages of youth and senescence, reached out to manipulate the game pieces. A boy with nascent stubble became a man, his beard turning grey, only to recede into the smooth face of youth within the span of a few moves. His sister across the table followed suit—her young vibrant eyes grew heavy with age, crinkled at the corners, before reclaiming their youthful sparkle. Each transition happened fluidly, mirroring the complex choreography of the chess game they were engrossed in.

Presiding over this tableau was Father Hishaya. Standing at the head of the table, he too was subject to the temporal flux enveloping the room. His bald head sprouted tufts of hair that greyed, receded, and then luxuriously regrew. His tribal tattoos blurred and resharpened as wrinkles crossed his face, disappearing as his visage rejuvenated.

The vision faded to white and then …

Elena, one of the original children who had grown into a sophisticated, matronly figure, gave birth. The air in the mansion's grand chamber was thick with both anticipation and incense as she cradled a newborn boy, swaddled in linen that seemed spun from moonlight. His tiny face peeked out, as innocent as dawn, and they named him Thomas.

Jonas, Elena's other son, stood at a respectful distance, wearing an expression of awestruck curiosity mixed with an undercurrent of trepidation. He had been an only child until that moment, and the weight of that change seemed to settle on him as he stepped forward. "Meet your brother Thomas," Elena had said, her voice thick with emotion. The dynamics of their family, like a complex musical chord, had added a new note. Jonas looked down at the infant, meeting his baby brother's eyes, and something ineffable passed between them.

The vision once again faded to white …

The family members donned their ceremonial robes, heavy and dark as the night sky. In a hidden, candlelit chamber lined with aged tomes and mystical symbols, they gathered around an altar. Father Hishaya presided, his countenance more inscrutable than ever. A sense of grim import saturated the air.

"The Collector walks among us once more," intoned Father Hishaya, his eyes hooded. Each family member cast a small, intricately carved token into a chalice to signify their vote. The tokens accumulated, clinking against each other in a chilling melody of finality. When Father Hishaya tipped the chalice to reveal the tokens, they spoke a unanimous yet heavy verdict: Thomas had been selected for 'sacrifice.'

Elena's hands trembled in her lap, her face a mask struggling to contain a tempest of maternal love and existential dread. Jonas stood there, frozen, his eyes meeting those of his newly born brother, whose life had just been decided in this shadowy conclave.

The vision faded and then …

The atmosphere fractured in an instant, splintering the room's dark solemnity with a sudden, malevolent force. Flames erupted from an unseen origin, exploding into a firestorm that engulfed the clandestine chamber in an inferno of blazing heat and smoke. The air turned acrid, heavy with the scent of burning wood and incense now reduced to cinders.

Screams ricocheted off the walls, distorted cries of horror and disbelief that perforated the night like staccato bursts of thunder. Robed figures scattered, their faces twisted masks of panic and confusion, vanishing into the labyrinthine corridors of the mansion, as if seeking refuge in its shadowy bowels. The fire roared, an insatiable beast consuming everything in its path: tapestries, wooden pews, the altar—each was devoured in the ravenous advance of the flames.

From the midst of the chaos emerged Eli, one of the family members who had cast his fateful vote. His arm was a grotesque vision, skin blistering and bubbling as the fire licked at it hungrily. The pain was excruciating, a searing agony that radiated from his fingertips to his shoulder, but it was the look in his eyes that captured the true horror: a blend of regret, fear, and something far darker.

Arthur, his brother, appeared beside him, his face grim but determined. He wrapped a piece of his robe tightly around Eli's burned arm, stifling a gasp as he did so. Together, they staggered through the collapsing doorway, barely evading a cascade of flaming debris that crashed down where they had stood mere seconds ago. Jonas was half-leading, half-carrying Eli, each step a battle against the disorienting blaze and choking fumes.

They emerged into the cooler air of a distant corridor, far from the chamber of doom but still close enough to feel its fiery breath. Eli collapsed against a wall, his breathing shallow, his face ashen …

… On a cliff that overlooked a raging ocean, Eli and Arthur stood with their eyes narrowed, faces hardened by suspicion and pain. Before them were Elena and her son, Thomas, who wore expressions of guilt and defiance, a complicated blend that offered no easy answers. The howl of the wind and the crash of waves below punctuated the tense silence, each natural force a reminder of the uncontrollable elements that had led them all to this precipice …

... *Before she could see any more, a scream so visceral it bordered on animalistic pierced the air, snapping everyone's heads in its direction. Lena's concentration was shattered momentarily, her focus yanked away from the complex array of memories she had been navigating.*

... *The scene shifted abruptly. Cars rolled by a sign that boldly declared* **Welcome to Rhymney***, the metallic bodies of the vehicles gleaming in the sunlight. It was as if the universe itself had hurled them into another chapter of this twisted narrative, the sign serving as both a welcome and a warning.*

Suddenly, the story plunged back into darkness. Thomas was now the focal point, lying on a cold, sterile table. His eyes darted around in sheer terror as he found himself surrounded by figures garbed in long robes, their identities obscured by grotesque rabbit masks. The room was imbued with a chilling atmosphere, a sense of ritualistic urgency that left no room for mercy ...

A brilliant flash of light suddenly engulfed the entire scene, so radiant that it blotted out all other sensory details. The air was filled with the anguished cries of souls in torment, a haunting chorus that spoke of irreversible fates and shattered lives. When the brilliance finally subsided, Arthur and Eli found themselves dramatically altered. They were no longer the hardened men shaped by years of family conflict; instead, they stood as young boys, their faces unmarked by the scars of time.

Arthur looked over the room's occupants. Astonishingly, the old, robed figures—the men and women who seemed to wield some unspeakable power—were now lifeless on the ground, their faces frozen in expressions of shocked disbelief. In stark contrast, the children, once subject to the whims of these enigmatic elders, stood unscathed and smiling as if released from some dark spell.

Confusion and terror wrestled for control of Arthur's young mind. Without a word, driven by an instinct he didn't fully understand, he turned and fled. His feet pounded the ground as he escaped, leaving behind the room ...

... Then it was 1995. Lena watched the scene unfold as if she were a spectator in her own life. Her younger self, a tiny five-year-old with innocent eyes, reached out to touch her father's forehead.

The instant her fingers made contact, she saw her father—Martin—jolt awake. His eyes turned an ashy hue, lifeless and void. Lena felt her stomach turn as she watched her younger self lose her grip and tumble to the ground when her father convulsed forward.

"Oh my God," she heard her mother Julia gasp in the memory. Julia's maternal instincts had kicked in instantly. Setting baby Reuben in the nearby crib, she rushed to scoop the young Lena off the floor.

When Julia turned back to look at Martin, his eyes had reverted to their normal colour. But Lena could see it—that unsettled flicker in her mother's eyes.

"Babe ... are you okay?" Julia's voice was laden with a tension that Lena now understood all too well.

She watched as her father seemed to stare through Julia, his focus miles and years away. She realized that in this moment, her younger self had opened a floodgate inside him. A torrent of memories—each a jigsaw piece of joy, sorrow, success, or failure—rushed through his consciousness. It was an overwhelming deluge that Lena herself had unwittingly unleashed.

And then she heard it—her father's scream. It tore through the fabric of the memory, a raw, guttural sound that seemed to embody every complex emotion he was feeling. For Lena, standing in the spectral viewing gallery of her own history, the scream echoed infinitely, magnifying until it filled every corner of her awareness ...

Startled awake, Martin suddenly lunged at his daughter, his eyes wide and wild. His instincts screamed danger, a reflex sharpened by years of living on the edge. But as he locked eyes with her, recognition flooded his face, washing away the momentary frenzy.

"Lena." He exhaled, his voice threaded with a palpable sense of dread. The colour had drained from his face, leaving him a sickly shade of pale. "W-What did you see?"

Her trembling form straightened, and she looked downward at him, a cataclysm of emotions roiling in her eyes. "I saw everything.

What did you do, Dad? What the fuck did you do?!"

She pivoted, intending to storm out of the room, but he lunged forward. His hand locked around her arm, and he pinned her against the wall of the stall.

"LET GO!" she shrieked, her voice shrill with terror and indignation.

"I understand you're upset!" he implored, his grip unwavering.

"Is that what they're going to do to me? You helped them do it for others, didn't you?!" Her eyes met his, a volatile blend of steel and vulnerability.

Arthur peered into her eyes, struck by the haunting reflections of innumerable memories she had just ingested, memories that were, damningly, his own. "I didn't remember anything that happened until you 'fixed' me," he confessed, imbuing each word with a tragic bitterness. "My mind was a fragmented jigsaw puzzle, pieces of lifetimes that wouldn't fit. But when you were five, the first time you used your powers, you made me whole again."

His shoulders sagged, weighed down by invisible tons. For the first time, Lena perceived the immense burden her father had been shouldering—a complex mesh of moral and existential crises that seemed poised to crush him entirely. "I spent my entire life being told that I was a monster for surviving being kidnapped … but I was an author of all the chaos."

Stricken yet suffused with a daughter's innate empathy, Lena stepped closer. Her arms encircled him in a comforting, almost maternal embrace. She clung to him, as if she could absorb some of his pain through osmosis.

"Dad. I still have loads of questions."

They separated just enough for their eyes to meet.

"Are you ready to talk about what happened? All of it?"

He nodded, his eyes finally steady. "I've spent most of my life shielding you from the truth. But you're going to need to know what happened all those years ago to finally beat them."

CHAPTER TWENTY-TWO

Present Day

Lena and Sophie, settled into the cosy embrace of their pyjamas and with glasses of champagne in hand, found themselves captivated by the unfolding drama on their TV screen. Their living room, typically a bastion against the world's turmoil, resonated with the grave tones of a breaking news report, starkly contrasting the mundane tranquillity of their morning. The presenter's voice, heavy with the gravity of recent events, pierced through their semblance of normalcy:

Back to our breaking story from last night. Last year, everyone in this country, including myself, was shocked by what happened to Martin Drake. How a man of simple origins could lose his life in such a way was something none of us understand. We hoped … no! We prayed that the family would be able to move on from this event. But today's top story has thrown that wish into the dark. This morning, South Wales Police confirmed that four bodies, including two police officers, were found in the Drake household. It's been confirmed that Martin's wife, Julia, has been taken to hospital after the incident. Police have also confirmed though that his son, Reuben, was not identified in the house. Currently, his whereabouts are unknown. Simon, you're there in the village now, could you tell us a bit more about what's happened?

The screen transitioned to a reporter, a tall, scarecrow-like figure in glasses, standing at a cordoned-off street that Lena recognized from her childhood. The sight of her former street sealed off and under investigation sent a chill down her spine.

Well, Tom. I've spoken to those living in Central Street who have painted quite a harrowing picture of the Drake household over the past few weeks. Mrs. Drake, who I've interviewed before, always came across to me as a strong individual with positive energy even with the circumstances of her husband's death. But what I've learnt is that this woman and her son have barely been seen in the past month. Some neighbours have told me of hearing screams coming from the house. Some have even informed me that they've seen mysterious men leaving the house in the early hours of the morning. It seems to me that this home was more broken on the inside than they wanted people to see.

The dialogue from the TV stirred a complex whirlwind of emotions in Lena. Sophie, sensing the weight of the moment, turned off the TV abruptly, unable to bear more.

"I've seen enough."

She moved to the window to collect her thoughts.

Lena watched her and wondered what was going through her mind. Sophie had woken up around four a.m. and had gone into the living room/kitchen to get a glass of water. It was there she found "Jamie" crying on the sofa. For the rest of the morning, Lena had been unravelling the threads of her life to Sophie, detailing the genesis of her powers, the painful choice to erase herself from her family's memories, her father's murder, and now, the abduction of her brother, Reuben. With each revelation, the weight of her secrets seemed to lift, only to be replaced by the gravity of the current crisis. Little did Lena know that her best friend was aware of the whole story.

"So that fight you had with Ian in the bathroom... that was you erasing his memory?" Sophie asked, curiosity lacing her tone. "Of us as a couple?"

Lena took a swig of her champagne, then shook her head, the weight of her secrets momentarily lifting with the alcohol's effervescence. "That wasn't what I was trying to do," she confessed, her voice tinged with a hint of regret and frustration. "There's this method I've tried which is almost like short-circuiting the brain."

Sophie threw her a look of horror, the implications of Lena's words sinking in.

"Christ. That sounds safe."

Lena sighed, acknowledging the sarcasm. "I basically remove the memory you have of a few seconds ago, causing confusion in the individual. The problem is that I don't have the control over my powers that I want. My Dad isn't around anymore to help me. It's like … I'm there with a fishing hook trying to fish out something of use and Ian's memories were the sea. But I wasn't strong enough, so I was dragged in with him. That's the best I can explain it."

Sophie stood up, driven by a mix of concern and a need for another drink, and walked towards the fridge. Her frustration was palpable as she realised, they were out of alcohol, the door slamming shut with a force that echoed her irritation. "I just can't wrap my head around him," she mumbled, turning back towards Lena.

"Who? Ian?" Lena asked, trying to follow Sophie's train of thought.

"No," Sophie responded, her frustration shifting focus. "Your father."

Lena was taken aback, confusion written across her face.

"Lena. He trained you to become no one. And for what? An old family feud over some superpower?" Sophie's voice rose with each word, her incredulity at the situation painting her face.

"It's not just a family feud if you remember all that I told you," Lena defended, her voice breaking slightly. "he protected me, Sophie He died for me."

"He didn't protect the rest of his family though, did he?" Sophie countered, looking back at the TV. "What are you going to do now?"

Lena swept her fingers through her hair, a manifestation of her growing desperation. "This might just be a bluff. Reuben could be far from danger, perhaps safe. Maybe this is nothing more than a ploy to draw me out," she pondered aloud.

"And if it isn't?" Sophie probed; her voice laced with concern.

"Then, honestly, the only plan I can think of is heading to the pub because I'm at a total loss," Lena admitted, her voice trailing off as she inverted her empty glass.

"I have a better suggestion," Sophie countered with determination. "Let's leave the city. Escape from all this."

Lena's response came with a burst of laughter. "You've definitely had one too many."

But Sophie, undeterred and serious, stepped closer, placing her hands on Lena's shoulders for emphasis. "Listen to me. If we stay, they'll find you, take you, and worse. We can get you out of this place. You won't have to face it alone."

"And what about my family? Do I just abandon them?" Lena shot back, gently removing Sophie's hands from her shoulders.

"With all due respect, Lena," Sophie corrected herself with a hint of frustration. "You wiped their memories of you. As of this moment, you're no longer family to them and they're not your family anymore either."

Lena was ensnared in a maelstrom of fatigue and indecision, unable to craft a rebuttal. Silently, she pivoted away, gravitating towards the remote control as if it were a lifeline, seeking to drown their bleak reality in the cacophony of the television. Her attempt to focus on the screen was palpable, yet she was acutely aware of Sophie's presence, almost hovering over her.

"Yes?" Lena's voice carried a hint of resignation, not turning to face her companion.

"Have you ever looked into my memories?" The question from Sophie was unexpected, piercing the veil of distraction Lena had tried to wrap around herself.

"What?" The inquiry seemed almost alien to Lena, catching her off guard.

"Tell me," Sophie pressed, her curiosity undimmed. "Have you ever delved into my memories?"

The absurdity of the situation almost coaxed a laugh out of Lena. When put into words, her abilities always seemed to border on the fantastical. She diverted her gaze, a gesture of evasion.

"No," she firmly responded after a brief pause. "I don't plan to either."

"Why?" Sophie wasn't deterred, sliding into the seat beside Lena, her presence now more pronounced. "Afraid you might see something you don't like?"

The question prompted Lena to lower the television volume, her attention momentarily captured by an episode of *The Fresh Prince of Bel-Air* flickering on the screen. A smile tugged at the corners of her mouth as she was transported to a simpler time.

"Me and my best friend from home, Emily, we used to watch this every day after school. We could watch episodes on mute, and we'd know every joke," Lena reminisced, her laughter a rare, genuine sound that seemed to momentarily lighten the atmosphere. But as quickly as it came, the laughter faded, leaving a trace of sorrow in its wake. She had not experienced such carefree joy in a long time.

"I haven't read your memories because, frankly, I don't want to," Lena confessed, the humour now draining from her voice. "These powers aren't a gift for me. They're a curse. The last time I used them on someone I considered my best friend, it destroyed them."

Sophie leaned in closer, her interest piqued by Lena's admission.

"Is that what happened to Emily?" she inquired, gently prodding her to unveil the story of the days leading up to when Lena Drake ceased to exist.

*

"Oh, hiya! What are you doing here?" Emily's voice rang out as she cracked open the door, revealing a sliver of her lanky figure framed by the entryway. Her cascade of red hair, a striking contrast against her pale skin, tumbled over her shoulders, framing a youthful face speckled with freckles. She was casually dressed in a sleeveless vest, high-waisted jeans that accentuated her slender build, and scuffed-up Converse sneakers that had clearly seen better days.

Bending down, Emily nudged aside the tower of moving boxes that barricaded the entrance, clearing a path for the door to swing open fully. As she straightened back up, she found herself staring into the face of her best friend of ten years, standing on her doorstep. The frenetic energy of the bustling Cardiff Street unravelled behind her, its clamour and chaos forming a jarring backdrop to her friend's palpable distress. Draped in an oversized black hoodie that clearly didn't belong to her, her face was tinged a ruddy hue, and her eyes, so red, looked like they were on the brink of releasing a flood.

"Oh my God, what's happened?" Emily's voice, tinged with a strong Swansea accent inherited from her father, radiated concern as she grasped her friend's hand, ushering her inside. "What's Derek said to you now? Want me to smack him?"

Lena gently disengaged her hand from Emily's grip, shaking her head. "I came to say goodbye," she murmured, her hand coming up to swipe away tears from her flushed cheeks.

"What do you mean, 'goodbye?'" Emily chortled, her arms folded across her chest, dismissing the seriousness of Lena's words. "We're not off to university until next month, you silly bugger!"

At the mention of university, Lena seemed to crumble inwardly. Her head shook involuntarily, a silent negation. It was a fragility Emily had never witnessed before.

"Lena ..." Emily's voice softened, her words delicately floating above the clamour of street noise seeping in from the outside. "Talk to me."

A tremulous smile flickered across Lena's face. "Well, I felt like I should say goodbye now. Thought it would be better than waiting until our final day before we all go."

Emily rolled her eyes, but her expression was fond. "Always the drama queen," she retorted.

"Oh, you can talk!" Lena shot back, her own arms now folded defensively.

"What do you mean?" Emily was genuinely perplexed.

"You were the one who stopped talking to me for two weeks because I went to the cinema without you."

Emily's face reddened, half in indignation and half in embarrassment. "It was Toy Story 3! We had promised to go together!"

"Two weeks, man!" Lena exclaimed, her eyes widening for emphasis.

They both laughed together.

Their laughter dissipated into the air, leaving behind a residue of warmth and shared history.

"I'm going to miss you too, you know," Emily said, her eyes meeting Lena's. "And don't ever think you can't just show up out of the blue like this. My door's always open for you."

"You sure about that?" Lena asked. The transient bubble of mirth had burst, its remnants floating away like wisps of smoke.

"Always, mate," Emily assured her. "Now come here, let's hug it out."

They enveloped each other in a hug, arms tight, and hearts tighter. Lena pressed her cheek to Emily's shoulder, fighting back the urge to dissolve into tears.

"I love you," Lena whispered into the fabric of Emily's vest.

Then Lena closed her eyes, diving mentally into the ocean of their shared past. Within that singular second, as if descending a cascading waterfall of memories, Lena began to relive every moment they'd spent together. The mindscape around her morphed into the turbulent currents of this waterfall—her consciousness plummeting from their first giggles in elementary school, past the shared secrets and challenges of middle school, descending through the rapids of their teenage years, each memory glowing with vivid luminescence before being snuffed out, absorbed back into the ether of Lena's being.

Inside this torrential mindscape, Lena screamed. She heard echoes of her father's teachings urging her to breathe, to maintain control, but the waterfalls of memory were too overpowering. Lena felt as if she were losing herself, becoming a lost voyager in this never-ending river of yesteryears.

Just as the vivid flash of red pulled Lena back to the present, she opened her eyes to see Emily staring back at her, a bewildered expression clouding her face. For a disorienting second, Lena wondered if Emily had shared the same tumultuous journey through their memories. Had her powers been accidentally revealed?

Emily opened her mouth to speak, perhaps to voice her confusion, but what came out instead was a horrifying splatter of blood. Her eyes rolled back, and her body began to convulse violently. Emily crumpled to the ground in a full-blown seizure.

"Oh God, what have I done?" Lena screamed, falling to her knees beside her best friend. Her hands hovered in the air, unsure of what to do, how to help. She looked up and saw Emily's Dad moving towards them.

"Emily! Oh my god!" He yelled as he lifted her from the ground and cradled her. His angry eyes fell on Lena. "What happened? What are you?"

There was no time to think. No time to mourn. No time for a human reaction. Lena simply reached forward and touched his shoulder. And just like Lena Drake, the real Emily Lewis was gone.

*

"And that's that ... I don't even know where she is now," Lena added, her voice a whisper laden with guilt and uncertainty. "She could be ... anywhere. In a hospital ... or worse." She shook her head, trying to dislodge her thoughts.

Sophie moved from her chair and joined her on the sofa, taking her hand.

"It's not your fault," she said. "You've put far too much pressure on yourself. You act as if you were left with a handbook on how to use this gift."

Lena laughed. "Gift? After all I told you, you think this is a gift?"

"It could be," Sophie replied, a spark of hope igniting in her eyes.

Lena let out a heavy sigh. "Sometimes, I just wish I could give it all back, you know? Release these memories that aren't mine to keep, stop losing myself in other people's lives."

"What if there's a way to do that? To return what you've taken?"

"What? You don't think I've tried that already?" she asked. "My dad didn't even give me the opportunity to try and help. It's always been about the Family. About the Blackwaters. All I want is a chance. A chance to break away from this legacy they've built for me. I'm tired, Sophie. Tired of running with no place to go, tired of no one knowing my own name, tired of not being able to call my Mum …"

She choked tearfully.

"Tired of avenging the man who made me destroy my own life."

Sophie reached out, placing her hand gently on Lena's back which quickly turned into a hug. "Everything is going to be okay," she whispered.

But as they sat there, Lena felt a deep, unsettling contradiction to Sophie's assurances. She knew the complexities of her situation couldn't be soothed away by simple words of comfort. The road ahead was fraught with challenges that Sophie's optimism alone couldn't erase.

The comforting embrace was abruptly severed by the sharp ring of Sophie's phone from the bedroom.

"Be right back," she muttered before disappearing into the other room.

Left alone, Lena's thoughts spiralled. Torn between despair and resolve, she felt an overwhelming urge to leave and search for her family. Each time she closed her eyes, haunting visions of her brother, ensnared in darkness and calling out for her rescue, played before her. The gnawing uncertainty of their safety and location haunted her, yet Sophie's advice resonated deeply. After all the turmoil, was further sacrifice worth it for those who no longer remembered her? Blame settled heavily on her shoulders, directed towards her father. She recalled a pivotal moment, sheltered in a makeshift camp by the M42 under a relentless downpour, when her father unveiled the grim secrets of the Blackwater Family.

Secrets so profound, she hadn't even shared them with Sophie. She had told her father she hated him and had disappeared into the storm, wishing for it to kill her.

This cascade of memories was abruptly halted by Sophie's hesitant voice, drawing Lena back to the present. Turning, Lena saw Sophie clutching her phone, her face drained of colour, a ghostly pallor betraying her distress.

"What's wrong?" Lena asked.

Sophie's response was barely audible, lost in a mumble of fear and uncertainty.

Lena's attempt at lightheartedness fell flat, her laughter tinged with anxiety. "Speak up, girl. What are you trying to say?"

As Sophie's grip loosened, the phone clattered to the floor, her voice finally breaking the heavy silence. "They're coming," she stammered, the weight of her words crashing into the room like a cold wave.

Confusion clouded Lena's mind. "Who's coming?" she pressed, the urgency in her voice sharpening.

Sophie, now visibly distraught, tears streaming down her cheeks, couldn't meet Lena's eyes. "I want you to know that I didn't want this. Not anymore," she managed through her sobs.

Lena's fleeting smile vanished, replaced by a dawning realisation of betrayal. "What's going on, Soph?" she asked, her voice barely above a whisper. "What have you done?"

The conversation was shattered by a jovial knock on the door. Lena looked between the door and Sophie, who couldn't bear to look at it. The second knock, louder and more insistent than the first, echoed a clear threat: they were not to be ignored.

Lena took a step towards the door.

"No," Sophie pleaded in a tearful whisper, trying to take her hand pitifully. But Lena didn't take it. Deep down, she knew why Sophie was so scared, but she didn't want to admit it. Not until she saw who was there.

Another knock, this one deafening, seemed to shake the very foundations of the room.

Lena's heart raced as she peered through the spyhole, her breath caught in her throat. The sight that met her eyes was menace incarnate—five figures, faces obscured by balaclavas, rifles in hand in a grotesque display of power. There was also a voice. A voice that came through the speaker attached to the uniform of the central figure. It was the voice of the men who killed her father.

"It's finally nice to meet you, Lena," Jonas Blackwater said through the speaker. "May we come in?"

CHAPTER TWENTY-THREE

Jonas gave her two choices.
"You can either open the door and invite us inside," he said. "Or we can break it down. I'll give you a minute just to be nice."

"Get into the bedroom," Lena commanded Sophie, backing away from the door.

Her flatmate stood there helplessly.

"I-I can help."

"I think you've done enough already!" Lena spat, not looking at her. "Do as I say!"

Without another moment of thought, the door broke off its seal. Lena jumped back. The first of the Blackwater soldiers stepped inside. Knowing how crucial the next steps were, she reached forward as if she was going to kiss the soldier and grabbed tightly onto his temple. A surge of memories drained into her—The soldier's life unfolded before Lena's eyes in a rapid montage: gruelling training sessions that forged him into a weapon, the harrowing brutality of combat in the Iraq War, filled with devastating scenes of conflict and loss. His subsequent discharge from the military was a disorienting return to a world he no longer felt part of, leaving him adrift until Jonas found him, offering purpose and belonging within the ranks of the Blackwater Family.

She let go, leaving his memories and arriving back in the room. The soldier dropped forward into her arms, exhausted by the process, and she took his rifle into her hands and pointed it at the rest of the soldiers.

"I think you're all aware that I now know how to use this, right?"

she said, pointing the gun back and forth to the remaining four assailants as they tried to circle the room.

"Ugh … what did I tell you all?" groaned Jonas over a small speaker with the tone of a child being asked to get up for school. "Don't get close to the girl who can access your memories! I apologise profusely, Miss Drake. You truly deserve a better adversary for your final stand."

"You're Jonas, right?" Lena asked, backing towards the bedroom door. "Dad always called you the mouthy one."

"I wouldn't take that man's words to heart, you know? He died like he lived. A liar. Think of how much suffering could've been avoided if he had just told you the truth. This situation with your mother could have been avoided."

"You don't get to talk about her," Lena said in a hushed, fierce voice. "She has no involvement in any of this. Neither does my brother."

"Correction. Your brother didn't have any involvement. But it still didn't stop him putting things together."

"Are you going to let him go?" she asked.

"What makes you think that we have him?" her cousin asked back. She could sense that he was smiling. "Of course, if you come with us, you will be able to find the answer to that question yourself."

"You think I'm stupid? Going with you? Sacrificing myself for the next cycle?"

All could hear him gasp over the speakers, and Jonas went quiet for a long minute. Something about what she had said had shocked him. Lena knew the last word of the sentence would provide this reaction.

"He told you everything?" Jonas asked, taking an extra space between each word. "About what you are?"

"Yeah, he did," Lena answered with gritted teeth. "So, if you think I'm just going to put this gun down and come with you, think again."

The room went eerily quiet. Someone had to make the next move, but right now, no one was prepared to take the risk.

"What happens next, Jonas? Are we going to wait and see whose arms get tired first?"

"I have an idea," Jonas said through the speaker. "Sophie. Come here."

And just as he requested, like a zombie, Lena's flatmate opened the door and returned to the room. They exchanged a sheepish glance.

"So, this is how you found me then?" Lena asked pedantically, snapping her head back and forth between her friend and the soldiers. "Now I'm starting to regret having never looked into that brain of yours. If I'm honest though, I probably don't want to see what else is in there!"

"I *never* told them anything," Sophie said, gazing around her apartment as if she was taking everything in. "I had my suspicions about you. I thought you might have been what they were looking for, but it's only a few days ago that I found out the truth."

"And that's why you disappeared to the room so you could call them—"

"No, I didn't."

"So you could tell them where I was—"

"That's not true—"

"DON'T LIE TO ME!" Lena screamed at the top of her voice, blackened in rage. Sophie jumped in disbelief as if she'd seen a ghost. The way she said it. The tone. The anger. It was like Ian was right there in the room with them. Lena regained herself and spoke again, the volume wasn't there anymore but the venom remained. "You were right. My dad did teach me to become no one. But he also told me to not trust anyone. I should have listened to him and remained off the grid. I should've stopped caring."

"Oh. Grow up," Jonas intervened. "Are you going to blame her for the bad weather as well? She hasn't been the one erasing memories and putting people in hospital left, right, and centre. We knew your powers were out of control once we saw the state you left your best friend in. Practically a vegetable now, if you're wondering. It was only a matter of time before you stumbled into someone else's life and completely messed it up. We just had to play the waiting game. When you went and put her boyfriend in hospital, it wasn't that difficult to put two and two together. All I did was ring that dear flatmate of yours to let her know that we were on our way. If we were ranking everyone in this room, including myself, with blood on their hands, she would be at the very bottom."

Lena's mind clouded with the thoughts of her best friend. Has she really done that? Was her friend now as good as dead? Jonas must be lying. He must be. She had to pull herself together. There must be a way out. There must be.

"Were you ever going to tell them about me?" Lena asked Sophie, less angrily. "Why didn't you?"

Sophie paused, tears in her eyes, and repeated what she had said to her:

"We take care of each other. That's the deal, remember?"

Lena couldn't bring herself to smile back. Her head was a mess. It was like she could barely hear the room, the sound of gunfire and bombs from a war long gone overwhelmed any other sense.

"What's going to happen to her?" Lena asked. "Is this the part where you negotiate my surrender to let her go"

Jonas laughed through the speaker and just like that, one of the soldiers moved their gun towards Sophie.

"What are you doing?" Lena asked, finally turned all the way around to face her friend, uncertain if it would be the last time.

"This was never going to be a negotiation, Collector," Jonas said. "Sophie over there needs to answer for not telling us about you sooner. We gave her everything and she gave us nothing in return. The only person who needs to leave this room alive is you."

Lena took a minute and thought of what to do next. She locked eyes with Sophie and smiled. It was as if the last night had never happened. All was normal.

"We take care of each other. That's the deal, right?"

Sophie nodded and smiled back, accepting that this was their final conversation.

"Yep," she answered. "Always."

Lena's smile dropped. Her eyes closed and she took a deep breath …

"Okay."

... she quickly removed the silencer, tucked the end of the rifle underneath her chin, and went to pull the trigger.

CHAPTER TWENTY-FOUR

It was chaos. Lena's desperate gambit worked. The mere sight of her holding a gun to her own head triggered a wave of panic among the soldiers. Their trained composure shattered into frantic pleas, their voices melding into a chorus of urgency, begging her to lower the weapon. But Lena, leveraging their distraction, angled the gun away at the last second, discharging a bullet into the flat's ceiling. The sound, deafening in the enclosed space, bought her precious seconds.

As confusion reigned, Lena retreated towards the bedroom. It was then, in a twist she hadn't anticipated, that Sophie stepped forward. She drew a concealed gun from her denim jacket. That same gun Jonas had given her for her birthday. The bullet found its mark across the room as one of the soldiers fell. With a last push of adrenaline and her back facing the enemy, she shoved Lena into her bedroom and slammed the door shut. Then came the sound of gunfire and the thud of Sophie's dead body dropping just behind the door.

Lena's heart pounded as she forced herself up from the ground. She immediately grabbed Sophie's bookshelf to the right and knocked it over in front of the door.

She's dead

She flung the window open, the hot midday sun assaulting her senses, making her squint as she scanned her escape route. She locked eyes with the drainpipe to her right. It was a long way down but also the only way to escape.

She's dead

She looked around Sophie's room. One last time.
She's dead, Lena. You killed her, she thought to herself.

The stark reality that Sophie was gone sliced through her, but there was no time to dwell, no time for tears.

Behind her, the sound of the soldiers hammering at the door had grown frantic, a countdown to breach. With a deep breath, Lena had slung the rifle over her shoulder and clambered out the window. She gripped the drainpipe tightly, beginning her descent.

She looked up and down frantically. She was waiting to see the soldiers peer out of Sophie's bedroom window. The voice came again:
You killed her
"FUCK!"

Her hands, slick with sweat and shaking from exertion, lost their hold. She plummeted, the ground rushing up to meet her. The impact when she hit the ground was a brutal embrace, knocking the wind out of her, pain radiating through every nerve.

Ignoring the pain and the dizziness, Lena forced herself to stand. The park across from her flat, usually a place of laughter and play, now offered a fleeting sanctuary. She stumbled towards it.

Collapsing onto the park bench opposite a set of swings, Lena began to cry. Sophie's scream and the sound of her body dropping drowned her thoughts. She sobbed through drawn breaths, unable to move any further, prepared for the soldiers to show up and take her.

"You should've pulled the trigger," she whispered to herself. "You should've pulled the trigger."

Lost in her turmoil, she barely noticed a child beside her until a small voice pierced her reverie.

"Are you okay?" the child had asked, innocence woven into every syllable.

The girl, clad in a bright blue coat, extended a carton of Ribena towards Lena, a gesture of childlike kindness.

Lena had managed a faint smile, declining the offer. "No, thank you," she murmured, her voice a whisper of its former self.

Suddenly, the moment of calm was shattered by a booming voice.

"Ruby! Get away from her now!"

A man in a green jumper stormed towards them. The father's face was a mask of warning as he grabbed Ruby, yanking her away from the space next to Lena.

She stuttered out an apology.

"I'm so sorry."

But the damage was done. She watched the father and girl storm to a dark blue car on the other edge of the park.

Left alone again, Lena caught her reflection in the park slide's polished surface. A skinhead with bulging manic eyes, half-dressed in pyjamas, carrying a gun on a bright summer's day. She sniggered at the sight. There she was. A harbinger of violence. She really was a Blackwater after all.

*

As the sun dipped below the horizon, casting the world in hues of fading gold and deepening shadow, time marched on indifferently. Lena, having sought a momentary escape in the dubious shelter behind a bin, awoke to the harsh reality of her situation. The stench assaulted her senses, a cruel reminder of her desperation, but she stifled the gag reflex and forced herself to focus. Clarity came with the realization that she must keep moving, her survival hanging in the balance.

The NCP car park, looming a few streets away, became her immediate goal—a temporary haven where she could regroup and plan her next move. Tomorrow she would return to the flat. Two scenarios played out in her mind. One where she would return to an empty flat and could collect her belongings before starting all over again. Or the other where she would return to face the soldiers in a final stand. She secretly wished for the latter. She wanted it to be over.

Navigating the evening streets, Lena was struck by their emptiness. The occasional drifts of drunks and the weary souls returning from work, their faces etched with the day's toll, mirrored her own exhaustion. They seemed just as zombified, moving through the urban sprawl in a shared daze of resignation. Remarkably, her visible armament, the gun slung over her shoulder, garnered no attention in the twilight. The city, it seemed, was too absorbed in its own survival to question hers.

Finally reaching the car park, Lena's footsteps echoed in the cavernous space as she ascended to level five, each level amplifying her isolation. The concrete structure offered cold comfort, a maze of shadows and dimly lit corners where she could conceal herself until dawn.

Settling into a concealed spot, her senses remained on high alert, the weight of the gun a constant reminder of the line she'd walked. Then, a sound shattered the silence—the distant rumble of footsteps.

Lena crouched low behind a sleek black sedan, the cold metal against her palms grounding her momentarily. She heard the heavy footfalls and saw suddenly a new set of soldiers moving at the end of the level, their voices a low murmur as they coordinated their search. Every so often, a flashlight beam would sweep across the lot, forcing Lena to shuffle from one car's shadow to another's. Each time the light came near, her heart would race, and her breathing would catch. The game of cat and mouse intensified with every passing second. Yet, amid the chaos, Lena's mind raced with potential escape routes and strategies. She needed a diversion, and she needed it fast.

The muted echoes of footsteps reverberated throughout the dimly lit car park, heightening Lena's sense of urgency. She darted between the rows of vehicles, her silhouette occasionally illuminated by the sparse overhead lights. Every shadow threatened to betray her, every rustling sound suggesting pursuit.

A burst of radio chatter sounded alarmingly close, causing Lena to duck behind a sleek sedan. She watched in tense anticipation as a flashlight beam panned across, briefly glinting off her red dress. She held her breath, praying the slight shimmer went unnoticed. The guards' murmurs came closer.

Lena eyed an exit sign, mapping out her next move. As the guards' attention shifted momentarily, she sprinted, weaving through the vehicles with newfound determination. The close call was a reminder that in this game of cat and mouse, any misstep could be her last.

Shadows lengthened in the car park, interspersed with sporadic bursts of light. Lena cautiously inched towards the far end, scanning for any sign of the guards. Their muttered frustrations painted a clear picture of their dwindling patience.

Taking a calculated risk, Lena emerged from her cover, feeling the cool concrete underfoot as she ventured towards the centre of the dim expanse.

A familiar voice sliced through the stillness, arresting her in her tracks.

"I've been looking for you."

She braced herself to confront another threat, but recognition dawned before she could complete her turn. Instead, she turned slowly, deliberately.

It was the last person she expected to see.

"Reuben?"

CHAPTER TWENTY-FIVE

The dim illumination of the car park played tricks on Lena's eyes, but as she fully registered the figure before her, raw emotion washed over her. It was as if she had been transported back to that darkened cinema, seated with her family, holding their hands, and saying goodbye.

"Reuben?" The name felt foreign on her lips, like a forgotten tune. Eighteen months might have seemed insignificant on paper, but facing him now, Lena saw the chasm of time etched onto her brother's features.

His hair, once a tousled blonde mop, was now cropped short. The playful twinkle that once danced in his hazel eyes had dulled, replaced with a steely determination that spoke of trials endured and battles fought. The soft boyishness of his face was now replaced with chiselled angles and a ruggedness that told tales of hardships and late-night missions. But beneath these stark transformations, the curve of his jaw, the familiar freckle on his cheek, and the essence of her brother remained, whispering to Lena that this was indeed her Reuben.

Their eyes locked, and Lena could see in his eyes the weight of countless stories yet to be shared. But for now, in this dim car park, the years of separation melted away. The world narrowed to just the two of them.

"We need to leave, now!" Lena finally urged, her voice firm with a hint of desperation. "I promise, I'll explain everything once we're safe." As she brushed past him, she instinctively reached for Reuben's hand, seeking that familiar reassurance. But he pulled away.

Lena's brow furrowed, concern evident in her eyes. "Reuben, what's going on?" she pressed.

He stood still, a stark contrast to the urgency of moments ago. The way Reuben turned, so methodical and detached, was unnerving. It was as if he was under some external influence, his movements precise and almost mechanical.

"You talk as if we know each other," Reuben remarked, his voice carrying an unfamiliar coldness, an iciness that Lena had never heard before. It was deeper, more detached, devoid of the warmth she remembered.

His finger jabbed towards his temple, his face contorting with a mixture of anger and pain. "You talk as if you never looked inside," he spat, his eyes blazing with accusation. "As if you didn't slice it open, digging around, taking pieces away." The vehemence in his tone was palpable, every word dripping with bitterness.

"I'm sorry." Lena hesitated, her mind racing with the choice to flee or to clarify. "I did it to shield you and Mum from—"

She made a move towards him, only for him to retreat a step, widening the gap between them. "Listen, we need to leave now! The people who killed Dad. They're after us. We need to move! We need to move!"

She pivoted, ready to make her escape. But his voice, cold and chilling, halted her.

"Lena. Who do you think I came here with?"

Lena's heart raced, refusing to acknowledge the truth staring her in the face. A wave of desperation washed over her. "You're lying," she protested, her voice quivering. Her memories of their shared past—of laughter, secrets, and sibling camaraderie—clashed violently with the figure that now stood before her.

He remained unflinching, the coldness in his eyes intensifying. Every ounce of affection she remembered seemed to have evaporated, replaced by a deep-rooted disdain.

A sob caught in her throat, her voice barely above a whisper as haunting memories resurfaced. "They … they killed our father. How could you?"

His expression was impassive, chilling her further. "Maybe he'd still be here if you weren't around," he said coolly. "Maybe if he were alive now, he'd be standing right here beside me."

Lena blinked back tears, her strength wavering.

"Don't cry for me, sister." Reuben laughed coldly. "I don't even know who you are."

Desperation laced her voice. "What did they do to you?"

"They told me the truth."

Lena's eyes widened.

"Yeah, that's right," he snapped back. "The Collector. The Blackwater Family. The cycles. Yeah. They told me *everything*."

"And you still side with them?" she choked out, disbelief evident.

As she moved closer, Reuben swiftly drew a gun. Lena's laughter was tinged with hysteria. "This is ridiculous. They need me alive."

Reuben's voice was chillingly calm. "I know." And he fired. The shot pierced Lena's shoulder, sending her to the ground in agony.

He aimed the gun once more, preparing to shoot again. But the distant echo of a door and approaching footsteps interrupted him. "Found her!" Reuben called out.

In that crucial moment, despite the searing pain in her shoulder, Lena reached up and grabbed his leg. Reuben watched as Jonas and the guards charged forward towards them. He looked down at Lena and watched her hand slip away. For a fleeting moment, a world of understanding and shared secrets passing silently between them. Gone were Lena's tears, replaced by a dawning realisation.

Reuben's astonishment was palpable, his voice barely audible amidst the escalating chaos. "You saw it. Didn't you?" he whispered desperately, urgency threading his words.

Behind him, the shadows of the advancing guards loomed closer, their intent clear. But for that fraction of a second, they existed in a bubble, isolated from the external threats.

Lena nodded, her voice firm. "Yes."

And then, with the ferocity of a storm, the guards descended upon her.

ACT THREE

CHAPTER TWENTY-SIX

October 30th, 1872

"Eddie! Eddie, wake up!"

In the claustrophobic confines of a decrepit cellar, thirteen-year-old Jason's voice cut through the silence, desperate and urgent. The air was thick with the musty scent of decay, and the cold, unyielding chains around their wrists seemed to echo the hopelessness of their predicament. The dim light filtering through a small, dirt-caked window barely illuminated their surroundings, casting long, menacing shadows.

Eight-year-old Eddie, his face streaked with dirt and tears, slowly opened his eyes, blinking in confusion. His once-white shirt, now soiled and stained with blood, clung to his small frame.

"J-Jason? Is that you?" he whispered, his voice tremulous with fear.

"Yes, it's me. We must be quiet and think. We need to get out of here," Jason replied, his eyes darting around the room, searching for any sign of escape.

The memory of their abduction was still vivid in Jason's mind, a haunting replay that refused to fade. The summer circus had arrived in town, a whirlwind of colour and excitement that promised a brief escape from the monotony of their daily lives. Initially, the allure of the circus was overshadowed by their secret plan to sip apple cider from the old flask hidden in Eddie's wooden toy chest. But eventually, the vibrant spectacle drew them in.

Their adventure turned sinister when Eddie disappeared in the bustling crowd. Jason's heart pounded as he searched frantically.

"Ed! Where are you?!" he called out, panic rising in his voice.

A man with a gaunt, pallid face and an unsettling aura approached him. His thin lips curled into a sly, knowing smile.

"Looking for your cousin, young man?"

"Yes, have you seen him? He's about this tall, brown hair, wearing a white shirt," Jason replied, his voice laced with urgency.

The man's eyes gleamed with a predatory glint as he subtly gestured behind him. Jason's eyes followed, and his heart plummeted. In the shadowy space near a set of bins, he saw Eddie. His cousin's small form was gripped tightly by a tall, sinister-looking man in a suit. The man's smile was chilling, his eyes cold and devoid of empathy, as he held Eddie close, whispering something into his ear. Panic surged through Jason, but before he could scream or run, a cloth was pressed against his face, and the world slipped away into darkness.

Now, in the eerie cellar, Jason's mind raced as he heard the distant sound of footsteps and coarse laughter above them. The prospect of their captors' return sent a shiver down his spine.

"We need to act when they come in. Be ready," Jason whispered to Eddie, his voice barely audible over the thumping of his own heart.

Eddie nodded; his eyes wide with fear but filled with a determination born from Jason's resolve.

As the cellar door creaked open, the two figures cast long, ominous shadows across the room. Their laughter was harsh, echoing off the stone walls. Jason tensed, ready to seize any opportunity. The chains around his wrists felt heavier, each second stretching into an eternity.

As the captors approached, their faces twisted in cruel amusement, Jason knew this was their only chance. With a burst of adrenaline-fueled courage, he lunged at the nearest captor as the chains loosened.

"RUN, EDDIE! NOW!"

Eddie sprinted towards the door, his small feet pounding against the cold floor. He glanced back just in time to see Jason grappling with their captors, his cousin's face set in a mask of fierce determination.

Bursting through the door, Eddie found himself in a grand, yet chillingly silent hallway. The Victorian elegance of the house contrasted starkly with the terror gripping his heart. He stumbled up the ornate staircase, each step echoing ominously.

Reaching the top, Eddie tripped, falling onto the hard floor. Pain shot through his body, but fear propelled him forward. He looked up to see a woman in a flowing blue silk dress, her long blonde hair framing a face that shifted from concern to utter horror.

"Please, help—" Eddie's plea was cut short as the woman's scream pierced the air, a sound that chilled him to the bone.

Eddie turned frantically, only to see the man in green, his earlier captor, looming over him. The corridors stretched out endlessly, a labyrinth with no escape. The last sensation Eddie felt was a crushing blow to his head, a final darkness enveloping him, a silence that would last forever.

The man in denim emerged from the upstairs room, peering down at his brother and the motionless boy on the floor. "Jesus Christ, you better not have hurt him! He's my pick, you know?"

The man in green, Eli, grunted in response.

"Maya! Will you cut it out?" he yelled, aggravated by the continued screaming.

The screaming ceased, replaced by a more playful laughter. "Sorry, Arthur," Maya replied as she sauntered into the hallway. "Just wanted to freak them out, that's all."

Her eyes settled on Jason's lifeless form. "He's cute, isn't he?" She looked up at the man in denim, Arthur, and winked. "It's going to be strange, staring at that face for the next few years."

Maya then turned to Eli, who was lifting Jason's body. "What do you think?"

Eli's eyes remained fixated on the boy in his arms. "What do I think? I think it's time to celebrate."

CHAPTER TWENTY-SEVEN

The walls closed in on Reuben, the plush cream carpet beneath his feet offering little comfort. To an outsider, the room might have appeared lavish—a modern-day palace tucked away in an upscale hotel. The king-sized bed draped in silken sheets, the muted gold accents catching the soft light, and a panoramic window offering a picturesque view of the city skyline. Yet, to Reuben, it was nothing more than a gilded cage. How long had he been here? He was sure it had only been a week since the car accident but there was no way to know for sure.

On the wooden coffee table, a collection of books lay scattered, their spines bent and pages torn. Titles of philosophy, art, and fiction lay mixed with magazines of the latest trends, now discarded in a fit of rage. The flat-screen TV, which once hung pristinely on the wall, now lay cracked on the ground, a testament to Reuben's desperation.

The velvet sofa, with its plump cushions that once promised relaxation, was overturned. Its accompanying mahogany end table lay beside it, a shattered vase and its wilted contents sprawled across the floor.

Reuben's frenzied reflection stared back at him from the large ornate mirror opposite the bed—his eyes red and swollen, his hair unkempt. His hoarse voice filled the air as he screamed, pounded on the locked door, and begged for his freedom. No matter how refined the room's trappings were, they couldn't mask its true purpose. It was a prison, and Reuben was its unwilling captive.

The word *fuck* pulsed in his mind like a relentless drumbeat, each repetition bringing with it a torrent of panic and regret. Images of Alice and his mother swirled incessantly. He imagined their faces, etched with concern, perhaps searching every corner, every shadow, hoping to find a trace of him. The image of his mother, drugged and defenceless on the cold floor, made his chest tighten with a mix of fury and guilt.

Bitter self-reproach consumed him. How could he have been so naive? Elaine Walker, with her reassuring smile and seemingly kind intentions, had fooled him. The very woman who had presented herself as a beacon of support during his darkest hour, the aftermath of losing his father, was the puppet master behind his current plight. The realisation stung sharply, a cruel twist in an already nightmarish reality.

As Reuben mustered up another bout of strength to pound on the door, it swung open, revealing Jonas. With his emerald shirt half-unbuttoned and neatly tailored brown trousers, Jonas exuded an air of casual menace. Reuben instinctively retreated a few steps as Jonas confidently strolled in.

"Calmed down now? You ready to talk?" Jonas inquired with a tone dripping in condescension.

Spying an opportunity, Reuben lunged towards the open door. However, Jonas was quicker. With fluid precision, he swept a leg behind Reuben's knees while simultaneously applying pressure to the youth's upper body, sending the boy crashing to the ground, his aspirations of escape halted in one swift motion.

Jonas rose gracefully, securing the door with an audible click. Reuben, still sprawled on the floor, wheezed as he tried to regain his composure. Meanwhile, Jonas meandered through the room, a smirk playing on his lips as he surveyed the destruction caused by Reuben's outburst.

He bent down, retrieving a damaged copy of a book from amidst the debris. Holding it up for Reuben to see, he waggled it playfully.

"You realise this was a first edition?" Jonas asked, feigning disappointment. His eyes twinkled mischievously.

Laying on his side like a baby, tears flowing from his eyes, Reuben's voice quavered, "I've told you everything I know. Why won't you let me go?"

The past days—was it five? In this place, time took on a twisted form—had seen Reuben blindfolded and hauled into an austere room where he was grilled relentlessly. The questioning came from an amorphous group of men, their voices often dripping with disdain and mockery, prodding not just for answers but seeking to degrade his spirit.

His father's stories, the mysterious cassette tape, the heartrending encounter with his mother, Maya's betrayal, the car crash—every memory, every truth was laid bare. To some, his candour might seem treacherous, a betrayal of those he loved. But Reuben was just a boy lost in a labyrinth of chaos and danger, yearning for the familiarity and comfort of home. Every answer he gave, every detail he spilled, was a desperate plea to end the nightmare and return to the life he once knew.

"TELL ME!" The plea erupted from Reuben's chest, filled with a blend of anger and desperation.

Jonas leaned in closer, and for a moment, Reuben tensed, anticipating a blow. But instead, Jonas's hand gently grazed Reuben's cheek. "Because we're family," Jonas murmured, his voice dripping with a tenderness that felt incongruous to the setting. "We take care of each other. That's the deal."

Reuben's eyes, still filled with mistrust, sought Jonas's. "Why do you keep saying we're family? What does that even mean?"

Pulling away, Jonas straightened up, his playful demeanour momentarily masked by a cryptic glint in his eyes. "Why don't you come and find out?" He extended a hand invitingly.

Reuben hesitated, emotions warring inside him. After what felt like an eternity, he placed his hand into Jonas's. He was immediately hoisted to his feet with surprising ease, a testament to Jonas's deceptive strength, which belied his flamboyant demeanour.

Jonas shot him a proud, almost patronising smile—the kind one would give a well-behaved child. "Atta boy!" he chimed, turning towards the door.

"When I open this door, can I trust you not to pull another reckless stunt?" His voice carried a hint of amusement.

Reuben, catching a glimpse of himself in a room's tarnished mirror, noted his ragged appearance—clothes crumpled, hair unkempt, and the distinct griminess of days without a proper shower.

"Don't worry," Jonas reassured him, "we'll get you cleaned up and in some fresh clothes."

As the door creaked open, it revealed a dim, elongated corridor, its expanse lit eerily by wall-mounted torches. The flames cast dancing shadows upon the damp stone walls, and the air was thick with a cold, earthy musk. As they walked, the soft echo of their footsteps was interrupted periodically by other sounds—ones that made Reuben's heart race. From behind heavy wooden doors emblazoned with numbers, came muffled cries, desperate pleas, and the unmistakable sound of anguish.

"Who are they?"

Jonas, seemingly unaffected by the chorus of despair surrounding them, replied cryptically, "All your answers lie just around the bend, kid. Just hold on a bit longer."

He paused for a moment, staring at the door he'd emerged from. Unlike the others, it bore the Roman numeral VI.

The narrow stairwell they ascended seemed to stretch interminably, each step echoing with a hollow resonance. Finally, they reached the top, and Jonas pushed open a heavy wooden door. The sudden burst of opulence that greeted Reuben's eyes was overwhelming.

The room was vast, with high vaulted ceilings supported by ornate stone pillars that rose to meet intricate gilded archways. A massive chandelier, festooned with countless gleaming crystals, hung in the centre, casting a shimmering light that danced across the room. The walls were adorned with vast, sweeping tapestries and paintings, each one a detailed masterpiece depicting scenes of mythic battles, grand banquets, and landscapes that seemed otherworldly in their beauty. Gold and deep blues dominated the colour palette, lending the room an air of regal sophistication.

The floor was made of polished marble, with intricate mosaics creating patterns of swirling designs. Each step Reuben took echoed in the vastness of the hall, magnifying his sense of smallness in this vast space. There were marble statues at intervals, some familiar and others foreign, their expressions frozen in time, watching over the hall with a silent vigil.

To one side, a grand staircase with velvet-lined bannisters spiralled upwards, leading to unseen floors above. By its foot, an indoor fountain bubbled serenely, surrounded by lush green plants and colourful flowers, providing a soft background murmur that was oddly comforting.

Reuben's eyes returned to the scrawling paintings that dominated the walls. They seemed to tell a story, but not one he could immediately decipher. Men and women in ancient garb, creatures of lore, and symbols that seemed both arcane and significant were depicted with meticulous detail. For a moment, he forgot the circumstances that brought him there, lost in the beauty and grandeur of it all. Beside him, Jonas watched with a smirk, seemingly enjoying the young man's reaction to the splendour around him.

Jonas steered Reuben into a small chamber that contained nothing more than two chairs and a gleaming marble table with a conspicuous red phone at its centre. As they settled in, an old man in a crisp suit came in, silently setting down a tray filled with hot beverages and an array of treats. As he left, Jonas helped himself to a pastry while Reuben continued to watch him depart.

"What's his deal? How much are you paying him to keep quiet?" Reuben asked, trying to keep his voice even.

Jonas laughed lightly. "He's not on payroll, Reuben. He's family. Been with us for years. He just … well let's just say he leads a quieter existence than ours."

Reuben rubbed his temples, exasperated. "Could you, for once, stop with the mysteries?"

Grinning, Jonas pointed at the red phone. "Things will become much clearer soon enough. I promise you."

Reuben looked down at the phone. "What's the deal with this?"

Jonas leaned back, locking eyes with Reuben. "I don't think we're going to get anywhere with the silent treatment. We need you to help us and we need to show you that you can trust us."

Reuben scoffed, "*You* need me?"

Jonas leaned back, swirling the liquid in his cup contemplatively. "You see, Reuben, power and wealth don't always equate to information or capability. Your sister, she's ... elusive. But you? You have a bond. A connection. Something inexplicable. It's not just about finding her physically. It's about reaching out to her emotionally, spiritually even."

"So, you kidnap me, keep me in a dungeon, then bring me to a posh suite and offer me tea? You have a twisted way of building trust."

Jonas chuckled. "Trust. A fickle thing, isn't it? But necessary. Believe me, if we wanted to harm you, you wouldn't be sipping on Darjeeling and nibbling on croissants."

Reuben's brow furrowed. "Couldn't you have just come into my house at any point over the last year to ask me if I knew anything about her? About Lena?"

Jonas's eyes locked with his and he looked at him as if he had grown an extra head.

"That's *exactly* what we did, Reuben," he answered. "Every conversation you have had with my sister, under the guise of DCI Walker, it was to find out if you or your mother knew anything. As far as we were concerned, you both were nothing more than victims of your father's secrets."

Reuben thought back to the many times he had spoken with her. All those conversations, all those times he shared his grief, were nothing more than a tick box exercise.

"It was only when you visited our sister's best friend, damaged by the very powers that your sister possessed, that we noticed you knew more than you led on. And it was only when you revealed the existence of your father's tape that we knew we had to act. If you're looking to blame anyone for the reason you are here, then you should be blaming Martin Drake."

The red phone on the table began to ring, interrupting their conversation. Jonas smiled knowingly. "Go for it."

Reuben eyed the phone suspiciously. "Who is it?"

Jonas leaned forward, pushing the phone towards Reuben. "Only one way to find out. Go on, answer it."

Reuben hesitated before answering.

"Hello?"

"Reuben? Is that you?"

For the first time in days, he felt warm.

"Alice?! Where are you? What's happening?"

There was a brief pause before she responded. "I'm okay, Reuben. I'm safe for now. But listen, your mother's alive."

His heart leapt. "Mum?! Where is she? Is she okay?"

"They're keeping her at your home. She's being watched."

His euphoria plummeted. "What do you mean *watched*?"

"You have to do what they tell you, Reuben," Alice whispered, and he could hear the anguish in her voice. "If you want to see us again, you will have to exactly as they say."

"Who are *they*?" he asked Alice but there was no point. He looked over to Jonas and saw him waving at him with a smile.

"Alice, I'm so sorry," he said, each word heavy with regret. "I never meant for you to get pulled into this. This is all my fault."

Alice sighed. "Reuben, I chose to help you okay. Remember? We're in this together."

"But it shouldn't be this way."

"Listen." Alice's voice was firm, yet gentle. "In a way, I'm still beside you. And we're going to get through this."

Reuben's resolve solidified, determination burning bright.

"Remember what I said …" But before she could finish, the line went dead.

Reuben slowly placed the phone back on its cradle, his mind racing with plans and vows, while Jonas watched him with an inscrutable expression.

Reuben's voice wavered slightly but the resolve was clear. "Is she telling the truth? That if I help you, they'll be safe?"

Jonas met his eyes evenly. "That's the arrangement. Your cooperation for their safety."

Reuben leaned in, eyebrows raised. "So why are you after Lena? What's this all really been about?"

Jonas paused, tapping his fingers on the table. "It's ... complicated. Part of a bigger picture."

Reuben threw up his hands in exasperation. "Great, more mysteries."

Sighing, Jonas stood up. "There's someone else you should meet before you make your decision."

Jonas's expression turned sombre as he said this. Clearly, this wasn't a meeting he relished.

"The man who killed your father."

CHAPTER TWENTY-EIGHT

As the door opened, Reuben was met with a staggering expanse of unspoiled landscape. An expansive sea of verdant green stretched endlessly in front of him, interrupted only by the sudden precipice of a cliff. Beyond that was a vast and unyielding expanse of water, its waves crashing relentlessly against the rugged cliffside. The salty tang of the sea filled the air, and the rhythmic sound of the waves seemed oddly soothing in the face of such uncertainty.

He had no idea where he was, and the vastness of the surroundings only magnified his feeling of isolation. The terrain seemed untouched, wild, and remote.

As they walked, his shoes crunched on the soft grass beneath. The open land felt infinite, and the horizon where the sea met the sky seemed to blur into one. All of it served as a stark reminder of how isolated he truly was.

As they continued their march towards the cliff's edge, Reuben couldn't resist stealing a glance back at where they had emerged from. A grand mansion stood there, seemingly rising out of the landscape. Its imposing stone facade was punctuated with tall, ornate windows that glinted in the sunlight. Ivy clung to its walls, and the mansion's spires reached for the sky, casting long shadows across the manicured lawns.

Despite its obvious beauty and grandeur, there was something foreboding about the edifice. It was a stark contrast to the natural beauty around it, a symbol of man's imposition on the wild. With its towering walls and secured entrance, it gave off an aura of being impenetrable.

The realisation made the weight on his chest heavier, reminding him of the vast distance between this unknown location and his home.

The juxtaposition between the serene, natural beauty of the surroundings and the looming, silent mansion was jarring. It felt as though the mansion was watching him, a silent sentinel in this remote location.

Ahead, near the very edge of the cliff, a solitary figure stood with his back to Reuben. He was dressed in a crisp white shirt that fluttered slightly in the sea breeze, paired with immaculate trousers. The man's posture was rigid, his attention fully consumed by the vast ocean in front of him. Beside him was a simple setup: a table and two chairs, looking almost out of place in such a natural setting.

The moment Reuben approached the chair, Jonas quickly turned on his heels and headed back to the mansion. Reuben's eyes narrowed, trying to piece together Jonas's sudden departure. Was he scared of this man?

The man, still looking out to the sea, spoke up. "Three days ago, when you first got here, I saw you from my bedroom window. Even from up there, you looked just like him. Just like your father."

He spoke slowly, each word carrying a heavy weight, as if every syllable held a lifetime of memories. The sombre seriousness of his tone made Reuben feel that humour had never touched this man's life.

"You were the man my father talked about on the tape," Reuben said softly. "You're Eli."

The author of his father's murder finally turned to face him.

As the sun highlighted the contours of his face, Reuben took in the details. Eli's face was lined with age, deep crevices carving out a history of hard choices and sleepless nights. His eyes, a pale shade of grey, were cold and unreadable, like a winter sea. But within them, there seemed to be a storm of emotions, all held back by a dam of restraint. The high cheekbones hinted at a once-chiselled jawline now softened by time. A rugged beard, streaked with silver, covered most of his lower face, and his lips were thin, always set in a tight line.

Reuben hesitated for a moment, then finally mustered the courage to ask.

"What happened to your arm?"

Eli followed Reuben's eyes to the stark burn marks peeking out from the sleeve of his crisp white shirt. "There was a fire here long ago," he began, a hint of bitterness creeping into his tone. "A farmhouse completely went up in flames. There were many people inside. Lots and lots of our family died that night. I had tried to save them. This was my punishment for doing so." He rubbed the scarred skin briefly, the action betraying a hint of vulnerability before his steely demeanour returned.

"So, you were the one who did it, right?" Reuben asked. "You killed my dad."

Eli's eyes settled back on the endless expanse of water. "I never intended harm to my own brother. Never," he said, the weight of genuine regret pressing down on each word. "If only he had told me where she was … he'd still be here with us. I genuinely regret that he's no longer in your life."

"Why is she so important to you?"

Eli motioned to the chair across from him. "Sit," he suggested gently.

With a hesitant sigh, Reuben settled into the chair, his sight drifting out towards the vast horizon. The sun, once brilliant, now hid behind gathering clouds, casting a subtle shadow over the scene.

"Do you believe that your sister possesses the ability to erase memories?" began Eli, choosing his words carefully.

Considering the recent bewildering events and the gaping holes in his own recollections, Reuben replied, "Given everything I've seen, or rather, not seen … and the lengths you're going to … I guess I can't really deny it."

Eli leaned forward slightly; his voice low. "What if I told you her abilities went far beyond what you know?"

Reuben shifted, looking directly into Eli's eyes, searching for clarity.

Eli continued, his voice almost a whisper, but its intensity palpable. "Our memories aren't just recollections. They're the very fabric of our consciousness. Every experience, every joy, every pain—it forms our identity. Each memory moulds and shapes our reactions, our decisions, our very character."

Eli paused, letting the weight of his words sink in before continuing. "Imagine, if every memory of Reuben Drake was stripped away, every joy, every heartbreak, every trivial moment—would I still be sitting across from Reuben Drake? Or just a shell that looks like him?"

Reuben shifted uncomfortably, feeling the implications of Eli's words deep within his core.

Eli leaned back, gazing again at the vast ocean. "If all the hurtful memories, like your father's death, were erased, would that truly give you peace? Or would it rob you of the very essence, the very experiences that made you resilient, compassionate, and unique?"

Reuben's breathing faltered as he wrestled with the enormity of Eli's words. "Are you trying to tell me that erasing memories isn't her true power?"

Eli, eyes intense, leaned closer. "She doesn't just erase. She can possess those memories, contain them, transfer them. Think about it, Reuben. If someone stripped away every memory, every experience that defines you, and handed them to another person ... would they not, in essence, become you?"

Reuben frowned, struggling to piece it all together. "So, you're saying ..."

Eli breathed a long sigh.

"Imagine a brilliant mind trapped in a body ravaged by age or disease. What if it could be freed? Transferred to a new, healthy vessel?" Eli's voice was filled with a fervour that unnerved Reuben. "Take my sister, for example. You knew her as Elaine Walker. I know here by her true name. Maya. Did she ever tell you during her time as an officer that she has terminal cancer?"

Reuben could feel his jaw slowly dropping. Her words from the house returned to the front of his mind.

I really wish we had time to discuss the ins and outs of who did what, but time isn't on my side.

He shook his head.

"No. No, she didn't," he replied simply. "Is that why you want to find Lena? Just to save her?"

Eli shook his head and looked at Reuben with a patronising glare. "To save us all," he replied.

Reuben didn't understand.

"Why go through all this effort?" he asked. "My father wouldn't have gone through all this just to stop you. There must be more."

Eli exhaled deeply.

"The procedure would be incredibly taxing on The Collector. Absorbing the memories of a single individual and transfer them is, to put it lightly, an ordeal. To undertake this for multiple people … it would be fatal."

Reuben acknowledged the gravity of Eli's words with a nod, though a sense of emotional detachment washed over him—like the numbing sensation he felt when he learned of his father's death.

Reuben's eyes widened. "And you know how? What, you've been running tests?"

Eli let out a laugh then, but it wasn't the warm, organic laughter of a person. It sounded mechanical, as if generated by an algorithm. A calculated series of notes that were almost grating in their inhumanity. Reuben shuddered at the sound.

"Your sister isn't the first person in our lineage to be graced with this gift. Roughly every seventy years, someone like her emerges …"

Eli slowly pivoted, and as Reuben looked into those eyes, it was like peering into an abyss of time. His gut dropped. They weren't just old; they were ancient, holding wisdom and weariness from multiple lifetimes. A chilling realisation washed over him: he wasn't looking at the eyes of one man but the collective experience of many.

"… And over centuries and centuries of time," Eli continued, his voice dripping with pride, "we have perfected this arrangement."

Reuben's throat tightened, and memories pierced him sharply. A conversation with Elaine—no, Maya, he corrected himself, resonated in his head.

Nothing was found until they came upon an apparent holiday home, seemingly deserted, belonging to a Mr. Richard Vaughan. They managed to get a warrant and broke in.

It couldn't be true.

Six men and women in their fifties and sixties, all deceased, and all wearing masks just like this one. And one child strapped to a cross.

Maya's voice came back once again.

They had disappeared in plain sight. Whatever happened to them, it was a tragedy.

The grim arithmetic was undeniable: Seven lifeless bodies. Six adults. One Collector. Six vanished children.

As the chilling realisation washed over him, he rose abruptly. A gust of wind caught the chair, sending it tumbling. In Eli's face, weathered by time and marked by experiences beyond comprehension, Reuben didn't just see the man who had taken his father from him. He saw the haunted visage of a child lost to time.

"You ... how many lifetimes?" Reuben's voice trembled. "How old are you, truly?"

"It's difficult to quantify. Ages meld into each other when you've spanned as many years as I have. I've watched the skies change, seen zeppelins draw awe from onlookers, and been the lone witness as cities crumbled under bombardments."

Standing tall, Eli's voice held a timbre of certainty. "The genesis of The Collector and our bloodline goes back a millennium. My duty, as I've come to understand it, is to ensure our family's eternal existence, to stand undaunted by death's shadow."

As Reuben staggered back, vertigo gripping him, fragments of memories surged. His father's enigmatic ways, the hints of a past layered in mysteries. The legacy that tied them all—Eli, his father, and himself—loomed heavy, binding them in an inescapable fate.

Reuben's legs gave way beneath him, dropping him to his knees as he gasped for air. Eli, ever impassive, rose and approached him, the weight of centuries behind his eyes.

"Listen closely, Reuben Drake," Eli began, his voice dripping with authority. "You will assist this family—your family—in locating your sister so we can commence our next rebirth. You will do what your father couldn't. If you do as I wish, I'll not only grant you a spot in our new cycle, but I will free your mother and your friend."

Reuben's vision blurred, but he managed to shoot Eli a venomous look. Eli responded by placing a heavy hand on Reuben's trembling shoulder.

"If you refuse to grant me what I'm rightfully owed, I will make you stand and watch as I burn them alive. Do we understand each other?"

The oppressive weight of Eli's hand, laden with the power of his intent, threatened to ground Reuben completely. He pitched forward, his forehead brushing the cool grass. The world around him dimmed.

"Your move." Eli's voice faded, leaving Reuben enveloped in darkness.

CHAPTER TWENTY-NINE

The air in the gallery room seemed colder, its silence echoing the weight of Reuben's recent confrontation with Eli. Illuminated under the muted light, the rows of artwork painted tales from different epochs. Yet, amid it all, there was one portrait that seemed out of place, that drew Reuben's fractured attention. A monochrome masterpiece, devoid of colour and contrasting the richly detailed surroundings, depicted a figure in a sleek black tuxedo.

He was lost in thought when Jonas entered the gallery. Taking in Reuben's dishevelled state and the new clothing that had been provided, Jonas remarked, "Seems they've gotten you into something more comfortable." But his jovial tone disappeared, replaced by genuine concern, upon seeing Reuben's trembling form and his intense fixation on the portrait. "You like that one?"

Jonas' eyes followed Reuben's as he scanned the painting.

"I painted these, you know," he murmured with a hint of melancholy and shyness. "Every single one of them."

The paintings, each imbued with an aura of timelessness, seemed as though they belonged behind velvet ropes in a grand museum.

"These works," Jonas continued, "represent our family's narrative, spanning countless generations. But this last one ... it embodies my deepest dread: everyone being gone and me being left behind."

Jonas fixed his sight on Reuben. "And if you fall short in your task, that reality may just come to pass."

Reuben let out a heavy sigh. "Well, no pressure then. So, you're telling me you're like, what, a hundred years old? A thousand?"

Jonas paused. "I'm not as old as Eli, but yes, I've been around multiple lifetimes. Enough time to build our wealth and our … protection."

Reuben's brows furrowed, a mix of confusion and anger. "And you're okay with this? Taking over someone's life? Erasing them? That's countless lives you've basically snuffed out!"

Jonas shook his head, and a wistful smile emerged, one that hinted at the weight of centuries. His demeanour suddenly reflected the age of an ancient soul trapped in a youthful form. "I remember when I truly was young, thinking just like you. Questioning the morality, the anguish we caused families. Imagining the pain of parents believing their children are gone forever. But with the passage of so much time, facing mortality again and again, those sentiments … they fade. The fear of death has a way of overshadowing those initial doubts."

Reuben looked to the monochrome portrait once more. "You sacrificed your humanity, became something monstrous … for what?" He pointed at the lonely figure in the painting. "You said this represents your fear of ending up alone. Haven't you realised? Maybe you already are." Without another word, Reuben turned on his heel, striding towards his room. Jonas, after a lingering, introspective glance at the painting, followed in his wake.

Reuben stormed into his room and Jonas was already there in front of the door he wanted to close. Facing Jonas, Reuben's voice was edged with accusation. "You're all monsters! You helped kill my father!"

The controlled composure that Jonas always maintained cracked. Swiftly, he cornered Reuben against the wall, holding him by the collar. His eyes, glistening with a rare vulnerability, met Reuben's fiercely. "I had a part in it, yes," he admitted with a choked voice. "But you must understand, it was never my choice. I loved your father. Every day, I wish I could go back and change what happened."

Reuben could only stare as the older man's grip on his collar slowly loosened. Jonas's breath heaved as he tried to control his own tumultuous feelings.

With one last pained look at Reuben, Jonas released him abruptly. Without a word, he turned on his heel, slamming the door behind him as he exited the room, leaving Reuben alone amid the heavy silence. The raw emotion in Jonas's confession made it clear that despite the countless lives he had lived, some regrets remained forever fresh.

*

As Jonas strode towards his room, he shot a firm glance at the guards. "Make sure he stays put," he ordered, his voice heavy with authority. With that, he pushed open the door to his chamber and, after a sharp slam, retreated to its shadowy corner, his gaze drifting over a section of paintings.

His chamber was nothing short of palatial. High, ornate ceilings crowned the room, with intricate gold leaf designs that glimmered in the muted light. Walls were adorned in rich, burgundy wallpaper with embedded gold patterns, giving the room a regal aura. Every corner spoke of history and opulence. Tall, expansive windows draped with luxurious crimson velvet curtains allowed the golden hue of the setting sun to seep through.

The room's centrepiece was a grand canopy bed with dark mahogany posts and royal blue silken drapes. Flanking it, an intricately carved nightstand bore an ancient oil lamp, its gentle flame casting eerie dances of light and shadow.

But what captured one's attention the most were the paintings. They seemed to span eras, some with figures in historical garb, others more abstract and modern. They depicted celebrations, sorrows, and moments that seemed to be frozen in time—likely a timeline of Jonas's long existence. It was in the presence of these silent witnesses that Jonas seemed to lose himself, reflecting on memories both cherished and haunting.

Jonas gradually moved towards one of the paintings, his fingertips nearly grazing the canvas. The piece in front of him was a vivid portrayal of a young man, his eyes filled with a mixture of hope and apprehension, cradling a baby boy beside a blonde woman. They stood in front of a stately eighteenth-century home, its architectural details meticulously rendered, complete with high windows, intricate cornices, and a looming presence that seemed to beckon the viewer inside. The young man and the woman were his mother and her brother, Arthur; the baby in the young man's arms, was Jonas himself.

As he stood there, his thoughts meandered back to that pivotal moment—the last time he had seen Arthur.

*

Jonas pushed open the heavy wooden door of the pub and was immediately hit with a cacophony of noise and the warmth of too many bodies in too small a space. Red, green, and white flags adorned every available surface, and the air was thick with the aroma of spilled beer and the sharp tang of fried food. It was a match day, and from the looks of it, every Welsh supporter in the vicinity had decided this was the place to be.

Rows of worn wooden tables were packed with raucous fans, their faces painted in the national colours. Groups huddled together, deep in animated conversation, while others stood, pint in hand, singing out classic Welsh anthems in hearty unison. Laughter echoed throughout the space, punctuated every so often by a cheer or a jeer as a game played out on the numerous screens around the pub.

Into this sea of passionate fandom, Jonas's entrance was like dropping a stone in a calm pond, causing ripples of tension to spread outwards. His tailored suit, a stark contrast to the sea of jerseys and casual wear, made him stick out like a sore thumb. Whispers began almost instantly, eyes darting from the unfamiliar figure to friends, seeking validation for their surprise.

"Who's the posh lad then?" one burly man with a bushy beard muttered to his mate, not bothering to lower his voice.

"Must've taken a wrong turn on his way to the theatre," another sneered, chuckling with his friends.

Jonas tried to keep his head high, ignoring the stares and the not-so-subtle comments. He approached the bar, the worn-out wood standing as a testament to the many years and countless elbows that had leaned on it.

"Vodka and orange juice, please," he requested, voice steady despite the clear feeling of being out of place.

In the pub, a stronghold of fervent Welsh rugby fans, Jonas felt the weight of numerous eyes on his back. Each individual seemed to dissect him, questioning his choice of drink, his clothes, his very presence in their domain. But Jonas, undeterred, exuded an air of confidence, even as the most out-of-place individual there.

"Oh. Where you from then?" a voice inquired from behind.

Jonas pivoted to face the speaker, a smirk curling his lips. The man behind him was a stereotypical local—grey-haired, with a pot belly, clad in a Welsh rugby top. He stood with his arms folded, a snarl etched on his face. "Does it matter?" Jonas retorted with a hint of defiance.

"Depends on your answer," the man, Jeff, shot back. "I've been coming to this pub for ten years. We don't like city folk bringing their ways here."

Jonas downed half his drink in one go and took a step forward, his grin broadening. "Look at you," he said loudly, ensuring the entire bar could hear. "You think your xenophobic rhetoric is original? Wearing that shirt, do you think you're part of the team? You're probably the type who fantasizes about being a hero in a war but is too scared for a game of paintball."

The local's lips quivered as a hush fell over the bar patrons. Jonas leaned in closer, his tone dripping with scorn. "You're all the same. Just man tits and a mouth of bollocks. It's not me bringing the place down. After all, it's just me. And there is so, so many of you."

As the situation teetered on the edge of violence, a calming voice interjected. "Jonas. Enough."

Jonas's eyes immediately found Arthur, a commanding presence despite the years that had passed. The shock on Jonas' face wasn't just from seeing Arthur again, but from the familial tone in his voice.

Arthur turned to the local, his expression apologetic. "Sorry about him, Jeff," he said, pulling Jonas back. "My nephew gets a bit overzealous after a few drinks. He means no harm."

With that, Arthur steered Jonas away from the escalating tension, leaving a stunned silence in their wake.

"You'll have to excuse Jeff," Arthur murmured, weaving through the crowd with Jonas in tow. "He's pleasant until pint number five."

Jonas smirked. "That's alright. Maybe I'll just show up at his deathbed—give him a proper scare at the end."

Arthur chuckled. "Always with the drama."

As they settled into a booth at the back, Jonas took a moment to really look at Arthur. The man before him bore only a faint resemblance to the boy he once knew. Age had etched itself onto Arthur's features: lines deepened by laughter, stress, and time. His once-lean physique had given way to a softness around the middle, a beer belly that strained against his green polo shirt. Faded jeans clung to his legs, and there was an undeniable weariness in his eyes. To Jonas, it seemed almost sacrilegious that Arthur had let his vessel deteriorate like this.

"It's truly you, isn't it?" Jonas's voice quivered with a mix of hope and disbelief. "You've returned."

Arthur sighed, massaging his temples. "In a manner of speaking," he admitted. "I have memories of both lives. Every detail of our existence, our actions … It's all there. At the same time, I have vivid memories of a typical boring childhood in Rhymney." He paused; his eyes distant. "Can you even fathom the turmoil of recalling your own abduction while also remembering orchestrating that very act? Having two sets of memories, overlapping from the same moments but from divergent perspectives. It hardly allows you a good night's sleep. Let's put it that way."

Jonas swirled the liquid in his glass before taking a sip. "I've experienced something akin. Occasionally, I recall moments that shouldn't belong to me. Just the other night, I painted a portrait of an elderly woman. When I finished … I was overcome with grief. Truly grieving for this stranger. I cross-referenced our records from the last cycle, and the woman I depicted is this vessel's grandmother."

Arthur raised an eyebrow. "When will you stop referring to it as a '*vessel*'? Does it help you distance yourself from the weight of taking those children's lives?"

Jonas hissed, eyes darting around to ensure they weren't drawing attention. "Lower your voice!" Yet, Arthur relished the tension, and leaning forward, maintaining his tone, he grasped his nephew's hands.

"Does refraining from acknowledging it as a body help you forget that it's truly yours now?"

Jonas jerked his hands away, knocking his drink slightly. A cheer of "watch it!" erupted from a neighbouring table of boisterous youths.

Jonas pulled himself together and focused on the conversation. "How do you remember all of this now? What happened?"

Arthur sighed, swirling his drink. "One night, I went to bed as Martin, as normal as any other day. But I woke up with this splitting headache, like my brain was tearing itself apart." He paused, seemingly lost in the recollection. "Everything came rushing back—every moment, every life, every soul I'd inhabited. I remember looking over and seeing my wife and daughter crying, terrified because they didn't understand what was happening."

Jonas leaned in, concerned. "And then?"

Arthur continued, "I rushed to the hospital, hoping it was just a bad episode or something. But even as they were running tests and scans, I stared at my reflection and realised the truth. I wasn't just Martin anymore. I was …"

Jonas twirled his glass, eyes pondering its contents. "Still can't figure how you forgot everything for all those years and why only now you've made your way back to us."

Martin's jaw tightened, exhaling a weary sigh. "It was Thomas."

"What?"

His hand brushed along his cheek, voice taut with restraint. "Your brother. That's the answer. Didn't piece it together then, but now …"

His finger absentmindedly stirred the ice cubes in his coke. "After your mum died and I took him back to the house, chained him to that ritual table …" Martin paused, lost in the dark maze of memory. "Father Hishaya had the kids thinking being The Collector was some noble duty. We all swallowed it. But not Thomas. He looked at me … all that burning hatred …" His voice trailed off. "Haven't had a night since remembering it all where I don't see that stare. Hear him whispering as I finished tying him up."

Jonas stayed silent, his standard way of navigating the treacherous waters of his mother and brother's final moments.

He said 'You were supposed to protect me, Uncle Arthur. Maybe it's time you felt as helpless as we did.' He took the life of Arthur Blackwater and locked it far, far away into the back of my mind."

Jonas blinked, slowly, absorbing the revelation. "I didn't think a Collector could do that."

With a steadier voice, Martin continued, "We all just trotted after Father Hishaya, didn't we? It's likely that none of us, not even The Collectors, really know what they can do."

Barely disguising his discomfort at the lack of knowledge, Jonas pushed the conversation back to the present.

"When you woke up after your memories came back, who was with you?"

"It was just my daughter and my wife," Arthur replied, a distant look in his eyes. "Why?"

Jonas sipped the last of his drink, setting the glass down deliberately. "Curious."

Arthur frowned; tension evident in his voice. "What are you implying?"

Jonas chuckled softly, aware of the loaded nature of his next words. "You know children in the Family develop their powers early on, often even before they're aware of it."

Arthur's expression morphed rapidly. The lines of his face deepened, his eyes darkening and narrowing into slits. The contours of his cheeks tightened, and his jaw clenched, making the veins on his temple more pronounced. It was as if an internal storm was raging, threatening to burst forth any moment.

"I'm going to suggest I misheard you," Arthur began, voice laced with a dangerous edge, "You know it's too early in the cycle for another child of the Family to become a Collector."

Jonas raised an eyebrow. "It's not unheard of. Our cousin, Frances, showed up as a Collector ten years before," he remarked.

Arthur's face turned cold, his voice carrying an icy edge. "How would you feel if we were talking about Thomas in the same way? Especially after what I just told you." Jonas's face tightened noticeably.

Jonas looked away, wrestling with the past. "For our extended lives, sacrifices have been made. My brother's sacrifice was commendable. As for my mother's choice to end her life …"

"Perhaps it was a choice she wouldn't have had to make," Arthur interrupted.

Jonas turned back, a challenge in his eyes. "What are you implying?"

Arthur sighed deeply, his defences momentarily down. "Throughout all my lifetimes, all the experiences I've been through, being Martin has been the most fulfilling. Living as a husband, a father—that's the only life that has felt truly real."

Jonas scoffed. "It's this life that's ruined the man you used to be."

Ignoring the jibe, Arthur leaned in, gripping Jonas's hand with conviction. "When you lie in your grand mansion tonight, surrounded by luxury, I want you to think—of all our numerous lifetimes, can you pinpoint a singular moment you genuinely treasure? Isn't it time to consider life beyond the Blackwaters? A life without Eli's influence?"

Jonas forcefully pulled his hands away. "I had hoped this reunion would lead to you rejoining us."

Arthur's expression was a mix of sadness and understanding. "And I had hoped to convince you that you don't have to be with them forever. That there's a life outside of cycles and tradition. Think about that, will you?"

Jonas rose, his chair scraping back noisily against the floor. He downed his drink in one swift gulp, the liquid fire burning a trail down his throat. "I'll relay your return to the Family," he said, voice cold. "Oh, and we'll be watching your daughter closely."

"Forever the errand boy," Arthur said. "Tell me, young nephew, in which lifetime are you going to start making your own decisions?"

Jonas's jaw tightened, but he didn't reply.

As Jonas navigated his way through the bustling pub, the raucous sounds of celebration became increasingly muffled, replaced by the weight of his own introspection. Each step seemed to echo a complex dance of his emotions—confusion, envy, but most palpably, discomfort. The Arthur that sat in the dim corner, swathed in the haze of ambient conversations and laughter, was far removed from the uncle he once knew. The familial warmth had been replaced with a world-weariness that Jonas couldn't reconcile with. Exiting the pub, the cold air embraced him, but it did little to alleviate the heaviness in his chest. The streets, bathed in the glow of streetlamps, seemed to stretch endlessly before him, mirroring the chasm that now seemed to exist between uncle and nephew. It was a long walk home, and Jonas felt more alone than ever.

*

Jonas swung open Reuben's door, anticipating the same disarray he had witnessed the previous day. To his surprise, the room was impeccably organised. Reuben sat on the bed, engrossed in a book, and looked up to greet Jonas as though he were a longtime roommate.

"There's something I want to show you," Jonas said, beckoning Reuben to follow him upstairs.

Upon entering Jonas's room, Reuben was immediately enveloped by a world of colour, history, and timelessness. The walls were adorned with an array of paintings, each one a window into the myriad lives Jonas had lived over the centuries. There were vast landscapes portraying ancient forests, unspoiled by civilization, under starry skies unmarred by modern light pollution. Cities rose and fell in other canvases, transitioning from a medieval stone fortresses to the modern steel skyscrapers of bustling metropolises. Interspersed among these were abstract pieces, with colours and patterns reflecting the changing moods and cultures of the eras Jonas had traversed. His portraits were especially captivating; faces from bygone eras, each with soulful eyes that held stories of love, war, peace, and transformation.

Reuben looked around, his eyes wide with wonder and realisation. He was not just in a room; he was in a living museum of a man who had seen civilizations rise, evolve, and fade away.

Jonas's voice softened; a hint of nostalgia laced with sorrow. "This is my mother," he whispered. "Elena. She was the one who taught me."

Drawn in by the portrait, Reuben took a step closer. "What happened to her?"

"She died a long time ago," Jonas said. Reuben watched him try and find the next words to say like a boy struggling to say his first sentence. "So did my youngest brother, Thomas. He was the last Collector. Only ten years old at the time."

Reuben's face fell, connecting the dots. He thought of Lena, who had suffered a similar fate, and he struggled to mask his emotions. "And your mother?"

Jonas swallowed hard. "When she learned that Thomas's powers would lead us to our new vessels, to your father becoming Martin Drake ... she couldn't bear it. She took my brother Thomas to the cliffs, to the very spot where you conversed with Eli."

Reuben's heart raced. "Who saved them?"

"It was Eli and Arthur. They reasoned with her, reminded her of the realities we all must face. The sacrifices that grant us continued existence. They questioned how she could suddenly decide it was too great a burden. The tale says that Eli and Arthur pulled Thomas away, and my mother ... well, she chose the depths."

Reuben hesitated, then murmured, "I'm sorry."

Jonas let out a dry chuckle. "I've held you captive, and yet you offer condolences?"

Lifting his eyes to meet Jonas's, Reuben replied, "Regardless of our circumstances, you lost a parent. I can't help but think you have the same regrets. The unspoken words, the moments missed."

There was a weighty pause, the past echoing in the silence between them. Shifting gears, Jonas said, "Tomorrow morning, Eli will invite you to join us. Use today to ponder your decision."

Reuben nodded. "Understood."

As they began to exit the room, Reuben hesitated. "Is there a painting of him in here? Thomas, I mean."

Jonas hung his head low. "It might take a few more lifetimes before I muster the strength for that."

With that, he guided Reuben out, gently closing the door behind them, sealing away memories and lifetimes within those painted walls.

/

CHAPTER THIRTY

Beneath the dim streetlight, Maya's car sat inconspicuously, its paintwork reflecting the subtle glow. Inside, the soft hum of the engine mixed with the aroma of the takeaway food she was about to indulge in. She was about to take a bite when a voice on the store's intercom snapped her to attention.

"Security to the front entrance!"

Looking up, Maya caught sight of a kid, no older than sixteen, bolting from the shop's exit. His hood concealed most of his face, and his grey top fluttered wildly as he sprinted. Close behind, a panting security guard shouted, "Stop! Thief!"

Maya's police instincts kicked in immediately. "Not on my watch," she muttered. Slamming the car door and leaving her meal behind, she darted after the hooded boy, her feet pounding the pavement with determination.

"Hey! Stop!" Maya shouted, weaving through the throngs of pedestrians and dodging obstacles. Every time she felt she was gaining ground; the boy would unpredictably change direction or hurdle over barriers.

Their chase took them into narrow alleyways, up short stairwells, and even across the road, forcing oncoming cars to screech to sudden stops. Horns honked and bystanders shouted, but the duo was too engrossed in their pursuit to care.

With the boy seemingly about to escape, Maya took a risky shortcut, hoping to cut him off. As she rounded a corner, they almost collided. The boy, shocked, skidded to a halt, losing his balance.

Maya lunged forward, catching him just as he was about to fall.

Their eyes locked, and time seemed to slow. Suddenly, haunting visions from Maya's past cycles consumed her. She saw herself, in various guises and eras, kidnapping children who wore expressions of pure terror and confusion. The weight of countless misdeeds hit her like a tidal wave.

The boy, sensing her distraction, tried to wriggle free. "Let go of me!" he spat, panic evident in his voice.

Shaken, Maya tightened her grip, her voice tremulous. "Sorry, mate. You're not going anywhere."

It wasn't long before the security guard arrived, panting heavily. "Thanks, Officer," he wheezed, grateful.

Maya slowly made her way back to her car, her every step heavy with the weight of the chase and her resurfaced memories. As she approached, she paused for a moment, glancing back at the scene unfolding behind her: the boy being escorted away, the gathered crowd dispersing, the city slowly returning to its nightly rhythm.

She opened the car door and eased herself into the driver's seat, leaning back and closing her eyes. The leather felt cool against her skin. Drawing a deep, steadying breath, she tried to shake off the haunting visions and the emotions they stirred.

Just as she was about to start the engine, her phone buzzed with an incoming text notification. Hesitantly, she picked it up, and the colour drained from her face as she read the message:

I know what you've been doing. 7AM. Gaffa Coffee

Nestled in a quiet corner, its facade was a mix of worn bricks and old wood, Gaffa Coffee hinted at the years it had seen. A rustic sign dangled precariously from an iron rod, creaking softly in the morning breeze.

As Maya pushed the door open, a vintage bell jingled overhead. The aroma of freshly brewed coffee wafted towards her, mingling with the comforting scent of baked goods. Flickering fluorescent lights illuminated the interior, casting a gentle glow on wooden tables and mismatched chairs. The walls, adorned with faded photographs of the town's bygone days, seemed to silently narrate tales of the past.

Inside, a group of construction workers sat huddled at one end, their orange vests contrasting sharply with the earthy tones of the cafe. They laughed and conversed in hushed tones, hands wrapped around steaming mugs. Beside the large windows, an elderly couple quietly shared a morning paper, their glasses perched on the bridges of their noses.

By the counter, a young mother tried to balance a toddler on her hip while ordering, and the barista, a tattooed woman with a warm smile, playfully winked at the child, making him giggle.

After placing her order, a latte with a touch of caramel, Maya's eyes swept across the room. And then she found him.

Sat at the back, almost hidden in the shadows, was a familiar figure. His hands, enveloped in the pockets of his worn denim jacket, betrayed no movement. His food, a traditional Welsh rarebit, lay untouched in front of him. But it was his eyes, intense and burning with rage, that gripped her. Arthur, her own brother.

She approached him with caution, taking a seat opposite him.

"You're not eating?" she ventured, trying to break the ice.

Arthur looked up, his eyes cold. "Lost my appetite after I heard a local police officer has been chatting with my daughter on her way to school."

Maya started, "It's not like—"

Arthur's hand came down hard on the table, making a few patrons look their way.

"I was willing to overlook you being here as a cop, thinking you were watching me. But her?!"

"If you didn't want anyone watching her, you should've stayed out of the picture. And you shouldn't have reached out to Jonas again."

Arthur's frustration was palpable. "I've told Jonas repeatedly, my daughter isn't The Collector. And while my son's just a toddler in nursery, you barely give him a second glance. So, if you're so convinced, she's The Collector, show me the evidence."

Maya leaned back, eyeing him coolly.

Arthur began, "You always toe Eli's line, yet you don't even try to—"

"Oh, cut the bullshit!" Maya's voice rang out, causing nearby patrons to glance over. She gave them a brief, indifferent look before locking eyes with Arthur again.

"Honestly, how dare you sit there on a podium and think that now, just because you developed a conscience, that you have no part to play in all of this. We have grown up and grown old together, brother. We have taken screaming children into the dark and told them they were seeing their family again, knowing very well that they were never going to. Yes, I follow Eli's orders. So should you. You had no problem in doing so before."

Arthur raised an eyebrow, a smirk tugging at the corner of his mouth. "You chastise me for developing a conscience, yet here you are, playing dress-up in your *Criminal Minds* day job."

Maya sipped her coffee, giving Arthur a dismissive glance. "Arthur, I've always just done what needs to be done. That's what sets me apart from the rest of you. I'm not holed up in an attic trying to emulate Van Gogh like Jonas, nor am I lurking in the shadows like Eli. And I'm certainly not having an identity crisis like you seem to be. So, I've chosen to be a cop in this life. What of it? By the next cycle, I might be a hip-hop sensation. Lighten up, will you? Life's too short, even for us."

Arthur leaned back, taking in her words. "You've always been the adaptable one, haven't you? But just remember, even in your various roles, our past will always be our shadow. No daylight job can change that."

Maya smirked, "That's the point, brother. I'm not trying to change the past; I'm just trying to live with it. One vessel at a time."

Arthur's face tightened. "Every lifetime has its regrets."

"Like the regrets you and Eli have over Elena?" Maya shot back.

Arthur's eyes widened, a raw vulnerability momentarily breaking through.

"What are you insinuating?"

Maya's gaze was unwavering. "I adored our sister. That woman meant everything to me. I would've sacrificed all these lifetimes if it meant she could have just one simple joy again. She was fierce, self-reliant, a beacon of strength to all of us. When I heard that this pillar of strength decided to end her own life ... It felt as surreal as one of Jonas's paintings. It just doesn't resonate with the reality I knew."

Arthur's jaw clenched. "I wish things were different, but they aren't."

"Sure," Maya said, her voice dripping with scepticism. "Just another decision you and Eli made without us. Won't be the last either."

Arthur's eyes flashed with anger. "I think we're done with this conversation. Don't you?"

Maya pushed her chair back, standing tall. "No, it's merely paused, Arthur."

His voice turned icy. "I warned you. Keep away from Lena. You won't appreciate what happens next."

Pausing at the door, Maya shot him a defiant grin. "You're not a Blackwater anymore, my dear. Whatever comes next? You're just a spectator now." She snatched up her coffee. "Oh, and try to enjoy your breakfast!"

*

Reuben's voice was firm. "I need to see her."

The nurses exchanged a glance, their expressions a blend of scepticism and uncertainty. "She might not be up for visitors," one began.

Reuben interjected, "Believe me, she'll want to see me."

A distant voice echoed through the corridor, interrupting them. "Let him in!" Eli's voice rang out. He appeared momentarily, his gesture emphatic. He shot Reuben a fleeting nod, inscrutable as ever, then vanished down the hall.

The nurse hesitated only a moment longer.

"Okay. Fine."

As the door swung open, Reuben was ushered into a lavish

home cinema. The scene was set for a movie night, but the mood was anything but relaxed.

Inside the dimly lit room, rows of plush seats stretched out, all facing a massive screen. The muted glow of ambient lights provided just enough illumination to navigate. This space, intended for leisure and cinematic enjoyment, was now heavy with an unspoken tension.

Reuben hesitated on the threshold, taking in the room. The gentle *whirr* of a projector hummed in the background, and the faint aroma of buttery popcorn was at odds with the scene before him.

At the centre, ensconced in one of the seats, was Maya. Medical equipment surrounded her, their soft beeps occasionally punctuating the silence. IV lines traced back to her arm, and half of her face was obscured by bandages, a grim reminder of the recent car crash. Where the bandages ended, hints of angry red scars peeked through. The side of her face that was visible held an expression of weary resignation, her eyes locking onto Reuben with a blend of pain, anger, and anticipation. The weight of his responsibility for her condition bore down on him, making each step forward feel monumentally heavy.

"Christ. You're brave." Maya remarked with a sarcastic edge. She shifted her eyes back to the screen.

Projected onto the large screen was a scene from Akira Kurosawa's *High and Low*. It showed a tense moment inside a lavish living room with panoramic windows, offering a breathtaking view of the city below. Two men sat opposite each other—one, in a crisp suit, looked distressed, his face etched with concern. The other man, equally sharp but with a calculating demeanour, laid out the stark choices facing his counterpart. The stark black-and-white contrast emphasised the intense emotions on the characters' faces, every bead of sweat and furrowed brow clear in detail. The ambient sound from the film was filled with the low hum of a summer day, the chirping of cicadas, and distant city noise, intensifying the gravity of the situation on the screen. The juxtaposition of the movie's tension with the real-life tension between Maya and Reuben added an eerie depth to the room.

"Favourite of yours?" Reuben ventured, lowering himself into a seat adjacent to her.

"Indeed," she retorted, a hint of irritation lacing her voice at his intrusion. "I met him once," she added, nodding towards the Japanese character on the screen. "Mifune. Spent a year in Japan during the '40s."

The room fell silent, with only the dialogue and ambient sounds of the movie filling the void.

Finally, Maya turned her head slightly, her injured side partially obscured from Reuben's view. "Why are you here, then?"

Swallowing the lump in his throat, Reuben replied, "I guess ... I came to ask why you didn't let me in on all this from the very beginning."

Inside the dim ambiance of the cinema room, Reuben's words echoed with an unsettling tone. "I considered you family. Was it all just ... an act? Were you just watching us?"

Maya's voice was eerily calm, cold, almost detached.

"Had I not been there to ensure you knew nothing about your sister, you and your mother would've found yourselves bound, confined to the shadows, with no hope of escape."

"Just like those people you have trapped in the basement?" Reuben's voice was laced with both fear and anger.

Maya's lips curled into a chilling smirk. "Their accommodations are even more luxurious than yours. They are our future vessels, the forms we'll take on once The Collector grants us rebirth. There is a girl down there. Dahlia. She is the person I will become once this is over."

"Eli told me you're dying?" Reuben asked nervously. "Said you had cancer."

Maya sighed in embarrassment.

"Yes, it's true. You won't believe it, but this is the first vessel I've had with one. Christ, I don't even smoke," she replied. "That's why as soon as I found out you knew about the tape, I had to take you in by force. People do crazy things when they know they're not going to be around for much longer. Your father is a good example of that."

Confusion clouded Reuben's expression. "Why target children in the last cycle? And why operate within such a confined space? A small valley in Wales? Sounds quite risky to me."

Maya tilted her head, the dim light catching her eyes in an eerie glow. "The risk is the point." She shrugged. "We wanted to see how close we could dance with death."

Reuben clenched his fists. "So this is all just a cruel game to you?"

"When you've existed as long as we have," Maya whispered, "everything seems like one."

Reuben reclined in his seat, eyes fixed on the screen before him. He hesitated to ask the looming question, fearing the answer, and avoiding Maya's stare as he spoke. "How did it all start? The Collector? The Family?"

Though he couldn't see her reaction, he sensed that Maya was probably smiling wryly. He had braced himself for yet another evasive response, but what he received took him by surprise. "Father Hishaya," she said. The astonishment in her voice matched his as he finally turned to look at her. "It began with him. A local priest who offered four lost siblings more than just shelter. Not the road to immortality, but a path to family. He lifted us from the squalor and brought us to Blackwater House, exposing us to its sordid secrets." She chuckled, and a tear traced its path down her cheek. "You wouldn't believe the chorus of voices this house once held."

"What became of him? And the others?" Reuben asked, noticing a shadow fall across her countenance.

"Elena happened. My sister," she said, her tone turning grave.

"Jonas and Thomas's mother?"

She looked intrigued. "So, he's told you."

"Her child was supposed to be the next Collector, wasn't he?"

Maya's eyes returned to the screen, its flickering light casting an ethereal glow on her bandaged visage. "Correct. We all voted to use his life as a bridge to our future. And she used that opportunity to try and burn us all to the ground."

"She killed them all."

Maya exhaled deeply, a weight in her breath. "And then there were four. Until your father decided to leave us too."

An oppressive silence hung in the air like a thick fog, until Reuben finally spoke. "Maya, when is all of this going to end?"

"You should already know the answer to that," she replied, her voice tinged with sorrow.

His head drooped, weighed down by a sense of irrevocable loss. "I had hoped—"

"Hoped what? That things could go back to the way they were? I wish that too, Reuben. I wish we could return to the days when I was bailing you out of pubs and sharing cups of coffee with your mother. But we're past that point now."

His eyes misted over as they locked with hers. "All that time, I thought you were shielding me from something."

They returned to the film.

"I was," she said softly. "From all of this."

CHAPTER THIRTY-ONE

Reuben squinted, focusing intently on the distant figure in the field. "Nope … a little higher … yep … that's it." Eli guided patiently, using two fingers to gently lift the end of the shotgun in Reuben's grasp.

With a nod, Eli stepped back, being careful of the squelching mud beneath their boots. Reuben took a steadying breath, and with a sudden motion, squeezed the trigger. A deafening blast echoed across the empty expanse. The bullet raced across the distance and hit its mark with precision. The scarecrow, once a guardian of the crops, now lay defeated on the ground.

A rush of exhilaration coursed through Reuben's veins. He threw his arms up and let out a triumphant whoop, a celebratory sound so intense it seemed it could carry all the way back to the looming mansion in the distance.

Two weeks had passed since Reuben had reluctantly aligned himself with the Family. "Improved since our last session," Eli remarked, a sly smile playing on his lips. His inner satisfaction was palpable; The Collector's impending return combined with having Martin's son under his influence was a double triumph. *I wonder, dear brother,* he thought. *Are you seething up in the heavens? Or perhaps you're stewing down below?*

As they approached the mansion, Reuben's eyes narrowed as he caught sight of a cluster of men in bright yellow hazmat suits. They were gathered around a patch of field near the edge of the mansion, tools and devices in hand, clearly engrossed in some sort of analysis.

He'd seen them before, on a previous visit, and had overheard one of them mentioning their boss.

"What are they doing over there?" Reuben asked, unable to contain his curiosity. "And what does VelourTech have to do with all of this?"

Eli glanced towards the men. "When my sister chose to burn down that part of the mansion, it wasn't only the lives of her brothers and sisters that were destroyed. Father Hishaya kept a selection of scriptures used in our ceremonies. Scriptures that have been around longer than any of us. After the fire, we used what we had left for the next cycle. We followed his instructions step by step but…our next cycle didn't come without its complications."

"What complications would that be?"

Eli sighed loudly.

"Oh well that would be your father" he replied. "I'm pretty sure not having the full scriptures were what caused him to not remember his identity. Edward Velour told me that his technology would allow us to recreate the missing pieces of the puzzle."

"Jesus Christ" Reuben said. "You're telling me this is all some sort of witchcraft?"

Eli laughed. He took a step towards Reuben and put his hand on the boy's shoulder.

"You are a still a bit young to know the full story."

Reuben stepped away from him and rubbed where Eli had touched him.

"And what did you offer them in return?" he asked.

"A place at the table for their owner, so to speak."

"Why follow the teachings of a man long dead? Why follow such teachings when you know they bring harm to others? Is being immortal that important to you?"

Eli turned to look squarely at Reuben, his eyes narrowing ever so slightly.

"What's your earliest memory?"

"I don't remember mine." Reuben hesitated.

"Well, I do," Eli replied, his voice dropping to a whisper. "I remember it as if it happened yesterday, even though countless years have gone by. We were just children, my siblings and I—too young to comprehend the world, let alone our plight. We were trapped in a tunnel so dark it felt like the very universe had abandoned us. It was a winding labyrinth with no sense of time or direction. I can still hear our tiny, desperate footsteps, echoing in that abyss."

His eyes took on a far-off, haunted look. "But it wasn't just the darkness that terrified us. It was the rats—scores of them, lurking in that eternal night. They were vicious, biting at our tender, unprotected feet as we wandered aimlessly. We could hear them too, their sinister little squeals getting closer, bolder, as they sensed our vulnerability. The pain was unbearable, but what was worse was the gnawing, relentless hunger that gripped us. It clawed at our insides like another beast altogether, making each step feel like a herculean effort."

Eli paused, swallowing hard, as if the very act of recalling that memory was a struggle. "But what truly broke us was the crushing, horrific sense of being utterly alone. Alone in a world that had neither light nor warmth, a world that offered no respite from our suffering. We were too young, Reuben, too young to be in a hell like that. I don't want to—can't—go back to that vulnerability, that fragility. Can you understand that?"

The atmosphere around them grew heavy, charged with the weight of Eli's revelations. Reuben felt a chill run down his spine, a cold dread settling in the pit of his stomach. "So that's why you've never erased it from your memory?"

Eli shook his head slowly. "How can one savour the pleasures of immortality if they've forgotten the depths of despair that make it worthwhile? That memory, as horrendous as it is, serves as my anchor, reminding me why I do what I do."

Upon reaching the front doors, the massive double entrance swung open, revealing the mansion's opulent interior. The butlers, dressed in crisp uniforms, greeted them with nods of acknowledgment.

"I'm off for a shower," Reuben announced, the sweat and mud from the training evident on his face.

Eli clapped him on the back, a pleased expression on his face. "I'm glad you chose the right side, Reuben. Truly."

As Eli turned away, Reuben's smile faltered for a moment, revealing a shadow of doubt or perhaps something more devious, had anyone been looking.

Making his way upstairs, Reuben paused by Jonas's room, knocking lightly on the doorframe. "Hey, Jonas," he began. "Got any paper? Thought I might try some drawing later."

Jonas looked up from his work, a sketch of what appeared to be an intricate landscape. He smiled. "Of course. And one of these days, I'll teach you a few things," he said, handing Reuben a neat stack of blank sheets and a sharpened pencil.

Reuben nodded appreciatively. "Sounds good. Thanks." With that, he continued down the hall and reached the bathrooms.

Steam billowed as Reuben turned the shower to its hottest setting. He took a moment, leaning heavily against the marble counter. The weight of the last few weeks bore down on him as he exhaled a breath, feeling he'd been holding it for far too long.

Every gesture, every word, every smile had been meticulously crafted to fit the image of loyalty. It was a role he played with a keen understanding of its significance. But beneath the facade, a storm of emotions churned. His heart ached with memories of his real family and the life he'd left behind, while his mind raced with strategy and determination.

Each interaction, each bit of information he gathered from the Blackwaters, was a piece of the puzzle. He had to know their strengths, weaknesses, and most importantly, their intentions. Only then could he unravel the plan that had been forming in his mind since he was forcibly introduced to this enigmatic family.

As the water cascaded over him, washing away the grime of the day, he allowed himself a moment of vulnerability. The hot water was therapeutic, almost cleansing him of the emotional weight he bore.

But Reuben knew he couldn't afford to let his guard down, not even for a second.

Drying off, he wrapped the towel around his waist and took one last look in the steam-covered mirror. His eyes moved to the paper, and he took the pencil and prayed that after he had flushed the remnants away that his plan would work.

He took the paper, set it down next to the sink carefully and began to write the message: (Break)

Lena - I hope this plan works.

I figure that there's going to be a time in the future where we will run into each other, so hopefully with what you can do, you'll see this. It's worse than I thought. These people are monsters, incapable of any humanity. But I don't think you can run from them forever. There's something we can use, something that I've noticed. It's about Elena. Jonas believes that his mum committed suicide, but I don't think she did. It matches the tape Dad left me. I think something else happened. And one of the people who knows is our father. I hope he shared something with you because I think if there's one thing that could bring this family down, it's a boy's grief. So, show him, Lena. If you can, show him what happened to his mother."

*

Present Day

Lena's hand slipped away from her brother's leg.

"You saw it. Didn't you?" he whispered desperately, urgency threading his words.

Behind him, the shadows of the advancing guards loomed closer, their intent clear. But for that fraction of a second, they existed in a bubble, isolated from the external threats.

Lena nodded, her voice firm. "Yes."

And then, with the ferocity of a storm, the guards descended upon her.

CHAPTER THIRTY-TWO

20th August 2018

As Martin ascended the steps, his heart pounded in a rhythm of dread, matching each of the football fans chants who crowded the platform. An unsettling sensation gripped him—the feeling of being observed. His eyes darted over his shoulder, scanning for any lurking presence. All he saw were the indistinct shadows thrown by the sparse streetlamps. Nevertheless, his mind whirred with anxious possibilities. Were they being followed? Stalked, even? The unsettling notion sent a shiver down his spine.

Gripping Lena's hand more tightly, he quickened his pace. Their immediate goal was the station, and they had to reach it urgently. Never before had he felt so nakedly vulnerable, as if walking into a web, already spun and waiting for them. But there was no turning back.

As they brushed past a bench near the station entrance, Martin's gut-instinct proved accurate. One of Eli's guards was perched there, his eyes icy and indifferent, yet piercingly focused. Martin felt as if those eyes were drilling holes through him, confirming that they were, indeed, in jeopardy. But retreat was not an option now.

Taking a deep, steadying breath, Martin swung open the station doors and ushered Lena inside. They were on their own, the point of no return crossed.

"Almost there," he assured Lena, guiding her through the throng of jubilant, boisterous football fans that filled the platform.

By this time tomorrow, we'll be far away from all this—safe with Jonas, he thought.

His daughter would soon question the indefinite nature of their escape. "How long will we be at this 'safe house'? Until I turn a hundred?" she'd likely ask.

Lena had a point. Martin had vowed to shield her from life's cruelties, a naive promise even at the best of times. Perhaps Jonas, always the insightful one, could offer a more sustainable solution.

"Any idea where he is?" Lena asked.

Turning, Martin looked at his exhausted daughter. Mud specks marred her face; signs of their gruelling journey. Her eyes were weary, barely open, and her expression was marred by fatigue—a fatigue that recalled his final, ghost-like days with Elena.

"He said he'd be on the platform," he answered.

Lena groaned. "I need the bathroom."

Martin gave her a questioning look, hinting that perhaps she could wait a bit longer.

"Waiting is not an option," she asserted.

"Alright, I'll find the restroom too," he agreed. "Let's meet by the vending machine, okay?"

Lena offered a tired smile, infused with youthful mischief. "Grab some snacks while you're at it, yeah?"

Martin gave a playful eyeroll and sauntered towards the men's restroom. He got to the entrance and saw a massive 'Out of Order' sign in front of the door. Before he could decide on where they should meet instead, a scrawny security guard with ginger hair came bumbling through the football fans towards him.

"Sorry, mate," he said with a smile that exposed a jagged section of yellow teeth. He reached into his side pocket, removed a key and a few seconds later, unlocked the toilet door. The man leaned in close to him. "Your nephew will be with you shortly."

Martin nodded in confirmation. He looked back and forth, thinking of Lena in the sea of football fans, hoping she wouldn't get lost.

He stepped inside.

Upon entering the somewhat grungy, whitewashed space, he found the lone cubicle already in use. Seizing the opportunity, he moved to the sink to wash his hands.

"The next departure from Platform 6 will be the 10:35 a.m. service to London Heathrow," boomed the station announcement.

That was their train. As the water cascaded over his hands, he stared intently at the droplets swirling away the grime, as if each one carried the weight of a redemptive act. In that fleeting moment of cleansing, he allowed himself to imagine the comfort of a warm bed awaiting him. It was then that the restroom door creaked open.

Martin pivoted sharply to find a slender, blond figure standing about five feet away.

"Hello, Jonas."

"Arthur. Been a minute. How you been?"

"Been better," he said. "You don't know how much I appreciate this."

Jonas said nothing. He seemed to just stare through him. There was no smile. No sarcastic quip. Something was wrong.

"Is everything okay?" he asked.

Jonas moved past him, patting his shoulder. "So where's the girl?"

"Drying her hands. she'll meet us on the platform. We should head there now," Martin said, turning off the tap and shaking the water from his hands.

Jonas hesitated, his eyes drifting.

"Is everything okay?" Martin asked again, this time a note of urgency colouring his voice.

Jonas seemed lost in thought, a shadow clouding his face. "I've been thinking about my mother recently. About the day she died. I've started to wonder if it was worth it. Losing her. Losing my brother. All for another lifetime."

Martin bowed his head.

"She loved you, Jonas. I hope once all this is over you can start living a life that she would be proud of."

"I almost can't wrap my head around it," Jonas said with a chuckle. "Death. The idea of having an end."

"There's nothing to be afraid of," Martin answered firmly. "You might find that you'll actually start to live."

Jonas turned to him. A soft smile broke across his face.

"It's really good to see you again."

He embraced his uncle tightly. Martin held his nephew closely before trying to part. But Jonas's face remained on his shoulder.

Jonas was crying.

"This is all on you," Jonas whispered.

The sentence hung in the air like a storm cloud, heavy with impending dread. Martin's instincts screamed that something was terribly, irrevocably wrong, but it was too late.

Martin felt a searing pain in his back. And then he heard that voice in his ear.

"Good morning, dear brother," Eli whispered.

He let go of Jonas and screamed. The pain was sharp and hot, like nothing he ever felt. He reached behind and felt the long thin object that had struck him. He returned his hands to the front and saw that it was covered in blood. He looked to Jonas for help, but he simply stood there as an audience for the massacre.

It was a heart stopping betrayal: Jonas had held him in place while Eli, hiding in one of the broken bathroom's stalls, plunged the knife into his back.

Eli sunk the blade further into his flesh with a dreadful intimacy. Eli's fingers gently combed through Martin's hair as he whispered, "Thank you for bringing her into this world." With a sickening ease, Eli withdrew the knife.

Martin crumpled to the floor, his strength ebbing away.

Just then, the bathroom door burst open. Eli whirled around, expecting to confront some hapless stranger. Instead, he found himself locking eyes with a young girl, her face contorted in sheer horror.

"JONAS! GRAB HER!"

Eli lunged at Lena, but with his final bit of strength, Martin jumped up and tackled Eli into the wall. Both men fell to the floor. Martin turned on his side, facing his daughter, and issued his final command.

"RUN!"

As Jonas sprinted after the fleeing girl, Eli and Martin tussled on the floor. It would've been a fair fight if not for Martin's wound. Eli used this to his advantage as he stuck his fingers into the wound, causing Martin to scream and drop on his back. Martin watched as Eli got on top of him, a devilish grin across his face. Martin flailed his hands at his brother to try and stop him, so Eli punched and punched until he lifted his arms no more. He then leaned over and grabbed the knife. The next few minutes were a blur of violence and emotion, but when Eli finally stepped back, Martin's blue shirt was awash in a sea of scarlet.

And he was gone.

Dropping his brother's lifeless form onto the cubicle floor, Eli bolted out of the men's room and onto the chaotic platform. He jostled through rowdy clusters of people, eyes darting to catch sight of the train pulling away. Desperation clawed at him as he sprinted alongside the departing train, peering into the windows. Then he saw it—a flash of a familiar blue backpack nestled beside a petite brunette woman. As the car containing the backpack slid past him and the train receded into the distance, his heart sank.

Whirling around, he found Jonas looking equally perplexed.

"Did she get on the train?" Eli demanded.

"I—"

"ANSWER ME!" Eli's shout echoed through the platform, silencing even the rowdiest of groups. "DID SHE GET ON THE DAMN TRAIN?"

Jonas offered no reply. Both uncle and nephew scanned the platform, their expressions a portrait of utter disarray, as if they were schoolboys who'd just missed the last bus home. Eli watched the train's taillights vanish into the horizon.

Before they could strategize their next move, a bloodcurdling scream erupted from the men's restroom. Eli's eyes darted to the commotion, where a cluster of shocked faces were shuffling in and out of the doorway. Their complexions had turned an ashen white, no doubt horrified by the gruesome discovery inside. Realising the danger of remaining, Eli swiftly pulled his hood over his head and melted into the descending staircase, vanishing from sight.

Just as Eli made his exit, Jonas hastily crossed over to another platform, his eyes scanning for an alternative route. As he boarded a departing train, he settled into his seat, peering out of the window just in time to witness a swarm of police officers ascending onto the platform.

Sequestered on Platform 7, a young girl garbed in an oversized green jacket cried into her hands. The setting sun gave way to twilight, yet her tears persisted, uninterrupted, for a full hour. Passersby averted their eyes, leaving her in her isolation; a harsh introduction to a world that would often look the other way. As the sky deepened into the inky blackness, she knew all too well from those frigid mornings at home, Lena dabbed her wet cheeks and rose from her perch. Her moment of mourning would have to be deferred.

All she could do was follow her father's final orders.

All she could do was run.

*

Lena swung back and forth on the chains, awaiting her fate. It wouldn't be long now before the ceremony would begin. The ritual would begin and the Blackwaters would use the black bible provided by Father Hishaya to transfer their consciousnesses into new bodies. And they would use her to do so. Her father told her that the verses would cast a spell on her and her powers would be used to empty the memories of their prisoners and refill them with the consciousness and memories of the Blackwaters. She had laughed when her father had originally told her this. She had said it sounded silly. But this situation that she once found so funny, so silly, had made her half an orphan and a prisoner. Why did it have to end this way? Why couldn't these powers be used for something better?

What if there's a way to do that? To return what you've taken?

Sophie's voice. God, she would give everything to hear her voice again. She had dismissed her suggestion of her power being used as a gift. But what if it could be a gift? A gift to save her brother. A gift to show the truth.

I think if there's one thing that could bring this family down, it's a boy's grief. So show him, Lena. If you can, show him what happened to his mother.

She had been using her powers for all the wrong reasons. To hide the truth. And by doing that, she had gotten lost in the nightmares of other lives. But if she had the chance to show Jonas the truth of what happened to his mother, it really could change everything. She closed her eyes and focused on no one's memories but her own. Emily's laugh. Sophie's smile. Her mother's embrace. Her brother's courage. Her father's words.

This was her final chance and she had to do it for him.

"Dad …" she said. "Whatever happens next, this is for you."

CHAPTER THIRTY-THREE

Present Day

With a final boom, the towering doors closed behind him. Delicate spring leaves floated down, settling onto the dull, grey stone path in front of him. Walking farther into the darkness, the torchlit path revealed a series of portraits. One depicted three soldiers in front of a bombed-out cottage, another a black and white image of two women looking up at a passing zeppelin, perhaps taken in the 1920s. The sight of these portraits produced a smile. Edward Velour had spent many fortunes on his quest for influence and it was finally within arm's reach.

Approaching another set of large doors leading to the mansion garden, silent nods were exchanged with two masked, armed guards. Edward reached into his jacket pocket, retrieving a small object: a mask carved from ebony wood into the face of a young boy. It was a tradition, a rule, those joining the Family must bear the sign of their junior rank.

Stepping through the doors, the senses were immediately flooded by sounds of merriment and celebration. More than fifty people milled about, all in fine suits and wearing similar ebony masks. Laughter, chatter, and dancing filled the space, accompanied by the melodies of a string quartet. Tables laden with an abundance of food and drink occupied the massive garden, set under the bright sun.

Yet despite the festive atmosphere, there was an insidious undertone. The collective morality, the collective conscience of this assembly, had eroded over decades, even centuries. Conventional morality held no sway here.

"Edward! Over here!"

He pivoted, finding Lisa beckoning to him. In her crimson dress and with her slightly dishevelled demeanour, it was evident she had already partaken in the evening's offerings.

"Lisa, we should be more discreet with our names," he cautioned, eyes darting around them.

She gave a rueful, slightly tipsy smile. "I know, I know. It's just … the ambiance, the wine, it makes me forget the need for secrecy."

Edward took a moment, absorbing the surroundings—the lavish event with masked guests, the low hum of conversations, and the clinking of glasses. "One can never be too careful, especially here."

"I can hardly grasp that we're actually here," she exclaimed, lifting her glass for a hesitant toast. "You made this possible! All your work for them was worth it."

He touched his glass to hers, eyes meeting over the brim. "It's surreal, isn't it? I wonder what my father would make of this. I don't suppose you've seen my assistant around. Have you?"

Lisa squinted, her eyes scanning the masked figures around them. "You know, it's odd. I haven't seen Sophie anywhere."

Edward nodded, a flicker of concern crossing his eyes. "Yes, her absence is conspicuous. What you might not know is that she played an even larger role in all this than I initially realized."

*

Lena's eyes flickered open, disoriented. The harsh reality of her surroundings quickly dispelled any lingering haze. She found herself confined in a prison cell; her wrists shackled to chains that dangled from the ceiling.

"Welcome home."

From the shadowed corner of the prison cell, a figure emerged, revealing that someone had been watching their interaction all along.

"Life as the Collector is a spiral," Eli said, stepping into the light. He was adorned in a long, scarlet-red ceremonial cloak, his hands clasped behind his back. "No matter how far you spiral outwards, how many lives you try to lead, you'll inevitably find yourself circling back to the origin. Circling back to me."

He looked up at Lena, who was shackled above him twelve feet in the air, a faint smile on his lips. "To think that you were only on the other platform, to think that you were still in the same city. You've done nothing but waste time. You know that? This could have all been over a year ago."

Lena's unflinching eyes locked with her enemy. "You talk about waste. Do you know what you could've done with the money, the resources, the time you've had on this planet … What have you achieved, Eli? You live just to move from one life to the next. All that precious time is spent only on trying to cheat death. What a waste indeed."

Eli looked at Lena, a veiled satisfaction in his eyes. "You may sound like your father, but your brother has been far more perceptive. He's matured impressively these past months. I'm pleased he'll be with us in our next life."

Lena lowered her eyes, her face obscured by her cascading hair, but a subtle smile was evident. "You envied my father, didn't you?"

For a fleeting moment, Eli's poised exterior seemed to crack.

"He managed to have a life without you. He found his independence, his freedom," Lena said.

Eli regained his composure quietly, but the brief lapse had already betrayed him. His eyes narrowed, the facade of amused detachment crumbling just a bit. "Jealousy is a petty emotion, beneath me."

Lena looked up, her eyes meeting his. "Is it beneath you? My father managed to escape this … this cycle you're so obsessed with. He built something—maybe not something grand or eternal, but something real. He had a family who loved him, a career, a life away from all this darkness. You couldn't let him have that, could you?"

For a fraction of a second, Eli looked unsettled. Then his veneer of control snapped back into place. "Your father made his choices, just as you've made yours. Don't presume to think you understand me or what I want."

"But I do understand," Lena said softly. "You're terrified of being left behind, of becoming irrelevant. My father found a way to live that didn't include you, and that's the one thing you can't stand."

Eli's jaw tightened, but he said nothing, turning away to hide the flicker of truth that crossed his face. He regained his poise, his eyes cold and unreadable. "The ceremony will begin soon." With that, he turned and opened the door. "We will see who is truly terrified then."

He shut the door behind him, leaving Lena suspended in her restraints, engulfed in the enveloping darkness.

CHAPTER THIRTY-FOUR

Edward was outside, mingling with the eclectic assembly of guests that graced the expansive lawn of the Blackwater mansion. The evening air was tinged with the scent of blooming roses, and the atmosphere was suffused with the subtle glow of strategically placed fairy lights. Crystal champagne flutes glinted in the hands of women in floor-length gowns, and men in sharp tuxedos engaged in hushed conversations. Classical music played softly from hidden speakers, adding an air of sophistication.

Edward was pulled from his thoughts when he felt a tap on his shoulder. He turned to find a young man. "Eli would like to see you," Reuben whispered into Edward's ear, as if safeguarding a secret that the wind itself shouldn't hear.

Edward felt a frisson of anticipation. "If you'll excuse me, ladies and gentlemen," he said, folding his conversations neatly like a book he planned to return to.

He followed Reuben through the French doors, entering the ornate interior of the mansion. The chandeliers were dimmed to a soft, golden glow, casting shadows that danced on the walls like ephemeral spectres. They navigated through a labyrinth of corridors adorned with portraits of ancestors who seemed to scrutinise their every move.

The door opened, and there Eli stood, his silhouette framed by the backlit room. "Edward," he greeted. "Come in, we have much to discuss."

Edward sank into the plush leather chair across from Eli's imposing mahogany desk, a room that bore the weight of generations. Lined with bookshelves filled with ancient tomes and contemporary works, artefacts that could belong in museums, and photographs that told stories of triumph and tragedy, it was a chamber of secrets and power. Nonchalantly, Edward stretched his legs and propped his feet up on an antique ottoman, a move that in any other context might be considered disrespectful. Eli shot him a glare but said nothing, opting to save his words for a moment that carried more weight.

Reuben stood at the back of the room, his posture rigid, hands clasped behind him like a sentinel. His eyes briefly met those of Jonas, who was leaning against a wall on the other side of the room, his arms folded across his chest. Jonas had a smug, almost predatory, smirk on his face—as if he were in on a secret that others in the room were not privy to. Reuben locked eyes with Maya. Sitting in a wheelchair, her face was still scarred but had healed considerably. She was wearing an all-grey suit, impeccably tailored yet muted in its statement.

Eli sat down, steepling his fingers, and looked at Edward. "Now that we're all here, it's time we talk about the upcoming transition and the roles we are all destined to play."

Eli leaned forward, his eyes sweeping over each face in the room as if he were assessing a board of chess pieces. "This marks the dawn of a new era for our family. Once, we were so numerous that this room couldn't contain us all. However, over the many lifetimes—some leaving by choice, others taken away from us—we have distilled down to the essence of who we are today: the individuals in this room."

His eyes settled on Jonas. "Jonas, our esteemed treasurer, my nephew. After the tumultuous events of the last cycle, one might have expected you to abandon our cause or become lost. Yet, here you are, wearing the Family's mantle. For that, I am proud of you."

Next, Eli turned to Maya. "My cherished sister, you have paid the steep price of physical sacrifice to bring us to this critical juncture. Your unwavering scrutiny of the Drake family has been invaluable. I owe you my deepest gratitude."

Finally, his attention pivoted to the room's newer member. "And then there's our final addition, Reuben. You haven't had to lift a finger to earn your place here; your birthright does that for you. It's regrettable that you've been detached from us for so long. But now, you're back where you bel-"

"Hang on just a minute!" Edward interrupted. "Aren't you forgetting someone?"

Eli scanned the faces of his assembled family, his eyes pausing briefly on Jonas, who seemed to stifle a chuckle.

"Ah, yes. My apologies," Eli said, clapping his hands twice.

At his signal, a set of grand doors swung open. Two guards, their faces obscured by masks, entered the room. One of them unmasked himself, revealing a balding, grizzled man in his fifties who bowed respectfully to the gathering.

"Oliver, my trusted guard," Eli began. "You've faithfully served me for many years. It's time for you to join our family. Your task is simple: eliminate Edward Velour."

Edward shot up from his chair, his face contorted in disbelief and rage. "What is the meaning of this? We had an agreement!"

Eli sighed theatrically. "We did have an agreement, Edward. But I've come to learn that you never truly believed in our family's mission. Jonas—remind me what Sophie told you?"

Edward's eyes snapped towards Jonas.

"I believe you told her, 'As long as the money keeps coming in, who am I to judge if it's real or not? I'll continue living in Jonas Blackwater's fantasy as long as I get to thrive as well.' Got to give it to the girl, she wasn't afraid to play each side against each other. God rest her soul."

Edward's mouth began to shake in horror.

"You're throwing away everything I've given you—my time, my resources, VelourTech's resources! I rebuilt your bloody scriptures for you! Without me, this ceremony wouldn't even be possible!"

Eli chuckled while Edward spun around, looking for a way out.

"What about my associates outside?" Edward's voice was tinged with desperation.

Eli sneered. "We'll give them a choice. They either hand the company to us, or we'll kill them. You know what will happen after that? They will hand the company over to us and then we'll kill them."

Before Edward could react, Oliver seized his chance. Swiftly drawing a knife from his pocket, he plunged it into Edward's neck with surgical precision. Reuben gasped, his face a mask of shock and dread as Edward clutched at his throat, staggering back in betrayal before collapsing onto the floor.

"We thank you for your interest in the Blackwater Family." Eli said coldly, stepping over Edward's convulsing body.

A chilling silence enveloped the room. It was a brutal, undeniable reminder of the dark path they were all irrevocably tied to, a path that promised to grow even darker as the minutes ticked down to the ceremony's beginning.

Edward gasped for air, choking on his own blood. Eli observed as the light drained from Edward's eyes and extended his hand to Oliver. "Well executed," he said. Oliver nodded curtly and retreated into the shadows.

"Jonas, bring Lena. Let's reconvene in the living room for the Curtain Call," Eli announced. As he stepped over Edward's lifeless form, he paused, catching Reuben's eye for a moment. Eli turned his back to leave.

"*Does he still not trust me?*"

Eli pivoted suddenly, wiping a solitary tear from his eye. He looked at the tear as if it were an artefact.

"The time has come," he whispered.

A shiver ran down Reuben's spine as he followed Eli out, his eyes lingering on Edward's lifeless body one final time. Time, it seemed, had run out.

*

Jonas stepped cautiously into the dimly lit room, his eyes locking onto Lena's despondent face. The air was thick, almost suffocating, heavy with the weight of what was about to unfold.

"It's time," Jonas uttered, the words clinging to the tension that enveloped the room.

Lena lifted her eyes, red-rimmed and brimming with tears, to meet his. "If it's time, then end it now. Kill me. I won't be a part of what comes next."

Jonas hesitated, looking to her shackled hand. A hundred thoughts seemed to cross his mind, each one a bullet in the chamber of decision. Slowly, ever so slowly, his hand moved towards the chain that bound her. The room was quiet, the air hanging heavy and thick. Even the sound of his fingertips brushing the metal of the shackle felt magnified, filling the room with a sort of thunderous silence.

Click. The first lock opened.

The knock at the door was sudden but soft, a timid interruption to the ominous quiet. Jonas froze, his hand hovering over the next chain.

"Excuse me," he said, moving cautiously towards the door.

When it opened, Reuben's face appeared in the narrow frame. "Come to say goodbye?" Jonas couldn't help but sneer, irony lacing his words.

Instead of a verbal reply, Reuben surged forwards, shoving Jonas with all the force he could muster. Off-balance, Jonas staggered backwards into Lena.

Her newly freed hand shot up, contacting Jonas's face.

"NO! GET OFF ME!" Jonas shrieked, a kind of raw, primal fear colouring his voice.

"Look at me, Jonas," Lena commanded softly, her voice almost caressing the words. "It's time you saw the truth."

*

The vision shifted, pulling Jonas away from the tension-filled room to a windswept clifftop overlooking a turbulent sea. Elena was there, her hair lashed by the wind, her eyes full of sorrow so deep it looked like an abyss.

"Mother."

She was holding the hands of a young boy, no older than ten or eleven.

Jonas felt a shiver crawl up his spine. He recognized the boy. "Thomas?" he whispered, the name escaping his lips like a haunted echo.

"Don't come any closer!" Elena yelled angrily at the two men who approached.

Arthur stood imposingly, his tall and broad-shouldered frame tensed as if preparing for battle. Although his face still bore the softness of youth, his eyes revealed a burgeoning intensity that presaged the hard-won resolve he would exhibit in the years to come.

Beside him, Eli, slightly shorter but no less formidable, was a study in kinetic energy. His eyes glinted with fervour as his hands cut through the air, punctuating his points. Although his visage was yet untouched by the years of strife that lay ahead, a subtle shadow, perhaps of a destiny not yet fully comprehended, clouded his countenance.

"What exactly do you think you're doing?" Arthur's voice sliced through the air, taut with incredulity and frustration.

"I'm doing what I have to—keeping him from the likes of you! Both of you!" Elena shot back, her voice challenging the approaching peals of thunder for dominance. "I won't allow it, Arthur. I won't let you use him as a sacrificial lamb. Thomas is not the Collector."

"I don't want to go … I don't want to go," Thomas whimpered.

Elena bent down, her eyes meeting his. "It's okay, sweetheart," she whispered, as the storm continued to gather around them.

"Stop this madness, Elena," Arthur implored his sister, his eyes narrowing. "We've all faced this agonizing choice. You've stood by before, watched as other children were chosen for the sacrifice. What makes this time different?"

Ignoring him, Elena smiled tenderly at her son, whispering, "Close your eyes, darling, okay?" Thomas obediently shut his eyes, and they both took a step closer to the cliff's edge.

"STOP!" Arthur's voice reverberated, filled with a blend of desperation and authority.

"You're being selfish," Eli finally declared, breaking his previous silence.

"Selfish? Absolutely," Elena retorted with palpable scorn. "Haven't we all been? Isn't that the bedrock of this twisted family saga? A lifetime of servitude to this house, to these archaic rituals. Don't we deserve something more? Something better?"

"So you killed Father Hishaya because you deserve 'something better?'" Eli's voice dripped with venom. "He was the closest thing to a parent we've ever had. You're willing to jeopardize everything for what? Your ego? The ceremony will proceed, whether you're part of it or not."

Laughing and crying in a manic duality, Elena responded, "I should've done it years ago. You remember how he found us, don't you? Homeless, famished, and abandoned, condemned to the gutters? He took us in, yes. But what did he make us into? Monsters. Sometimes, when I close my eyes, it's clear. We're still there, still lost in xthat same gutter."

"Enough," Arthur interjected, extending his hand towards her. "Come home. We can discuss this. We'll find a way."

Elena looked at her brother's outstretched hand, then back at the cliff, the weight of her decision hanging in the air like the gathering storm clouds.

Engulfed in the vivid memory, Jonas felt an overwhelming urge for it to cease. He knew the impending tragedy: his mother would thrust the boy aside and leap into the abyss, severing herself from any cycle of rebirth.

"Please stop," Jonas muttered, tears unexpectedly forming in his eyes. "I can't bear to watch anymore."

His mother, Elena, positioned her son in front of her and then—defying Jonas's memory of events—stepped back, away from the precipice.

"Mother, I'm sorry."

Elena, her eyes misty, almost sank to her knees. "Alright," she whispered, her voice tinged with an emotional weariness. "Alright.

Let's go home."

"What?"

Arthur exhaled a sigh of relief as he took Thomas into his arms. The young boy began to weep, clutching at Arthur's legs. Arthur looked down at him, his eyes icy but satisfied. The gateway to their next existence was now controllable, within their grasp.

As Arthur reached out to grasp Elena's hand, Eli moved, interposing himself between them.

"No," Eli declared, his voice cold and final. "You can never go home again."

Elena's eyes flickered from Arthur to her son, Thomas. Was there a glimmer of premonition in that split-second of confusion? Did she sense the dreadful act that was about to unfold? Her last wish was to see her son's face, and in that agonizing moment, Eli violently shoved her off the cliff's edge.

Arthur watched in frozen horror as Elena's eyes widened, and her mouth opened in a cry that was abruptly swallowed by the abyss below. Her scream reverberated, a chilling echo that punctuated her sudden, dreadful descent—then nothing but the mournful roar of the waves crashing against the cliffside.

Arthur's face contorted in a mixture of rage and disbelief as he tackled Eli to the ground. "What have you done? What have you done?!" he roared, his fists pummelling Eli's face with each anguished word.

He struck Eli repeatedly until he noticed a spatter of blood and teeth mingling with the grass. Yet Eli looked up, his swollen face breaking into a deranged smile as he gasped for breath.

"I saved us," Eli rasped, his voice tinged with perverse satisfaction.

"She surrendered the boy, Eli! She wasn't going to act against us! Why did you do it?"

Eli's smile died, and a vacant look replaced the earlier gleam in his eyes. "The moment that boy was born, she ceased to be one of us," he spat out, blood dribbling down his chin. "That kind of love can bring down empires, Arthur. Don't you agree?"

Arthur raised his fist again, trembling with the effort to restrain himself.

"Do you want to lose another sibling today, dear brother?" Eli taunted.

Arthur's fist hung in the air, a moment stretched in time, before he redirected it, slamming it into the ground next to Eli's face. He stood, shaking, and took Thomas into his arms. The young boy clung to him, burying his tear-streaked face into Arthur's shoulder as they made their way back towards the house. Eli remained on the ground, a crumpled, bloody heap at the cliff's edge.

"Please, Uncle Arthur, don't let them hurt me!" Thomas sobbed into Arthur's shoulder. "Please don't let them hurt me!"

*

Finally, Lena lifted her hand from Jonas's face. He was trembling, visibly undone, his eyes darting between the two Drake siblings. It was in that gut-wrenching moment that the devastating truth hit Jonas like a sledgehammer: the narrative he'd accepted about his mother's suicide was an intricately woven lie. And the architect of that falsehood, the man responsible for robbing him of his mother, was the very person to whom he had devoted his life. Jonas realised right there and then on the cold hard ground that he was a prisoner, and like all prisoners at Blackwater House, he started to scream.

CHAPTER THIRTY-FIVE

The night had cast its inky shroud over the land. It was a time of impending transformation. A thick fog, almost spectral in its eeriness, enveloped Blackwater House like a shroud. All its windows were dark, save for a mysterious light that bled from the bottom floor, casting ghostly patterns through the mist that clung to the estate.

Inside, the living room had undergone a metamorphosis that hinted at arcane rites and secret gatherings. The room's usual furnishings, the tables and chairs that spoke of everyday domesticity, had been pushed against the walls, leaving a vast emptiness at the centre. A long red carpet unfurled across this void, stretching out like a sanguine river.

But it was the candles that truly transformed the room. Scores of them, varying in size and shape, flickered in carefully orchestrated placement around the room. Their flames danced as if moved by some unseen wind, or perhaps the breath of spirits, casting both light and shadow in an intricate choreography. The illumination was soft yet strangely intense, revealing the room's high arches and heavy drapes. The flickering light seemed to make the very walls come alive, their aged wood and stone taking on the appearance of ancient, watchful faces. Here, in this room, a sense of grandeur and dread filled the air, a palpable tension that whispered of things both majestic and malevolent. Time itself seemed to hold its breath, waiting for the ritual to begin.

To the room's left rear corner sat a congregation of spectral figures—Edward Velour's associates. These were men and women accustomed to the sober atmosphere of boardrooms and the stiff mechanics of negotiation. Tonight, however, they found themselves part of an altogether different assembly. Each was garbed in a flowing gown that seemed to drink in the candlelight, rendering their forms almost indistinguishable from the encompassing darkness. The eerie transformation was complete in the masks they wore brown, rabbit masks, the signature visages of the Blackwater family.

Unbeknownst to these associates, they were unwittingly slated to become the quarry in a macabre hunting party as the night unfolded. Far from being observers or judges in some solemn ceremony, they were, in fact, lambs awaiting a slaughter they could not yet perceive.

As the doors creaked open, a burst of light swept into the room, momentarily banishing the lurking shadows. On the floor lay an unsettling yet fascinating sight—a simplified diagram etched into the stone beneath them, its design reminiscent of the Kabbalistic Tree of Life.

Eli was the first to enter, his presence immediately commanding the room. He was draped in a resplendent red robe, its deep hue enhanced by the soft flicker of the surrounding candlelight. What caught everyone's attention, however, was his mask: a gold metallic version of his usual disguise. The mask seemed to emanate an almost mystical power, absorbing and reflecting the room's ambient light in a dance that was both ethereal and unsettling.

Four additional figures followed Eli, each robed in a winter blue that seemed to chill the atmosphere even further. Their masks were striking—half-formed skeletons that abruptly halted at the nose, each one a haunting metaphor for the transformation yet to come. Among them were Reuben, Jonas, Maya—whose gait faltered as she hobbled—and Oliver, the surviving fragments of the enigmatic Blackwater family. With a sense of ceremony, they assumed their places around the table, its circular shape seeming to underscore their unity and unbroken lineage.

Then came the vessels. Clothed in simple gowns but devoid of masks, their faces laid bare their raw emotions. Some wept softly, others whimpered, and a few unleashed guttural screams that reverberated off the stone walls.

Lastly, borne aloft by guards, came The Collector, now reduced to a shadow of her former self. Encased in a golden mask, akin to Eli's, she was attached to an intricate wooden apparatus. As she was hoisted into the room, she displayed no struggle, no attempt at escape; whatever will she'd once had seemed utterly broken. The guards carefully detached her from the contraption and reverently placed her upon the circular table.

Simultaneously, the prisoners—the designated vessels—were led to their grim destiny. Each was handcuffed to a different member of the Blackwater family, their shackled hands forced into an eerie semblance of an embrace. This chilling tableau seemed the final act of bonding between captor and captive, their fates now inexorably linked in the dark ceremony to come.

With a palpable sense of relief, Eli surveyed the room from his central vantage point within the circle. Everything was perfectly in place, down to the most minute detail. Clasping the hand of his unnamed shackled prisoner, he allowed himself a moment of exultation and a rare, almost beatific smile graced his features.

He looked to the young prisoner before him—a young man, perhaps in his early twenties, with dishevelled brown hair, pale skin marred by streaks of dirt, and eyes so blue they seemed to glow even in the dim light. Those eyes were now filled with raw fear, and tears streamed down his cheeks. An unexpected thought flitted across Eli's mind; the young man's vulnerability and terror bore an uncomfortable resemblance to Reuben's demeanour when he had first joined the family. Like this young prisoner, Reuben too had once been an outsider, shackled—figuratively and now literally—to Eli and the dark legacy they both carried.

The sight of the young prisoner seemed to electrify Eli, not with remorse, but with a heady sense of anticipation. In the young man's fearful visage, Eli saw not just a terrified human being, but a vessel— his future vessel. This realisation was exhilarating, filling him with an almost ecstatic sense of impending triumph. For Eli, this was more than just another ritual; it was the dawn of a new existence, the promise of a life renewed in another's flesh.

"My esteemed guests, members of my lineage, bear witness to the renaissance of our illustrious family. Upon the completion of this sacred rite, the veil shall be lifted, and all our enigmatic truths revealed. Let us commence."

Eli unrolled the newly reformed ancient scrolls and began to chant the esoteric dialect, the words designed to ensnare Lena's mind and spirit.

Just as the incantation reached its crescendo, the room was suddenly awash in the grandiose strains of orchestral music. Eli froze, his masked head tilting to the side in confusion. A mistake, surely, he thought, his mouth turning dry as parchment.

"Jonas!" he bellowed; his voice tinged with a nascent apprehension. "Would you kindly investigate this anomaly?" The room remained eerily still; there was no sound of footsteps, no sense of movement at all. His eyes darted to where Jonas should have been standing. The figure was unmoving, as if paralyzed.

"Jonas?" Eli's voice wavered, betraying a hint of vulnerability, like that of a young boy afraid to face the night alone.

In that fleeting instant, a chilling realization washed over Eli—something had gone terribly wrong.

"Do you recognize this music, Uncle?" He did but couldn't bring himself to admit it. "No," he lied.

Jonas removed his skeletal mask to reveal a triumphant grin. "For those amongst us not versed in the finer points of classical music—and thus woefully deficient in taste—this is Beethoven's 'Ode to Joy.' A universally recognized masterpiece of course! But within the Blackwater family, its significance transcends mere aesthetic appreciation."

"What are you doing?!" Eli's voice shattered the room's calculated composure as he yanked off his own mask. For the first time, a palpable sense of panic clouded his demeanour.

Jonas relished the moment, his tone that of a charismatic game show host. "You see, this melody has a specific connotation for our family; it's bound to a particular pact, an agreement if you will. And oh, how timely its interruption is!"

The room's atmosphere, already thick with tension, became suffocating as everyone awaited Jonas's next move.

"Every soul in this chamber knows that our family fears one thing above death itself: capture, and the subsequent unmasking of our dark lineage," Jonas began, his voice seeped in eerie gravitas. "So we made a solemn pact: if ever we found ourselves on the cusp of capture, we would make our collective exit, not with a whimper but in a blaze of infernal glory."

As he spoke, he felt the confusion swirling beneath the disguises of those present. One by one, the masks were removed, revealing faces twisted in fear.

"Buried beneath this grand and ostensibly genteel mansion, precisely where we've kept our prisoners, lies a staggering cache of explosives" Jonas continued, relishing each word. "And it's rigged for a rather theatrical send-off."

"No," Eli breathed, horror distorting his features.

Jonas glanced at his watch. "Our flair for drama necessitated an equally dramatic trigger. And that, dear family, is synced to the final note of this iconic symphony."

"WHAT ARE YOU DOING?!" Eli howled in terror.

He snapped his fingers, summoning Oliver to seize Jonas. But before Oliver could reach him, out of nowhere, Lena intercepted, laying her hand upon him. Oliver collapsed in agony, retching onto the floor.

Eli's eyes returned to Lena, who was now shedding her cloak. A sense of dread overwhelmed him. Frantically, he reached for the person he had assumed was The Collector, ripping off her mask. It was Dahlia. They had switched places. The room's atmosphere, already laden with tension, had now reached a breaking point, teetering on the edge of unspeakable chaos.

"So, to clarify for those who might have missed the subtleties," Jonas grinned, revelling in the tension, "by the time this song ends, we will all be dead." Pandemonium erupted, the room devolving into a chaotic scramble for the exits. Desperate cries and shrieks filled the air.

Eli fumbled with a key hidden in his wristband, unshackling himself from the terrified young man beside him and ruthlessly kicking him aside. Maya approached Jonas, demanding an explanation, but he merely shoved her away, cackling gleefully.

"Come on!" Reuben shouted to his sister, gripping her hand. "Jonas said it would be over here!"

As they started to make their way, Reuben felt a forceful tug on his cloak. He turned, meeting Eli's frenzied eyes. With a primal scream, he summoned all his strength and landed a solid punch on his uncle's face, sending him reeling back.

Eli lunged at him again, but this time Lena intervened. "Not a chance," she hissed. Her fingers clasped around Eli's face, and suddenly he was a captive audience to a cinema of her memories. He witnessed her life in vivid flashes—moments with her mother, her time with Reuben, and the complex tapestry of their family history.

"You've always been petrified of genuine happiness, haven't you, Eli?" she said, her voice laced with both pity and scorn.

"The happiness we've found—my brother, myself, our parents—I want you to feel it, even if it's just a fleeting glimpse," she said. Their eyes met, separated by just a finger's breadth. "I'm not a collector. I'm not an object. I am a Drake."

Releasing her grip, she watched as Eli staggered backward, collapsing to his knees, visibly shaken by the torrent of memories she'd shared. Desperate, Reuben and his sister fumbled along the wall, searching for the hidden switch Jonas had mentioned — the one that would reveal the passage to the library and their sanctuary. But their fingers met only cold, unyielding stone. No switch materialised.

As dread settled in, they turned to find Jonas striding toward them through the chaos, a grim look in his eyes.

"Jonas, where's the switch?" Reuben's voice edged with panic as the music approached its finale.

"What switch?" Jonas replied, a melancholy sigh escaping his lips. "The one to the tunnel to the safe house, the one you promised us!"

Lena insisted, her eyes wide with desperation.

"I apologise. There isn't one," Jonas said, his face reflecting a sorrow like that of a parent breaking the news of a pet's death to a child.

"What?"

"Your abilities allowed me to see my mother one more time. But look at the cost— the lives ruined; the monstrosities birthed. Our family is doomed to betray and consume each other over this power. It's a heart-wrenching cycle I don't want to perpetuate."

"Jonas" Reuben lunged forward, grabbing the collar of Jonas's shirt. "What are you saying?"

"I'm sorry, Reuben. But you and Lena are going to have to die too."

Reuben's grip weakened, his fingers gradually releasing Jonas's shirt. "What?"

"The Collector has to end. The Blackwater family must end. And tonight," Jonas gently removed Reuben's hands from his collar, "it will."

Turning away, Jonas retreated into the mayhem enveloping the room.

Frantically, Reuben pivoted back to the wall, his fingertips skimming its surface as if he could coax a hidden switch to reveal itself. "No, no, no! It's got to be here somewhere! Lena, help me! Lena!"

"Reuben…"

"It's just here! Maybe it's some sort of—"

"Reuben!"

She seized his face, her hands cupping his cheeks to guide his eyes into hers.

"It's over," she whispered, her smile teetering on the precipice of tears.

"No, we can still—"

"It's okay," she assured him, pulling him into a trembling embrace as they both sank to their knees amid the unfolding chaos.

Tears slipped down their cheeks as the music swelled, its notes like the very heartbeat of the mounting dread. "I know you don't know me like you used to," Lena's voice trembled, "but I'm so glad you found me."

Reuben, engulfed in a euphoria of desperation, listened to the climax of the orchestral piece, his prayers now directed toward its imminent finale. "I'm glad too." he choked out, closing his eyes and waiting for the end. "I'm glad too…"

As the song reached its final crescendo, Jonas yanked Eli up from the floor. Eli stared at him in disbelief.

"Why, Jonas? Why would you betray us? I loved you."

Jonas's tearful eyes blazed with fury as he spoke.

"Nothing you have ever done has been based on love! You killed my mother, Eli! YOU KILLED MY MOTHER!"

Eli opened his mouth to speak, but it was too late—the final note hung in the air, a haunting lullaby for the end of their world. Jonas grabbed Eli and held him tightly in one final embrace.

"I'll find you in the dark"

And then, with a deafening roar, the mansion erupted in flames.

CHAPTER THIRTY-SIX

Darkness engulfed Reuben, swallowing him whole. For a brief, disorienting moment, he believed he had crossed over, that he was marooned in the inky abyss of the afterlife. The thought flickered in his mind: *Is this it? Is this death?*

His senses seemed suspended, floating in a liminal space where time lost meaning and space lost dimension. A terrifying stillness enveloped him, a silence so complete it felt like an existential vacuum. Even the air felt void of substance, as if the molecules themselves had evaporated in the explosion's heat.

As his vision sharpened, a shape materialised before him, hovering just inches from his face. It was calling his name.

It was Lena.

Her eyes were wide with a mix of panic and relief, her features bathed in the dim light that seemed to grow steadily brighter. She was lifting something off his face, a weight he hadn't even realised was there.

"Are you okay?" Her lips moved, forming the words, but the sound seemed to reach him as if through a thick wall of water. "Can you hear me?"

Then, with a sudden, jarring intensity, his hearing snapped back into focus, as if a cosmic drum had been kicked. The muffled sounds rushed in with a clarity that was almost painful—most notably, the wails and cries that filled the air, raw vocalisations of human terror and confusion.

Instinctively, Reuben tried to lift himself up, to get his bearings, but as he put weight on his arm, a searing pain shot through him.

"Ah!" he cried out, collapsing back onto the ground. His arm was clearly broken, a realisation that came with its own wave of despair.

Lena's face tightened at his cry, her eyes scanning his form for injuries. Despite the surrounding chaos, despite the pain coursing through him, despite the sheer incomprehensibility of what had just occurred, they were there together, they were alive.

With a strength that seemed at odds with her slender frame, Lena hoisted Reuben up by his shoulders. As he gained a better vantage point, he took stock of the devastation around them. The floor had splintered and buckled, caving in upon itself as if swallowed by some subterranean maw. Half of the wall had crumbled away, showering debris over—

Reuben's words caught in his throat. "Oh, Jesus," he finally managed to mutter, averting his eyes.

Beneath the rubble lay the twisted forms of VelourTech employees, their fates sealed in the very moment of the explosion. The sight was too horrific to dwell on, a brutal tableau he had no desire to fully absorb.

Reuben scanned the semi-intact structure around them, baffled. "What happened? Shouldn't this place be flattened?"

Lena surveyed the surrounding destruction, noting how the walls, though scarred and smouldering, had somehow remained upright. "Seems Jonas exaggerated the scale of the explosives," she replied.

They navigated around what was left of the main room. The blast had ravaged the living room, leaving a skeletal framework where luxury and excess once thrived. But remarkably, the perimeter walls endured, albeit engulfed in rampant flames that danced like malevolent sprites.

"No …"

Reuben's eyes widened as he saw a figure begin to materialise from the smoky haze.

~~Time seemed to slow, each second stretching into an eternity as the Drakes saw what was coming for them.~~ From the depths of the inferno, a nightmarish figure emerged, his silhouette framed by flames that danced like malevolent spirits. It was Eli, holding Jonas's lifeless body in a twisted, grotesque embrace—a danse macabre bathed in the hellish glow. His eyes locked onto Lena's, and in that moment, an abyss of soul-crushing darkness opened before them. The sheer weight of his eyes seemed to compress the air, as if reality itself recoiled from the malevolence he embodied.

With a movement so casual it defied the gravity of the situation, Eli unceremoniously let Jonas's body drop to the scorched ground. The sound it made as it hit—a soft, chilling thud—was a punctuation of finality that echoed in the ears of all who heard it.

This was no mere gesture; it was a declaration, a gauntlet thrown in the face of decency and humanity. The air itself felt electrified, vibrating with a dread so palpable it was almost a living thing, a monstrous entity birthed from the sum of their fears, regrets, and sorrows. As Eli stood there, framed by the consuming fire, it was as if he had torn open the very fabric of the world, revealing a chasm of darkness beneath.

Now with a knife glinting ominously in his hand, Eli limped closer, his voice tinged with a manic intensity. "First, I'm going to make you watch me kill your brother!" he roared. "And then, we're going to start this family again!"

"We must move! Now!" Reuben's shout broke through his sister's grief. Without a moment's hesitation, Lena clutched her brother's good arm, and together they staggered towards what remained of a doorway, its outline licked by rampant flames. The floor beneath them creaked ominously, weakened by the prior explosion, as they moved as swiftly as their bodies would allow. Behind them, Eli's limping footsteps reverberated hauntingly, the distance between them closing with each harrowing moment. Flames danced and roared like demonic sentinels, eager to engulf them as they navigated the fiery maze their home had become. The heat was relentless, scorching their eyes and searing their lungs, but adrenaline and dread urged them forward.

"Keep moving! We're almost there!" Reuben gasped, his breaths short and shallow in the oppressive heat. Glancing back, he saw Eli, relentless in his pursuit, his silhouette wavy through the heat and rising smoke.

Both siblings broke through the final wall of flames, feeling the blistering heat scorch their backs, and stumbled into a less ravaged part of the mansion. For a fleeting moment, hope sparked within them that they might have eluded their twisted uncle. Yet, as they risked a final backwards glance through the haze of flames and ruin, they saw Eli—still advancing, the knife in his hand aiming to end the one thing stopping him from having Lena. Her brother.

Adrenaline surging, Reuben and Lena scrambled towards one of the mansion's side doors, their breaths shallow and quick. As they ran, Reuben's eyes darted around the chaos, and he felt his heart sink further. Maya's wheelchair sat ominously empty by the crumbling wall—she was nowhere to be seen.

"It's jammed!" he hissed just as Lena sensed a sudden movement behind them.

"Watch out!" she screamed.

Whirling around, they barely dodged Eli's lunging form. His knife glinted menacingly, catching the flickering light from the fires that still raged throughout the mansion. The blade sliced through the air, inches from their faces. With a quick sidestep, they evaded his thrust, but not entirely— the blade grazed Reuben's arm, drawing a thin line of blood.

Ignoring the pain, Reuben yelled, "Upstairs, now!"

They bolted for the grand staircase, each step amplifying the thumping of their own hearts. Eli was right behind them, but it wasn't just his presence that startled them. His face was horribly burnt, patches of scorched skin glaring in stark contrast to the unaffected areas, and clumps of his hair were missing, creating a ghastly mosaic of agony. His ragged breaths mixed with the cacophony of their pounding footsteps.

They rounded the corner onto the second floor and darted into one of the mansion's lavish kitchens. Reuben and Lena ducked behind a marble counter, their backs pressed against wooden cabinets, as they tried to muffle their ragged breaths.

The sound of footsteps grew closer, each one weighted with

dreadful anticipation. The siblings locked eyes, a silent understanding passing between them. Eli was near, his warped determination palpable in the thick, smoke-laden air.

Suddenly, the kitchen door burst open, and Eli staggered in, his eyes scanning the room, knife still clutched tightly in hand.

"Where are you?" he seethed.

Holding their breath, Reuben and Lena stayed as still as statues, their hearts pounding in their ears. The tension was nearly unbearable. Then, as if guided by some malevolent intuition, Eli began to approach their hiding place, the knife raised and ready.

In that fraught moment, every outcome seemed possible—and none of them good.

"Oh, come on! You don't bring the guy holding a kitchen knife to a kitchen full of knives!" Eli yelled with a chuckle, a macabre delight warping his burning face.

Eli paced before the counter where Lena and Reuben crouched, his knife glinting menacingly. He turned to his nephew.

"I was going to give you the keys to the kingdom, and you threw them back in my face! Truly your father's son!"

Seeing their moment, Lena and Reuben dashed into the adjoining room. As Eli stepped through the threshold, Lena swung a glass bottle she'd grabbed earlier, smashing it directly into his face. Glass shards splintered, temporarily blinding him.

Eli howled, clutching his face with one hand while wildly swinging his knife with the other.

Lena and Reuben now found themselves confined to a cramped library, shelves lining the walls and a heavy, immovable door behind them. There was no other way out. Eli, though temporarily blinded, was still a formidable threat. His anguished screams filled the small room as he flailed his knife through the air, each swing a chaotic promise of violence.

Eli's voice had fractured as he screamed, the knife in his hand slicing through the air in erratic, dangerous arcs. As he lunged, he collided with objects—a vase shattered here, a picture frame toppled there. "You don't understand!" he howled, his eyes alight with a madness that terrified Reuben and Lena. "I can't die! I can't end!"

Just then, the door had creaked open. Reuben and Lena's hearts sank into their stomachs as they locked eyes with the newcomer: Maya. Time seemed to slow as she stepped into the room, her eyes meeting theirs in a way that was almost disconcertingly calm amid the chaos. With her finger pressed to her lips, she gestured for silence, her eyes inscrutable.

She then pointed towards the floor. Reuben and Lena instantly grasped her silent command. They dropped to their hands and knees, their hearts pounding so loudly they feared Eli might hear them over his own frenetic movements.

The room felt impossibly small, each inch they crawled laden with the potential for disaster. Eli continued his erratic dance of destruction, still brandishing the knife like a talisman of his unhinged intent. With every swing that brought the blade perilously close to their hidden path, the siblings held their breath, eyes widening in terror.

Maya, standing like a statue, locked eyes with them once again, urging them forward with the slightest nod. They moved in nerve-racking synchrony, painfully aware that a single sound—a creaking floorboard, a rustle of fabric—could bring Eli's wrath down upon them.

As they neared the threshold of the room, the air seemed to grow thinner, each inhalation a struggle. Eli whirled around suddenly, as if sensing the shift in the room's energy. For a heart stopping second, Reuben and Lena froze, their eyes meeting in mutual dread. But Eli scanned past them; his attention captured by some invisible demon only he could see.

Taking advantage of this brief lapse, they redoubled their efforts, inching over the final stretch of floor. The moment they crossed the threshold, Reuben and Lena rose to their feet, trembling.

As Reuben prepared to stealthily depart, he couldn't resist casting one last glance back at Eli. The sight seared into his memory: Eli, caught in a whirlwind of anguish, had wielded the knife with the fervour of a tormented artist lost in his twisted creation. His anguished screams and tears had merged into a harrowing cacophony of despair. Reuben found himself wishing that Eli had been claimed by the initial explosion, sparing him the sight of this grotesque unravelling. With a heart heavy with sorrow, Reuben turned away, leaving Eli to his bleak, self-inflicted solitude. Behind him, Eli continued his frenetic dance, his knife slicing the air, tracing unseen patterns known only to his fractured mind.

The trio moved swiftly through the rooms, the distant echoes of Eli's screams spurring their urgency. No longer was cautious tiptoeing an option; speed was of the essence.

Reuben's eyes caught a spreading dark red stain on Maya's grey hoodie near her abdomen. "You're hurt."

Glancing down at the expanding blot of red, Maya forced a wry smile. "I think we both know I've suffered worse," she said, her face betraying the severity of her pain.

"Where are you leading us?" Lena asked, her voice tinged with wariness.

Maya, struggling to speak through the evident pain, responded in a hushed tone. "There's a hidden passageway out of the mansion."

Following Maya's guidance, they descended a narrow, antiquated staircase to a cramped pantry. "Help me … open this," Maya whispered, her voice strained.

Reuben and Lena worked together to open the door, revealing a tunnel lined with stone, descending into darkness. As the door swung wide, Maya stumbled back, leaning against the wall for support. Reuben reached out to steady her, but she resisted.

"The mansion is unstable. The second set of bombs are going off," she insisted, urgency in her voice. "You need to leave. Now."

Reuben, still distrusting, asked, "Why are you helping us?"

Maya sighed, her eyes reflecting a complex mix of emotions. "Look around us. The party's over, isn't it? I can't see any reason for you to suffer anymore."

"Come with us," Reuben implored, a flicker of hope in his eyes.

Maya laughed, a sound filled with irony and acceptance. "Trying to save the life of the woman who dragged you into this. You truly are insufferable, Reuben Drake."

He reached out his hand, but she didn't take it.

"It's okay," she answered softly. "I'm ready."

Their eyes met, sharing a silent moment of understanding. "Go now," Maya urged.

As Reuben and Lena headed towards the tunnel, Maya called out, "Reuben! One more thing!"

He quickly returned to her side. Maya leaned in and whispered something to him. His eyes widened in shock, but before he could respond, Lena's urgent call from the tunnel snapped him back to reality.

With one last, profound look at Maya, alone with her choices and fading strength, Reuben followed Lena into the tunnel, leaving Maya in the fading light of the crumbling mansion.

The distant tremors had persisted, intermingling with faint, desperate screams that reverberated through the decaying mansion. Gathering what little strength she had left, Maya pushed herself off the floor and stumbled back through the pantry, making her way onto the mansion's second level. Clutching her wounded side, she limped through the labyrinthine corridors.

This way! This way!

The memory of Arthur's youthful voice called out to her, echoing in her mind as she recalled the simpler times when they played chase through those very halls. The comforting aroma of her mother's cooking came back to her.

"So, this is it?" she murmured to herself. The finality she had always dreaded—the end, death—somehow didn't intimidate her now. All she felt was an enveloping sadness, a soft melancholy that she could almost touch.

As Maya navigated the convoluted passageways of the mansion, she encountered a young man and woman, their faces etched with a mix of confusion and terror. They were struggling to carry an unconscious girl between them, Dahlia, her chosen vessel. For a split second, she mourned the body she could have taken over and dreamed of the world she would see.

"Can you help us?" the boy pleaded, desperation lining his voice.

Without a further second lost, Maya began to direct them. "There's a hidden passage. Go down that staircase over there; it leads to a small pantry. From there—" Her words were abruptly cut off by a more violent tremor that shook the mansion's very foundations. Plaster fell from the ceiling and the air grew thick with dust and tension.

"Hurry! Go now!" she urged them, her own words punctuated by the mansion's creaking lament. They nodded, urgency quickening their steps as they rushed towards the staircase, leaving Maya to continue her own solemn journey.

Limping along, Maya finally found her way back to the room where Eli remained. He was facing away from her, his hand gripping the knife as if it were his last connection to a world he could no longer see.

Gingerly, Maya tiptoed behind Eli, gathering enough courage to speak.

"Brother."

Caught off guard, he instinctively spun around, his knife slashing through the air to meet its mark. The blade pierced Maya, eliciting a sharp gasp from her. His face contorted in horrified recognition as he heard the familiar gasp.

"Maya?!"

He quickly withdrew the knife, his hands trembling. "Oh God … what have I done?"

With a final surge of strength, Maya reached for him and pulled him into an embrace. "It's alright," she whispered, her voice imbued with a calm surrender, even as the knife's sharp betrayal marked its presence between them.

The rumbling throughout the mansion intensified, punctuating their tragic moment.

"I can't see," Eli sobbed, his voice breaking, reverting to the vulnerability of a child lost in the dark. "I can't see, sister."

"It's okay," she whispered once more, comforting him in the enveloping darkness.

The mansion's rumbling crescendo reached its peak, filling the air with an almost unbearable tension. "I can't see ..." Eli repeated, his voice tinged with despair.

"You will again, very soon," Maya whispered, her lips curving into a gentle, reassuring smile. "I promise."

Cradling him in her arms, she began to sway him back and forth. Softly, she hummed a familiar melody, one that had once been a lullaby sung by their mother, before she and their father left them to rot in that tunnel all those years ago. The rumbling amplified, reaching an almost deafening volume. Eli clung to the tune, allowing it to drown out the chaos around them.

As the top floor crumbled, collapsing in an avalanche of debris onto them both, Eli held fast to the fading strains of that haunting melody and, in the engulfing darkness, felt a fresh set of arms reaching out to embrace him.

*

Reuben and Lena ventured into the unlit, narrow passage, feeling the oppressive darkness close in around them like a shroud. The distant rumbling of the mansion reverberated through the walls, making the ground beneath them quake. Each echoing boom amplified their fear, filling the confined space with an ominous sense of impending doom.

For a moment, they both froze, convinced that the labyrinthine passage would become their tomb. The thought that they might be buried alive, mere steps away from freedom, gripped them with paralyzing terror.

Just then, Reuben felt Lena's hand clasp his own. The touch reignited their resolve. They gathered themselves and pushed forward, their steps quickening as they yearned for the escape that lay somewhere ahead.

Navigating the rocky contours, they continued, driven by a new sense of urgency. A faint glimmer of light beckoned in the distance, a pinprick of hope piercing the darkness …

Emerging into the dim glow of what appeared to be early dawn, they found themselves at the edge of a desolate lakebed, its water long vanished, leaving a stretch of barren land bordered by towering trees. Wordlessly, they followed a forested path that wound between gnarled trunks and overgrown foliage.

Their journey took them up a gradual incline, their muscles burning with exertion and hearts pounding with a mixture of fear and hope. After what seemed like an eternity, they summited the hill, finally breaking free from the forest's claustrophobic embrace.

Pausing for a moment to catch their breath, they turned to the right. There, in the distance, stood the Blackwater mansion, its grandeur now engulfed in a roaring blaze. Firelight flickered through the broken windows, a dying star in the predawn light.

Reuben and Lena reached the summit of the hill, their eyes drawn to the spectacle of the burning mansion below. As if guided by the same impulse, they both lowered themselves onto the soft grass, sitting side by side. Together, they watched in solemn silence as the Blackwater mansion was consumed by flames, its grandeur reduced to smouldering ashes and rising smoke.

"You know what's going through my head right now?" Reuben finally said, breaking the thick silence.

"Please tell me you're thinking about us getting McDonalds?" Lena replied, trying to lighten the mood.

"Nah. I'm just wondering, how the hell are we going to explain all this? We're so far from home, I'm not even sure we're in the same country anymore," Reuben admitted.

"That's rich, coming from you. At least you 'exist' on paper. How do I even start explaining myself to—oh God. Mum. Is she—"

"She's fine." Reuben cut her off, sensing her rising panic. "I talked to her on the phone."

A visible wave of relief washed over Lena. Then her eyes started to mist. "But she has no idea who I am. Fuck ..."

Reuben placed a reassuring hand on Lena's shoulder. "We've got a lot to unpack with Mum after all this. We can navigate the weirdness together, okay?"

Lena managed a half-smile, her eyes drifting back to the ruins of the mansion. "It's really over, isn't it?"

"It is. And now? We get to choose what comes next," Reuben answered. His eyes caught sight of a trio of figures approaching from a distance. "Look, over there!"

Lena's eyes followed his pointing finger and spotted the three survivors making their way towards them. "Let's go help them," she declared, already sprinting in their direction before Reuben could even nod his agreement.

As Lena dashed off, Reuben took a moment to survey the landscape. The sun was finally breaking through the cloud cover, its rays no longer obscured by the looming presence of the mansion. A thought occurred to him, triggered by the memory of Jonas's many family portraits.

"Hey, Jonas. I think I've figured out what was missing from the family paintings," he said, following the trail of smoke to the dark blue sky. "An adult."

CHAPTER THIRTY-SEVEN

Sometime later

Lena pulled her winter coat tight around her, tucking her gloved hands deep into her pockets. The biting chill of the air seemed to seep through the fabric, prickling her skin with goosebumps. The forest was hauntingly quiet, save for the crunching of snow beneath her boots as she made her way towards Larkhill Manor.

Each step felt like a journey back in time. She had come home with Reuben, had tried to find a semblance of normalcy in the chaos of reunions and explanations. She had stared at her reflection in the mirror and talked to her mother about trivial matters while a torrent of unspeakable things lurked just beneath the surface. But no matter how hard she tried to move forward, something pulled her back, a gnawing feeling of unfinished business.

As she reached the entrance of the manor, her heart pounded in her chest. The grand structure loomed before her, its walls lined with ivy and windows like soulless eyes, watching, waiting. She pushed the gate open; it creaked mournfully, as if lamenting the dark secrets it kept.

Lena hesitated before walking up the stone path that led to the front door. Her mind wandered to the awkward conversations she'd had with her family since her return. Talking to her mother about places they'd been, meals they'd shared, Christmases and birthdays, only to be met with puzzled eyes. Trying to reminisce with her brother about adventures they'd had, jokes they'd laughed at, and challenges they'd faced together, and hearing him say, "I don't remember any of that."

The thought flickered through her mind again: should she run away? Would it be kinder to her mother and brother to allow them the grace of a life not burdened by the truths they couldn't even remember?

Every night, she lay on the makeshift bed in what used to be her living room—now transformed into an unrecognizable space by her father's pre-emptive actions before their family was torn asunder. She would stare up at the ceiling, each imperfection in the plaster a metaphor for her own tangled thoughts. They had succeeded in erasing everything, scrubbing away every trace of a life her family no longer knew. It was as if she walked through the remnants of a story where all the key pages had been torn out.

As she approached the imposing gates of the Manor, Lena felt a gravitation pull that surpassed nostalgia or duty; it was as if the very stones and trees whispered that this was an encounter that could not be delayed or avoided.

Regardless of what she chose to do next—whether to run or to stay and piece together her fragmented family—Lena knew that there was one thing she had to do, one person she needed to see before making that life-altering decision. This moment, she knew, could not and would not be erased.

Shivering from the winter chill that seemed to follow her inside, Lena stepped into the dimly lit reception area of Larkhill Manor. The ambiance mirrored the grey outside world, a palette of muted colours softened further by the diffused glow of antique sconces mounted on the walls. The effect was oddly cozy, as if the building itself were swaddled in a wintry haze.

"I'm here to see Emily Lewis," Lena announced to the receptionist, a middle-aged woman whose look of surprise suggested that foot traffic was rare in these conditions.

"I'm sorry, we're not allowing visitors after recent events," the receptionist replied cautiously, her eyes flicking to Lena's backpack and weather-beaten appearance.

"I was invited here. Her brother invited me," Lena insisted, her voice carrying a subtle tremor as her anxiety began to build.

The receptionist sighed, her fingers dancing across the keyboard to check for confirmation. The silence of the room was punctuated only by the soft tapping of keys and Lena's own heartbeat, which seemed to grow louder in her ears.

Finally, the sound of footsteps echoed down the corridor, and a young, familiar man emerged. Luke, Emily's brother, stopped a few feet away, his eyes locking onto Lena's.

"You're her," he said, his voice tinged with a combination of relief and disbelief, his smile tinged with melancholy. "From the photo."

"The one my brother showed you, right?" Lena echoed, her own smile fragile, a delicate blend of nostalgia and yearning. She couldn't help but think of all the times she had seen Luke over at Emily's house. Those memories felt both close and yet impossibly distant.

"It feels like years ago that he was here," Luke mused, his eyes taking on a faraway look. "So, you're here to see her. You said that you used to be friends?"

Lena nodded, her head dipping involuntarily as she fought back a sudden swell of tears. Yeah, we knew each other before," she managed, her voice quivering on the edge of breaking. "If that's okay, mind you. I don't want to disturb anything."

"I pray every night for something," Luke admitted, his voice softening. "A miracle, maybe. Hopefully, you're something halfway there."

The dimness of the corridor seemed to deepen as Luke led Lena through it, each door they passed by adding another layer to her escalating sense of tension. Her heart thudded erratically, like a frantic bird against a cage, as they finally stopped in front of one door. He opened it with a quiet click and gestured for her to enter.

Stepping into the room was like stepping into another world. The walls were painted in soft, soothing colours, and the lighting seemed deliberately muted. A single desk was set up against the far window, sunlight filtered through closed blinds casting dappled shadows on the floor. And there, facing away from her, seated facing the window, was a redhead—Emily.

For a split second, Lena was overwhelmed, nearly undone by a tidal wave of emotion. She wanted to sprint across the room, to throw her arms around Emily, to reclaim a piece of her lost past. But then reality settled back in, cold and unyielding: Emily didn't remember her. With that thought, her feet felt like they were rooted to the floor, and Lena stood there, her heart a confusing jumble of joy, sorrow, and the sharp pang of what could have been.

"Do you mind if I stay here while you talk?" Luke inquired, a hint of concern lacing his words. "Especially after what happened last time?"

Lena's eyes shimmered with a complex blend of emotions she couldn't fully articulate. "Of course," she said softly. "And I'm really sorry, Luke. For everything that's happened."

Luke chuckled; the sound imbued with a gentleness that momentarily lightened the room's atmosphere. He placed a comforting hand on Lena's shoulder. "You have nothing to apologize for," he assured her. "I know Emily better than anyone, and I can already sense that her spirits have lifted just knowing you're here."

Lena took a deep breath to steady herself and began to slowly approach Emily. She half-expected to hear Emily's voice break the silence but the room remained painfully quiet.

She finally reached Emily's side and paused, taking in the sight before her. Emily was seated at the desk, her red hair cascading around her face like a halo of forgotten memories. Her eyes were fixed on something outside the window, but as Lena followed her gaze, she realized there was nothing to see—just the dim winter sky and the bare trees standing sentinel in the chill air.

It struck Lena with a raw, aching force: Emily was looking, but not seeing; present, yet so far away. Her friend had become an empty vessel, a shell made for the family who had ruined her life.

Lena carefully leaned down to Emily's level, her voice a tender whisper, almost brittle in its vulnerability. "Hi, Emily," she breathed out softly, laden with an emotional depth that could move mountains. "I'm Lena."

She paused for a beat, letting the gravity of her next words fill the space between them. "I am your best friend," she continued, her voice tinged with both conviction and sorrow. "And I'm the reason you're here."

Emily looked up, her eyes an unfathomable canvas of confusion, echoing the abyss that had swallowed her once-effervescent spirit. It was as if Lena's words were abstract shapes, their meaning elusive to Emily's altered state of being.

Gathering her strength, Lena ~~delicately~~ placed her hands ~~on either~~ near side of Emily's forehead. Panic ignited in Emily's eyes; her body instinctively tensed, recoiling from Lena's touch. At that moment, Emily seemed like a terrified child, her circle of trust reduced to one soul—her brother, Luke.

Sensing his sister's unease, Luke moved quickly, joining her bedside to take her hand in his—a sanctuary in the shape of a sibling's grasp. "It's going to be okay," he assured her, his voice a calming balm steeped in love and fidelity. "I'm right here, and I promise, nothing bad is going to happen."

With Luke's reassurances acting like an anchor, Emily's tightly wound form began to relax, her eyes softening. She looked at her brother, as if siphoning comfort from the deep well of their shared history. After a moment of hesitant stillness, she nodded. It was a slight, almost timid gesture, but it gave Lena the permission she had been seeking.

Lena's eyes lingered on Emily, studying the face of her friend, now a pale reflection of the vibrant girl she used to know. A kaleidoscope of shared memories flickered in her mind, punctuated by the sound of Emily's laughter that once coloured their days with joy.

"I hope this begins to make things right," Lena murmured, her words a fragile bridge spanning between remorse and hope.

Taking a slow, grounding breath, she extended her hand towards Emily's temple. Her palm hovered there, laden with intention and tinged with desperation. Then, in the silent recesses of her thoughts, she heard her father's voice—not as Arthur Blackwater, the dark spectre who had wreaked havoc, but as Martin Drake, the loving man who had married his best friend and raised two children in the warm embrace of family and love.

In her mind's eye, she saw that version of her father reaching out to her, offering his hand as both an anchor and a lifeline. She imagined taking it, as if doing so could ground her to the love that remained from the curse bestowed on them all.

~~With her hand extended towards Emily, Lena drew from a deep reservoir of courage and hope. She touched Emily's temple.~~

Time seemed to suspend, the air charged with an electric energy, an unspoken language reverberating between Lena and Emily. The room felt as though it was pulsing with the weight of history, and the possibility of redemption.

Memories, radiant and full of love, flowed from the depths of Lena's consciousness. These were not solely her recollections; they were the shared tapestry of a friendship that once illuminated both their lives. These moments—each one a woven strand of laughter, trust, and shared secrets—didn't belong to her alone. They were a mutual narrative, a cherished history that defined them both.

And then as Lena's hand parted from her head, Emily's eyes returned to their original deep blue. They looked at each other, and in that fleeting moment, a spark of recognition ignited between them. The room and the people in it were joined together in a feeling of quiet astonishment, as if the scattered pieces of a shattered puzzle had finally realigned.

EPILOGUE

"What can I get for you?"

"A large Coke and a pack of Minstrels for me. And she'll have popcorn," the young man said, pausing to glance at the young woman beside him.

"You're spot on," she affirmed with a smile.

"And a medium Coke for her!"

"Wait, did you just—"

"Large Coke! I meant a large Coke. My mistake!" the young man hurriedly corrected himself.

The theatre usher, Simon, chuckled and began assembling their order. Placing the drinks on the counter, he took a closer look at the hooded young man. "You seem familiar. Are you that kid they found in Holland?"

The hooded figure exhaled deeply before grinning. "Could be, could be."

"Ronald, was it?"

The girl stopped herself from laughing.

"It's Reuben."

"Ah, sorry man," Simon said, setting down the drinks.

"No worries. It's all good."

Simon finalised the order and looked up. "That'll be twelve quid."

The young man passed over a twenty-pound bill, his eyes meeting Simon's.

"You were abducted, huh?" Simon ventured cautiously, glancing at the headline of a nearby newspaper. "Heard it was some sort of cult. Sorry if I'm prying."

The young man's eyes narrowed for just a second, but then he relaxed, flashing another quick grin. "I'm sure it'll be a Netflix show some day, pal. Take it easy."

Navigating through the expansive cinema lobby, Reuben and Alice passed under glowing chandeliers that cast soft, golden light onto the plush red carpeting below.

"Ugh, am I ever going to get used to this attention?" Reuben muttered, catching a few lingering stares from other patrons.

"You're practically a celebrity now, Ronald," Alice quipped, grinning.

"Don't go getting any ideas," Reuben shot back, half joking, as they handed over their tickets to the usher and ventured down the dimly lit corridor.

Alice shifted topics. "So, how's Lena adjusting to all this—to normal life?"

"As well as can be expected," Reuben sighed. "She feels like there's a lot she needs to make amends for."

"And your mum? How's she coping with everything?"

Reuben hesitated, collecting his thoughts. "Well, she's sort of in a holding pattern right now. It's a lot to process. Losing a husband, being kidnapped, discovering you have a daughter you can't remember—it's overwhelming. But me and Len are working on it."

"Working on it? How so?"

Reuben's eyes lit up a bit. "Dad and the Family suggested that Lena should be capable of restoring memories. She's going to see if she can do it for Mum. And if that works, she can restore mine as well."

By this point, they had taken their seats in the cinema room. Apart from them, the room remained empty.

Alice took a deep breath, her posture tense. "So, it's finally over then?" she murmured, breaking the silence.

Reuben leaned back in his chair, the weight of his thoughts evident in his furrowed brows. "Not entirely," he admitted. "Something's been gnawing at the back of my mind."

Alice shifted, turning to face him. "What is it?"

"It's something Maya said to me" Reuben started, his eyes searching Alice's for understanding. "Just before we escaped the mansion, she whispered something to me. Something about my father."

He repeated the same thing she had whispered in Reuben's ear: "That mask me and your mother found. It's not your father's."

Alice looked away, seemingly lost in thought.

Her hands, which had been wrapped around her drink, now seemed to shake slightly.

Reuben continued, his voice laced with a mix of confusion and suspicion. "Doesn't make sense, right? My dad hated the Blackwater Family. So why would he have kept that mask? And even if, by some far-fetched notion, he did, wouldn't my mum or I have come across it earlier? The placement, it's as if ... it was deliberately positioned there, almost staged."

His eyes sharpened, locking onto Alice. "There were only a handful of people who had access to my home, and of those, only two come to mind who would have the motive. Do you know what I'm talking about, Alice?"

Alice seemed to recoil slightly, her face a shade paler. She remained silent.

Reuben fixed his eyes on Alice, his voice tinged with both disbelief and a desperate need for answers. "Looking back, there's something else that struck me. My mum was kept hostage in her own home and used as leverage for me to work with the Blackwaters to find my sister. But you? They let go. Just like that."

Alice turned away, her body trembling. Was she crying? Reuben couldn't tell.

"They asked you to plant the mask, didn't they?"

Alice faced him again, tears streaming down her cheeks.

"It was when I came back for your father's funeral."

Reuben sighed in disappointment.

"I remember seeing you and your mum entering the funeral room … but your sister wasn't there. I started asking people, 'Where's Lena? Why didn't she come?' And everyone looked at me like I'd lost my mind. When I returned home, that's when the head of The Family found me and asked me to help."

A heavy silence followed.

Reuben looked at Alice, his expression a mixture of hurt and betrayal. "My mum was kept hostage in her own house, Alice. She could've died. I could've died."

Alice dabbed at her eyes, a remorseful tremor in her voice. "I'm so terribly sorry, Reuben. I can't even express how much I regret it."

A heavy, suffocating silence settled between them, each lost in their own world of what-ifs and recriminations, both aware that some mistakes are too grave to be easily forgiven, and some trusts too shattered to be quickly mended.

"So what's next?" Alice asked, her eyes searching his face. "Are you going to get your sister to erase my memory? Or worse?"

Reuben shook his head, the weight of the decision settling into his features. "I don't think we are planning on doing anything like that," he answered. "If there's any hope for us to be able to lead normal lives, we can't act like them. Like the Blackwaters."

"I'm so sorry, I never would have—"

He interrupted her by gently taking her hand. "From now on we need to be honest with each other. No more lies. If we do that, we can move on. Okay?"

Alice wiped away her lingering tears. "If that's what you want."

The air between them lightened, just a bit.

The cinema's screen lit up with previews for upcoming films, casting an ethereal glow on their faces.

"You know what's strange?" Reuben broke the silence, his eyes still on the screen. "I had a dream about my dad last night—the first one since he passed away."

Alice, who was still dabbing at her eyes, looked over at him. "Really? What was it about?"

"I found myself in that dark passageway again, the same one we navigated to escape Blackwater House. Only this time, Lena wasn't there; it was just me. The air was so cold it seemed to slice through me, and the darkness was almost tangible. I put my hands out in front of me, fearing I might trip and fall. Then, as if stepping through a portal, I suddenly found myself in my parents' bedroom. The lighting was soft, almost nostalgic, and there stood my dad. We didn't exchange any words. We just hugged, and he gave me a reassuring pat on the shoulder. There was this newfound lightness about him, a tranquillity I'd never seen when he was alive. I was just about to ask him something and he stopped me, he just took my hand in both of his and just held it. He smiled once more … and then I woke up."

Reuben nodded solemnly. "He was still my father. Unlike Eli, he chose to be a different person."

Alice looked puzzled. "Who's that? Eli?"

Reuben looked at her with the same puzzled expression.

"You said the head of the family came to see you in Barcelona."

She shook her head. "That wasn't the name they used."

His heart quickened. "Well, then who was it? Jonas? Maya?"

Again, she shook her head worryingly. "No one by those names came to visit me in Barcelona."

A chill seemed to fill the room. "You said it was the head of the Family," Reuben said, his voice tinged with a rising sense of dread. "If it wasn't them, then who came to see you?"

She hesitated, then spoke softly, her eyes meeting his.

"The person who came to visit me went by a different name," she said. "Does the name Father Hishaya mean anything to you?"

ACKNOWLEDGEMENTS

I would like to express my deepest gratitude to the following individuals for their invaluable contributions to the editing and production of this novel.

To Elizabeth Ward, for her meticulous work on the developmental edit. Your insightful questions and guidance helped shape this story, and your encouragement gave me the confidence that it was one worth telling.

To Ciera Cox, for your exceptional copyediting. Your attention to detail and commitment to perfection ensured that this book is in the best possible form.

To Barış Şehri, for bringing my vision for the cover and artwork to life. Thank you for embracing my ideas and translating them into a design that truly captures the essence of this book.

Printed in Great Britain
by Amazon

50496679R00178